North

Is the

Night

North Is the Night

Emily Rath

EREWHON

an imprint of Kensington Publishing Corp.

erewhonbooks.com

Content notice: *North Is the Night* contains depictions of fantasy violence (kidnapping, blood and gore, torture, on-page death), religious persecution, forced conversion, and themes of colonization and cultural genocide. Multiple characters experience abuse (mental, physical, emotional). There is one scene of attempted sexual assault. While there is no sexual violence between any of the main characters, there's room for readers to question consent due to the uneven power dynamics.

EREWHON BOOKS are published by:

Kensington Publishing Corp.
900 Third Avenue
New York, NY 10022
erewhonbooks.com

All Kensington titles, imprints, and distributed lines are available at special quantity discounts for bulk purchases for sales promotions, premiums, fundraising, educational, or institutional use.

Special book excerpts or customized printings can also be created to fit specific needs. For details, write or phone the office of the Kensington sales manager: Kensington Publishing Corp., 900 Third Avenue, New York, NY 10022, attn: Sales Department; phone 1-800-221-2647.

Erewhon and the Erewhon logo Reg. US Pat. & TM Off.

This is a work of fiction. All of the characters, organizations, and events portrayed in this novel are either products of the author's imagination or are used fictitiously.

ISBN 978-1-64566-220-4 (hardcover)

First Erewhon hardcover printing: January 2025

10 9 8 7 6 5 4 3 2 1

Printed in China

Library of Congress Control Number: 2024932751

Electronic edition: ISBN 978-1-64566-167-2 (ebook)

Edited by Sarah T. Guan. Interior design by Kelsy Thompson and Cassandra Farrin, adapted from the artwork of Finnish painter Joseph Alanen (1885–1920). Special edition endpapers and case design by INKfluence. Author photograph by Jennifer Catherine Photography.

To my mummi,

Bernice,

who first told me the stories and songs.

Finnish Gods, Spirits, and Heroes

Ahti | god of the seas, water, and fish; husband to **Vellamo**

Aino | the sister of **Joukahainen**; she drowns herself rather than marry **Väinämöinen**

Ajatar | an evil forest witch who lures people into getting lost in the woods

Akka | goddess of fertility; wife of **Ukko**

Hiiden hevonen | the Horse of Hiisi; a goblin-made creature of stone and iron that breathes flames, forged from the mountains of Tuonela

Iku-Turso | a malevolent sea monster defeated by **Väinämöinen**

Ilmarinen | the great smith, god of iron, sky, and winds; designed the Sampo, the mill of fortune which can make flour, salt, and gold out of thin air

Ilmatar | the All-Mother; goddess of air; mother of **Väinämöinen**

Joukahainen | the main adversary of **Väinämöinen** in the *Kalevala*; he offers his sister as a prize to **Väinämöinen** in a singing contest and loses (see **Aino**)

Kalma | goddess of death and decay; lingers in graveyards with **Surma**

Keijulainen | death sprites; small, flying creatures that resemble snowflakes or birds of fire; they haunt graveyards, roads, and rooms where people have died

Kivutar | goddess of suffering; boils the suffering of mortals in a big pot

Kiputyttö | goddess of pain; turns a stone over in her hand to inflict pain on mortals

Kuutar | goddess of the moon; weaves fabric of pure gold taken from the moon's light

Liekkiö | the spirits of murdered children who haunt forests and lure travelers from their paths

Lemminkäinen | an adventurer and friend of **Väinämöinen** who tries to steal a swan from Tuonela

Loviatar | goddess of illness and disease; mother to the nine diseases of men and a nameless tenth child, a daughter; she is canonically blind

Mielikki | goddess of the forest; wife of **Tapio**

Nyyrikki | god of the hunt; son of **Tapio** and **Mielikki**

Otso | the spirit of Bear; the bear is sacred to Finns. If a bear is killed, the hunter must offer a feast to **Otso** called a peijaiset

Päivätär | goddess of the sun; weaves fabric of pure silver taken from the sun's light

Revontulet | the Firefox; a mythical black fox that runs so fast across the snow, his tail leaves sparks, creating the Northern Lights

Surma | a terrifying beast described as a wolf or dog with a snake-like tail; embodies sudden, violent death; companion of **Kalma**

Tapio | god of the forests and hunting; husband of **Mielikki**

Tellervo | goddess of the forest; daughter of **Tapio** and **Mielikki**

Tuonetar | goddess of death; Queen of Tuonela

Tuonen tytti | the ferrywoman who rows all souls to Tuonela

Tuoni | god of death; King of Tuonela

Ukko | god of thunder, weather, and the sky; he wields a magic hammer called Ukonvasara; husband of **Akka**

Ututyttö | the mist maiden; she uses her powers to control mist and fog, protecting animals and slowing the passage of men

Väinämöinen | the hero of the *Kalevala*; a shaman, minstrel, and warrior who was born an old man with all the wisdom of the ages; son of Ilmatar

Väki | groups of spirits that represent or otherwise protect various natural elements, like water (veden väki), fire (tulen väki), death (kalman väki), and forests (metsän väki)

Vammatar | goddess of evil and misfortune

Vellamo | goddess of the sea; wife of **Ahti**

Elements of Finnish Paganism

Henki | one part of the Finnish three-part soul; the essence of the self that must remain in the living body at all times; it is the piece of the soul that goes to Tuonela at death

Hiisi | a sacred grove within a forest, like an open-air temple; typically includes an **uhrikivi**, or offering stone; used to leave sacrifices for the gods and the ancestors (see **uhrikivi**)

Itse | one part of the Finnish three-part soul; a physical manifestation of the self that can be sent across the realms

Kantele | a traditional Finnish plucked stringed instrument; the oldest forms typically have five or six strings made of horsehair and a wooden box carved from one piece of wood

Kuppikivi | cup-stones; a shrine comprised of a large stone that has rows of cup-sized recesses drilled into the face, used for leaving offerings to ancestors and spirits (also see **uhrikivi**)

Linnunrata | the path of the birds, i.e., the Milky Way, thought to be the path the birds followed to reach **Lintukoto**

Lintukoto | a warm place at the edge of the world where birds live during the winter

Luonto | one part of the Finnish three-part soul; takes the shape of a bird and represents the strongest parts of our personality

Shaman | their roles were typically to heal and prevent illness, but they also helped with farming, fishing, hunting, and dealing with issues related to witchcraft. They could use drumming to cast out parts of their soul to travel the realms and grow their knowledge; the greatest shaman is Väinämöinen

Shaman Drum | a painted drum used by a shaman to go into trances or release one of their souls

Sielulintu | a soul bird; a wooden bird-figure used to protect souls while they sleep. It is believed that a bird brings the soul to a newborn baby and the same bird carries away the soul at death

Tuonela | the Finnish underworld; an underground realm, surrounded by a river, where all souls go to find eternal rest; sometimes called Manala

Uhrikivi | a large stone or boulder uses as a sacrificial stone typically found in a **hiisi**; not to be confused with cup-stones (see **kuppikivi**)

Note

North is the Night is inspired by Finnish mythology and folklore, but this book should be read as a fantasy. Creative license was taken interpreting the *Kalevala*, as well as interpreting certain aspects of Finnish shamanism and paganism. The author also took creative license in determining which of the gods of the Finnish pantheon to include, which to combine, and which names to use for them.

North Is the Night

Part One

O how beautiful thy childhood,
In thy father's dwelling-places,
Nurtured like a tender flower,
Like the strawberry in springtime.

—Rune 22. *The Kalevala.*

Siri

A CHILL AUTUMN WIND whips at my face as I stand on the lakeshore, hands on my hips. Aina waits dutifully at my side. Together, we watch as my father calls out to us in greeting. He pulls in his oars just as the bottom of our wooden boat crunches against the pebbly beach. Flipping my braid off my shoulder, I wade in shin-deep and hold the boat steady for him. The water is icy cold, soaking through my socks and the hem of my woolen dress. I bite my lip against the pain. Father hops out, and we grip the sides, giving the small boat two sharp tugs.

"A good catch today," he says proudly.

We give the boat one more heave, pulling it fully up onto the beach.

I peer inside. It *is* a good catch. And thank the gods for that. We need more fish if we're to survive the winter. Father managed to fill a whole basket with perch. The other basket is a mix. Zander, a skinny pike, a handful of roach. A few of these will be set aside and given to Mummi, my grandmother, for tonight's supper, but the rest must be salted and stored in the njalle for winter.

Father wipes his hands on his breeches. "Your brothers will stay out a bit longer. Help them bring in their catch too. Understood?"

"Yes, Isä," I reply.

Glancing up at the sky, he judges how much daylight is left. There are still more chores to do before nightfall. "Remember not to stay out too late, Siiri. You, too, Aina. Get yourselves home well before dark."

We nod, and he leaves us with the baskets.

I don't fault him his curt manner. Everyone in the village is on edge. A few days ago, some of the menfolk returned from the southern market with chilling news: More young women have been going missing up and down the lakeshore. Strange tales of screams heard in the dark woods, creatures with eyes that glow red, a lingering stench of death in the air. People always talk of such things, but never so close to us, never here. And none of the girls have been found.

These are dark times. If Father could spare me, he would probably make me stay nearer the house with Mummi and my little sister. But winter is coming, and I have two strong hands. We both know he needs me. There's no time for worry, not when our worries seem endless now.

Once, these forests were a safe haven. The gods give of their bounty, and we Finns take. We *must* take. And that which is taken is always shared. When the harsh winter comes, and the long, cold night sets in, we sit by our fires and warm each other with good food and stories of summertime. I have golden memories of sitting on my mother's lap as she told us stories of the old gods—Ukko and the making of his stone hammer, Ahti the seafaring warrior, the clever shaman Väinämöinen and his magical kantele. Summer is the time for hard work and sacrifice. Winter is for stories and family and a quietly lived life.

That was before.

Before the gods went quiet, abandoning us here in these woods. Before bards stopped strumming kanteles and singing the songs. Before Swedish settlers arrived on our shores, stealing farmland across the south, uprooting thousands of us, including my family. We left my mother there, buried in the cold ground outside Turku. No one remains to tend to her grave. No flowers. No songs.

And that was before the whispers of a new god whistled darkly through the woods. Every day, the Christians grow bolder, challenging our gods and threatening our way of life.

In a few short years, the Swedes have turned these forests from a haven into a hell. Powerful men in robes of white now call out from their great stone houses in the south, offering gold and silver to any Finn who would provision them— meat, fur, timber, grain. Our forests are full of thieves who dare to take more than they need, leaving little enough for the rest of us. Each summer, the fight for land becomes bloodier. They slash and burn large swaths of acreage for their cattle. They thin our herds of free-roaming deer and elk. They claim the best of the farmland for their wheat and barley.

Before long, they'll take even the mushrooms. We Finns will be left with nothing but the brambles in the fens and the bark on the trees.

I gaze down at the baskets in my father's boat. The Swedes may be trying to claim everything, but Ilmatar hear me, they will not have our small, regular haul of fish. Lifting my hands, I close my eyes and offer up a blessing to the sea goddess. "Vellamo, righteous in beauty, thank you for your bounty."

Next to me, Aina offers up her own quiet blessing.

"You don't have to help me." My tone is half-apologetic,

half-hopeful. As much as I know we need these fish to survive the winter, I hate salting them. It's probably my least favorite chore. With a heavy sigh, I pick up the first basket.

Aina just smiles, taking the other basket. "I don't mind. You're always helping me with my chores."

I lead the way over to our salting station. A few of the older women are seated together, gossiping quietly as they work. They nod in welcome, their expressions worried, if a little curious too.

Aina frowns, the basket of fish still balanced on her hip. "It's as if they expect one of us to be taken next."

"Ignore them," I mutter, giving the women a fake smile and a wave. "They're just jealous, because they know no man wants a catty old fishwife with salty fingers in his bed." I drop down onto a stump and select a crock, preparing it with a base of salt. This is the worst part. The salt finds every scrape and blemish on my skin, burning and stinging so sharply, my eyes water. I hiss, waiting for the sting to numb, as I pick up the first fish, roll it in salt, and layer it in the bottom of the crock.

We'll have to repeat this whole process in a few days. Once the fish are all repacked, they'll last for up to nine months. Come winter, we'll stay warm by our fires eating stews of perch with barley and dried mushrooms.

I try to hold my breath as I work, because the briny smell of the fish makes me gag. Also, I hate the feel of their slippery bodies as I roll them in the salt. On the stump next to me, Aina laughs. When I cast her a glare, she flicks a little salt my way with her fingers. "Don't," I mutter, in no mood to be teased.

"You're such a goose. You like to eat fish, right?"

"Of course."

"Well, you won't be eating anything this winter if you don't salt these first."

I grimace, packing a layer of salt over the first row of perch. "What does it look like I'm doing?"

She turns her attention back to her own work. After a few minutes of silence, she glances my way. "What if these girls aren't really missing? Perhaps they simply chose to leave."

My shoulders stiffen. "Why would someone do that? Just disappear like smoke in the wind without a word to anyone? All because you fancy a new life for yourself?"

She huffs, rolling another fish in salt. "Well, I wouldn't, but other girls might. Not everyone has a mother as kind as mine . . . or a mummi as protective as yours."

True.

I smile, thinking of my grandmother, of her warm hands and her cold glare. That woman was born with iron in her spine. She protects her grandchildren with the ferocity of a mother bear, and she loves us just as fiercely. And there really is no kinder woman than Aina's mother . . . except perhaps Aina herself.

"You've made this point already," I tease. "More than once."

"Well, it's as true now as it was this morning," she counters. "We've heard these stories for years. Women go missing, Siiri. Too many women die in childbirth, and that leaves too few of us unmarried women left. And men get lonely—"

I snort, peering out at the boats. "Oh, do they? You wouldn't know it from Aksel."

She follows my gaze. We both know how decidedly *not* lonely my brother is, most nights. If my father catches him with a girl in the barn again, he's likely to strap Aksel's hide clean off.

"Fine, *some* men get lonely," she clarifies. "And then they get desperate. I'm not saying it's right," she adds quickly. "I'm only saying I bet if someone went out and looked, they would find every one of those missing girls scattered somewhere along the lakeshore, adjusting to her lot as a lonely man's wife."

Now my grimace has nothing to do with the salt burning my hands. "Gods, why does your theory sound even more horrifying than the one about witches and blood sacrifice?"

She purses her lips, trying to hide her smile. "Perhaps because you are singularly opposed to even the idea of marriage? For you, a woman choosing to marry is as disturbing as being kidnapped by a witch or fed to a stone giant."

I snort. "Surely I'm not that bad?"

"You are worse, and you know it. No man will ever be good enough for you, Siiri. You're smarter than they are, funnier than they are."

"True," I joke.

"Not to mention you always best them in every contest of will. It's quite maddening, I assure you."

"Maddening? For whom?"

"For them."

"How can you know how they feel about it?"

"Because they *tell* me so," she replies with a laugh. "Repeatedly. They call you the pickled herring."

I laugh, too, puffing a little with pride. "Well, perhaps they should try harder to impress me."

"And since no man is good enough for *you*," she says over me, "you've decided no man can possibly ever be good enough for *me,* either. You've scared away my last three suitors—"

"Stop right there." I waggle a salt-crusted finger in her face. "If you call that duck-brained Joki your suitor one more time, gods hear me, I'll marry you to him myself. See how well you like it when a year from now he's still telling you the same story of the time he *nearly* felled a ten-point stag."

She laughs again despite herself, tossing another fish down

on her bed of salt. Leaning over, she gives my knee a gentle squeeze. "Be at peace. I don't want to marry Joki."

The tension in my chest eases a bit at her admission.

"But I will eventually marry someone," she adds, turning back to her work.

Her words stifle the air like a blanket tossed over a fire. I can't look at her, can't let her see my face.

"I want a family," she says, her tone almost apologetic. "I want a home of my own. Gods willing, I'll have children."

"Gods willing, you'll survive it," I mutter. Too few women do. We lost our dear friend Helka just last month. Her and her baby. That's three mothers and three babies this summer alone. Just another one of the curses plaguing our land. I swear, sometimes it feels like the gods are laughing at us . . . if they bother to see us at all.

Maybe my brother Onni is right. Maybe our gods really are dead. What else could account for this cruel, senseless suffering?

But my sweet Aina is ever hopeful. "I'll have children and a husband who loves me," she goes on. "A home of my own. A family. A purpose. Don't you want that for me, Siiri? Don't you want it for yourself?"

I stare down at my fingers, red and stinging and swollen with salt. *A family and a home of my own.* That's supposed to be the dream, right? Children. A warm fire and full bellies. My own njalle stocked with provisions to last us the long winter. A man in my bed to warm my back and keep the wolves at bay.

I shake my head. All my life, I've tried to see that future for myself. It's what my mother wanted for me . . . before she died bringing my little sister into this world. It's what my grandmother wants for me. Now, it's what Aina wants for us both.

But what do I want? What do I see when I close my eyes and dream of my happiest self?

I take a deep breath, gazing out across Lake Päijänne, my home for the last fourteen years. The days are getting shorter, the nights colder. I can taste autumn in the air, that crisp smell of drying leaves. The lake is changing too. In summer, she's as bright as the blue of a jaybird's wing. In autumn, the lake darkens as the fish sink to her depths. She grows quiet and secretive as she waits for spring.

Watching the boats bob, the truth unravels itself inside me like a spool of golden thread. I want to live the life I already have. I want long summer days running through the forest, hunting deer and snaring rabbits. I want quiet winter nights in Aina's hayloft, cracking walnuts and laughing until we fall asleep. I want to swim naked in the lake, my hair loose and tangled around my arms. I want us to stay just like this, happy and free forever.

"Siiri?" Aina's hand brushes my arm. "Are you well?"

Sucking in a sharp breath, I turn to face her. Bracing myself with both hands on her shoulders, I search her face. Her lips part in silent question, her brows lowered with worry.

"Aina, I want you to be happy," I say at last, giving her shoulders a squeeze. "That's what I want. Tell me what will make you happy, and I'll get it for you. If you want to marry Joki, the fish-faced farm boy, I will be the first to light a candle in the great oak tree."

She rolls her eyes with a soft smile.

"If you want to leave our village and go on that adventure in search of a new love, I will leave with you—"

She leans away. "Siiri—"

"I *will*," I say in earnest. Taking her salty hands in mine, I hold them fast. "Aina, you are my oldest and dearest friend. I don't care about finding myself a good man and settling down. I am perfectly content being my own good man. What I cannot bear is the thought of losing you or making you unhappy. So please, just tell me what you want, and I'll get it for you."

She blinks, eyes brimming with tears as she searches my face. I fear what she might see in me. She's always seen too much—the parts I hide, the parts I pretend not to have. My weaknesses, my fears. She knows me better than any person living or dead.

Slowly, she sighs, shaking her head. "I guess . . . I wish there was just some way you really could be happy for me if I pick a life you wouldn't pick for yourself."

I drop her hands. "What do you mean?"

"I mean . . . " She groans. "Gods, you know, I wish I knew whether there was even *one* person out there who you thought was good enough for me. I could never marry without your blessing, Siiri, so I need to know. Is there no man living you could bear to see me wed?"

I consider for a moment, heart in my throat. Does she want me to say Joki? The poor man is duller than lichen on rocks. My brothers are both clever enough, I guess, but they're all wrong for her. They're both too independent. Aina needs someone who really sees her, someone who listens, someone who *needs* her.

She watches me, waiting, still searching my face. I can't sit here and have her looking at me with such hope in her eyes. Taking a deep breath, I hold her gaze. "You want a name? Fine. Let it be Nyyrikki."

She blinks. After a moment, she laughs. It bubbles out of her like foam off a stream. Before long, she's gripping her sides with salty fingers. I join her, and we both laugh, tears filling our eyes.

"Nyyrikki?" she says on a tight breath. "God of the hunt

and prince of the forest? That's where I must set my standard of matrimony?"

"You said any man living. And you'd never be hungry," I add with a shrug. "There would always be game for your table. And he's supposed to be of famed beauty, with a head of flowing hair . . . and he lives in a forest palace with gates of wrought gold. You could do worse, Aina."

She laughs. "Well, next time I stumble across his palace in the woods, I'll just give those golden gates a knock, shall I?"

"We'll both knock," I tease, catching her gaze again. Aina has the most beautiful eyes, bright like new blades of spring grass. She has freckles too, though not so many as me. Hers are soft and small, scattered over her pointed nose. Wisps of her nut-brown hair frame her face, tugged loose by this wind. I want to tuck the strands behind her ear. I want to touch her face. I want to brush my fingertips over the freckles on her nose.

"What is it?"

Looking at her now, I can see the truth so clearly: I don't want things to change between us. And marriage *will* change her. It always does. It's the way of things. Once children come, they will be her world, and I'll lose her. I'll lose everything. Call me selfish, but I'm not ready. Not yet. I want just one more summer of being the first in her affections.

I curl my salted fingers until the tips of my nails bite into the meat of my palms.

"Siiri?"

"It's nothing," I mutter, turning away.

She drops her hand from my thigh, reaching for another fish. "And . . . who shall we find for you, then?" She keeps her tone light, trying to move us past my awkwardness. "I don't believe Nyyrikki has a brother . . . "

"I don't need to marry."

"Ilmarinen could spin gold for you," she offers.

I huff. "So can the moon goddess. And she'd likely darn her own stockings. Clean up her own messes too. Now, no more talk of god-husbands. Let's just get this done."

Before long, I'm packing the last perch into the top of my crock. Aina is crouched over at the water's edge, washing her hands. She stands, shielding her eyes with her hand, as she gazes out across the lake. The setting sun is casting a glare.

"What are they doing?" she asks.

I glance up, squinting. My brother Aksel is perched in the front of our other fishing boat, waving at us. "Maybe they caught a massive pike," I say with a shrug. It doesn't make me happy. It's just more work.

"They'll have the boat over if they keep rocking it like that," Aina warns.

I look up again. Aksel isn't so much waving as gesturing frantically. Cupping his mouth, he shouts across the water. Meanwhile, Onni faces the opposite way, rowing as hard as he can. I rise to my feet. "What the . . . "

"*Run!*"

I join Aina at the water's edge. What is he saying?

"*Siiri, run!*"

Screams erupt behind us. Up and down the beach, the others scatter. My heart leaps into my throat. On the shore, not fifteen feet from me, stands a woman. No . . . a *monster*. She has the body of a woman, draped in heavy black robes. The cloth is soiled and torn, dragging on the ground, hanging off her skeletal frame. Her face is painted—a band of mottled white across her eyes and nose—while her forehead and exposed neck are smeared with what looks like dried, flaking blood. Perched on her head is a set of curling black ram's horns.

She looks at me with eyes darker than two starless skies.

They dare me to leap into their depths. Sucking in a breath, I blink, breaking our connection. Her mouth opens, showing broken, rotting teeth. She hisses, taking a step forward, and one thought fills me.

Run.

Grabbing Aina by the hand, I take off down the beach.

She asks no questions. She just holds my hand, and we sprint. Our feet crunch against the pebbles. I chance a look over my shoulder as I pull her towards the trees. The creature slowly turns and raises her tattooed hand, pointing right at us. In a swirl of black smoke, a monstrous wolf appears at the creature's side. The jaws of the beast open wide as it pants, exposing rows of sharp white teeth. The glowing red eyes track us like prey. With a growl, it leaps from its mistress's side.

The chase is on.

"Ilmatar, help us," I cry to the heavens. "Aina, *run.*"

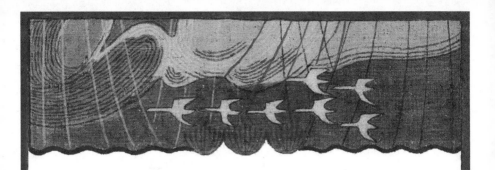

Siiri

"**WHAT IS THAT CREATURE?**" Aina cries as soon as we slip under the cover of the trees.

"My guess is that's the thing stealing girls," I pant. "Not some lonely fisherman and not a scurrilous Swede."

I pull us deeper into the forest, Aina's hand clasped firmly in mine. It's darker here. Too dark. We should have been home already. Behind us, I can still hear the screams of the people on the beach. The men will soon be out in droves, bows and axes at the ready. They'll come for us. They'll help. We just have to find a place to hide.

"You're faster than me, Siiri." Aina pulls on my hand. "I can't keep up. Just go—"

"Not a chance."

Through the dim trees, the underbrush rustles and twigs snap. As we burst into a clearing, I stop and drop Aina's hand, still holding tight to my little filleting knife. Chest heaving, I put a protective arm up in front of her. Something is coming, and Aina's right, we can't keep running. Better to stand and catch my breath. Better to die facing my foe.

"That thing is here for one of us. Siiri, you need to *go*." She gives me a shove. "Keep running."

Too late.

In another swirl of billowing black smoke, the horned woman appears before us on the other side of the clearing. Her head tips to the side at an impossible angle, more owl than human, and those black eyes gauge us, as if she's deciding which of us to kill first.

"Stay behind me," I rasp, stepping in front of Aina.

She clings to my hips with both hands. I can feel the warmth of her breath on my neck.

The creature's mouth opens wide, and I can't help but gag. Once, when I was hunting with Onni, we came across a dead deer washed up on the beach. The carcass was bloated and rotting, bugs eating away its eyes. The waves slowly pushed it back and forth against the pebbles. The smell of that mangled, bloated deer carcass emanates out of this creature's cavernous mouth. Moist decay, sour rot. I can't breathe. Can't think. My eyes sting. My nose and throat burn. Behind me, Aina makes a choking sound.

A low growl comes from behind us both, and I know what I'll see if I turn around. That monstrous wolf will be there, those glowing red eyes watching me. With one hand on Aina, I adjust my stance so I can face both monsters at once.

"Stay back," I shout, swiping the air with my little knife.

The horned woman steps closer, so close her shadow towers over us. She makes no sound when she moves. Not a single whisper or crunch over the fallen leaves. That rune-marked, skeletal hand extends towards me.

"I said stay back," I cry, swinging wildly with my knife. The blade connects with the meat of the creature's palm, and she pauses. Next to her, the wolf growls, flicking his serpent-like tail. A sickening smile spreads across the woman's face, as if she's surprised and delighted to see I would dare attack her. With a sweep of her arm, she launches me off my feet. Her hand doesn't even touch me, and yet I'm breathless, my vision spinning as I fly through the air and slam against a tree. I crumple, body aching.

"Siiri," Aina cries out, somewhere to my right. "Don't hurt her," she screams at the monster. "Take me. *Please*, take me instead!"

Never.

Darkness creeps in from the corners of my vision as I scramble to my knees. That creature is not taking Aina away from me. Warm blood oozes from my cut brow and down my cheek, dripping onto the fallen leaves. My breaths come short and fast as I paw at the ground, desperate to find my knife. I grasp a small rock. The fingers of my other hand wrap around the sharp metal of my knife blade. Stumbling to my feet, I throw the rock. It strikes the horned woman on the side of the head. She turns to face me, letting out an unearthly hiss.

"Aina, run," I shout.

But Aina is rooted to the spot.

With a feral cry, I throw my knife. It spins through the air, handle over blade, landing hilt-deep in the chest of the horned woman. "Now, Aina," I call. "Run!"

She shakes her head, tears slipping down her cheeks. "Not without you."

The monster doesn't even blink as the knife pierces her heart. Slowly, she raises her hand and jerks it free. With her haunting gaze locked on mine, she drops the knife to the ground at her feet. Still looking at me, she steps to the side and reaches out, her rune-marked fingers gripping Aina's exposed forearm.

Aina's scream rips through me, stealing the air from my lungs.

Torches bob around us in the night, flashes of golden yellow. Men run towards her screams. The monster gives me one last lopsided smile before disappearing in a swirl of black smoke, drawing Aina with her.

"Siiri—" Aina's cry is cut short, lost to the shadows.

"Aina!"

As the smoke dissipates, the giant wolf lunges, crossing the clearing in one leap. It follows Aina and the creature into dark oblivion. I stumble forward, waving my hand through the wisps of shadow, but they're gone.

I sink to my knees, heart thudding in my chest. My eyes are fixed on the point where Aina just disappeared. She could have run, but she wouldn't leave me. Given the choice between her and me, she let the monster take her.

The black void that swallowed her whole fills me, growing, growing inside me. My heart pounds as the truth sinks into my chest, coiling around my very bones. Aina is gone. I couldn't protect her. I failed her. She sacrificed herself to the monster to save me.

I collapse on the forest floor, the moss now a pillow for my aching head. *It's my fault Aina's gone, so let me die here in these woods.* I close my eyes, my cold hand pressed against the soil. "Take me," I whisper to the ground. "Ilmatar, take me with her. I am nothing without her."

The All-Mother answers my prayer as blessed darkness overtakes me.

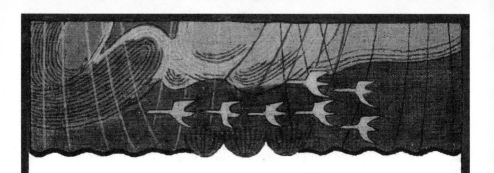

Siiri

I'VE NEVER THOUGHT MUCH about dying. Death, certainly. It seems to me an exciting new adventure. It's a long and perilous journey to the northern gates, the journey all souls must take. Through fen and forest, over meadow and marsh, through the ever-rising woodlands. Past brambles, then hazels, then on through the juniper wood. That's the song the bards sing. That is the road to Tuonela.

I want to see it all. I want to take that journey and see what only the dead have seen.

I'm ready.

But first I have to get up. I have to begin my last walk.

A cool hand brushes against my brow with the comforting touch of a mother. I lean into it, desperate for the feel of one last embrace before I go.

"Get up," whispers a soft voice.

No, this is all wrong. One must take the road to Tuonela alone. Death's journey is my own. I cannot have another here with me.

"Get up," the voice says again.

I groan, pulling away from her gentle touch. No, I wanted to die. Aina is gone, and it's my fault. I failed her. I mean to walk that lonely road all the way to the gates of Tuonela.

"Men are coming," whispers the voice. "Do not let them find you defeated."

I hear them marching through the trees—crashing, breaking, snapping. Let them come. Let them see how I've failed. They shout to each other. They shout for me, voices raised in alarm.

"Siiri!"

"Aina!"

The cool hand brushes my brow again. "You must get up."

I open my eyes. Darkness has settled all around. A woman kneels over me. This close to the new moon, the sky is dark, and there is little light for me to see. I don't trust my vision anyway. I blink, trying to make out her features.

"Who are you?" I reach out. She leans away, rising silently to her feet. She's tall and willowy, but I can make out nothing of her features, for she wears a hood. It casts her face in deep shadow. All I see is a black braid. Her hair is so long, the tip of her braid reaches her ankles.

"Return to us," she whispers. "We need you."

My mind feels fuzzy. The forest floor seems to tilt as I try to place her voice. This is a small village, and I know every woman in it. I don't know this voice. I push up on my elbows, panting through the pain. "Who are you?" I say again, my voice more forceful.

"The time has come," she replies, her voice ringing with prophecy. From deep within the folds of her hood, her eyes gleam pearly white, like two moons in the darkness. I choke on her magic as it drifts in a white mist from beneath her cloak. "Save us," she commands, her tone both a warning and a plea. "Before it's too late."

I cough. "Wait—"

Bright lights suddenly blind me, forcing me to close my eyes. I raise an arm. When I open my eyes again, the woman is gone.

I'm alone.

"Wait—come back," I call through my cough, glancing around the dark clearing. I struggle up to my knees, swaying in my dizziness. I put a trembling hand to my head, wincing at the pain. When I pull my hand away, there's blood coating my fingers. "She's gone," I whisper. "My Aina is gone—"

"Siiri!" My brother Aksel breaks through the last of the trees. He drops to his knees at my side. "Are you all right?"

Many voices now. Bobbing lights, blinking torchlight. I think I'm in shock. All I hear is a humming in my ears and my own broken heartbeat. *Gone. Gone. Gone.*

Aksel gives me an anxious shake. "Siiri—"

"It took her," I say. "It took Aina."

People loom all around me. The bearded faces of men, come too late. Above their heads, torches flicker, casting long shadows. I try to peer through their legs, looking for the woman who gave me comfort. She's a witch, perhaps. Or a goddess. A shamaness. Where did she go? What did she mean? I don't see it with my eyes, but I feel it in my bones. She's gone too.

"Siiri?" Onni drops to my other side, settling a supportive arm around my shoulders. He's massive, built like a bear. His arm curls around me like the trunk of a mighty tree. Our father jokes that on the night he was conceived my mother went walking in the winter moonlight and mated herself to Otso, the god of bears. He scoops me up as if I weigh no more than a leaf.

"Where's Aina?" a man shouts, his voice frantic. "Oh gods, where's my Aina?"

I know that voice. It's Taavi, Aina's father. I close my eyes tight, fresh tears coming. Gods, I can't look at him. "I'm sorry," I whisper, unable to face his grief.

Another shout. "Siiri? Siiri!"

"Father!" Onni bellows back. Wrapped in his arms, I feel the rumble of it through my whole body. "Over here!"

"We have her," Aksel calls.

The men make room as Father barrels between them, sharpened axe in hand. The edge glints in the torchlight.

"What happened?" asks he asks, pulling me out of Onni's arms.

I take a deep breath, swaying as I gaze up at his concerned face. He looks so much like Aksel. They're both tall and narrow, with shaggy blond hair and beards. The only difference is age. Father has creased crow's feet lining his eyes and more weathering on his strong hands.

"My child, I need you to tell us what happened," he says, gently cupping my face. He winces, inspecting the blood at my brow. The forest stops spinning. The torchlight doesn't feel quite so painfully bright.

"The woman . . ." I swallow, still tasting her stench in the back of my throat. "The creature . . . she was behind us on the beach. We ran for the trees. I tried to protect Aina. I tried—" My words break on a sob.

Onni's arm is back around my shoulders. "No one blames you, Siiri."

"I had my knife," I go on. "I cut her, but she didn't even flinch. I threw the knife, and it struck her in the heart. She just smiled. . . . Then she took Aina from me. They're gone."

"Oh gods," her father cries, digging his hands through his hair. "Oh, my Aina."

Another man puts an arm around his shoulders, keeping him on his feet.

I can't look at him. I can't see his tears. I look to the other men instead. They're all watching me with expressions of shock and horror. Some are stepping back. Others exchange worried glances with each other.

Father draws himself up to his full height, glancing around the clearing. "You did the best you could," he declares. "No man here could have done any better."

A few nod their heads.

"But what *was* it?" one of them asks.

"A witch!"

"A monster!"

"I'm telling you, it was Ajatar," shouts another. "The forest witch of Pohjola. It's why she wore a serpent's face."

Old farmer Aatos shakes his head. "No, no, it was a Lempo, a demon spirit."

"Was it a kalman väki?"

"Or Kalma herself," another man offers.

A shudder of worried exclamations passes through the assembled men.

"All-Mother, protect us," Aina's father cries, touching a hand to his forehead, then his chest. A few other men repeat the gesture. More than one man makes the sign of the Christian cross.

"I'm taking my daughter home," Father calls to the group. "Go tell your womenfolk what happened here. Until we know more, lock your doors and stay by your fires. We'll speak again tomorrow."

The men reluctantly part in twos and threes.

"Come," Onni says gently. "Let's get you home."

I let myself be steered through the darkness back to our homestead. It rests on the edge of the lakeshore—a small, pinewood house situated a stone's throw from the water, and a looming barn behind. A few outbuildings and njalle are scattered around the yard, along with our family sauna.

Father leads me right up to the house. The high windows are all shut tight. Golden light glows around their frames, and smoke billows from the chimney. He pounds on the door with his large fist. "It's us," he calls.

There's a scraping sound as my mummi lifts the bar and swings the door inward. "Oh, praise the All-Mother," she weeps, reaching out with greedy hands to pull me inside. I fall against her breast, her hands in my hair as I cling weakly to her apron-covered hips.

Father bolts the door. "Check the shutters," he directs Aksel.

My brothers skirt the perimeter of our one-room house, reaching up high to check the fastenings on the shuttered windows.

Meanwhile, Mummi steers me to the fire. Our great stone hearth takes up one whole wall of the house. Pegs pounded into the stone hold all manner of cookware. The wooden table is laden with an evening meal—creamy salmon soup with potatoes and carrots, seasoned with dill. A basket of cloudberries waits next to a pile of barley loaves. There's a pitcher of reindeer milk too, and a blackberry tart.

"Sit yourself down," Mummi murmurs, her strong hands guiding me onto a stool.

I sink down. Everything is spinning again. My head aches.

"She's bleeding," my little sister Liisa whispers from her spot at the end of the table. Her grey cat sits curled in her lap. "Why is she bleeding?"

"Go upstairs." Father brushes a hand over her wispy, white-blonde braids.

Liisa grips the sides of her stool in defiance. "No. Why is Siiri bleeding?" She lets out a squeal, and the cat scampers away, as Onni grabs her from behind, shaking her loose from her stool. It clatters to the floor, and she kicks her skinny legs and cries as he carries her over to the ladder leading to the sleeping loft.

"Go to bed," he barks, hoisting her over his head nearly to the top rung.

Liisa climbs up the ladder with a huff.

Mummi presses a wet rag to my face, gently wiping away the blood. She gestures to my soiled outer dress. "If you take this off, I'll wash it for you."

I stand on shaky legs, untying the braided belt that holds the simple wool garment together. My fingers tremble as I pull the shell over my head. Mummi dabs at my wound again. When she nears my eye, I flinch away from her touch.

"This eye will probably blacken." She looks to Father and the boys as they all make their way to the table and sit down. "What happened?"

Father frowns. "Do you have the strength to tell it again? Your mummi has a right to know."

I nod. Mummi listens, not interrupting as I start my story on the beach and end with, "And then they brought me back home."

Mummi looks from me to my brothers. "You saw this too?"

"We saw her, Mummi," Aksel replies. "We saw her even before Siiri did."

Mummi returns her attention to me, tucking a loose strand of my hair behind my ear. "Siiri, my brave girl, I believe that tonight you met a goddess. From what you describe, it can only be Kalma."

A chill seeps through me. Kalma, goddess of death. She haunts graveyards with her malevolent guard dog, the evil Surma, guardian of Tuonela.

Gods, if she's right, what am I to do? How am I to save Aina?

It's clear Onni isn't ready to believe, even knowing what he saw. He spends too much time with the Christian priests. Aksel looks uncertain too. He leans forward. "Mummi, you said nothing can leave the realm of the dead. You said that when Mother died. You said she can't come back."

"The *dead* cannot come back," she replies gently. "But Kalma and her sisters have the ability to cross realms. They are powerful witches, my boy. Their magic is deep and ancient, as old as the hills on which this forest stands. Older."

I fight a shiver, meeting her gaze for the first time this night. "But what would Kalma want with Aina?"

"And don't forget the others," Aksel adds. "The disappearances this summer are all the work of Kalma, yes?"

"Undoubtedly," Mummi replies.

Aksel glances around at each of us. "Where would she take them?"

Next to him, Onni shrugs. "Maybe a graveyard."

"But why?" Aksel replies.

"Maybe she eats them . . . or Surma does—"

"Onni, don't be crass," Father warns.

Mummi ignores them all, clearly lost in thought as she watches the fire. My father and brothers continue to argue, but I watch Mummi. I watch and I wait. Of all of us, she knows the most about the old gods and their ways.

"Tuonela," she whispers at last.

"What?" I say, dread coiling in my chest. Did I not think my own path would lead me there this very night? Did I not wish for it?

My father and brothers go quiet.

Mummi glances from my father to me. "I believe Aina is

in Tuonela. All the girls. They've surely crossed the river into the land of the dead. It's the only thing that makes sense."

My heart stops. "Wait—you think Aina's dead?"

"No," she corrects, her grey gaze level. "They are in the realm of the dead . . . but I believe they may yet be alive."

"Why?" Aksel asks again.

"I don't know," she admits. She places her fingertips against her temples, massaging in small circles. "Kalma may have some need of them, I suppose. And the Witch Queen is a devious woman. She loves to torture mortals with her Beer of Oblivion—"

I grip the table with both hands.

"Kaisa," Father says, casting a pleading glance my way.

Mummi glances at me too. "Oh—oh, my dear girl, I'm sorry." She wraps her strong arms around me. "I shouldn't have said that out loud. I was merely thinking—"

"But you think that's what happened to her." Holding back my tears, I push away. "You think she's been taken to Tuonela, to what end? To be tortured?"

Aksel reaches across the table, squeezing my arm. "Perhaps Aina has been *chosen*," he offers. "She and the other girls may have been selected to be handmaidens for the death goddesses. They could even serve Tuoni himself. It would be a great honor." He glances from Mummi to our father. "It's possible, right?"

I look to Mummi, anxious to see her face. Mummi raised me on stories of Tuonela. The stories don't tell of the Witch Queen's supper parties. They tell of torture and strife, violence and death.

In these last few years alone, their need to cause pain and suffering seems unmatched. So much senseless violence, so much cruel, wasteful death—young women in childbirth, hunting accidents, a boy drowned in the stream, his little lips so pale and blue. Animals inexplicably sicken and waste away. Even our crops suffer.

It's as if death has forgotten the importance of life. It chokes us, the ever-firm hand at our throat. And in the chaos of all this overwhelming death, the Swedes and their bloodthirsty god swept in with a vengeance, preying on our weaknesses, dividing us like sheep before the slaughter.

I stare blankly into the depths of the hearth, not feeling its warmth. This is all my fault. Kalma was after me. If only I hadn't chosen to fight. Why do I *always* fight? Why can I never yield? I should have sacrificed myself to the goddess. Aina would be safe, and I would be in Tuonela right now, fighting with every breath to escape.

Will Aina do the same? Will she fight to return home to me?

I want to believe. Gods, I *have* to believe she has the strength to fight. Everyone likes to dismiss Aina, but they don't know her the way I do. Yes, she's quiet. She's patient and reserved. She keeps her opinions to herself, especially in company. But she has them. She's never held back with me, never been afraid to speak her mind. Unlike me, however, she doesn't trample people to do it.

Can she survive in Tuonela? Or will her kindness be her undoing?

I can't risk it. I can't sit idly by and wait to see if she frees herself. "I have to save her," I whisper, letting the words fortify my very bones.

Father sighs, his weathered hand brushing my hair. "Your passion does you credit, Siiri. But if a death goddess has indeed taken Aina, we should pray they are merciful to her . . . and then we should grieve with her family as they mourn her loss."

"I'll bring them a haunch tomorrow," Mummi offers. "Some eggs and bread."

"We can bring it for you," Aksel says with a nod at Onni.

I glance between them, my eyes narrowing in disgust. Oh gods, *gods*. They're planning Aina's funeral! My hands shake as I push onto my feet. "Stop."

"Siiri—" Father reaches for me, but I step away. "My child, you must accept—"

"No! She's not dead until I see her body with my own two eyes." I turn to my grandmother. "Mummi, you said it yourself, she's in Tuonela, and she's alive." Taking a deep breath, I square my shoulders. "And I'm going to bring her home."

Behind me, Onni huffs, arms crossed over his barrel chest. He's been spending too much time with those damned Christian priests who haunt our village every summer. Just two nights ago, he sat at this very table telling us that the old gods are dead. Now he's seen a goddess with his own eyes and he's still choosing not to believe?

"I feel sorry for you," I say to him. "Onni, where is your faith? Where is your hope?"

Next to him, Aksel looks just as incredulous. "What will you do, little sister? No mortal can get into Tuonela, not if they plan to come back alive."

"I don't know," I admit, crossing my arms and turning back to stare at the flames. "Not yet. But I *will* save her. Ilmatar hear me, I will save Aina."

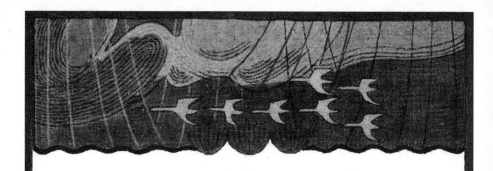

Siiri

4

I STAY UP FOR most of the night. Curled by the hearth, I try to recall every story Mummi ever told us about Tuonela and the death gods: the black river, impassable except by the ferrywoman's boat; the twin witches of pain and suffering; horses made of goblin fire; armies of the restless dead.

By the time my father and brothers wake, I've prepared the porridge, and I'm seated at the table waiting. "I need to go see Milja," I say as soon as Father sits.

He heaves a sigh. "Best to give it some time, I think."

"No. Now. This morning. I need to get to Milja before the village gossips do," I explain. "Please, Father. After Mummi, Milja is the closest I have to a mother. She deserves to hear from me directly. You know you would want the same from Aina," I add, holding his gaze.

"I will take her," Onni says. "I'll not leave her side, Father, I swear it."

After a moment's deliberation, Father nods. "There and back.

And speak to no one else, do you hear me? Onni, make sure of it. I don't want your sister getting into any more trouble."

"Trouble?"

He sets down his spoon. "All this talk of death gods and Tuonela, it bodes ill, Siiri. We must be careful now. I think you should limit who you speak to and what you say."

"What can you mean?"

"I mean that you should say nothing of your suspicions as to who took Aina and why."

I share a surprised glance with Aksel. "But—you believe Mummi, don't you? You believe me? You believe it was a death goddess who took Aina and the other girls?"

Father groans. "I wasn't there, Siiri. I didn't see it."

"Aksel saw," I declare, pointing to my brother. "And Onni, he saw too."

"I saw a strangely dressed woman on the beach," Onni corrects. "I know how I felt, but I saw no magic. She was there and then she wasn't—"

"That *is* magic," I hiss at him. "And did you not see Surma appear in a cloud of black smoke?"

He keeps shaking his head. "There was a glare. The sun—"

"Oh, don't be a coward," I snap. "Do not run from this, Onni. Do not hide like a frog in the mud, pretending the winter is not happening all around you. The gods are *real*."

"I refuse to believe that every roar of thunder comes from a god in the sky swinging a hammer," Onni counters.

"Kalma took my dearest friend!"

"Enough." Father pounds his fist on the table. "Siiri, you may tell Milja of your suspicions, but no one else. Do you understand me? If anyone asks, you are to say you don't know what you saw."

My indignation burns white-hot. "But—"

"No, Siiri. This is how it must be. Give your brothers and

me time to ask around the village. Let us determine how they're responding to these events. Then we can decide what our next step forward shall be."

I cross my arms, glaring at him. "So, you ask me to lie?"

"No, I ask you to say nothing," he corrects. "Keep your eyes down and your mouth shut. Can you do that? Say yes, or I'll lock you in this house with Liisa and the cat."

Casting him a glare, I give a curt nod.

"Then Onni will take you to see Milja after breakfast. And you will both return directly home."

Onni and I take the long way through the western woods, weaving along the outskirts of the village. We each carry a basket of food prepared by Mummi on our hips. At my father's insistence, I wear a hood over my hair to hide my face. The cut on my brow is dark and swollen, fading from purple to mottled yellow around the side of my eye.

Aina's father is chopping wood in the yard, while her younger brother Jaako stacks the cut wood next to the house. Taavi first sees Onni's massive frame emerging from the stand of pine trees. His gaze then drops to me at my brother's side.

"She's here to see Milja," Onni explains. "Will you allow it?"

Taavi's gaze lingers on my swollen eye. After a moment, he nods.

Onni gives me a little push. "I'll wait for you here."

Taking a deep breath, I slip past the men, crossing the yard and stepping through the open back door. The interior is a house and barn in one. All the animals are out grazing, so the doors to their stalls stand open, letting in the weak morning sunlight.

The hearth burns with a low fire. Along the wall, a ladder

leads up to the family's sleeping quarters above. Aina's hand loom rests on a stool in the corner. I can't bear to look at it. I turn away. Milja sits at a narrow table in the middle of the room, a steaming cup of tea clasped between her hands. As I step closer, I catch a whiff of mint, her favorite.

Milja's eyes are red-rimmed, her face swollen from all her tears shed. "Hello, Siiri." Her gaze sweeps over my bruised and blackened eye. "Taavi said you fought the creature with your bare hands. I see it must be true."

I lower my hood and drop down onto the stool opposite Milja. When my own mother died, I cursed the goddess of illness for taking her from us. The fevers burned through her for three days and nights before she faded away. I was so mad and so alone. With each year that passes, I remember less of her face, her smile, her warm embrace. Memories of Milja have slowly begun to replace memories of my mother—green eyes instead of blue, pointed chin instead of round. And Milja has taken it all in stride, loving me as a mother loves a daughter.

"Milja, I'm so sorry. I'm so—I did everything I could to protect her—" My words stop short. I can't give excuses, not to Milja. "I shouldn't have fought," I say instead, eyes brimming with tears. "I should have let it take me. I think it wanted me at first. Oh gods, it's my fault she's gone—" The rest of my apology dies in a weak, broken sob.

Milja reaches across the table, wrapping her hands around my wrist. They are warm from cradling her cup of tea. "I don't blame you, Siiri. I don't blame anyone. The gods demand sacrifices of us. If Aina was required, there is no stopping the gods from taking what is owed."

"You believe the gods took her?"

She offers me a weak smile. "I know your mummi raised you right. My mother taught me the stories and songs too, just as her mother taught her, on and on back to the time the songs were first sung. The gods are here, Siiri," she says, glancing around the room. "They watch us. They intercede in our prayers. And sometimes they teach us lessons."

"Milja, I believe Kalma is the one who took Aina," I say. "Mummi and I think Aina is in Tuonela. All the girls."

Slowly, Milja nods. "Yes, it was surely Kalma who came last night. For what purpose, I don't know." She slips her hand out of mine, dropping it to her lap. "I only know I shall never see my Aina again."

"My father doesn't want me to tell people what happened," I go on. "I think he's afraid of what they'll do if they know Kalma was here."

"Jari is right to be afraid," she replies. "For so long now, we've been told all our gods are dead. We opened the door to this misery with our lack of faith. Now the gods punish us for it."

"Does Taavi believe?"

She blinks back fresh tears, wrapping her slender hands once more around her steaming cup. "He doesn't know what to think. Aina was his pride and joy. Parents aren't supposed to have favorites—and our boys are such sweet little lads." She gives me another weak smile. "But my Aina . . . she was something special, wasn't she?"

I lean across the table, gripping her wrist. "Milja, I'm going to save her."

Milja blinks, looking up. "What?"

"Don't you see? The Christians are wrong, and Kalma just gave us the proof. Our gods aren't dead, Milja. If Kalma was here last night, then they're *all* here—Ukko in the sky pounding out lightning with his hammer, Ilmarinen at his forge, Tuoni on his throne of skulls. If one is real, they're *all* real."

Her green eyes widen. Slowly, she shakes her head. "Siiri . . ."

"Besides," I press on, "I think the gods need us as much as we need them."

"What do you mean?"

"They need us to believe in them," I reply. "They need us to stop indulging in this damned complacency. And they need us to stop letting foreigners invade our land telling us that we're as powerless as they believe our gods to be. They are *real*, Milja. I saw one last night. She looked in my eyes. She showed me her face." Holding her gaze, I make my oath. "If Kalma can take Aina away, another god will bring her back."

"Oh, Siiri," Milja whispers, a fresh tear slipping down her cheek.

Searching her face, I see the truth. She's terrified—and broken. She doesn't dare let herself hope. It breaks my heart to see her so defeated. I must have enough hope to sustain us both. I give her wrist another gentle squeeze. "Do you trust me enough to at least let me try? Please, Milja, hold on to hope for a little while longer. I will bring Aina home."

"My brave Siiri . . . they call your brother the bear-child, but it is *you* who shares the spirit of Otso." She smiles weakly. "I believe you can do anything you set your mind to, whether because you have the strength to achieve it . . . or because you simply have the will to never give up. You have my blessing, child. Go if you must. And may Ilmatar go with you."

Siiri

ONNI LEADS THE WAY through the woods back towards our house. I walk behind him on silent feet, a basket of vegetables from Milja on my hip. The building to our left is a small structure with a thatched roof. It used to be a barn, but the family moved north two summers ago. The Christian priests use it now. Onni takes a deer path that brings us closer to the side of the building.

"We should stay away," I warn.

"This way is faster," he replies, not slowing down.

I peer through the trees, noting the new addition on the roof. A large wooden cross casts its shadow over the clearing. An ominous feeling of wrongness tickles the back of my neck. "Onni, please, let's go around."

Onni stops, and I nearly walk right into him. He puts out a hand, catching me by the shoulder. I tense, my gaze locking on Brother Abbiørn at the far end of the clearing, standing on an oaken stump. A dozen villagers stand between us, listening to him speak.

This priest started showing up several summers ago. He travels up and down the lakeshore, visiting different villages, always talking with the young men. He's short, with large, round eyes. He wears his hair in an odd style, with the top of his head shaved. And he has no beard. He wears a long dress like a woman, tied at the hip with a corded belt. A small cross hangs around his neck on a leather cord. His crisp, baritone voice carries over the crowd to Onni and me on the path, no longer concealed by the trees. Instinctively, I adjust my hood, trying to hide my face.

"This is a warning, brothers," the priest calls out. "It is a sign of the Devil's power over this place. But it is also a victory cry to the Believer. God will take the wicked and cast them into the pit of eternal darkness, but the righteous of the Lord will be sent heavenward."

"Is he talking about Aina?" I hiss at my brother.

"But why was she taken?" one of the men calls out.

Brother Abbiørn turns to him. "The Devil will always claim the wicked. We must have faith that all those who walk in the light of the one true God will be free of the powers of darkness!"

Rage courses through me as I drop my basket of vegetables. "Aina was *not* wicked," I shout, startling some of the gathered men.

"Siiri, don't," Onni warns.

Brother Abbiørn gazes across the crowd, his dark eyes settling on me. Slowly, he smiles. "You saw the Devil last night, didn't you, child? You felt the hot breath of Hell on your face." Looking around at the group, he points to me. "All of you, look now! The Lord placed His hand upon her head and spared her from the wrath of Satan. The good shall always be spared."

"Are you saying Aina wasn't good?" I shout. "Are you saying she deserved what happened to her?"

Onni grabs my arm. "Siiri, stop."

I jerk myself loose, taking two full steps into the clearing. My hood slips back, revealing the ugly bruise on my face. Those closest to me move back.

"We are all sinners, child," Brother Abbiørn replies from atop his stump. "In word and deed, we have sinned. But some of us can be spared. *You* were spared. The Lord is not done with you yet."

My hands curl into fists. "And where was Aina's sin? She is the truest person I've ever known. I defy any man here to disagree!"

A few mumbles of assent reach my ears.

"If she is so pure of heart, why did the Devil take her?" Brother Abbiørn challenges.

Squaring my shoulders, I make the sign of Ukko with my left hand and shout, "By Ukonvasara, I swear that the first person to side with this scheming foreigner and blacken Aina's name will get a knife in the back, courtesy of *my* hand!"

Anyone in my reach edges away.

"No Christian devil took Aina last night," I go on. "It was Kalma! I was there, I *saw* her. Please, you have to believe me!"

"Siiri, enough," Onni growls, wrapping both arms around me from behind. He lifts me clean off the ground. A few men chuckle as I fight and kick, trying to get myself free from his iron grip.

"Onni, put me down," I snarl, but he just backs away.

"The Lord has plans for you, girl," Brother Abbiørn calls after us. "He spared you from the fires of Hell!"

"It's called Tuonela, you ignorant swine!"

Now the villagers are muttering, backing away from us. Onni tightens his grip.

"It was Kalma," I shout again, pointing at the priest. "His god is not here. *Our* gods still rule this land—"

"Siiri, come *on*." Onni drags me down the path towards home, our boots squelching in the mud.

"You will be His acolyte in the end, Siiri Jarinsdotter," Brother Abbiørn calls through the trees. "You will be a true Believer!"

That afternoon, the door to the cabin snaps open, and Father marches in. His eyes narrow, a deep scowl on his face as he takes me in, sitting on the floor before the hearth with Liisa's cat asleep in my lap. "What have you done?" he bellows.

I flinch as the terrified cat scampers off. "Father?"

He jerks his axe out of his belt, slamming it down on the table. "Did you insult the priest? Did you threaten him?"

I glance over at Mummi, who sits quietly peeling carrots, only recently returned to the house herself from a visit to Milja. Then I rise to my feet. "Father, listen—"

"Don't bother denying it," he shouts. "Onni told me everything."

I knew he would. He dragged me home and all but threw me inside the house, slamming the door shut and threatening to sink me in the bog if I dared to leave before Father came home. I cross my arms. "Father, that priest called Aina wicked. He said she deserved what she got. You would expect me to do nothing?"

He groans, dragging both hands through his sweaty hair. "Gods help me, you're not a child, Siiri! You're a woman grown, and it's time you started acting like one."

Indignation hums through me. "And is a woman not allowed to stand up for the honor of her friends?"

"A woman should know when to hold her tongue!"

I gasp, reeling back. "You believe a woman can have no voice, then?"

"I believe that *priest* believes it should be so," he counters. "Did you see a single woman in that crowd assembled today? Have you *ever* seen the Swedish priests take women aside and share with them any mystical truths about this formless god?"

I let the truth of his words sink in. No, never once has Brother Abbiørn sought out the women of my village to speak with us about his god.

"There is no place for women with the Swedes and their one god," he goes on. "It is a god of men, Siiri. A god of wars and conquest. A god of blood and death and destruction. And if it keeps moving north, it will swallow us all. Why do you think I left Turku when I did? You think I wanted to leave? You think life is easier for us out here in this godsforsaken wilderness?"

My eyes go wide. "Wait . . . you're not running from the Swedes at all, are you? You're running from their god. You're running for us."

"Of course I ran for you," he replies, his tone softening. "For Liisa, for your mummi, for your brothers and their future wives and children. Our gods demand balance, Siiri. They believe in justice and fairness and equality. The Swedish god stands against everything I hold most dear. It is jealous and vindictive. It demands total fealty and seeks only subjugation and violence. I fear the only way to stem the tide will be to meet it with more violence. And we're not ready. The Finns aren't ready to face a people united under one bloodthirsty god. We're not ready for a war."

I glance from Mummi back to him. "So, what happens now? How do we get the people ready?"

He sighs. "We don't, Siiri. It's not possible. All I can do is keep you all alive. I'll keep you fed, keep you sheltered, and the Swedes will come as they will. Brother Abbiørn must be allowed to say and do what he wants. You must not antagonize him further. It's not safe, Siiri. Do you see that now? Please tell me you understand."

I narrow my eyes at him. "I suppose we're to be a family of rabbits, then, always hiding, always giving ground." I huff in disdain. "I thought Finns were the brothers and sisters of Otso. We are bears, Father. We don't run from a fight. We are strong. We protect our land—"

"We are not bears, we're *men*," he shouts. "And we are weak . . . and hungry . . . and few. And our gods have abandoned us."

I shake my head, not wanting to believe him.

He lets out a heavy breath. "I need you to go to that priest, Siiri. I need you to apologize to him."

"Never," I hiss, angry tears stinging my eyes.

"Godsdamn it," he bellows, slamming both fists on the table, rattling the wooden cups and bowls. "What do you think will happen when that priest travels south in a month and tells the Swedes in Turku that the people of Lake Päijänne are saying the old gods have returned?"

I cross my arms again. "Maybe they'll finally leave us alone."

Father scoffs. "That dream is as futile as a flower blooming in winter. Brother Abbiørn *will* return, and he won't be alone. Where there was one meddlesome priest, there will now be three. And if we don't listen to their bleating and pretend to care, more will come: five . . . then ten. They will burn our sacred groves and smash our cup-stones to dust. If we don't supplicate ourselves before that priest now, he'll tear this village down around us. Mark me, Siiri, he will never forget the insult of a girl who claims to have seen Kalma."

"I *did* see Kalma! Father, you know I did—*ah*—"

He lunges forward, smacking the unbruised side of my face, knocking me backwards. Tears sting my eyes as I touch the spot on my cheek with a shaky hand.

"Enough, Jari," Mummi calls, getting to her feet at last.

I can see in his eyes that he's just as shocked by his actions as I. He blinks twice, grunting with frustration. Then he points a finger at me. "You'll go first thing in the morning and apologize to that priest. You'll ask him polite questions about his god and listen quietly as he explains."

"Father—"

"This you *will* do, or by all the gods, Siiri, I'll belt you until your backside matches your face!"

Mummi steps forward. "Jari, that's enough—"

"Quiet," he snaps at her. "Better my belt on her stubborn back than militant priests putting a rope around her neck." Chest heaving, he holds my gaze. "I'll give you the night to think it over, and pray you make the right choice." With that, he takes his axe off the table and storms out.

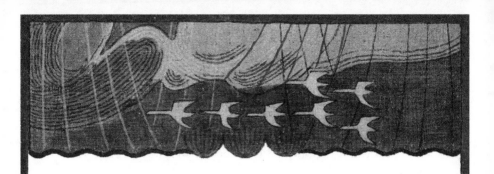

Siiri

"ARE YOU ALL RIGHT?" Mummi reaches towards me, but I shrug her away, moving in the other direction around the table. "What are you going to do?" she calls after me.

I shake my head, my heart racing.

"Forgive your father, Siiri."

My indignation mingles with my embarrassment. "He hit me."

"He's afraid," she replies. "Nothing he said now is untrue. Your father left Turku to offer you all a better life away from the Christians. But no matter where we go, they follow."

"So we should stand and fight! When a bear is backed into a corner, it stands tall, and it fights to the death."

Tears rim her eyes. Hopelessness lurks inside her too.

"Oh, Mummi," I whisper. "Where is your heart?"

She offers me a sad smile. "Apparently, it beats in your strong chest."

"Do you think I should apologize to the priest? Should I

lie to everyone and say it was not Kalma on the lakeshore but some devil of the formless God?"

Mummi considers, her blue-grey eyes searching my face. "No," she says at last. "I don't."

"You think I should take the belt? I should let Father humiliate me?"

Before Mummi can respond, the door rattles open and Liisa bounces in, followed closely by Aksel. "I fed the chickens, Mummi," my sister announces, going straight to the ladder in search of her cat.

Aksel plops a brace of rabbits on the table, already skinned and ready for the pot. "For supper," he says with a grunt. Then he moves to the back of the cabin and begins stripping out of his soiled clothes. "I'm going to the lake to wash."

"I want to do sauna tonight," Mummi calls. "Will you cart in the wood?"

Aksel huffs, his head stuck inside his shirt. "It's not sauna night."

"It is if I say it is," she counters.

He peels himself out of his sweaty shirt, leaving him in only his elk-skin breeches. "Mummi, I stink and I'm tired. I'm going to wash. We'll do sauna tomorrow."

"Never mind. Siiri and I will do it," she replies with her own huff. "Siiri, come."

I reach out my hand, letting her take it. I know what she's doing. Inside the sauna we can speak with no one around.

Aksel shrugs, and we all step outside into the weak afternoon light. All around us, the green of the leaves is starting to change to yellow, brown, and red. Autumn is here, and it won't last long.

Aksel marches off in his breeches and bare feet towards the lakeshore. Mummi and I veer right, walking hand in hand towards the sauna. Liisa doesn't dare follow, lest she be put to work carting wood.

Mummi and I gather several logs from the pile outside the door. Inside the sauna, the aromatic smell of pine fills my nose. We remove our boots, keeping the door open to allow light into the windowless room. I drop to my knees before the small hearth, ready to layer in the logs. Behind me, Mummi watches. "Milja told me what you said," she begins. "She told me what you plan to do."

I go still, a split piece of wood balanced in my hands.

"Siiri, you can't go alone on some quest looking for proof of the old gods."

I drop the wood, gazing up at her. "I don't need proof. I have it already. Kalma took Aina, you said so yourself."

"And you think because Kalma revealed herself to you, another god will do the same? Who are you that the gods of old will show you their faces?"

"Another god already did," I challenge, rising to my feet.

"When? Why did you not say anything?"

"I'm not sure what I saw," I admit. "It was in the woods after Aina was taken. It was dark, and I heard a voice. Someone was there with me, Mummi. She helped me. And then I blinked, and she was gone, just like Kalma."

"You took a rather hard blow to the head," she offers, not unkindly.

I glare at her. "She touched me, Mummi. She spoke to me."

"What did she say?"

"She told me to get up. And she told me to return. She said, 'Return to us. We need you.'"

"Perhaps it was a villager saying that you should return home—"

I raise a hand. "I didn't recognize the voice, Mummi. It

was a woman's voice. You tell me if there is a woman's voice in this village that you wouldn't know even in the dark."

She sighs, conceding defeat. "So, you think another goddess was with you in the woods?"

"I know she was. I just don't know *who* she was. But perhaps she'll come to me again. Perhaps she'll help me save Aina."

Mummi narrows her eyes at me. "Just tell me your plan, child."

"I mean to go north," I reply. "There's a hiisi, a sacred grove. It's a two-day walk up the lakeshore. Father took us there years ago, do you remember?"

She nods again.

"I will go and pray to the gods for help. They will answer, Mummi. I know they will."

"Siiri, you can't just wander the wilderness, looking for a sacred grove. It's dangerous. There are hunters and trappers, and beasts of the forest, to say nothing at all of this fickle weather."

I smile, placing a hand on her shoulder. "I'll be gone a week at most. I'll go to the hiisi and make my prayers. I'll beg a god to help me bring Aina back. I have to try. I promised Milja."

"She would never hold you to it," Mummi replies gently.

I search her face. "What do you mean?"

Mummi sighs, brushing a hand down my arm. "She knows it's impossible. She just doesn't have the strength to break your heart. But by all the gods, Siiri, I *do* have that strength." Her grip tightens on my arm. "If Aina were anywhere but Tuonela, things might be different. But Kalma took her, Siiri. She's no longer in this realm. No god can help you now, for none can do what you seek. Aina is gone. You must accept it."

Shrugging away from her touch, I sink onto the empty bench. *Is this really the end? Is there no hope for my dearest friend?*

All the memories of long nights spent around the table listening to Mummi tell us stories swirl in my mind. Stories of Lemminkäinen, the wayward adventurer who traveled to Tuonela and paid the ultimate price. Stories of the frost giants and the gnomes and the kings of Kalevala. But my favorite stories have always been the tales of Väinämöinen, son of Ilmatar and the greatest shaman of legend. He planted all the trees of the earth, battled the great sea monster Iku-Turso . . . and he used his shamanic magic to enter Tuonela. There, he learned the secrets of death, before tricking the death gods and crossing the realms back into life.

He returned *alive*.

"Väinämöinen." I whisper his name like a blessing, a prayer.

Mummi goes still. "What about him?"

I smile, looking up at her. "You're right. I don't need a god to get into Tuonela, I need a shaman. I need Väinämöinen."

She shakes her head. "Siiri, he died a long time ago . . . if he ever really lived at all. The songs say he left these lands to sail the inland sea—"

"But he will *return*," I press, rising to my feet. "The songs say he will return—" I gasp, piecing it all together. "Oh gods . . . and when he returns, he will bring back the true religion. That is the prophecy, yes?"

"Siiri—"

"Suns will rise and set in Finland, rise and set for generations." I repeat the words of the ancient song. "He *knew* we would forget about him. All the gods knew. But he will return to save his people. He will restore all that was lost to us—his teachings, his wisdom. He will bring back the true religion, and we can be one Finland again. We can be united, as we were in the days of Kalevala. No more senseless death, no more violence. And if there is to be a war with the Swedes and their god, we can rise up as one to meet them. We can fight back. With Väinämöinen at our side, how can we lose?"

"Have you forgotten about Aina?" Mummi says with a raised brow.

"Of course not," I reply. "I'll find Väinämöinen, and he can help me save Aina. Then I can bring him back here. I can bring them *both* back."

"Oh, is that all?"

"Mummi, the gods are stirring. I know you feel it too. This hopelessness, this apathy, this godsdamn acceptance—it is not who we are. It is not who we ought to be. And the Swedes are advancing. They think us weak. They think us ready to fall to their power. The time is now. Väinämöinen *must* return to us—"

As soon as I say the words, we both gasp, gazing at each other.

Mummi squeezes my hand. "Oh child, what did the goddess say in the woods?"

"'Return to us,'" I repeat. "'We need you.' And she said 'The time has come. Save us.'"

"Oh, Siiri . . . "

I smile through my tears. "Do you believe me now, Mummi? That was a message from the gods. I am meant to do this. I am meant to find him. Will you help me?"

Her own smile falls. "I don't know where he is," she admits. "I only know what the songs say. He got in his copper-bottomed boat and sailed away from the lands of Kalevala. He could have followed the path of the inland sea north, but no one knows where it ends."

"I was planning to go north anyway," I say. "I will go to the sacred grove. There I will pray and beg for a god to intercede. They must want Väinämöinen to return as much as we do. They want their land back, their people. They want our prayers, our devotion. They want us all to wake up, Mummi. They'll help me."

After a moment, Mummi nods. "If you are going, you must leave tonight. The longer you delay, the better the chance is that your father will try to stop you."

My heart skips a beat. "Tonight?"

"You know the way well enough," she replies, dropping to her knees and shoving the rest of the wood inside the small hearth. "Have an offering ready for the uhrikivi. A token of fresh game is good, but gold or silver is better."

My gaze traces the curve of her hunched back. "Wait—this plan is mad, Mummi. Why aren't you trying to stop me?"

She pauses, glancing over her shoulder. "Because our lives are measured by the risks we take to help those in need when their need is greatest." She gets to her feet, turning to take my hand in both of hers. "I know how much you love Aina. And I know you love your family too. I know you love your people. You were born to love with your whole heart and to protect fiercely." She smiles, stroking my freckled cheek. "My wild Siiri. There's never been any stopping you at anything you wish to do . . . so go. You have my blessing."

"I will come back. Look for me at each sunset returning from the north."

She nods, her hand still on my cheek. "Men have long been the heroes of our tales. Show the people what we women can do to fight for those we love. Go north. Find Väinämöinen if you can. Save Aina. Then return to us. We need you," she adds with a smile.

"I think I might be afraid," I whisper, letting her hear my deepest truth.

Leaning forward, Mummi kisses my forehead. "You'd be a fool not to be afraid, my brave girl . . . but you'll go all the same."

Part Two

Now my mind is filled with sorrow,
Wanders through the bog and stubble,
Wanders weary through the brambles,
Roams throughout the dismal forest,
Till my life is filled with darkness,
And my spirit white with anguish.

—Rune 4. *The Kalevala.*

Aina

7

MY DREAMS HAVE BEEN so dark of late. I dream about a forest. It's night, and there's no moon. Clouds cover the stars, and I'm running faster than I've ever run in my life. My bare feet pound the ground as I take panting breaths. I feel everything under my toes—soft moss, crunching leaves, roots, and rock.

I'm not running. I'm *fleeing*. The monster keeps pace with me, an enormous, shaggy black wolf with glowing red eyes. That color haunts me, like two droplets of blood. Feathered branches slap at my face. I cry out in fear, my voice breaking with the chill of the air. Why am I running? Why am I alone? Where is Siiri? The details of the dream slip away until a sharp pain in my forearm tears me from my sleep.

I'm awake.

This is my body, arms and legs weighed down by heavy blankets. I blink my eyes open, turning my head to either side. I'm in the middle of a large bed, toasty warm under a pile of furs. I've never slept in a proper bed before, not one built on a wooden frame, raised off the floor. I sit up, the furs slipping down around my waist. I'm in a strange room. The bed sits in the middle of one wall, the frame hung with thick curtains. On the far side of the room, a hearth glows with a welcoming fire. To either side of the hearth are two small, shuttered windows. The only other furnishings in the room are a small wooden table and a single chair.

I wrap one of the furs around my shoulders and slip my feet out the side of the bed, and my bare toes touch the cold, wood-planked floor. Why are my feet bare? The last thing I remember, I was wearing socks and my thick boots. I unfold the fur from around my shoulders and look down. My sturdy woolen dress is gone. Now, I'm in a white gown. The neckline is cut into a V, and the gown falls in folds to my ankles. It feels soft against my skin, but the feeling doesn't soothe me. Someone had to strip me naked to clothe me.

Is this still a dream?

I pinch my arm and wince. Nothing else happens.

"I'm awake," I murmur.

Moving over to the door on soft feet, I lift the latch and give it a little push. The door doesn't budge. I rattle the latch again and push with my shoulder, but the door is locked. My chest tightens as I fight my growing panic. What would Siiri do?

Find a way out.

I drag the chair beneath a window and glance up, measuring the distance. It will be a difficult climb, but fear and courage pulse through me in equal measure. I step up onto the chair and pull the shutters inward. Cool night air blasts inside, making the fire spark. I tip up onto my toes and can only just peek out over the sill. It's a rare moonless night, not a star in the sky. The same night from my dreams? From this angle, I can't quite see the ground. Are there other houses close by? A forest? A lake?

Taking a deep breath, I pull up with all my might, scrambling to find a foothold with my bare feet. My right foot slips, and I cry out. I sink down to the chair but miss, dropping to the floor with a clatter, jarring my elbow painfully. "Ow, ow, ow." A large splinter sticks out of my heel. I carefully pull it loose, grimacing as I set it aside. Blood flows freely from the wound.

Try again, you fool.

I let Siiri's voice in my head give me strength.

Stop crying and get up. Don't die in this room, and don't wait for your captor to find you.

I climb back onto the chair and jump, pulling my head and shoulders towards the ledge. It's working this time. I'm nearly there. I'm—

"Ahhh, it's hot!"

I screech in pain, dropping back to the chair. Heart racing, I look down at my aching hands. My palms are bright red, as if I'd just wrapped them around a burning log. The red color fades, my palms returning to normal. I inspect the area where the splinter pierced my heel. The skin is smooth. No blood, no pain. I glance back up at the sill, my panic rising. I can't get out. This room is my cage.

I slam the window shut. Turning away, I gasp in fright, both hands clutching my chest. Moments before, the table had been empty. Now, it contains a jug and a tray of barley bread. The smell of the bread makes me salivate. How long has it been since my last meal?

I pad on cold feet over to the table. The golden tray holding the bread glistens in the firelight. I pick up the jug first and sniff its contents. Just water. The moment I touch it, a cup appears next to the golden tray. I set the jug aside to examine the cup.

It's made of horn, but the bottom is gilded, finely etched in a feathered pattern. I've never seen ornamentation so delicate on such a simple object. I pour myself a cupful of the cold water and down it in a gulp, already feeling a little better.

Setting the cup aside, I reach for a loaf of barley bread, my stomach growling. I take a bite and hold back a moan of pleasure. This is the softest, most finely milled bread I've ever tasted. With my eyes closed, I feel like I'm standing in the field where the barley was grown. I can feel the sun warming my cheeks. It's truly magical. If I reached out my hands, would they touch the bristled tops of the barley?

As soon as I swallow the bread, the sensation ends. I take another bite and gag, choking on the taste of slick, pungent mold. I spit out the piece in my mouth, looking down to inspect the rest. It looks like a perfectly normal loaf of bread.

Two other loaves wait on the golden tray. I set the moldy-tasting bread down and take up another loaf. That first bite is even more exquisite. Tears fill my eyes as I swallow the delicious morsel. But then I take another bite and gag, the foul taste of rot once more filling my senses. I set the bread aside, too afraid to try the third loaf. If I only get one bite, I'll have to wait. I don't know when I'll be fed again.

Suppressing a shiver, I glance over at the bed. The pile of furs waits for me, enough to keep me warm in this strange place.

Tap. Tap. Tap.

My heart races as I look to the high window. Someone's out there. Someone's tapping at my window. Slowly, I take a step forward. A raven's plaintive caw breaks the oppressive silence, and I let out a shaky breath. It quickly morphs into a nervous laugh.

There's a raven on my windowsill.

I hurry over and pull open the shutter. The handsome

raven ruffles his feathers and clicks his large beak, turning his head from side to side. One of his eyes is clouded and white, like a little full moon. The other is black as night. The black eye holds my gaze, and he caws loudly, clicking his beak again.

"Hello there," I whisper, taking a step back.

The sharp talons on his scaly black toes scratch against the sill as he hops back and forth, still glancing around. Will the magic of this room keep him out, just as it keeps me in?

"Are you hungry, friend? Would you like some bread? I have plenty to spare." Stepping over to the table, I pick up one of the loaves and tear off a small piece. The raven follows my every movement. He's easily twice the size of a normal raven, almost the size of an eagle. He watches me with that curious, unblinking eye. I rise up on tiptoe and set the piece of bread on the sill. "Here you go, friend."

The raven flutters his wings and squawks indignantly . . . but he stays.

"You're such a handsome fellow," I whisper. "My mother taught me the stories about Raven. You were born on a charcoal hill, with eyes like a mussel's pearl. Your beak is made from a goblin's sharp-tipped arrow . . . or some such nonsense. She says you're a bad omen."

The raven cocks his head at me. He almost looks affronted.

"I disagree with her, of course," I add quickly. "I think ravens are lovely, clever birds. And here in this dark place, you're my only friend."

That seems to satisfy him, and I smile. His wings are glossy, the iridescent sheen almost glowing in the light of the fire. It is green and purple and blue at once, like the foxfires that light the sky in the far north. He's beautiful. He makes quick work of my little offering, pecking the morsel of bread to pieces and cawing at me indignantly when it's gone.

"How do you feel?" Even though he ate more than one

bite, it doesn't seem to be making him ill. "Just me then," I say with a tired sigh, and then smile at the open expression of hunger on his face. "Greedy thing. Would you like some more?" I get another piece of bread and return to the window, lifting it up to the ledge.

As soon as he finishes his meal, he flaps his wings and disappears into the dark.

"Oh, don't go," I cry. "Please, don't go. Please!"

But the raven doesn't come back.

My room is freezing with both windows thrown open wide, but I don't care. I'm waiting to see if Jaako will return. That's what I've named the raven. Like my younger brother, he's black of hair and seems just a little bit mischievous. By my guess, it's been two days since he was last here. Two days with no sunrise. No sunset. The bread remains cursed so that each bite I take after the first tastes like mold in my mouth. My stomach aches with hunger, and I'm tired. But I can't sleep. I don't dare waste my water to bathe. At least my fire never dies. Just when I think I've burned my last log, a new stack appears.

Trapped in this room, I've done everything I know to escape. I tried picking the lock, removing the door's hinges. I even tried climbing out the other window. I abandoned that plan after I fell and nearly broke my leg. Desperate, I took to knocking. Then I pounded on the door, rattling it in the frame. I've screamed out my windows until I thought my throat would bleed. I've spent hours listening for movement beyond the door.

Nothing.

I see nothing. I hear nothing. Not even the nighttime crickets in the grass or frogs at the water's edge. No howling of wolves in the distant hills. No laughter from a neighboring homestead.

I'm alone.

It's the strangest feeling. I don't think I've ever felt so utterly alone.

"I used to pray for solitude," I say to no one at all. "Just a moment of peace without the prying eyes of Siiri or my family." I let out a little laugh, feeling a pang of guilt at the admission. "Now, I'm praying for the attention of a raven." My fingers pause. "Gods, I must be going mad."

I laugh again, unable to help myself. Before long, tears are in my eyes and I'm short of breath. It's in that moment, doubled over on the bed, that I hear it—the gentle rustle of wings. I look to the window, scrambling to the edge of the bed as the raven appears. He lands on my windowsill and greets me with a caw.

"Hello, Jaako," I say, breathless.

The beautiful bird tips his head at me, curious.

"Oh, I gave you a name," I say. "I hope you don't mind." He clicks his beak, and I smile. "Won't you come in?" I gesture to my table and chair as if he's a traveler in need of refreshment.

Jaako hops forward, ruffling his feathers.

"It's all right," I soothe. "I can't go out, but I think you may be able to come in. I'd like it so very much if you would. I'd like to have a friend. Shall we break our fast together?"

He hesitates, hopping on the sill in nervous agitation. Unable to resist the allure of my barley bread, he flutters in off the windowsill, landing on the back of my chair.

My heart thrums with excitement. "Oh, Jaako, you did it."

He clicks his beak, seemingly just as delighted to learn the magic can't keep him out. It feels significant somehow, having him in the room with me rather than just on the sill. Now I'm truly not alone.

"I wish I had another chair," I say. "Then we could sit and chat like old friends. What I wouldn't give for some hot tea too. My mother makes the most delicious teas—blackcurrant leaf, dried nettle and lemon balm, raspberry mint. Do you like tea?"

The raven hops off the chair onto the table, his talons clicking on the wood until he situates himself on the table's edge. He bobs his head at the empty chair, and I grin.

"Is this chair for me? Thank you, Jaako." I take a seat, pouring myself a cup of water. "I'm sorry to say my options are quite limited. Your choices are barley bread . . . or barley bread. But since you so kindly offered to join me, I'll let you pick the loaf."

Jaako glances at the barley loaves with his good eye, flashing me the pearly white one.

"Did you hurt yourself?" I murmur, noting the appearance of a scar cutting over the eye. "Can you see out of that eye?" I reach my hand out to the side and wave it. "Can you see this?"

Jaako tips his head, letting his black eye spy my hand, and clicks his beak in assent.

I smile again. "Cheater. If we're to be friends, you have to behave. Have you picked which loaf we'll share?"

He hops forward, tapping a loaf with his beak.

"Good choice," I say, reaching for it. That I'm talking to this raven, and that he seems to understand me, is a problem I'll solve on another day. For now, I'm just desperate for the company. "I hope you don't think me rude, but I'm going to take the first bite." The raven watches as I take the largest bite I can fit in my mouth. I stifle my groan, savoring the taste as I let the aroma of the barley fill my senses. I chew and swallow, setting the bread between us on the table. "The rest is for you."

He cocks his head at me and clicks his beak.

"I don't mind, really. Take as much as you'd like. I can't eat any more."

Jaako hops forward and taps the loaf with his beak, trying to nudge it closer to me.

"No, I can't," I say again. "I can only take one bite."

He stills, glancing up at me with his good eye, a question written on his impish face.

"I think it's cursed," I admit. "The first bite tastes like . . ." I close my eyes and breathe in deeply, conjuring the taste in my mind. "It tastes like the first barley ever milled by the great Sampo. It tastes like sun and earth and water. It tastes like . . . life itself." I open my eyes, blinking back tears, my smile falling. "But every bite after tastes like death. The bread crumbles like rot in my mouth. It spoils and makes me sick."

The raven clicks his beak, clearly agitated, then hops forward and lets out a soft caw.

"It's all right." Reaching out a hand, I stroke his silky head. "It's not your fault. I have three loaves a day. That's three bites to fill my belly. And it leaves me enough to share with you," I add, giving him a weak smile. He nudges my hand, and I stroke him again, letting my fingers trail down his strong back. I lower my face closer to him, focusing on his good eye. "Where am I, Jaako? What is this dark place? Am I in danger?"

He gives me a pitying look, and I know the truth. I've known it from the moment I woke in this strange place.

Yes, he says without words. *You are in danger.*

I swallow my fear, leaning back in my chair, still stroking his feathered back. "You're a clever bird, Jaako. Clever even for a raven. You understand me, don't you?"

He bobs his head. In any other situation, I might find it

charming. But some dark magic is keeping me trapped in this room. Magic is starving me slowly. And now magic has gifted me this raven. I glance down at the handsome bird. "I think my mother may be right," I whisper, letting my hand drop away from him.

He cocks his head at me, watching me, a question in his eyes.

"I think you may be a bad omen."

Jaako casts me an indignant glare.

I lower my face to his, one elbow on the table. "If you're not . . . prove it. Help me, Jaako. Whatever magic is here in this place, use it to help me escape."

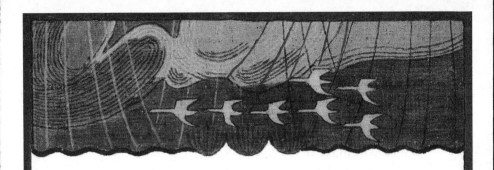

Siiri

SUPPER WITH MY FAMILY is a painfully quiet affair.
Father won't look at me, and the boys take his lead. Even
Liisa seems to know better than to break this determined silence. I choose to embrace it. If I'm quiet, I won't give myself
away . . . or land myself in more trouble. I sop up the gravy
at the bottom of my bowl with a chunk of bread, nodding to
Mummi as she refills my cup with more reindeer milk.

"Is the sauna ready?" Aksel mutters through a mouth full
of stew.

Mummi nods.

"We'll all go after supper," Father replies, taking a deep
gulp of beer.

"I'd like to stay here," I say, breaking my silence.

All eyes turn my way. My brothers glance warily between
me and our father.

Father glares at me from down the table. "Why?"

I shrug. "My courses have come early. But if you'd rather I
join you—"

"No," he says. "Stay here."

My father and brothers glance quickly away, and Mummi casts me an approving look. Nothing will make the menfolk capitulate faster than a mention of your courses.

I help Mummi clean up the evening meal as the men head outside to wash in the lake. Liisa clears all of two bowls before she races naked outside to join them. As soon as the front door rattles shut, Mummi turns to me. "I think you should go now, while they're all in the sauna."

I set down the stack of bowls in my hands. "Now? But I haven't prepared—"

"I prepared everything for you this afternoon," she says. "Go into the barn, behind the first haystack. You'll see everything there waiting for you. And take Halla. She's strong, and she won't make a fuss. She'll also give you milk, should you need it."

I shake my head, suddenly nervous. "They'll see me."

"They won't. Leave through the south woods and circle 'round. I'll tell them you went to bed, and I'll make Liisa sleep down here with me."

Tears fill my eyes. "He'll find out you helped me and be so furious."

She huffs. "I'm not afraid of my daughter's husband." Slipping a hand into the pocket of her apron, she pulls out a pair of silver bracelets. "And here, take these as well." I've seen her wear them many times before, at weddings and feast days. They're woven to look like braids.

"I can't—"

"You *can*," she presses, closing my fingers around the bracelets. "Help from the gods never comes cheap. This is all the silver I have."

"Thank you, Mummi."

She cups my face, kissing each cheek. "Stay safe, my wild

girl. And remember—sometimes the bravest thing you can do is *not* fight. The bear is valiant, Siiri. But it runs too. It hides; it lives to fight another day."

"I'll be careful."

"And come home to me."

I smile, slipping the silver bracelets onto my wrists. "I'll come home."

With Mummi's help, I sneak outside and around the back of the house. The new moon is here, so I race across the dark yard, ducking inside the barn. I make quick work of digging through the haystack, pulling out a pair of heavy leather packs. Father uses them to travel south for market days. They hold a bedroll, foodstuffs, and some basic cooking utensils. If I know Mummi, she packed me enough food to last a week.

She has also left me a pile of clothes on the crate. I shrug out of my old woolen dress and pull on a pair of elk-skin breeches. They're a good fit in the waist, if a bit long in the leg. They must have been Aksel's. I layer a pair of blue wool socks over them. Then I stuff my feet back inside my reindeer-fur boots with the thick leather soles. The shirt is blue, a long-sleeved wool blend with leather ties at the neck. It falls almost to my knees. Over the shirt, I tug on a fox-fur vest. I secure the shirt and vest with a leather belt and attach my favorite knife to my hip. I stuff a pair of mittens lined with rabbit fur into my belt pouch.

The last item is a simple blue cap trimmed with an em-broidered band of flowers. My eyes fill with tears. It belonged to my mother. I still hold memories of her wearing it, wisps of blonde hair framing her face. I bring the cap to my nose and take a deep breath, hoping it might still hold some scent of my mother, some memory. But it just smells of hay. I slip it on over my plaited blonde hair.

Ready at last, I fasten the packs onto the harness of Halla, a young, snowy-white reindeer. The last thing I grab is my bow and quiver. I strap the quiver to my opposite hip and sling the bow on my back. Taking up Halla's guide rope, I give a little click with my tongue. The reindeer follows me willingly out into the dark of the forest.

I journey north all through the night and most of the next morning, only resting so Halla and I can drink water at each stream we cross. She's a sturdy girl, quiet and attentive. She plods along at my side. As we walk, I glance around at the thick canopy of trees overhead. This autumn will be short; I can feel it in the air. It's crisp and cold, stinging the tip of my nose. In a matter of days, all these leaves will fall.

By the time the sun has reached its peak, I've already foraged a meal of mushrooms, edible clover, and a clutch of wood sorrel as I walked. I washed it down with a few strips of dried fish from my pack and several swigs of water from my waterskin.

Halla and I make our way through a sparsely populated birch forest, the narrow white trunks reaching up into the hazy blue sky. I keep a loose hold on her lead, letting her pluck mouthfuls of grass. She pauses, her nostrils flaring in alarm.

"What is it, girl?" I whisper.

Halla snorts, tugging on the lead. Tucking the loose end into my belt, I pull an arrow from the quiver and slip my bow off my shoulder. It's difficult to see. All the bending white trunks play tricks on the eyes, confounding my depth perception.

Then, I hear it.

"Oh Tapio, great lord of the forest, protect us," I pray, my fingers clenching around the feathered end of my arrow.

Through the trees comes the low, grunting moan of a bear. It sounds close. Too close. If Halla can hear and smell it, there's no doubt the bear can hear and smell us too. I think quickly: My packs are full of food the bear might find enticing. I could leave a bag of the dried fish, scattering the morsels on the ground, then run in the opposite direction. I can only hope it will stop to investigate, lured by the pungent smell.

The problem is that Halla makes a much sweeter prize. A reindeer on her own, boxed in by the woods and unable to run? A hungry bear readying for winter will happily tear her apart.

I hear again the strange moaning. The bear sounds afraid . . . and in pain.

The bear is sacred to Finns. *Forest brother*, we call him. *Honey palm.* It is our duty to protect him, to share the forest with him. I can't hear his distress and walk past if there might be some way for me to help. The gods would never forgive me if I didn't try. As I intend to ask the gods for a favor, I have to at least investigate.

"Wait here," I say, tying Halla to a tree.

The reindeer grunts in frustration, tugging on the lead.

"I don't think you'll like this," I warn.

Keeping an arrow nocked in my bow, I approach on soft feet. The bear continues to grunt and groan as I make my way through the spindly birches. The sounds are coming from the depths of a man-made pit. I inch towards the edge, wary of the soil giving way. The last thing I want is to end up at the bottom next to a starving, scared bear.

When I'm sure the ground will hold, I peer cautiously over the edge. There, at the bottom of the deep, earthen pit, stands a young brown bear. He's caught my scent and looks up at me with anxious eyes. His fur is golden brown around his face and ears, darker at his snout. His massive claws are thick with mud. He pants with fatigue. He's clearly been trying for quite a while to free himself.

"Hello there, forest brother," I call down into the pit.

My indignation grows as I look around. Who would make a pit out here, and why? There are no villages nearby, which means the bears are no threat. And Otso is a proud and vengeful god. As the spirit of the bear, he feels each of their deaths. If a Finn kills a bear, he must offer a feast in honor of Otso. The clever hunter will lie to Otso and make him believe the bear died of natural causes. If the god is not appeased, he will rain down his wrath.

You have to help him, Siiri.

It's Aina's voice in my head. I hear her words as clearly as if she were standing at my side. She's always had such a heart for animals, for any wounded thing.

"I'd like to be alive when I join you in Tuonela," I mutter, glancing around at the trees framing the pit.

You have to at least try.

I sigh, knowing she's right. It's the only thing to be done. Dropping to my knees, I lean over the edge of the pit. "Forest brother? I need you to know that I have a reindeer up here, and I need her. I'm going to help get you out, but I need you not to eat her, and I *really* need you not to eat me. If you go your way, and I go mine, I'll give you all the dried fish in my pack. Do you agree to my terms?"

The bear makes a soft grunt that I take for assent.

I scramble to my feet and pull the hatchet from my belt, cursing Aina under my breath. Then I march over to the closest sapling. "This is, by far, the maddest thing I've ever done." I look up to the heavens, spying the blue of the sky beyond the leaves. "Otso, please tell me you're watching. Let this not lead to my death."

Gripping the hatchet with both hands, I take a swing,

slamming the blade into the trunk of the young tree. With deft strokes, wishing all the while that I could borrow the strength of Ilmarinen for the task, I gradually hack the trunk in two. When it starts to teeter, I give it a shove with both hands, guiding the path of its fall. Tucking the hatchet back into my belt, I grab the trunk with both hands and drag it closer.

"Look out below," I call. "I'm dropping this end down to you."

Dirt and leaves shower down onto the bear as I give the felled tree another heave, and it crashes trunk first into the bottom of the deep pit.

"Are you all right?" I call, peering through the branches.

The bear grunts in reply. The hacked end of the trunk is speared into the mud, while the rest of the tree is angled, the top branches clearing the edge of the pit. The bear pants through his open mouth, sharp white teeth on display as he surveys the tree.

"See if you can climb out now," I call down to him. "And here's your prize." I reach into the pocket of my fox-fur vest and tug out the little satchel of dried fish. I shake the bag at him. "Climb out, and you can have some delicious fish."

The bear watches me with puzzled eyes.

"Come on," I groan. "I don't want to leave you trapped down there. Climb out so I know you're safe."

The bear rises up onto his back paws and climbs on the trunk. The birch sapling sags under his heavy weight.

"Best to do it quick as you can," I shout. "You're too heavy. The sapling will break, but I can't move a bigger tree on my own."

It feels silly to talk to a bear, but I swear he looks up at me through the branches and nods like he understands me. In moments, he's braving the climb. I stand back, one hand gripping the top of my hatchet.

"That's it," I say. "You can do it. Quick as you can—*ah*—"

I scramble backwards as the great paws of the bear clear the top of the pit. The branches rustle, and the trunk bends and snaps, the sound echoing around the forest as the head and shoulders of the bear emerge. He claws his way out, grunting and groaning, pulling himself onto firmer ground.

My heart pounds. Oh gods, what have I done? Now I'm standing just feet away from an angry, scared bear. He faces me, snorting through his nose as drool drips from his open jaws. His eyes are a warm brown as he looks at me. Neither of us moves.

Slowly, I raise my hand holding the satchel of fish. "Here you go, friend. Your prize." I shake the contents of the bag out onto the ground and then back several feet away, making no move to touch my weapons. "I'll not hurt you, brother. I've just proven that to you. Please don't hurt me."

The bear's massive snout drops to sniff the pile of dried fish. With a grunt, he noses away the leaves, exposing all the pieces. Then he starts to eat.

"If you see Otso, will you tell him what I did for you?" I say, giving him one last nod.

I don't dare wait for him to finish. I keep backing away until I can no longer see the bear through the birch trees. Heart racing, I spin around and run back to poor Halla. She snorts, eyes wide, as she watches me approach.

"Come on, girl. We have to get out of here. That bear will still be hungry."

We run side by side, putting distance between us and the bear. As I run, I pull an arrow from my quiver and press the tip of it into my palm hard enough to break the skin. I squeeze my hand tight, letting a few drops of blood fall to the forest floor. "Great Tapio, if you're listening, know that I saved your cousin Otso in good faith. Please don't let him hunt me down."

Next to me, Halla picks up her pace, her eyes still bulging in fear.

"Good idea." Returning the arrow to my quiver, I pull out my hatchet. With that in my left hand and Halla's lead in my right, I run faster, determined to put as much distance between us and the bear as possible. "Are you happy, Aina?" I say through panting breaths as we jog. "You better be alive when I get to you. And when I do, we'll have a nice long chat about how I think you've become a bad influence on me."

At my side, Halla just snorts.

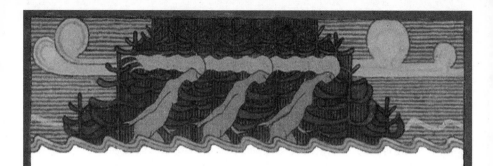

Aina

I HAVEN'T SEEN JAAKO in two days. He left after our last little feast, just after I begged him to help me escape. Meanwhile, nothing in this room has changed. Bread and water. Bread and water. The sun doesn't rise. No birds call. Not even a wind in the trees.

I'm alone.

Impossibly, wretchedly alone.

I'm just about to get out of bed and eat a bite of bread when suddenly the entire room changes around me. Where before there was a plain table and chair tucked along the far wall, there is now a grander table and a large, fur-covered chair. It's almost throne-like in its proportions. And the table is laden with a meal fit for a feast day.

I scramble off the bed and cross over to the table. Hands on my hips, I warily examine the feast—whole roasted duck on a golden platter, a silver pike seasoned with rosemary and coarse salt, tureens of boiled root vegetables, lingonberry tarts, game meat pie, fresh rye bread with butter and seeded berry jam, a carafe of wine and a jewel-encrusted cup.

The fine meal isn't the only change. In the corner of the room near the fire, there's now a large copper tub filled to the brim with hot water. Steam spirals off the surface. There's a stool, too, a cloth, a comb for my hair, and a thick block of soap.

It's a bath.

Glancing around at all this splendor, I could weep with relief. A squawk from the windowsill has me turning. I take in Jaako on the sill, his chest puffed out with pride. "Is it not cursed?"

He shakes his feathered shoulders, and my heart skips a beat.

"Wait—did you do this, Jaako? Is this your magic?"

He bobs his head.

I sink down onto the chair as he flutters into the room. The tips of his feathers brush my shoulder as he lands on the table's edge. "How did you do this?" I whisper, stroking his strong back. "Can you open the door for me? Can you not let me out?"

He stills, his gaze mournful as he clicks his beak.

I blink back my tears of frustration. "Well, it's enough," I say, not wishing to seem ungrateful. "For now, gods know this is more than enough." Closing my eyes, I lift my hands in gratitude. "Ilmatar, blessed mother, thank you for this bounty. And thank you for my friend, Jaako."

We share the feast together. Every bite is delicious. The duck all but melts in my mouth, the skin of the pike is crispy, the lingonberry tart is sweet. If I could, I would eat everything. Like a rock giant, I would open my mouth wide and swallow the table whole, candles and all. That's how hungry I am after so many days of bread and water.

My spirits restored as I eat, I tell Jaako stories of Siiri and our many misadventures. The summer we found an abandoned litter of fox kits and raised them by hand. The solstice we got drunk on her father's barley beer and danced naked under the full moon. I speak of my precocious little brothers and tending to my mother's herb garden.

The raven listens intently to every word. I think he's an even better listener than Siiri. He must be, because Siiri has the ability to speak, which means she's constantly interrupting me to embellish my stories and laugh at her own expense.

By the time I sink into the warm bath, I'm talking of Lintukoto. "They call it a paradise," I say, easing myself back into the hot water. "The dwarves tend to the trees, making the place ready for the birds to return each year. They say all the birds fly there in the winter, following the path of the stars in the sky to the farthest edge of the world. Have you ever been?"

From his perch on the stool, Jaako ruffles his feathers.

I sigh, dragging the bar of soap up and down my arms. "No, you wouldn't have, would you? Ravens don't leave in winter. You're like me, like all the Finns. We stay when we should leave. The harsh winds bring ice and snow, everything withers and dies and still we stay. Even the sun abandons us."

A sharp pain in my arm has me wincing. It's the same pain I felt on first waking in this room. I lift my arm out of the water, tipping it in the light of the fire. My forearm is bruised. Faint marks, in four long strips. Dropping the soap to the bottom of the tub, I sit up and reach out with my left hand, covering the marks.

Finger marks.

I gasp, dropping my hand away. I carry the bruises of being grabbed and held against my will, but I have no memory of how I got them or why. The only dreams that haunt me are dreams of a wolf in the darkness, chasing me with his glowing red eyes.

But wolves have no fingers . . .

Jaako gazes at me somberly from his perch, his black eye locked on my bruises. I can almost feel the anger washing over him.

"I have to get out." When I lean forward, the water sloshes, spilling over the edges of the copper tub. "Jaako, food and a bath are lovely gifts, but they're not enough. Surely, you must see that. You have to help me escape this place."

He clicks his beak, glancing warily from me to the door.

I go still, heart in my throat. "Jaako . . . can you open that door? Is it in your power?"

He ruffles his shoulders in what I think is frustration.

I consider for a moment, searching his handsome face. "They say ravens are messengers. They say you hold deep magic, from before the time of the stories and songs. You are forged by the goblins, their clever creature. Do they wait beyond the door, Jaako?"

He looks at me with those mismatched eyes.

I grip the edges of the copper tub. Steam swirls in the air between us. "No day and no night exist in this place. No whisper of wind in the trees. Is that because there are no trees? Is there no night because I am simply not outside to see it? Tell me now, friend, am I in the depths of a mountain? Is this some dark goblin hold?"

Jaako clicks his beak as if to say no.

I lean back against the wall of the tub. Wrapping my arms around my knees, I gaze at the handsome bird. A tight feeling coils in my chest. For the first time since meeting him, I fear I can't trust him. "If I'm not deep inside a goblin mountain, and I'm not in Lintukoto, then I am in some other dark realm." My skin prickles as I let myself say out loud the thought that has kept me awake. "Jaako, am I dead? Is this death?"

The words are no sooner spoken than the raven alights

from the stool and flies through the open window, disappearing into the endless night.

"No, Jaako—*wait*—" I stand, water splashing everywhere. "Jaako, please come back!"

I feel so close to an answer. I have to know where I am. I have to know what's happening to me and why. Surely, if I'm dead, I would remember dying. But I remember nothing. I turn to retrieve my dress from the bed and go still. My white dress is gone. In its place is a new garment made from a cloth like woven gold. I inch closer to the bed, touching the fabric with a cautious hand. Is this another gift from Jaako?

"Oh gods." My fingers brush over the dress. It is like nothing I've ever seen, like a master weaver found a way to spin solid gold into thread . . . but the fabric doesn't feel metallic or heavy. It's lighter than air. Artful embroidery covers the bodice in a pattern of acorns and oak leaves. A panel of forest-green fabric peeks out from the front of the skirt, embroidered in silver thread.

It's the most beautiful dress I've ever seen. Strangely, the laces tie in the back. How can a woman wear a dress that must lace from the back? With trembling hands, I loosen the laces and pull the dress on over my head. It falls around my hips and down to the floor with a whisper, ending at my feet. It's a perfect fit. I have to do an awkward stretch behind my back to reach the strings and pull the laces tight.

Two more gifts wait for me on the bed. The first is a pair of blue, leather-soled slippers with ribbons for ties. I sit on the edge of the bed and put them on. They, too, are a perfect fit. I wiggle my toes with a smile. The last gift on the bed is a beautiful, white, fox-fur stole. Atop the stole rests a short gold chain with jeweled clasps, great glittering stones in black and green. I once saw a wealthy tradesman's wife wear something similar. I slip the stole around my shoulders and pin it in place across my chest with the jeweled clasps.

The sound of Jaako's flapping wings makes me turn. "Was this you too? Jaako, they're beautiful. I—"

He squawks, fluttering into the room to land on my chair.

"What's wrong?" I step towards him.

Jaako's eyes are desperate as he takes in my new dress. He hops agitatedly on the back of the chair.

"Jaako, what—"

His feathers ruffle before he takes flight, swooping to the door and back to the chair.

"Jaako—"

Cawing in distress, he does it again.

My heart drops. "No . . . no, this was you, wasn't it? The dress, the shoes . . . it was you."

He shakes his head.

"Oh gods," I whisper, my hands brushing down the soft fur of the stole. "Jaako . . ." I know the truth now. I see it so clearly. "You don't want that door to open, do you? You don't want it to open, because you know I'm safer in here . . . don't you? Is someone coming, Jaako? Is the door about to open?"

His gaze darts from me to the door. He knows what's coming. He knows *who* is coming.

I step forward, reaching out for him. "Please don't leave me again. Stay here with me."

Behind me comes the unmistakable sound of metal scraping against wood. Someone is removing the heavy bolt. The door is about to open. Fear threatens to overpower me.

"Do not leave me, Jaako," I whisper. "Whatever comes, we face it together."

But with a last mournful caw, the raven takes off again through the open window, leaving me alone to face my fate. The door creaks open.

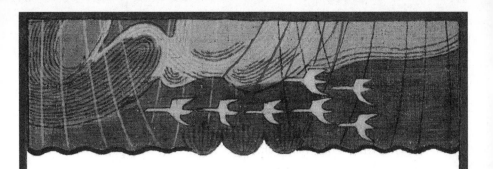

Siiri

I'M MAKING GOOD TIME. It helps that I spent the whole of yesterday running like a bear was chasing me. Bears don't typically bother with humans but one can never be too careful. I'm sure I made poor Halla nervous with how often I glanced over my shoulder, looking for any sign of the hungry beast on our trail.

But the bear was yesterday's problem. Today is the day I find the sacred grove.

"What happened to us, girl?" I ask the reindeer, sharing with her the last of the apples I found along the trail. The reindeer crunches into the juicy flesh, dropping little chunks into the moss as she walks at my side.

"We used to have kings," I tell her, patting her shoulder. "And gods who walked among us. They dined with us like old friends, tended to our wounds, mourned our dead. We had a magic mill that turned grain into gold. We built castles of stone. We were warriors. We fought great battles and won.

Who are we now, Halla? How do we find ourselves again if our gods hide their faces from us?"

The reindeer just snorts.

"None of this looks familiar," I admit, gazing at the trees all around. "When I came here with Father, it was spring. The forest looks so different from one season to the next. And it's been nearly ten years," I add. "But we must be close."

I can feel it; some sharpness stirs the air. It raises the fine hairs on my arms. There's a taste on my tongue, sweet but metallic, like blood. I remember this feeling. I remember this taste in my mouth. One hand grips my bow, the other Halla's lead, and I take an even breath. We pause at the same time, both our heads turning. Her ears perk up as my eyes narrow, peering through the trees. The leaves are thick overhead, and the sun is weak today, hidden behind storm clouds. The smell of snow is in the air.

I wrap my fist more tightly around Halla's lead. "Do you hear it too?"

Halla's nostrils puff as she softly grinds her teeth.

The birds have stopped twittering in the branches. Usually this happens before a storm. But I smell it in the wind: the snow is hours, if not days away.

Halla and I exchange a glance.

"Come on," I say, giving her lead a tug. "We're definitely close."

She resists the pull of her lead, her face still turned to look between a pair of elm trees. I follow her gaze, wishing more sunlight might filter through the canopy. The wind suddenly changes directions, blowing straight through the elms, pushing at my back. Sucking in a sharp breath, I let myself really look at the pair of trees. They stretch far above us, their branches meeting, twisting together to make a natural archway.

My heart flutters faster as I inch closer to the nearest of the two. Reaching out, I trace the faded design carved into the trunk. It looks like geometric scrollwork. The pattern is mirrored on the other elm. "It's the doorway," I say to the reindeer. "Oh, clever girl. You found it."

I tug on Halla's lead again, willing her to step forward with me. We pass under the arch, and all the fine hairs on my arms bristle again. I pause, glancing around. Nothing has changed, and yet everything feels different. I peer back through the elms. The forest looks just the same. But the air is thicker here, and not one bird twitters in the trees. The silence is deafening, almost reverent.

"Come on," I say to Halla.

The trees continue in a row, creating a clear path for us. The ground to either side is blanketed in lush green ferns, dotted here and there with lichen-covered rocks. I walk on soft feet, my gaze darting around as my eyes adjust to the darkness. "I still don't remember this place," I admit to her.

Directly ahead, a third massive elm tree stands in our path. I take in the shadows at the base of the mighty tree. It's not one elm tree; it's *two*. The trunks were planted side by side and made to grow around a stone archway. The archway remains, twisted and crumbling, folding inward from the weight of the trunks. It's barely wide enough for a single person my size to pass through. A man Onni's size would never fit.

The underbrush is thick all around the elms, the shadows deep, blocking my view of what lies beyond. With a sigh, I turn to the reindeer. "I'm sorry, girl. You'll have to wait here." I drape her lead rope over her neck and drop to one knee, hobbling her. I use the trick knot Aksel taught me. If she pulls hard enough, she'll get herself loose.

Giving her another pat, I turn back to the massive elm. I keep my bow slung on my pack, pulling out my hatchet and my long hunter's knife. I can't shake this feeling that I'm being watched.

With my hatchet in my right hand, knife in my left, I crouch and inch sideways through the narrow, crumbling archway. "Ilmatar, protect me." I nearly trip over a tangle of thick roots. Finding my footing, I grip my weapons more tightly and peer around. I now stand in a glade of alder trees. Their spindly, lichen-dusted trunks stretch high into the sky, packed so tightly together they almost make four walls of a great outdoor temple. Their branches form the roof. Weak, storm-grey light filters through the leaves. They sway in the silent wind all across the clearing, like I'm underwater.

"It's so beautiful." My heart pounds as I do a half turn.

They say the alder tree can feel as people do. It bleeds like us, a red resin that drips from its injuries like blood from open wounds. The stories say the fae use the alders to turn change-ling babies into giants. Back home, we boil the bark to use in paints and dyes. Aina's mother taught us the leaves of the alder tree can act as a ward against witchcraft and bad luck.

I narrow my eyes, searching the clearing. The ferns are large, some growing nearly to waist height. A woman's muted sobs meet my ears, cutting through the unearthly quiet. Knife and hatchet in hand, I take a few steps closer. At the far end of the grove, a woman rests on her knees. She blends in so well. As she sits up, her dark brown hair flows freely down her back. Her body remains hidden in the ferns.

"Hello?" I call out softly.

Her shoulders go still, her sobs cut short. I wait as she rises to her feet. Her unbound hair is dark like the soil, snarled by twigs and leaves. If she dropped back down to her knees, she would disappear before my eyes. Only her crying gave her away.

Where did she come from? Mummi tells stories of witches

that live in these forests. Witches like Ajatar, who hunts the hunters, confusing their paths and luring them deeper into the woods. She steals children too, hiding them under thick blankets of moss. Even if you were standing right beside the child, you wouldn't hear their screams.

I fight a shiver. I won't let go of these weapons for anything. "Are you all right?" I call, taking a step closer.

"You should not be here," the woman replies, still with her back turned.

"A hiisi is a sacred space," I say. "All may stand before the uhrikivi and seek communion with the gods."

"There is only one god here now," she replies, her voice trembling with rage. "And he does not commune with the likes of us." Slowly, she lifts her hand, pointing to the resting place of a large stone altar.

I peer past her and gasp, heart sinking. "Oh gods, what have they done?"

The woman spins around, her hauntingly beautiful face contorted with anguish. Her eyes are black as night, her skin pale as milk. She takes me in with a scowl.

I stare right back, noting the odd, moss-colored robes hanging from her narrow shoulders. But they don't just look like moss; they *are* moss. They're shaggy and green, dusted with lichen. A necklace of feathers frames her neck, seemingly made from all the birds of the forest, with smaller feathers around her shoulders and longer ones below, ending with a spray of golden eagle feathers that dangle past her breasts. Tangled vines weave around her waist to form a belt, trailing down to her feet.

"They defiled it," she shrieks. The sky above us darkens, and wind shakes the trees.

Rage burns inside my chest as I take in the new addition perched atop our sacred stone. There, illuminated by the weak sunlight, is a cross, right in the center of the uhrikivi, casting an ominous shadow over it.

The Christians were here. Is this what they do whenever they travel between villages? Are they searching for our sacred groves to claim them all for their god? Father warned me of this. "I'm sorry," I say to the woman. "I'm so sorry—"

She snarls at me, the sound like the snapping of tree branches. "Your apology is worth as little to me as an acorn that will not sprout."

"Please, what can I do—"

"They desecrated my father's house!" she screams. Her face darkens, her milky white skin transforming before my eyes into the bark of a tree. Her eyes turn blacker still.

Recognition flows through me, rooting me to the spot as if I, too, were a tree. I open my hands, dropping both my weapons. "Goddess, please," I entreat. "Let me help you—"

She sweeps forward, wrapping her bony hand around my throat. "I do not need your help, faithless one."

My hand grasps her wrist as I take in her haunting eyes, black like Kalma's. But unlike those of the death witch, a soul burns bright in these eyes. She is not a goddess of death but a goddess of life. I believe she may be Tellervo, daughter of Tapio, king of the forest. She is the shepherdess of the trees.

"You're here," I say, hopeful tears stinging my eyes even as she holds me in her viselike grip. "You came back—"

"I never left," she hisses. She smells sweet, like sun-ripened raspberries and juniper. "The mortals do not deserve us," she adds, shaking me by the throat. "Like worms they toil in the mud, tearing my trees up from their roots. They used to live as one with nature. Now they only take." With each word, she squeezes my throat tighter. "They will take until there's nothing left."

"Then teach them how to live as one with you again," I

offer. "Come back to us, Tellervo. Show us your kindly face. Extend the hand of mercy—*ah*—"

She snarls again, her strong arm lifting me off the ground as if I were little more than a squirrel caught in the boughs of a tree. "They don't need me anymore," she shouts. "They have their new god that ravages this land like a raging fire. He will consume us all, burning us to ash." Her words ring with prophecy as flames dance inside her black eyes. "They left me here to rot."

My vision blurs, and I slap at her hand feebly. I need air. "You—left us—first," I rasp.

She opens her hand, and I fall to the ground. "You dare!"

I sputter and cough, rolling to my feet. I back away while massaging my throat. "You left us first, Tellervo. Without you, we are nothing. Without you, we weaken and wither, like fruit left too long on the vine. Return to us. Teach us your ways, goddess."

She hisses again. "Humans are ravagers. They are root-renders. They're not worthy of my mercy!"

"Then we are not the only ones who have lost our faith," I counter.

She blinks, the bark of her fingers curling into fists at her sides.

I take a cautious step forward. "But there is one who could help us, goddess. One who could restore all our faith . . ."

In a rush like the fluttering of a great many birds' wings, Tellervo transforms back to her human form, her skin pale, her dark eyes wide and curious. "Who?"

"Väinämöinen. The great shaman of legend, keeper of the wisdom of the ages."

She flinches away. "That shaman is lost. He abandoned us to this fate long ago."

"But you could help me find him," I say, crossing the distance to her side. "The songs foretell his return. He will restore all that was lost. We will be one people again, Tellervo."

She shakes her head. "I don't know where he is."

"But do you know where he went?" I press. "Did he sail north on the inland sea? If I keep going north, will I find him?"

She narrows her eyes at me. "You would go north . . . even as the harsh winter sweeps south? You would go in search of Väinämöinen when you have no proof that he still lives?"

"I would do anything to protect those I love," I reply, defiant in the face of her doubt.

She considers for a moment, taking me in from head to toe. Her dark gaze settles on my bruised brow. Her bony fingers brush against my cut. I wince, trying to hold still. "I am not the first immortal you've encountered," she whispers, her breath cool on my cheek. Leaning in close, she inhales deeply, the sound rattling through her chest. "I smell my cousin's death magic on your skin. Rancid, foul rot. Did she touch you?"

I hold my head high. "She tried."

Tellervo smiles, almost as if she's impressed.

"Please, goddess. I need to find Väinämöinen. My friend is lost too," I admit. "I must find her. I must bring her home. He can help me—"

"I said no." She drops her soil-stained fingers from my face. "I am sorry, brave one, but a lost shaman cannot be found if he is truly lost."

"Well, then, he can't fulfill his prophecy either," I reply, my frustration rising. "And one is only lost *until* he is found."

"A shaman is only lost because he does not *wish* to be found," she corrects. "And my path does not lead me north." Her voice rings with finality.

"But does it lead *me* north?" I ask, daring to grab her arm. "Can you see my future, goddess?"

Her gaze moves from my hand on her mossy sleeve, up to my bruised face. She scowls. "Unhand me, mortal. I am shepherdess of my father's forest. I'm not a soothsayer or a prophetess that you can command me to see what is unseen or know what is unknown."

I drop my hand away from her. "But—well, you just foretold your own future. How do you know your path does not lead you north?"

"Because I do not wish to go there." With a last nod, she walks away.

"Please, *wait*—"

She barely takes three steps before she disappears in a swirl of birds' feathers. They flutter to the ground at my feet.

"Tellervo?" I call into the silence. I look everywhere, but she's gone. My shoulders sink, and I fight the urge to scream. I'm on my own. Meanwhile, Aina waits for me to find her, enduring unimaginable horrors. I feel powerless, and I hate it. I want to *do* something. I narrow my eyes at the symbol of the foreign god. With a growl, I march forward, pushing through the ferns to the base of the altar.

Placing my hands on the lichen-marked stone, I scramble atop it. From my knees, I inspect the cross. It's about three feet tall, made of a lighter stone than that of the uhrikivi. I flick my braid over my shoulder, brace my hands on the cross, and push.

Nothing happens.

"Come on," I mutter, giving the stone another shove.

The cross doesn't move.

I look to the sky with a shout, peering up through the alder branches at the swirling grey clouds far above. "Ilmatar, can you hear me? Either help me find your son or help me move this false—ugly—piece of rock—" I shove at the cross with each curse.

At last, the cross tips forward, and I shriek, falling with it. In a thunderous crash, it cracks in two against the top of the altar. Panting, I roll off, looking down at my handiwork. The false god's idol is broken. This hiisi belongs to the old gods again.

Behind me comes a soft chuckle and a familiar voice. "I don't think the foreign god will take kindly to you desecrating his temple."

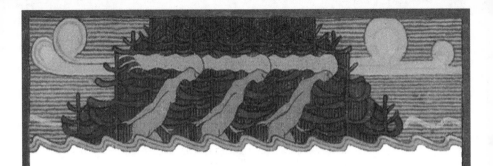

Aina

MY DOOR SWINGS OPEN to reveal a dark hallway. No one is standing there—man, monster, giant, or goblin. The doorway is empty. My breath leaves me in a huff, my shoulders sagging with relief . . . and disappointment. I stand still, staring at the open door. This is what I wanted, right? I wanted this door to open. So why am I just standing here?

Because you're a scared goose, comes Siiri's voice.

If I were Siiri, I'd already be out the door. But I'm not Siiri. I'm just Aina. And I'm afraid.

I take a candle off my table, inch closer to the open door, and peek outside. One end of the hall vanishes into shadow. The other is lit with a glowing torch. I glance over my shoulder one more time, looking in at the confines of my room. My window stands open, but Jaako is gone.

Suddenly, a voice cries out. "Hello? Oh please, someone. Hello!"

It sounds like a frightened young woman. It's her fear that

has me stepping through the open door, although I'm still afraid myself. Holding my candle aloft, I walk towards the voice. As I pass a dark hallway, the young woman appears, limping in my direction. Like me, she wears an elegant dress, this one sky blue with a rich, red fox fur around her shoulders. Blonde braids frame her youthful face.

"Are you my captor?" she asks, her eyes wide with terror. "Or are you . . . like me?"

I drop my free hand away from my thrumming heart as I lower my candle. "It's all right," I say, gently. "I'm like you. I've been locked in my room for days."

"Where are we? Why are they doing this to us?"

"I don't know." I give her the support of my arm. "What happened to your ankle?"

She shakes her head, her bottom lip trembling. "I don't know. I-I can't remember. I w-woke with it aching days ago. It was p-purple and swollen."

"Come, let me help you. Let's keep moving towards the light."

"No," she rasps, pulling on my arm.

"We won't learn anything staying in our rooms," I assure her. "Lean on me. We'll go together."

Slowly, she nods, gripping my arm tightly as we creep down the hall.

"My name is Aina."

"I'm Helmi," she replies.

"Where are you from, Helmi—"

"*Shhh.*" She pulls me to a halt. "What's that noise?"

We both listen. From farther down the hall comes a humming sound.

My heart flutters as my steps quicken. "Come."

"Aina, *wait,*" she begs, pulling on my arm.

"I think it's people."

It sounds like a gathering of some kind: many voices, raised in celebration. On cold winter nights when the villagers all gather in one barn to celebrate a wedding or death, these are the sounds I hear. The sound swells as we creep out of the dark hallway into a large room with a closed door at the other end. Five young women stand huddled together. They turn at the sight of us, surprise and fear etched on their faces. They all wear queenly dresses and furs without any confidence. I know they must be simple village girls like me.

"More girls," one whispers.

"You've been locked away?" another calls. She flicks her dark curtain of hair off her shoulder, her icy blue eyes narrowed at us.

"Yes," I reply. "I'm Aina. This is Helmi."

"I'm Riina," says the black-haired one.

"Satu," offers a short girl with curly brown hair tied in two loose braids.

"I'm Salla," says a beautiful, freckle-faced woman with flowing red hair.

"And I'm Lilja," says an angry-looking woman, her blonde hair tied in one long braid. She reminds me so much of Siiri, it takes my breath away. But where Siiri has blue eyes, this Lilja has brown. And where Siiri has a face of freckles, Lilja has none. Still, her gaze darts around the room as if she's looking for anything she might use as a weapon.

Helmi and I turn to the last young woman. She's tall and willowy, with pale grey eyes and white-blonde hair that holds as much life as her sallow skin. "Inari," she mutters, her lips barely moving.

I look around the room, taking in as much detail as I can. It's an antechamber, clearly leading to a great hall. The hum of voices comes from behind a pair of wooden double doors. They're carved with ornate patterns of forest animals and fruiting trees. I smell roasted meats, spices, and fresh-baked bread. The rest of the room is bare of furniture, but the walls are decorated with embroidered tapestries. They're like something out of the songs—golden-horned stags racing through a sunny wood, maidens with flowers in their hair bathing in a pool. Everything is light, everything is golden and green and teeming with life.

"It's going to be all right," I whisper to Helmi, squeezing her arm.

The great double doors creak open, and we all gasp, spinning as one to meet our fate. The noise from the feast slams into us—deep, boisterous laughter, the clatter of plates and cups. After so many days of isolation, my ears ring with it. Inside the hall, every surface glitters with gold and candlelight. The tables overflow with a bountiful feast. Men and women drink and carouse, all as finely dressed as we are. They're so engrossed, they don't even notice that the doors have opened.

A man with beady eyes shuffles towards us. He wears robes like the those of Christian priests, except his are the deepest of bloodred, the sleeves trimmed in richest blue. "Stand up straight," he barks. "Shoulders back, chins up. You're about to meet the Queen."

Helmi and I drop our hands to our sides, weaving our fingers together.

Riina scoffs. "Finland has no queen."

The man raps Riina hard on the shoulder with a thin rod, making her shriek. "Face front, you. Do not dare avert your eyes from her honored majesty."

A horn blasts near the huge doors, making us jump. All faces within the hall turn as one, locking eyes with us. The benches and tables screech and creak against the stone floor as the revelers get to their feet. Some stand on their benches, curious to get a better look at us.

The man turns, rod raised in the air, and marches into the great hall, clearly expecting us to follow. We shuffle forward, my hand still gripping Helmi's. I gaze up in wonder as I walk. The sharply arched ceiling angles so steeply that the apex is lost to the shadows. Three colossal antler chandeliers hang down on thick metal chains. They hold hundreds of dripping candles each, illuminating the vast interior of the wooden hall.

The walls are adorned with all manner of weapons: sword and shield, lance and axe. It reminds me of the stories Siiri's mummi would tell of the kings of Kalevala. In summertime, they lived in the deep south, right at the edge of the sea. Their palaces were used for hunting and fighting and making merry. They had winter palaces in the north too, great structures of stone and ice with fires that burned blue.

The longer sides of the hall are dotted with massive hearths, three on each side. Each one is so large, a pair of men could dance inside. They blaze with fire. I follow the line of the hearths down to the far end of the room. There, behind the top table, sit two throne-like chairs, decorated in furs. The large throne sits empty, but the smaller throne is filled by a woman of enchanting beauty.

My steps slow as I take her in. Her blonde hair is piled high in intricate braids adorned with silver clasps. Atop her head sits a silver crown. Like me, she wears a dress of spun gold. She tips her lips in a knowing smile, not breaking her hungry gaze from us as we make our way closer. Then she raises an elegant hand, and a hush falls over the room.

"Welcome, my children," she calls. "What a terrible time you've had. Come forward. Join my daughters and me in our feast." Her voice is sweetness itself, dew on a spring flower, as she gestures to a pair of benches placed on the opposite side of the high table before her.

The other girls hurry, but my steps are slow. None of this is right. I don't want to sit with my back to the room. I glance to either side of the thrones to see four young women dressed as richly as the queen. The woman sitting directly across from me has sullen features, carelessly sipping from her goblet of wine as if she's bored by the whole affair.

"Yes, come, come," says the queen. "Take your ease at my bountiful table."

The other girls are already sitting, so I feel I have no choice. I sink onto the bench between Helmi and Satu. I can feel every eye in the great hall boring into my back. I flinch as a servant appears behind me, reaching over my shoulder to fill my goblet with wine. I lean away from him, trying to keep a smile on my face as the queen and her daughters survey us. The princess across from me makes me ill at ease. She keeps staring, her face utterly expressionless.

The queen remains standing, lifting her jeweled goblet with a flourish. "A toast to your health," she croons. She holds her goblet aloft, clearly waiting for us to do the same.

As one, we pick up our cups and hold them up.

"Kippis," she calls out. Tipping the goblet back, she drains it in two gulps.

"Kippis," a few of the girls say.

I raise the goblet to my lips, but I don't drink. Jaako's fear is still fresh in my mind. All is not as it seems.

Behind us, the crowd raises their own cups and goblets, toasting our health in a great chorus of cheers. The queen resumes her seat, which signals the hall to do the same. I flinch again, gripping the table, as, behind me, a host of two hundred people move benches and rattle plates, and the sounds of conversation and merriment grow.

"You all must be famished," says the queen in that simpering voice, cutting through the revelers. "Please, make my home your home. Eat and be merry."

None of us move to taste the food, though it sits tantalizingly close. In front of me rests a whole roasted chicken, fish stew, a shaved leg of lamb, and what looks like a dish of mashed turnips. But I'm not hungry, for Jaako already fed me more than my cursed barley bread.

I cast a furtive glance down the table. I can't know if the other girls had Jaako visiting them and bringing them food too.

The queen pulls a disappointed face, tsking. "You don't appreciate the feast I had prepared for you. This surprises me. Are you not all tired of barley bread?"

I go still, as do several of the other girls down the table. Yes, not all is as it seems. This is still a prison, and we are still trapped.

Don't eat the food, comes Siiri's voice in my mind. *Starve first.*

I don't need her warning. I won't touch a bite of this feast.

The queen slaps down her knife with a haughty sniff. "Well, I suppose I'll have the servants clear all this away, and my guards will escort you back to your rooms. We'll see how you feel about accepting my hospitality in a few days—"

"No," cries Lilja, clearly in agony over being so close to such a feast after days of spoiled bread.

"We'll eat it," freckle-faced Salla adds. "Please, don't send us back to our rooms." Hers is a different fear then. I sense that, like me, she's afraid to be alone.

Riina is the first to reach for a few select morsels, piling them on her golden plate. The other girls follow her lead. Riina and Salla each take a bite of fish. Their eyes close, savoring the delight of tasting something other than barley bread.

I reach tentatively forward and pluck the leg from a chicken, bringing it to my lips. But I watch first, waiting for Riina and Salla to take their second bite. As soon as they do, they sputter and gag. Up and down our side of the table, the girls squeal and choke. I shriek as the chicken leg in my hand begins to squirm. I drop it, watching as it transforms into a slimy, green frog, which hops across the table, scattering a plate of maggots in its mad dash to escape.

Then the whole illusion shatters.

I glance wildly around the hall, eyes blinking in the sudden darkness as the light from the antler chandeliers disappears, taking all their warmth too. Now the cold room is lit by only a few flickering lampstands. All else is lost to darkness and shadows. No more are the walls adorned with a hunter's armory. Now they're thick with skulls, human and animal alike. Some are twisted into screams of terror, their jaws unhinged, locked forever in the moment of their terrible deaths. The crowd of revelers is gone, leaving us alone with the queen and her daughters.

I spin back around, swallowing a groan of horror to see that our "feast" is creeping and crawling away. Frogs hop and spiders skitter over the plates. The platter I thought was a roasted leg of mutton is now the rotting head of a lamb, tongue lolling, eyes clouded and unblinking. By my left hand, maggots swarm over the carcass of a chicken. Next to me, Helmi makes a sound somewhere between a retch and a sob.

Across from us, the queen cackles, rising to her feet, her body framed by a massive throne of skulls. She holds aloft a slender willow wand in her hand. She gives it a flick, and I nearly topple off my bench in panic. At first, I don't know what I'm seeing. Her hair transforms to beautiful grey locks that hang in cords around her face. And her dress of spun gold changes to robes of silver, pure and bright as woven starlight . . . but the rest of her beauty melts away. Where there was youth and warmth, there is now only withering decay. The face she reveals to us is that of a haggard old woman with blackened teeth. Her skin is thin and lined and grey, sagging around her eyes to show the sunken shape of her skull. Her eyes are like two glowing embers. The hand holding her wand is now little more than skin and bone.

She cackles again, and the sound rattles in my rib cage. "What's wrong, my children? Is the feast not to your liking?" Her bony hand slaps the table with mirth as her daughters share in her laughter, cruel twisting sounds that steal my breath.

My gaze sweeps the table, stopping at the creature sitting across from me. What moments before was a sullen young woman is now a monster. She has a painted face, white around her coal-black eyes, while her neck is smeared with dried blood. Her dark hair is matted with debris and hangs lankly around her face like her tattered, stinking robes hang off her body. Black horns curl away from her skull. She looks at me with those lifeless eyes, her mouth tipping into a broken smile.

"*You*," I cry, the word strangled by fear.

She lifts her jeweled goblet with her rune-marked hand in mocking salute. This time I really do fall off the bench. I land on the dais and scramble backwards, unable to look away from this terrifying creature. Instinctively, I slap my left hand over the bruises on my forearm. As if dragged underwater, I'm pulled into a sea of my own memories, Siiri's voice filling my mind . . .

"Run! Aina, run!" Siiri screams.

I'm panting, lungs seizing, legs aching. "You're faster than me, Siiri. Go!"

"The wolf is that way—"

It's the wolf from my dreams, with his bloodred glowing eyes and swishing, serpent-like tail. All I taste is panic. Dread. Fear.

Death. The creature is death, and the wolf is her minion.

"Stay behind me," Siiri commands, her strong hand on my arm, pulling me back.

The monster approaches us on silent feet.

"Aina, run!"

Too late. My heart constricts in my chest as I'm struck breathless. I can save Siiri. I can let it take me. I see the hurt in Siiri's eyes when she knows my decision is made. The creature grabs my arm, her touch searing. Her stench envelops me. I'm choking, coughing, gasping for air. She reeks like a thousand rotting corpses. I feel nothing but loss as the darkness closes in, and I watch Siiri's face as I lose her. Forever.

Darkness takes me to the deepest depths.

I open my eyes and stare down the creature still seated across the table. All at once, the pieces of this nightmare fit together in my mind—the creature and her wolf hunting us in the woods, six young women gone missing, my magic room, this strange world of endless night, a cackling witch with monstrous daughters who reek of death. I scramble to my feet and point with a shaking finger. "Tuonetar," I cry out, tears thick in my throat.

The witch turns, manic eyes locked on me. I'm trapped in the underworld, standing before Tuonetar, the goddess of violent death.

Siiri

I SLIP DOWN FROM the stone altar as I scan the sacred alder grove for the source of the voice. There, standing where I'd dropped my weapons, is the woman from the woods. Like Tellervo, her beauty is breathtaking. She wears robes of white that drape around her slender shoulders. Her night-black hair falls in a glistening sheet down her back, almost trailing on the ground. It's parted perfectly down the center, framing her child-like face. The blue of her eyes glows almost white, the hint of a smile tipping her lips. In the woods, I wasn't sure if she was a goddess or a shamaness. But now that I see her face, I know. She's another goddess.

She tsks her tongue, looking at the broken cross. "Do you not fear the wrath of the foreign god?"

I square my shoulders at her. "The foreign god can get on his longboat and sail back to Sweden. We have no need of him or his zealots here."

Her smile falls as she considers me, tilting her head slightly to the side. "The old gods are dead, hadn't you heard?"

"Then tell me how you're standing here."

"Maybe I'm a witch," she muses.

"You were with me the other night. In the woods, after Kalma took my friend. You got me to my feet."

"You got yourself to your feet."

"You helped me."

"You helped yourself," she counters. "I did nothing."

"You were there," I press. "I wanted to die, and you called me back from the brink. You gave me the hope to stand, to keep fighting."

"You already had hope. I just reminded you of where you'd temporarily misplaced it."

I search her face. "Who are you?"

"A friend." As if to prove her point, she lifts her hand from her side, holding out my discarded hatchet.

I tense, not having realized she'd picked it up. She had it hidden in the folds of her robes. Crossing the clearing, I tuck it back in my belt. She holds out my knife with her other hand, and I do the same, slipping it back in its sheath at my hip.

She watches me adjust my belt. "Do those help?"

"Well, they can't hurt," I reply, grateful to feel their weight at my hips again.

She shrugs a narrow shoulder. "Where I'm from, they're not very useful."

"And where is that?"

She ignores my question. "I heard you're looking for Väinämöinen. I assume my cousin wasn't forthcoming with her aid?"

"No, she wasn't."

She nods, lips pursed in curiosity as she surveys me. "She's angry. And bone-weary with grief. Don't judge her too harshly."

"Why does she grieve?"

"A life-giving goddess will always grieve death," she replies. "And there is so much death now. It infects everything. She is powerless to right the balance, so she grieves."

"And what if Väinämöinen could help restore the balance? What if he could return order to life and death? Would you help me find him?"

"You assume life and death are out of balance."

I blink, confused. "But you just said—"

"I said she is powerless to right the balance, and she is. There is no one in this realm who can mend what is broken. Not even your lost shaman."

My shoulders sag with frustration. "Well, then, it's hopeless."

She lets out a little laugh. "My, how changeable you are. You're worse than a spring morning. Rain or snow. Rain or snow. You can't make up your mind."

I glare at her, and she just smiles.

"Why do you seek the lost shaman, Siiri?"

"I—" My words fall silent. "You know my name?"

"I know many things."

There's no point in lying to this goddess. "Kalma took my friend to Tuonela," I explain. "For what reason, I don't know. I need Väinämöinen to help me get her back. Once I do, I intend to convince him to return south with us. I want him to fulfill his prophecy to bring back the true religion. It's time. You said it yourself."

She gives me a searching look. "You ask for too much. He will say no."

"Then I'll ask again."

"He will deny you again."

"I'm persistent."

She smiles. "'Stubborn' is the word he would use."

I sigh, glancing around the clearing. "Look, he can call me whatever he wants, so long as he helps me save Aina. She sacrificed herself for me, and now she's in Tuonela. Even if there was no life debt between us, I would still go to her."

"Why?"

I hold her gaze. "Because she's my oldest and dearest friend. And because she would do the same for me. Only Väinämöinen can help me reach her now. And despite all your questions and riddles, I think you mean to help me find him. Why else would you appear to me twice?"

"I appear where I'm called," she replies with a shrug. "As I say, you are stubborn, Siiri . . . and quite loud."

"Are you Ilmatar?"

"The All-Mother would not concern herself with following the aimless wanderings of one lost girl."

"My wanderings won't be aimless, if you help me." She walks away and I follow. "Goddess, *please*." I hold out one of Mummi's bangles. "I have silver—"

"I have no need of silver."

"Will I find Väinämöinen if I keep walking north?"

"You cannot find someone who wishes to remain lost," she calls over her shoulder.

"Tellervo just said the same thing. But you know where he is—"

She spins around, glaring at me. "Väinämöinen is the most powerful shaman ever to have lived. To stay lost for all these years, he's worked his magic on even the gods. Tellervo cannot help you because she doesn't know where he is. And neither do I." She ducks through the stone archway between the elms and calls back, "Väinämöinen must be willing to be found."

I follow, grunting as my bow catches. "But how—gods— *ouch*—Goddess, how do we do that?"

She walks right up to Halla, procuring a carrot from the

air that she offers to the little reindeer. Halla sniffs it before taking a bite, her ears flicking as she chews. The goddess smiles fondly, giving the animal a pat. "I've always liked reindeer."

I search her face. "Do you think he'll reveal himself to me?"

She nods.

"Why?"

"Because you're stubborn . . . and he likes stubborn."

I rub my brow with a tired hand. "Can you not just give me a straight answer?"

She turns away from the reindeer, her icy blue eyes locked on me. "Follow the bear, for he is the key. He will unlock the door to Väinämöinen."

"Follow the—wait, which bear? The one from that pit? But that was two days south of here. Are you saying I should turn around—"

"No, you must continue north."

I growl in annoyance. "You're not making any sense."

She lets out another little laugh, flicking her long sheet of black hair off her shoulder. "Continue north, Siiri. When the bear is ready to reveal himself, I believe he will. Then you must follow him to Väinämöinen."

"Continue north but find the bear I left in the south? That's all you can give me?"

"That . . . and this." The goddess flicks her hand, and Halla grunts. My eyes widen as I take in how much heavier her packs have suddenly become. Now the poles of a tent emerge from the back of her harness. "Supplies for your journey," the goddess explains. "Autumn will fade quickly, Siiri. The winter snows will be harsh. Do not tarry. Do not slacken your pace. Keep walking north. And, try very hard not to die. This will all be for nothing if you die."

I search her ageless face. "Who are you? Are you Mielikki?"

"The Queen of the Forest has golden hair."

"Kuutar then, goddess of the moon? No—Akka. Are you Akka?"

Her smile falls. "Stop guessing, Siiri." She slips Halla's lead off the branch of the tree and offers it to me. "You have less than an hour of daylight left. Start walking. And don't die."

I take the lead from her hand, and she steps back, leaving my way clear. I glance through the thick trees, then back to her kind face. She's cryptic and irritating, but it's been nice to have her company. She makes me miss the easy familiarity of walking with Aina always at my side. I'm not ready to say goodbye. "Will you not walk with me awhile? I promise I won't try to guess your name again."

I can see from the set of her shoulders she's going to say no.

"This is your journey, Siiri. Whatever comes, you must stay the course and stay alive. When you begin to doubt, remember that Aina waits for you. We all do. You must not fail us." Slowly, she raises her hand and points due north. "Siiri, go."

Turning away from the goddess, I click at the reindeer with my tongue, and we continue north. I don't look back over my shoulder. I don't need to. I know the goddess is gone.

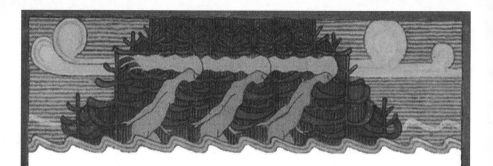

Aina

THE WITCH QUEEN OF Tuonela smiles at me, her cracked, blackened teeth filling me with dread.

"You are Tuonetar," I gasp, dropping my trembling hand to my side.

"Clever girl," she sneers, tucking her willow wand back into her robes. She gestures magnanimously at the dark hall, adorned with the skulls of the dead. "Welcome to Tuonela."

Several of the girls shiver, and poor Satu lets out a panicked sob. From beyond the walls come faint screaming and wailing. It sends a chill through me. I turn my attention to the monster seated at the left hand of her mother. "And you are Kalma," I say, my voice little more than a whisper. "You took me from my home and brought me here. I remember everything."

The black eyes of the goddess don't blink. She tears the leg off a roasted fowl crawling with maggots. As we watch, she takes a bite, crunching the maggots along with the spoiled meat. Some of the maggots drop to her empty plate and squirm. To either side of me, Helmi and Satu make pitiful retching sounds, which makes the other goddesses laugh.

"Sit, child," Tuonetar orders me.

But I can't move. I can hardly breathe. My mind still spins with the memories of running from Kalma through the woods—Siiri's strong hand on my arm, her daring fight, the look in her eyes as I was pulled into darkness—

"I said *sit*," the Witch Queen shrieks. Pulling out her willow wand, she gives it a flick.

Invisible hands jerk me forward, smacking my shins into the hard wood of the bench. I cry out, tears filling my eyes, as I am forced down onto the bench, Helmi and Satu making room for me. I'm shoved into a sitting position, back straight, hands clasped tight in my lap, head bowed so low my chin digs into my chest.

"Good girl," Tuonetar says with a wicked smile, pocketing the wand again.

The other girls shift nervously down the bench. Next to me, Helmi copies my posture, tears slipping silently down her pink cheeks.

Tuonetar resumes her place on her throne, her hands balanced atop two human skulls. Reindeer skulls frame the top of the throne, their antlers casting sharp shadows along the wall. Next to her throne is an even larger one, meant for the king. His throne is topped with the massive skull of a bear.

"You're no doubt wondering why you've all been brought here," Tuonetar says, reaching for her jeweled wine goblet.

"Are we dead?" Satu whimpers. I can feel her shaking like a leaf.

Lowering her goblet from her lips, the Witch Queen turns to stare at Satu, her expression becoming almost sympathetic. "Yes," she whispers.

Satu and Helmi both sob. I think Riina may join them.

But then Tuonetar cackles, slamming her goblet down. Bloodred wine sloshes onto her hand. She brings her hand to her mouth and sucks it dry. "Of course you're not dead, you *stupid* child. What use would you all be to me dead?"

The other goddesses snicker at this too.

"You've been selected," Tuonetar continues. She smiles over at Kalma with an almost fond, motherly expression. "My clever daughter brought you to me. You are here to fulfill a grand purpose. You *do* want to fulfill your grand purpose, don't you?"

"What purpose?" Lilja dares to ask.

The Queen's red-rimmed eyes narrow. "All will be revealed in good time. For now, know that I have done my duty as the law of hospitality requires. I have sheltered you, fed you, and offered you a seat at my table. You can expect no more comfort from me."

I close my eyes, fighting back tears.

"Why are you doing this to us?" Riina cries. "Tuonela is for the dead, not the living. What can you need from mortal girls except our deaths?"

The Queen cackles again, rising to her feet. "Of *course* you have come here to die. Did you really think there could be any other end to your pathetic little lives?" She slips her hand back inside her silvery robes, pulling out that cursed willow wand again. "All life ends in death. Whether in one day . . . one year . . . or one thousand years, you will die, my sweet little doves. And then you will be mine. Now, be good and return to your rooms to await my pleasure." She gives her wand another little flick with her wrist. "Guards, take them."

A chill wind sweeps through the hall, and then the sound of stomping feet and rattling metal rings through the silence. The girls all shriek, turning their backs on the Witch Queen to meet this new threat. "No, please," Salla begs.

The magic holding me releases, and I'm able to turn too.

Soldiers march out of the shadows. They move with odd, shuffling gaits. Some are skeletally thin . . . and the *smell*. I gasp and cover my nose with my hand. The soldiers are all *dead*. As they approach, I can see some of them are rotting away, missing flesh and bone. Only magic holds them together.

All down the table, the girls shrink away as the rotting hands of the corpse soldiers reach for us, dragging us to our feet. The one in front of me has an arrow sticking through his eye, his jaw hanging loose on one side like he's trapped making a soundless scream for the rest of his undying existence. Reaching for Helmi's hand, I pull her off the bench with me. The soldier's weak, clammy hand grips my arm right over Kalma's marks, raising gooseflesh over my body.

"This isn't real," Helmi murmurs at my side, her eyes shut tight.

Down the table, the other girls are dragged to their feet. Some of the dead are harsher than others. A massive soldier with a cleaved face holds Lilja by her braid, lifting her off the floor as she flails and shrieks, batting at his bony hand. "If you're going to kill us, just do it now," she shouts at Tuonetar. "Where is your honor? Give us a clean death, you rotten witch—"

She chokes and sputters, her words cut short as the soldier's free hand wraps around her throat, squeezing it tight.

"Courage will get you nowhere in Tuonela," the Witch Queen warns. "There's no call for it here. The dead are my creatures." All the while, Lilja hangs in the air, choking, her legs kicking feebly.

And then Tuonetar lunges across the table like some huge, horrible spider. Cups and plates clatter to the floor as she sweeps forward, silvery robes billowing. She hops to the floor before Lilja, pointing at the poor girl's reddening face. "Do you see this, little doves? Do you see how she struggles, holding on to the fragile tendrils of her life with her grasping little fingers?"

I know I'm not the only one trying to look away when I lock eyes with Riina. She shakes her head, leaning away from the soldier who holds both her arms.

"*Look at her,*" the Witch Queen shrieks, her words echoing around the room, shaking dust from the rafters, and making me tremble.

We all turn reluctantly to face the struggling Lilja.

"Do you think I do not know how she plans to escape me?" says the Witch Queen with a sneer. "She wants a noble end. She wants control of her fate . . . but that is a fool's dream in Tuonela." Reaching out a gnarled finger, she brushes it down Lilja's freckled cheek. "Let go of this fantasy, child. That's not what death is. Death is beautiful violence. Death is unbridled chaos. Death is . . . me. And there is nothing I like better than watching the life drain from mortals' eyes."

The Witch Queen nods, and the soldier holding Lilja opens his hand. The poor girl drops like a stone to the floor. Her rasping sobs are the only sound in the room. Tuonetar smiles down at her. "That's a good girl," she coos. "Yes, breathe deep. Fill those lungs, my pet. And know with each breath you take that your death will come soon. For there is nothing I like *less* than misguided nobility."

Lilja goes still, holding back her sobs, as we all absorb Tuonetar's words.

The Witch Queen drops to her knees, bringing her face level with Lilja's. "I will kill you," she declares. "And it will be beautiful." Her tone is almost gleeful. "Your days are numbered, dove."

The dead soldiers pull us towards the set of looming

double doors. I cling to Helmi's hand as we're dragged back into the arrival hall.

"Don't lose faith," Riina calls out softly. "Stay alive."

"Lilja, are you all right?" Salla tries to reach for her.

"Everyone, stay alive," Riina says again.

"Aina, don't let go," Helmi begs, her breath warm on my cheek.

I hold her fast, my grip tight enough to make my hand ache. But the soldiers jerk us apart.

"Aina," Helmi cries, her face a mask of pain as her solider wraps bony, broken fingers around her middle and pulls her away from me.

"Helmi—"

"Aina, please don't leave me," she sobs.

Hating myself, I loosen my grip, letting her slip through my fingers.

"Aina—"

The soldiers drag her away down the dark hall.

"Stay alive," I call after her, echoing Riina.

Inside my own head, a different voice says the words. *Stay alive.* I can almost feel Siiri standing at my side. I pretend it's her tight grip on my shoulder.

Whatever you do, stay alive.

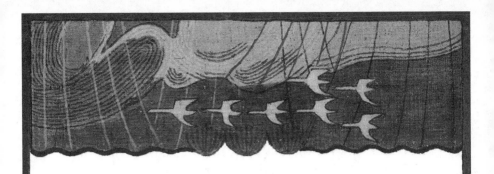

Siiri

14

THREE DAYS PASS, AND there's no sign of a bear anywhere. I've tracked all manner of animals—rabbits and squirrels, wolves, foxes, a lynx. I even spied what I was sure was a metsän väki running through the woods. He was small, no larger than a child, and so fast I could hardly make him out through the trees. But he laughed and rustled the branches, scaring Halla and teasing me, before throwing rocks at us and running off.

But no bears.

"The goddess's instructions were clear," I say to Halla for the hundredth time. "Go north. When the bear is ready to find me, he will. I have to keep the faith."

Glancing around this grassy bogland, it strikes me again how very far from home I am. I've never traveled so far on my own. I promised Mummi I would return from the hiisi two days ago. She must be worried sick. I imagine her pacing in the yard, sending my brothers up to the north end of the village to watch and wait for my return.

But I can't return yet, not when there's still a chance to save Aina. Not when there's a chance Väinämöinen can save us all. I feel the hand of fate on me now, holding me in a fist as strong as iron. A new story is being told, and I'm at its center. "Maybe they'll sing of this one day," I say, giving Halla a pat. "Brave Siiri and her noble Halla, off on a daring quest."

The reindeer just snorts.

"You know, in Mummi's stories, the women are always waiting for things to happen to them. The princess waits for her suitor by the roadside, the sister waits for her valiant brother's return, the mother waits for news of her son's untimely death." I give the reindeer another pat. "This is a new kind of story. I'm not waiting for the shaman to find me. I'm striding out into the world, bow at my back and fire in my heart. I'm going to find the shaman and make him help us. We're done waiting for the menfolk to hurry up and change things. If we want change, I think it must begin with us."

I narrow my eyes at the grey sky. "Those storm clouds are getting thicker. We should stop and make camp before the storm descends. And I could do with a proper meal."

Around midafternoon, we come through a stand of trees to find a stream crossing our path. It pools deep in spots before babbling around the bend of a low hill. It's the perfect place to fish. Perhaps I'll even indulge in a bath.

The goddess said not to tarry.

Aina's voice in my mind makes me groan.

"Would you have me starve?" I say at the trees. Even as I speak the words, my stomach grumbles, squeezing in pain at its emptiness. I've only been eating what I can forage as we walk, saving the best of the foodstuffs for my return journey.

The reindeer gives me a doleful look. She's used to a hearty dinner of piled hay every night. No doubt she's hungry too.

"Two hours," I say at last. "We'll stop and rest here for two hours only. That hardly counts as tarrying."

Halla just snorts.

I work quickly to remove her heavy packs, setting her loose to graze. Within the hour, I've caught three small trout. I make a fire and set the trout to roasting on a hastily made spit. Then I take out my cookpot and pour a handful of the dried potato bits into it. I add a few dried mushrooms and some seasoning from my mummi's little leather satchel. I fill the pot halfway with water and set it at the edge of the fire to warm.

Once the meal is cooking, I go to the edge of the stream and strip down to my waist, shivering in the autumn chill. I shuck my boots and socks, rolling up my pantlegs. I wash my feet first before kneeling at the water's edge. Sensing that I'm alone, I dip my head in the water and scrub my scalp with calloused fingers. Pulling the ties from my braids, I let my long hair flow free. It tangles in the grasses, slipping along mossy, wet rocks.

Before long, I'm shivering. I tie my soaking wet hair in a knot atop my head and inspect my brow in my reflection off the water. It's healing nicely. Most of the purple bruising is now a mottled yellow brown. The swelling is all but gone. If I had Milja's poultice treatments, it would be healed already. You just have to be ready to smell like wood garlic for a week. I smile, thinking of how Aina would turn up her nose, even as she applied the paste—

"Come on out of that stream," a low voice calls from behind me.

My heart drops.

"Nice and slow," calls another voice.

Slowly, I rise.

Two men stand behind me on the bank. One holds my

quiver and bow; the other holds Halla's lead. They're trappers, dressed from head to toe in skins and furs. The man holding my bow is taller, with a russet beard and a weathered face. The shorter man has beady eyes and strands of peppered grey hair sticking out from under the flaps of his hat. Beyond the fire, their own pair of reindeer stand hooked to a sled piled high with a summer bounty's worth of skins and furs.

Godsdamn it. Careless, reckless, Siiri! In my haste, I'd collected leaves and wet kindling. Smoke from my fire spirals high into the sky, a beacon these trappers undoubtedly followed straight to me. "I caught three fish," I say, gesturing to the fire. "One for each of us. And the pot has potato porridge. You're welcome to share my food and fire. Then we'll part ways as friends."

"We'll share with you," the tall man says with a nod.

His friend watches me, his eyes trailing down my half-naked form.

"I'm cold," I say. "Let me dress, and I'll join you by the fire."

"By all means," the tall man replies, gesturing to my shirt and boots with an open hand.

His friend just smirks, giving Halla's neck a pat. "We keep the weapons though. We'll not have you gutting us like those fish."

I hurry over to my small pile of clothes and jerk my shirt over my head. I don't bother with the vest or socks. I only want my boots. I slip them on, careful to hide the knife along my right ankle. *Ilmatar, protect me*, I pray to the heavens.

As I dress, the men settle around the fire. The tall man turns the fish on the spit, oils from the fish skin dripping into the flames, making them pop and hiss. The shorter man lifts the lid off my cookpot, inspecting the potato porridge.

"We should stir it," I say. "I have a spoon in my pack—"

"Don't," says the tall man, his hand dropping to the axe at his belt.

I stop, my gaze shifting from his hand on the sharpened metal, back to his face.

"We'll get the spoon. You go over there and sit," he says, pointing to the fire's edge. "Paavo, look in the pack. And make sure there are no other surprises in there."

Paavo rummages through my pack. "She's got good supplies," he mutters as he passes the taller man. Then he sticks out his hand, offering me the spoon. "Here, girl. Cooking is women's work."

I snatch it from his hand. "If it's women's work, I wonder why you've both not starved and died already. However did you last the season?"

"We get by," Paavo replies. "But you're here now. You'll make the meal."

The smell of the rehydrated mushrooms makes my empty stomach tighten and groan. *Please gods,* I cry out in my mind. *Let me eat this meal. Let me regain my strength.*

"What's a girl like you doing so far north?" asks the tall man.

"And why are you alone?" Paavo adds.

"I'm not alone," I reply.

Both men go still. Then they glance over their shoulders, peering into the shade of the trees all around us. Paavo huffs. "You lie."

"Why would I lie?" I give the pot another stir. "My husband Joki and I separated yesterday morning. He caught the tracks of a stag, and he means to fell it. He should return soon. My smoke was meant to signal him, not you."

"Then he is welcome," says the tall trapper. "We'll make room for him at the fire." He hands me three wooden bowls, watching as I scoop some of the potato porridge into each one. Then he uses a knife to slide the roasted fish off the spit, giving me the smallest trout.

I don't wait for him to sit before I'm shoveling the food into my mouth, desperate for the strength it will give me. The porridge is so hot it burns, but I don't care. I tear into my trout, crunching the tiny bones, swallowing the white, tender meat.

"Easy," the tall man says with a laugh. "Slow down before you choke, girl. We're not going to take it from you."

On the other side of the fire, Paavo watches me, spitting out his larger fish bones. "Tell us more about this man of yours. What's his name? Josti?"

"Joki," I correct, taking a sip of cool stream water. It soothes the burning roof of my mouth. "And he's a hunter," I go on. "We're both hunters. We travel south for the winter. We have family living along Lake Päijänne."

"You hunt too?" the tall man asks, a bemused smile on his face.

"I do," I reply. I can tell they don't believe me. Squaring my shoulders at the tall man, I give a nod to my bow resting behind him. "I can fell a deer at thirty yards."

Paavo snorts again. "You lie."

I glare at him before turning back to the tall man. "That's the second time your friend has called me a liar. If he does it a third time, I'll begin to think he means it."

Paavo smirks, spitting out another bone. "You *are* a liar, little girl. Know how I know?"

I turn my glare back on him. "How?"

"Because I just looked inside your pack," he replies, his gaze triumphant. "You're packed for one, not two."

"Then you didn't check both my packs," I counter. "Joki will come. And if I tell him you've been anything less than kind to me, he'll put an arrow through your eye faster than you can blink."

Lies. Joki couldn't hit the broadside of a barn at twenty paces. I can see it on their faces: they don't believe me. The tall one did, but now he doesn't.

"I think we all know what happens next here," says Paavo, spitting another bone into the fire.

"I wash the bowls for you?" I say, playing ignorant.

"You can do that after," he replies.

His words sink in my belly like a stone.

"We don't want to hurt you," says the tall man.

I scramble to my feet. "Then finish your meal and be on your way."

"Times are hard," he replies, rising to his feet as well. "It's been a long summer."

"And men have needs," Paavo adds, leering at me with those dark, beady eyes.

"Summers are never long in this wilderness," I counter. "Go south to a village and find a willing woman you can pay. Leave me in peace, as any man of honor would."

The tall man almost looks like he's considering it. But then Paavo laughs, tossing the carcass of his fish into the flames, making them crackle and hiss. "Why would I waste precious coin on a tip in the hay, when I can tip you now for free?"

Iron resolve hardens in my gut. I'm telling my own story now. I escaped the clutches of a goddess. I stared into the eyes of Surma, and death stared back. I am on a mission to walk into the very depths of Tuonela to rescue my dearest friend from the clutches of the death gods.

I am Siiri, and I am no man's prey.

I am the hunter.

"We'll let you choose the order," the tall man offers.

The thought of either of these men touching me makes me sick. But I can't fight them both at once. "You first," I say, pointing to the tall man. "But I don't want him to watch," I add, jabbing my thumb over my shoulder at Paavo.

Paavo laughs again. "You don't get to dictate terms here, little girl."

"Shut up," the tall man snaps. He looks at me with hungry eyes. Something else is there too, just a flicker before he hides it away. Loneliness. Life truly is harsh in this vast wilderness. If he weren't about to attempt to rape me, I might almost feel sorry for him.

"It will be as you say," the tall man says, offering his hand. "Stay and mind the fire," he adds to his friend.

Paavo huffs, leaning back against my packs. "Take your time," he says, slipping a whetstone from his pocket. Then he pulls free his hatchet, giving me a wink.

Bile rises in my throat. "I can walk myself." Balling my hands into fists, I storm away from the fire.

The tall man follows. "Wait—girl—I don't even know your name."

"Goddess, if you're listening, I could use a little help," I mutter, looking for anything I can use as a weapon—a rock, a fallen branch—

"Who are you talking to?" he calls.

"Come *on*," I whisper. "Goddess, help me—"

"Hey—" He grabs my arm. "Where are you going?"

"I just—I—don't want him to see us."

"He won't bother us," the man soothes. "We can take our time."

I go still, heart in my throat, as he steps closer to me. *Goddess, please . . .*

He gives the knot of my hair a little tug and my damp tresses fall down my back to my waist. With one hand holding my arm, he gently takes a handful of my hair with the other, lifting it over my shoulder. Then he leans in closer still, lowering his face to breathe deeply, nestling his nose against my hair.

Help me.

"Gods, girl, you smell like a forest after a rain," he says, his voice low with longing.

"And you smell like a half-dead bear," I mutter, my back stiff as I fight the urge to pull away.

He laughs, wrapping his arm around my waist and pulling me closer. Lowering his face, he kisses my cheek, my neck. His beard bristles against my throat, raising the fine hairs on my arms. Gods, he really does smell awful. I arch away, not allowing him to reach my lips. All around us, the woods stand quiet, empty. The goddess isn't coming to save me. I'm on my own. Is this a punishment for stopping? She told me not to tarry. She told me not to die too. Is this a test? Am I strong enough to survive it?

The trapper's hands roam, taking what I haven't offered. The feel of his lips is almost unbearable. Each kiss feels like the slap of a wet fish against my skin. I swallow back my rage.

Not yet. It's Aksel's voice in my mind now. He taught me everything I know about hunting. *You'll only get one shot. Be patient, Siiri.*

The man undoes his thick leather belt with fumbling fingers, letting his knife and axe fall to the ground. Then he's pushing me forward, leading me over to a mossy spot between two large rocks. "I'll be gentle," he says, his voice growing desperate. "I swear, I won't hurt you. You might even enjoy it."

He pushes on my shoulder, and we drop to our knees. I'm not breathing. I think I may have forgotten how.

Breathe, Siiri, comes Aksel's voice. *A sloppy hunter forgets to breathe.*

I suck in a sharp breath as the trapper pushes me back, his hands still touching me over my clothing. I let myself fall away, lying on my back on the cool moss. A root rests under my shoulder; it's hard and knotted. Above my head, the branches of the trees reach for each other with bony fingers, their leaves blocking out the sky. They hide me from the All-Mother. She cannot see. She cannot help me.

I'm alone.

The man pushes up on his knees. "What's your name?" he asks, dropping his hands to the tie of my pants. I close my eyes as he jerks them down.

Wait . . .

He crouches over me, his breath hot on my face. The pain is sharp in my shoulder from the root, and my unbound hair is caught under me, pulling my neck back. I try lifting my leg to make sure I can reach inside my right boot. Panic rises sharp and fast in my throat. "Oh gods—" I gasp, my body going stiff. With my pants around my knees, I can't bend my leg.

I can't reach the knife.

He presses on top of me, his weight forcing all the air from my lungs. He fumbles, still kissing my neck as he tries to get his hand between us.

"Ouch—you're hurting me!"

He grunts in frustration when I elbow him. "Stop wriggling like a fish—"

"Please—just—here, let me take my pants off first."

He sighs and pushes up with both hands. With his weight off me, I have the room I need. I twist my body under him, leaning down far enough and wrap my hand around the hilt of my knife inside my boot.

Do it, Siiri. Take the shot. Make it count.

With my brother's voice echoing in my head, I throw my left hand behind his head and dig my fingers into his hair, holding him still. In the same breath, I drag the sharp blade of the knife across his throat, pushing up as I pull him closer to me. It's a clean cut, deep and deadly.

The trapper grunts as his blood spills down onto my face and neck, drenching me. "You—bitch," he gurgles, pushing up to his knees, both hands at his throat.

Pulse racing, I scramble to my feet and dart out of his reach.

Blood coats his mouth as he tries to keep the wound closed. He whimpers and I know he knows the truth. "Help me—"

"Never," I hiss.

Mercy, Siiri.

I wince, pushing Aina's voice away.

You're a hunter, not a killer. Show mercy.

"Help me," he pleads again.

I step closer, my bloody hand gripping my knife tight. "You're going to die."

He looks up at me from his knees, eyes wide with fear.

"Take your hands away," I soothe. "It'll be faster if you just let go."

He drops his hands from his mangled neck, holding my gaze as he sways on his knees. "Finish it."

I gasp. "No, I'm a hunter, not a killer—"

"You've just killed me," he grunts, his icy gaze locked on me. "Finish the job, girl."

I look down at the blood coating my chest and hands. *His* blood. "I didn't ask for this." Angry tears burn my eyes. "Why couldn't you just leave me alone?"

"I'm a hunter and a killer."

I shake my head in disgust. "You would make me do this? You would make me be like you?"

He sways, swallowing against the pain at his throat. "Give me—a clean—death," he wheezes. "I'll forgive you—like the men on the cross."

I go still. "What men?"

"The sinners," he gurgles, his color draining. "With Jesus—on the cross."

I search his face. It's only then that I see the leather cord around his neck. Stepping forward, I tug at it, freeing the charm nestled under his bloody tunic. There it is, the sign of the cross, made from a pair of blacksmith's nails. "You're a Christian?"

"Forgive me. I'll—go—heaven—"

Ice fills my veins as I glare down at him. Grabbing him by the hair, I tip his head back, opening his wound. "You were trying to rape me. Nothing was going to stop you but my blade at your throat. You want my forgiveness?"

"I was—desperate—"

"And now you're dead. And there is no heaven," I add, tightening my grip in his hair. "When you die, you will go to Tuonela. And you go without my forgiveness. May you find no rest there." With that, I slam the blade of my knife through his eye, granting him his quick death. His body goes limp as he falls.

I stand there, chest heaving. The madness of the moment fades, and suddenly I can hear the birds sing. I feel the wind on my face. I'm sweating, and I'm cold. I'm wet. Not wet. "Blood," I say, with a voice not my own. I raise my hands. They're red with it, the cuffs of my shirt stained. I stand over the body of a dead man, covered in his blood.

"I just killed a man," I whisper to the trees. "Goddess, I just—"

Breathe. Focus, Siiri.

There's no time for panic now. I pull up my pants with trembling hands. Then I drop to one knee and jerk the knife free from the dead man's skull. I wipe the blade clean on the grass before tucking it back inside my boot.

Stumbling to my feet, I take his long hunting knife and his short-handled axe. Leaving the dead man on the ground behind me, I peer through the trees, looking and listening for any sign of Paavo. If I were smart, I'd leave now. I'd run through the trees and disappear. But I need my gear—the food, the tent, the extra layers of clothes. I'll die without them, and so will Aina . . . so I'll die trying to get them back from Paavo. I have no choice. And right now, I have the element of surprise.

As I move forward on soft feet, the tall man's words haunt my every step.

I'm a hunter and a killer.

Now, thanks to these men, I am too.

Aina

JAAKO CAME TO ME in the night. He let me hold him while I cried, my fear of Tuonela and the Witch Queen stealing all thoughts of sleep. But sleep must have come at some point, for I wake with the comforting warmth of the raven nestled against me. My peace shatters when I realize it was a loud knock at my door that woke me. Jaako hops up, ruffling his feathers.

"Go," I whisper, fearful of him being found. I don't want them to take him from me, my only friend in this dark place. The bolt on the door rattles, and I slip off the bed, still wearing my fine gold dress and the fox-fur stole. "Go now," I hiss at the raven. "Fly."

Jaako gives me a last longing look before he swoops past my shoulder and out the window, clearing the sill just as my door swings open. I brace myself to face my menacing dead guard, but a young woman stands in the doorway instead. I catch the whiff of decay from her flesh. She's dressed plainly, in a homespun dress much like what I would wear. She has glassy eyes, and her hair is falling out in patches. She looks young, perhaps the same age as me. My heart breaks for her, and I wonder how she died. Slowly, the dead woman raises a bony hand and curls her finger. *Come.*

I glance around, unsure of what to do. Can I refuse to follow her? What happens if I do? Taking a shaky breath, I put on my slippers and follow the dead girl out of the room. We walk silently down the hallway. My guide directs me left instead of right at the waiting chamber. We step through an open doorway, and I gasp, the fine hairs on my arms rising. I loosen the fur at my shoulders. For the first time in days, I'm outside . . . at least I think I'm outside. I can feel the crisp autumn air against the skin of my neck and arms.

The sky above is nothing but impenetrable darkness. It's a void so deep I almost fear looking up, lest I float away into it. I focus on my feet instead. I'm standing on large flagstones set in a path through a courtyard. We're in a walled garden lit from all sides by torches casting golden light.

In the corner, standing before a large weeping willow tree, a witch waits. She watches me approach, smiling the same cruel smile as the Witch Queen. Where her mother is haunting in her ugliness, this witch is beautiful, her walnut-brown hair flowing down her back in waves. Several braids wrapped like a crown around her head keep the tendrils away from her face. This death goddess has decorated her crown of braids with bits of bone. Human or animal, I can't be sure. A necklace made from human teeth encircles her slender neck. The teeth look dipped in silver, so they glitter in the torchlight.

I don't notice that the witch isn't alone at first. Quiet Inari stands at her side like a ghost. The women say nothing at my approach, and I take their cue to remain silent. I wait by Inari as the rest of the girls arrive. The other girls look as poorly rested as I feel. Poor Satu looks like she spent the night weeping. Lilja looks determined. Tuonetar promised to kill us. I wonder if this is the day.

As soon as we all stand before her, the witch speaks, her voice high and melodic. "The time has come for you to be of some use to us. You've taken advantage of our hospitality for far too long." She scowls at each of us, as if it were our choice to be locked away for days and fed cursed bread.

"What will you do?" Helmi whimpers. "Will you kill us?"

The witch glares at her. "Kill you? What use would you be then?"

"They mean to work us to death," says Lilja. "How is that any different from our lives among the living?"

"The loud, foolish one is correct," the witch replies. "From today, you will all be assigned a task. No one in Tuonela may be idle. You will work . . . or suffer the consequences."

Lilja scoffs. "The Witch Queen promised to kill me anyway, so why not just be done with it—" She shrieks, dropping to her knees as blood gushes from the side of her head. She clasps a hand over the wound, crying out in pain. We all back away as the blood seeps between her fingers, down her neck, staining the fur of her stole. The witch holds out a hand, revealing Lilja's severed ear. My stomach twists as the witch laughs.

"I didn't think you had much need of this, since you never listen." The witch tosses the ear to the ground, utterly indifferent to Lilja's pain. "Your tongue is next if you don't learn to bide it. Speak again, foolish one, and it will be *your* teeth I wear around my neck."

Lilja whimpers, but says nothing, her hand clasped over her bleeding ear.

The witch turns to face us. "You two," she barks, pointing at Satu and Inari. Satu nearly jumps out of her skin at being addressed directly. "Can either of you cook?"

"Y-yes," Satu stammers.

Next to her, Inari nods.

"Take them to the kitchens," the witch says with a wave of her hand.

From behind us our dead guides appear, ready to lead them away. Satu and Inari have no choice but to turn and go. I watch them leave, unsure if I'll ever see them alive again.

"And you two." The witch points beyond me to Riina and Helmi. "Go tend to the animals. My mother is particularly fond of pork. Pay special attention to the care of her pigs."

In quick succession, the group goes from seven to three. I'm left with Salla at my side and Lilja on her knees. The witch casts a glance between us before pointing a rune-marked hand at Salla. "You, take this one who likes to talk so much, and bring her to Tuonen tytti. She'll no doubt find some use for you both."

I go still, thanking my stars that I'm not being taken to serve the ferrywoman of Tuonela. She transports all the dead across the river of death in a boat made from the bones of a giant pike. I don't think I could bear watching scores of the newly dead massing on Tuonela's shores, eager for entry, when I know I can never leave.

Salla does as she's told, helping Lilja to her feet as their dead guides step forward to lead them away. I'm left alone before the willow and the witch.

"My sister usually abhors taking in any of our mother's strays," she says, "but apparently she finds herself in need of assistance. Can you weave, useless thing?"

I nod, heart in my throat. "Yes, goddess."

"Good. Then go. And do try to be useful," she warns. "It is not unheard of for my dear sister to snip the fingers off clumsy hands." She turns to leave.

"Goddess, wait," I call after her.

The witch stops and glances over her shoulder. "If you're about to ask me to spare your miserable life, you're wasting your breath."

"No, I—I stand before a goddess, and I am ashamed to admit I don't know her face," I admit. "My mother would never forgive me if I didn't ask your name."

Her eyes narrow as she considers me. "You wish to know my name?"

I nod, praying I look sufficiently guileless. There is power in a name. I will need all the power I can gather if I'm to survive this place. Luckily, I'm an excellent forager. "All the gods deserve our devotion and admiration," I say, echoing my mother's words. "As a death goddess, your power is boundless, your reach is limitless, and your control over my life is as inevitable as the night all around us. I would know your name to offer you all due respect."

After a moment, the witch smirks. "I am Vammatar."

I blink, breath frozen in my chest. I stand before the goddess of evil.

"Now, go on," she sneers, that necklace of human teeth glinting in the torchlight. "Show me the respect I'm due."

I drop to my knees. Bending forward, I press my palms flat to the ground, bowing my head. "Goddess."

She lifts the hem of her dark blue robes. "Kiss my boot, worm."

Crawling forward, I let my lips brush the top of her boot.

The witch cackles, kicking me back like a dog. I swallow my whimper of pain and curl away from her. With that, she leaves. I wait on the ground, listening to her distant, mocking laughter. From somewhere beyond the walls, sharp moans and howling wails make the fine hairs on my arms stand on end.

My guide nudges me with a bony hand. I get shakily to my feet, wiping my mouth with the back of my hand. With another curl of her broken fingers, she beckons for me to follow. I try to memorize our path across the walled court-yard, passing under a large archway into a smaller, spiritless courtyard. It is nothing but four stone walls and a stone floor, open to the black sky above. One wall contains a massive set of thick double doors. Is that the way out of the palace?

We pass through the smaller door set in the opposite wall from the garden. The view from the doorway of this third courtyard stops me in my tracks. Not only is it brighter than the other two, lit with twice as many torches, but it hums with activity. Busy people and wriggling dogs, cages of squawking chickens, the tantalizing smell of roasting meats, the metallic clang of hammer to anvil. All the animals are alive. How did they get here?

The strangeness of the scene becomes clear as I take it in. There is no laughter, no chatter, no shouted calls or hurried words. The people are all silent as the grave . . . because they're all dead. They move silently, performing their tasks with all due diligence, exchanging not a word or a look with their fellow man. There's something so deeply lonely about it.

On the far side of the courtyard, Helmi and Riina are al-ready hard at work. Riina sits on a milking stool, tending to a cow. Helmi gives me a reassuring smile as I pass, tossing slop into a pen of grunting pigs. I follow my guide to a small building. She opens the door and gestures for me to go inside. Taking one last look at the bustling courtyard, I step through.

It takes a moment for my eyes to adjust to the dimness. The room is only lit by a small handful of tallow candles. It's long and narrow, taking up half the length of the courtyard, and filled with two-beam looms. Some stand empty, but most carry cloth in some stage of progress. I pause to admire the work on the first loom I pass. The weaver has chosen light and dark threads for a lovely, contrasting geometric pattern.

From the back of the room comes the soft *clack, clack* of a loom at work. I peek around one of the looms and spy the weaver. I can tell by the set of her shoulders and the cleanliness of her hair and clothes that she's alive. Her sleek black hair is so long, it nearly touches the floor. It's braided in a single, thick plait. Vammatar said this was her sister. If the stories are true, Kiputyttö and Kivutar, the twins of evil and suffering, live atop the Kipumäki, the hill of pain. I have a feeling I know who this is . . .

The witch never stops the movement of her hands—back and forth, deft fingers constantly checking the tightness of the weave. I still as I notice the runes tattooed on the backs of her hands. Kalma and Vammatar have them too, but the Witch Queen doesn't. I've only seen such tattoos once before, on a traveling bard who strummed a kantele. What do they mean? Do they serve some godly purpose?

"You know how to weave, mortal?" the goddess asks without turning her head. Her voice is low and melodic.

I clear my throat and step forward. "Yes, goddess. My mother taught me . . . though I'm afraid some of these projects may be beyond my skill," I admit, glancing around at the looms.

Clack. Clack. Clack. The warp weights sway as the goddess weaves the wefts back and forth, moving her heddle rods as she goes. "You have nothing but time to learn and improve."

She's right . . . as long as they keep me alive. "Where shall I begin?"

"Begin at the beginning."

I smile. This feels a bit like speaking to Siiri's mummi. "Must I begin on a loom?"

"Begin wherever you begin," she replies, apparently wholly indifferent.

Making my second bold move of the day, I step closer. A

clever forager knows when to take. "Might I begin with your name, goddess? My name is Aina."

The weaver's hands pause on the heddle rod. I swallow the nerves in my throat, waiting to see if she might kick me as her sister did. "I am Loviatar," she says at last.

Loviatar, goddess of illness and pestilence. The stories say that when she was a young woman, Loviatar was raped by the north wind, and from her womb—and her rage—sprang nine sons, the nine diseases of men. Some storytellers like to say Loviatar had a tenth child, a daughter. This child was Envy, who must go unnamed, lest the speaker be consumed by her.

There is another aspect to Loviatar's stories. All mortals know the witch is—

"Yes, I'm blind." The goddess turns to face me.

I blink, struck by the beauty of her face. While Kalma has black eyes, Loviatar's eyes are cloudy white, like two pearls. I'm not sure what else I expected. Perhaps because Tuonetar and Kalma are so monstrous, I imagined the goddess of illness's face would be riddled with boils and sores. But her skin is soft and smooth, with gentle lines framing her mouth and creasing her brow. There are streaks of grey at her temples. She looks austere . . . and sad. Those pearl eyes stare at me, unblinking.

My heart flutters. "How did you—"

"Because you are mortal," she replies tonelessly. "And mortals are painfully predictable. Now, are you going to weave anything today? Or should I call my vapid sister back here to hammer nails through your thumbs or find some other such uninspired torture?"

I move quickly over to the rack in the corner of the room where a large collection of yarns wait ready for weaving. I pick up a ball of deep red yarn, the color of wine. The cord is thick. It would make quick work to knit a pair of socks. I fish through a basket and pull out a pair of needles. Returning to Loviatar's side, I drag a stool closer to her loom and sit.

Loviatar's head turns to follow my movements. As I sit next to her, she frowns. "What are you doing?"

"I'm knitting," I reply. "The light is best here by your candles. I suppose they must be for warmth?"

Her frown deepens, creasing her forehead still further. "What are you knitting?"

"You said to begin at the beginning. Well, the first thing I ever learned to knit was a stout pair of socks. You see, the trick is—"

"I *can't* see," the witch corrects.

"The trick is to do this special row of stitches at the toe and again when you make the turn for the heel," I say. "It saves hours of work later."

We settle into silence as I begin. Once I have a good inch of knitting complete, I reach for Loviatar's hand. The goddess jumps at the unexpected touch. "What are you doing, little mouse?"

I set Loviatar's fingers on the knitted fabric. "See—I mean, can you *feel* the thickness of the sock here?" I smile as Loviatar moves her fingers over the stitches. "That will make a good pair of socks," I say proudly.

Loviatar just huffs, returning to her work. I do the same. The cloth she's weaving is a beautiful blue scroll pattern on a bed of white, like liverleaves peeking through the snow in spring. I watch in awe as the blind witch works, weaving her pattern without the need of sight.

I can't explain why, but I feel comfortable with Loviatar, at least more comfortable than in the presence of Kalma or the Witch Queen. She's certainly less menacing than Vammatar, who took an ear off Lilja's head just for annoying her and kicked me for asking her name.

For the first time since waking in this dark realm, I feel almost at peace.

When I can stand the silence no longer, I lean forward on my stool. "And what are you working on?"

"Cloth for the servants," Loviatar replies, never stopping the movement of her hands.

This surprises me. I never expected the death gods to care what a dead servant has to wear. All the dead I've seen so far seem barely able to hold themselves together. They wear soiled clothes, their bodies bent and broken. "Why would the gods of Tuonela care about clothing for dead servants?"

Loviatar stills, her head turned away. "This is not Tuonela. Not anymore."

"What do you mean?"

The goddess keeps working her wefts through the warps. "All is not as it seems, little mouse. You come to Tuonela in its darkest hour. Only chaos reigns here now."

Some answers at last. The forager in me leans forward eagerly, ready to collect more kernels of information. I have to find a way to keep her talking. "Who made my dress?" I ask, keeping my knitting needles clicking.

The goddess slow-turns to glare at me. "How easy it is for you to forget that I'm blind."

I wince. "I'm sorry, goddess. The clothes appeared in my room as if by magic—"

"It *was* magic, you fool. You are in Tuonela."

"This dress is like spun gold," I explain. "I've never seen its like. It's beautiful beyond words. Did you weave it?"

"No," comes her soft reply.

"Will you teach me how to work the loom to weave cloth like gold?"

She huffs. "Prove you have any skill first. Then we'll discuss plans for your improvement."

I throw in a few more rows of stitches, working the needles like my mother taught me. The question I've wondered about every hour of my waking sits on the tip of my tongue. Finally, I ask it. "Why am I here?"

"You're here to weave, foolish girl," Loviatar replies.

"No, why am I *here*?" I repeat. "Why was I brought to Tuonela? I know we're not the first group of girls brought down here. There have been many. At first, we thought the girls were going missing, or simply running away from home. But you took them . . . didn't you?"

"I did nothing," she hisses. "I take no part in any of this madness."

I lean forward on my stool. "What does Tuonetar want with us?"

Slowly, Loviatar faces me, her milky white eyes unblinking. "My mother wants you to die. She only ever wants mortals to die."

"Why?" I whisper, fighting to keep my voice from breaking.

"Because she is death."

I think of the great hall last night. I picture the larger of the two skull chairs, empty and forlorn. The arms of the chair were dusted with cobwebs. "And Lord Tuoni?" I ask. "The King of Death? Where is he? Does she not share power with him? Does he want us all dead too?"

Loviatar scowls, her rune-marked hands unmoving on her loom. "Do not speak of my father, little mouse. Not in this place. Not if you value your miserable life."

I glance around. "I cannot speak of him in his own home?"

"This is not his home anymore."

My knitting needles go still, silence filling the space between us. "Where is he?"

"Gone."

"Meaning Tuonetar rules alone," I murmur. "She is wholly unchecked by his influence. Is that why the magic of this place feels so . . . off?"

She says nothing.

"We feel it in life, too, you know. Her chaos spreads like a plague. Why has Lord Tuoni abandoned his realm to the whims of a madwoman?"

"You speak too much, silly girl," Loviatar hisses. "You want to stay alive? Keep your mind on your work and your mouth shut. Do not draw the attention of my mother and sisters. Do not draw my attention either. You are a mouse now, little mouse. You are neither seen nor heard. *That* is how you survive."

"I understand."

She narrows her eyes at me. Then she huffs, turning away. "You understand nothing. How could you?" Her hands go back to her weft.

We work in silence for several hours, and I ask no more questions. I have them, to be sure. My mind is full of nothing but questions, but I worry about pressing my luck too far. A good forager knows when to harvest, but she must also know when to wait, leaving treasures to ripen and grow. By the time my guide returns, I've knitted a pair or thick woolen socks.

"Here," I say, reaching forward to set them on Loviatar's knee.

The goddess stops her work to feel the socks. "What is this?"

"I made them for you," I reply. "Everyone should have a good pair of socks, even a goddess."

Loviatar's hand stills on the socks. Her face is turned away, so I can't read her expression. The goddess says nothing, returning to her weaving with the socks balanced on her knee.

"May I make a pair for myself tomorrow?" I ask, rising to join my dead maid at the door. "My room is quite cold . . ."

Loviatar is silent for so long, I think she will not speak. But as I turn to leave, she says, "You may keep making socks."

"Thank you."

The witch turns to face me, reading me with those unblinking eyes. "At least your feet will be warm when you die."

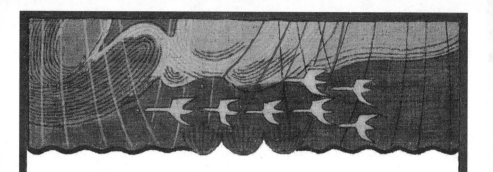

Siiri

PAAVO SITS ON THE far side of the fire, still leaning against my pack. He has the whetstone in hand, sharpening the blade of his axe. The sound of metal on stone echoes across the clearing. A soft wind blows through the trees, rustling the leaves. The scene is peaceful, almost idyllic, with the babbling stream and the grazing reindeer.

But an agent of death stalks these woods, and her name is Siiri. I watch from the edge of the clearing, my bloody hands pressed against the trunk of a tree. I can't take him by surprise. The distance is too far, and he's facing me with his back to the stream. Maybe if I ran forward a few feet, I could throw my knife and strike true, but a man's chest is protected by thick bones. It's easy to miss his heart. I got lucky with Kalma, and it didn't even hurt her. The witch hardly blinked.

There's only one option. I step out of the trees.

"Kyösti?" Paavo takes in my frightening new appearance, soaked in his friend's blood.

"Kyösti is dead," I call. Raising the dead man's axe, I point it at Paavo. "You're next."

A wicked smile spreads across his face as he sets his whetstone aside. He rises slowly, his own axe balanced in his practiced hand. "You're brave for a dead girl."

I hold his gaze, stalking closer. "I've met Kalma already. She gave me this," I reply, gesturing to the faint bruise over my brow. "She doesn't scare me. I bet she scares you to death."

He smirks. Then he lunges forward, closing the space between us. I dip left and bob, dancing with him, hoping to tire him out as he takes massive swings, blade singing through the air.

"Godsdamn it," he barks. "Fight me!"

I raise my axe and step forward, deflecting his blow. Our wooden axe handles clack and slide until the blades scrape together. He grins with yellow teeth as he presses down with his axe. Reaching behind me, I jerk the dead trapper's knife free and stab Paavo in the gut.

He stumbles away with a grunt, his free hand pressed over the bleeding wound. "You foul, stinking bitch."

"My bite is far worse than my bark," I say in challenge, flashing him both blades. "With these metal teeth, I will shred you limb from worthless limb."

With a grunt, he swings high with his axe. I duck it easily, darting to the side. But in a feat of strength and skill, he corrects the blade mid-swing. The shaft cracks the side of my skull, dropping me to the ground. I lose control of my axe as I fall, the forest spinning around me . . .

Get to your feet.

I scramble away, blinking through the pain in my temple. I search for my axe. Paavo grabs me by my loose hair. I'm on my knees in the long grass, fingers inches from the axe shaft.

Goddess, please—just a little closer—

I cry out in pain as Paavo jerks my head back. He stands behind me, his body pressed against mine, as I feel the sharp chill of his axe blade against my throat.

He pants through the pain in his side. "You're a brave little thing, I'll give you that. You look like death's own mistress all covered in Kyösti's blood."

I try to wriggle free, desperately reaching for my axe.

"Don't fight now," he grunts, jerking my hair again as he presses into my throat with his blade. "You'll cut your own neck if you fight, and I'm not ready to kill you yet. Turn over."

No. Please, gods—

"I said turn over." Grappling with me, he forces me down, flipping me on my back until he's straddling my hips, the sharp weight of his blade still pressing into my neck. I can feel it cutting into my flesh, breaking me open the same way I just killed Kyösti. A tear slips down my cheek as I gaze up at the storm clouds swirling overhead. *Goddess, protect me*, I pray to the heavens. *I can't do this on my own. I surrender to you.*

Paavo laughs. "Did Kyösti at least get a taste before you killed him—*argh*—"

A roar splits the air. I feel the ground tremble beneath me, and then a massive form barrels over us, knocking Paavo aside. I pant, my body prone in the grass, bleeding from my neck and brow. Above me is nothing but grey sky.

Another roar. I roll onto my side and can't quite believe what I'm seeing. A large brown bear has pinned Paavo to the ground. The trapper screams in terror, uselessly punching the giant's face as it claws at him.

Then, the bear lowers its hulking snout, teeth bared, and rips the scream from Paavo's throat, silencing him forever.

I lie there, winded. My head pounds; my limbs shake. Paavo had me pinned. I was facing the moment of my death. I had failed. *Again.* Now Paavo's dead, and the bear's soulful dark eyes take me in. With a low grunt, he steps over the dead trapper, blood dripping from his open mouth.

I scramble backwards, trying to stand, but I only manage to get to my knees, swaying. I cover my throat with one hand, feeling the severity of the cut. It won't be fatal, thank the gods. I reach out with my free hand, desperate for my axe, but pause, hand pressed to the cold grass.

The goddess's words echo in my mind: *Follow the bear.*

"Oh gods . . ." The golden-brown fur on his muzzle and around his eyes glows brightest at the tips of his fuzzy ears. "It's you." Ignoring my axe, I crawl forward. "You followed me all this way?"

The bear grunts again, closing the distance between us until I can feel and smell his hot breath. In an act of pure faith, I raise a hand towards his face. "They made me a killer," I whisper, voice trembling. "They forced my hand. Otso, hear me, I'll not harm your servant. May you strike me down if I ever raise a hand to you in anything but friendship."

The bear steps into my hand, letting me stroke his face.

"I saved you from that pit," I say, brushing my fingers over his thick fur. "And now you've saved me. A life for a life. The gods have linked us together, friend." I swallow a startled scream as the bear licks my face from chin to hairline. He does it again, his stinking breath hot on my skin.

He follows me back over to where Paavo lies dead in the grass. He's sprawled out, a gaping hole in his neck, eyes fixed. Inches from his lifeless hand, the handle of his axe waits. The sting of it still burns at my throat.

I'm a hunter and a killer.

So much senseless violence. So much needless death. This is my Finland now, a cold land where Finn turns on Finn. Where is our spirit? Where is our community? Out here, I can only trust the animals of the forest and the gods others presume are dead.

Dropping to one knee, I take Paavo's axe. The memory of his fist twisted tight in my hair makes me sick. I shiver as I remember the feeling of Kyösti pinning me down, my long hair tangled, trapping me. In a fit of madness, I take his axe by the blade and slice through my hair with a sharp jerk, cutting it all until it hangs just above my shoulders. Holding back a sob, I drop my severed locks and the axe onto the dead man's body. My blonde tresses cover him like a shroud.

"Keep it," I say, spitting on his corpse. No man will ever use my hair as a weapon against me again.

From across the small clearing, the bear watches me.

"You found me for a reason," I say to him. "I believe we're meant to help each other." The bear grunts his assent, and I smile. "You should know I travel north in search of Väinämöinen."

The bear goes still, closing his mouth and narrowing those soft eyes.

"I'm told you know the way," I continue. "I'm also told the shaman doesn't wish to be found. But he's my only hope. Without him, I will lose the person who means more to me than my own life. You see now what I'm willing to risk." I point down at the dead trapper. "Only death will stop me. Will you go north with me? Will you help me find the shaman?"

The bear considers for a moment, studying me with his knowing eyes. Slowly, he nods.

"Very well, then. Let's go, friend. Northward."

Aina

DAYS HAVE PASSED, AND I'm still alive. My nights are spent in quiet comfort with Jaako. He still feeds me, using his magic to provide me with meals of roasted waterfowl and meat pies, sweet berry tarts. My father says ravens are messengers of death. They can cross the realms, taking away sickness and pain, sharing secrets of Tuonela.

I'm hoping, if I prove myself his friend, Jaako will send a message for me. I have to reach Siiri. She has to know I forgive her everything, that I would do it all again to spare her this fate. I need her to know I love her and I'm sorry I took away her choice. But I'm not sorry she'll get to live. She deserves such a long and happy life.

Each night, I look to the raven, my request on the tip of my tongue. But I'm afraid of his refusal. He's my only hope. I can't bear to ask. Not yet. I'm not ready. But I also know I can't tarry for too long. Each moment here could be my last.

And yet, each night, I curl up with the raven in my arms, and I stay silent.

Maybe tomorrow night . . .

Maybe . . .

My dead guide is actually a handmaid. She comes each morning to deliver me to the weaving room. I've decided to give her a name—Kukka. It means flower. The name has helped to disarm some of my feelings of disquiet at always having the dead girl beside me. She's not a specter of death meant to monitor my every movement; she's just Kukka.

We arrive each morning to the weaving room, and Loviatar greets me in her cold manner. We're not always alone. Sometimes the dead help us. One woman in particular seems just as skilled as Loviatar. The weaver specializes in using the metallic threads. She creates the most beautiful cloth of silver, copper, and gold.

True to her threats, Loviatar treats me like a mouse, preferring when I'm neither seen nor heard. But on the second day, she lets me keep a pair of blue wool socks. And on the fifth day, she shows me through the door in the corner of the weaving room. It leads to a large storage room filled with shelves, each stacked with piles of clothes—stout men's tunics and breeches, wool dresses, peplos-style overdresses, all manner of fur and wool capes.

The goddess tells me I can take my pick of anything in the room. "The dead don't mind what they wear."

As much as I love my beautiful golden dress, it's highly impractical for everyday use. I switch it out for a stout wool dress of bellflower blue. I style a green peplos over it and belt both with a bit of woven cloth. I even find a pair of fingerless wool mittens and an extra pair of socks. The last piece of my new winter outfit is a knit wool hood that can rest around my neck like a scarf while I work.

"Tell me about Tuonela," I say, daring to speak as we sit side by side at a loom. She's begun to teach me, now that she feels confident in my knitting. "I feel the seasons changing, but there is no sun or moon. Is it autumn now? Will winter come soon?"

"Seasons are seasons everywhere," the witch replies. "Not too tight," she warns, her fingers brushing over mine as she checks my work.

"Where do the animals come from?" I ask, passing her the weft through the warps. "They're alive, too, right? The dogs, the chickens, the pigs, the ravens . . ."

Loviatar makes no response.

"And the food . . . are there farms in Tuonela? How do plants grow? Is it all magic? The stories say Tuonela is a vast land of mountains and meadows and great palaces. Can I see it—"

"Focus, little mouse," the witch chastises.

I try to bite my tongue, but I have so many questions. Jaako can't answer me the way Loviatar can. "What is your favorite thing about Tuonela?" I say, handing her the batten.

"The silence," she says, tapping the weave tight.

I smirk. "Yes, silence must be a rare gift in a realm where the dead sleep eternal."

"Do you have any family, little mouse?"

My smile falls as I try to stop my mind from conjuring an image of my parents and my young brothers. It's too painful to think of them. "Yes," I whisper.

"Do you have any sisters?"

I close my eyes, thinking of Siiri. "Yes."

"Then you know what it means to crave silence," the witch retorts.

I can't help but smile again. It's true, there have been many moments where I've wanted to stuff Siiri's mouth with socks just to hear myself think. "Tell me about your sisters."

"You want a fond tale of sisterly affection," she replies, her rune-marked fingers brushing over the warps. "But my sisters and I are witches, Aina. We were made by the All-Mother to fulfill a divine purpose. With our power comes great suffering and even greater pain. Mortals fear us, for they fear death. But they are foolish to do so. Like all the dead now resting here, you will soon learn the greatest truth in life."

I glance her way. "And what truth is that?"

She turns her face. Her striking eyes gleam in the candlelight. "That there is power to be found in embracing death. Do not run from it, little mouse. Do not hide. Meet it head on. Treat it as your equal, and it will see you as such."

I huff a little laugh. There is no mirth in the sound. "Clearly, you haven't heard the tale of my capture. Did Kalma not tell you?"

"Kalma does not speak," Loviatar replies.

"Why can't she speak—"

"I said she doesn't speak," the witch corrects. "There's a difference, little mouse."

We're quiet for a moment, our hands working in rhythm together on the loom.

"Tell me." Her voice is soft.

I swallow the emotion thick in my throat. "Kalma appeared to us at the lakeshore," I begin. "It was nearing sunset. She had her eyes set on Siiri."

"Who is Siiri?"

I smile weakly, tapping the weave to tighten the knots. "My dearest friend. It was her Kalma wanted . . . until Siiri fought back."

The witch raises a dark brow, stark against the paleness of her skin. "She fought Kalma?"

"Yes."

She shakes her head. "Stupid girl."

"She was brave," I correct. "And selfless. She was fighting

Kalma to protect me, to give me a chance to run. I had that chance. I could have let Kalma take Siiri."

"But you didn't?"

I blink back my tears. "To use your words, I met death as my equal. I offered Kalma my hand. I let her take me, praying she would spare Siiri this fate."

Next to me, the goddess grows impossibly still, her hands splayed on our shared weave. Slowly, she turns to cup my cheek, her cold fingers brushing along my jaw. "Little mouse . . . answer me very carefully now. Are you saying you *chose* this fate? You chose to come to Tuonela?"

Before I can reply, the door to the weaving room slams open. Loviatar drops her hand away from me. Vammatar sweeps into the room, her walnut-brown hair piled high on her head in intricate braids. She wears flowing robes of bloodred, a wool shawl around her shoulders the color of charcoal. "Sister," she says with a nod to Loviatar, her long fingers brushing wispy tendrils of hair back from her face.

Loviatar just scowls. "What do you want?"

"I'm here for the bonebag," she replies, gesturing to me. "Mother has set them all with a delightful new task," she adds with a devious glint in her eye.

Holding the witch's gaze, I know with all surety that I cannot leave this room. To leave this room is death. No matter what Loviatar says, I'm not ready to truly meet it as my equal.

Next to me, Loviatar tenses. "Use one of the others. I don't feel like parting with this one. She's a skilled worker."

Her hesitancy only confirms my fears. If I walk out that door with Vammatar, I'm not coming back. As if she knows exactly what we're both thinking, Vammatar laughs. "Oh, little sister. You've always been so sentimental about your pets. It really is your curse. Don't worry, you'll get her back . . .

probably." Sweeping forward, she grabs me by the arm, gripping it like a vise. "Let's go, bonebag. We can't keep the others waiting."

I look desperately from Vammatar to her sister, waiting for Loviatar to do something. She could fight for me to stay. She could use her magic. We could escape together right now. Cross the river and—

"Just let this one keep all her fingers," Loviatar calls, her tone flat and dismissive. "She'll make a fine weaver, alive or dead. At least dead she won't talk so much."

Vammatar snorts as my heart sinks. "Yes, they really do bleat more than goats, don't they?" She gives my arm another sharp tug. "Let's go."

Knowing my fate is sealed, I let the witch drag me from the weaving room.

Vammatar leads the way through the maze of courtyards back to the walled garden. I'm grateful for my new clothes in this crisp autumn chill. I flip up the hood of my cowl, covering my hair. From my pocket I pull my pair of wrist-warmers and slip them on.

I follow Vammatar down the path. There, behind the willow tree, set into the wall of the courtyard, is a small wooden door. The witch waves her hand, and the door swings open on creaky hinges. The light from the courtyard stops abruptly beyond the door.

"Come *on*," Vammatar growls, pulling me forward.

I pass through the narrow doorway and blink desperately to encourage my eyes to adjust. An eerie mist, almost silver in the half-light, floats over the grass. Before us, not twenty yards away, looms a ghostly forest. The trunks of the birch trees are heavy with knots. Like so many unblinking eyes, they watch as we approach. It's unnerving. I feel like the trees know I'm walking to my death.

I cast a wild look behind me, letting myself take in the full sight of Tuoni's palace. The high stone walls are lit from the inside, making the whole structure glow. I can see the roof of the massive hall where Tuonetar received us. To either end of the hall are two stone towers. I stumble over a root as Vammatar pulls me into the trees. "I—goddess, I can't see," I admit.

"You don't need to see," she snaps. "Move your worthless feet."

We step between a pair of thick trees and my stomach twists in a painful knot. There, beneath an orb of eerie light, wait Kalma and another dark-haired witch. This one earns the name. She is weathered and rotting, her hair falling in thin, greasy strands around her face. Like Kalma, she dresses in black. Her shoulders are hunched, her pale eyes red-rimmed and lifeless as she stares at us, unblinking. She must be one of the twins. Either she is Kivutar, the goddess of suffering, or her twin Kiputyttö, goddess of pain.

Three other girls huddle together nearby. Lilja and Satu hold hands, both of them looking pale and underfed. Behind them, tall Riina looks resigned. Like me, she assumes this is the moment she will meet her end. I freeze, a strangled shriek of fright caught in my throat, as the great, hulking form of a red-eyed wolf slinks through the trees. He is Surma, the death-bringer. His bright eyes watch me as he stalks over to the side of his mistress. Kalma reaches out a bony, tattooed hand, scratching between the monster's pointed black ears.

"Finally," Vammatar's sister rasps, her voice like rocks scraped along a boat's hull. "Let's get on with this." Next to her, Kalma stands silent as the grave.

"Patience, Kivutar," Vammatar replies in that light, teasing tone. "All good things to those who wait."

My shoulders sag in defeat. If the goddess of eternal suffering is here, this can only end horribly. The witch and I join the circle of light, and she lets me go, giving me a shove towards the other girls. Satu and Riina each take one of my gloved hands.

"You lot are spoiled rotten," Kivutar growls. "Worthless to the core, I don't know why we keep you at all."

"Come, sister," Vammatar says with another laugh. "Surely, they're not all so bad. Loviatar says the mousey one is quite skilled at weaving."

I go still as all three witches stare at me. Loviatar is over-generous in her praise, but I'll take it if it keeps me alive. The goddess of suffering, her skin so ancient and lined it looks like it may fall off the bones of her face, glares at me. Vammatar steps out of the light, leaving us with only Kivutar and Kalma.

"We're tired of doing all the hunting for you spoiled kits," Kivutar says. "And my father's forests are teeming with life. If you want meat to eat, hunt it yourselves."

From the darkness behind her, Vammatar drags forward a large wooden box. She flips open the lid to reveal an assortment of weapons. "Take your pick," she says with a wave of her hand. "You must all be sick of barley bread by now. Whatever you kill, you may cook and eat."

Next to me, the other girls look confused. I can hear their stomachs groan at the thought of fresh meat. Satu all but whimpers with relief. What new game is this? Even before the Witch Queen's haunted welcome feast, I've enjoyed a varied diet of game and fruit pies, and warm salted nuts. Twice now, my cup even filled with a sweet, red wine. I see now that I must be alone. The way Lilja and Riina cling to their quivers and bows, I can only imagine they're not eating roasted perch every night. Jaako's magic is feeding only me.

This feels dangerous in the extreme. I have a secret I'm keeping from everyone, even the other girls. I can't give myself away. Not until I speak to Jaako again. I have to understand why he's helping me . . . and whether his help will get me killed faster. Swallowing my nerves, I step over to the box and choose a hatchet. Lilja and Riina look far more confident wielding their bows and axes.

"Move quickly and quietly," Vammatar cautions. "Keep your aim straight and true."

"But be careful, little mortals," her sister adds. "For more than animals roam these dark woods. Beware the kalman väki and the keijulainen. Beware the walking dead."

Next to me, Satu trembles. Lilja just narrows her eyes, ready to face any beasts or monsters prowling these dark woods.

"Stop when you reach the river," Vammatar directs. "And if you get any ideas, just know we'll be watching. Surma doesn't take kindly to naughty little girls who break the rules."

Next to his mistress, the wolf gives a low growl, making poor Satu jump, nearly dropping her axe.

"Get on with it," says Kivutar, pointing at the trees.

I exchange a worried look with Satu, but Lilja and Riina take off running. They hold their bows confidently, arrows nocked. Satu and I hurry after them, chased by the witches' mocking laughter. Poor Satu trips on the hem of her dress, nearly falling on her face, and the witches cackle louder.

"Lilja," I rasp. "Riina, wait—"

The girls pause, glancing over their shoulders. I wince at the bloody bandage over Lilja's missing ear.

"Are you well?" I ask. "Are the others alive?"

"Salla lives," Lilja replies as Riina nods.

"Inari too," Satu adds.

I breathe a sigh of relief. "Then we're all still alive."

"Not for long," Riina mutters. "This is a test meant to kill us."

Satu's eyes widen. "What can you mean?"

"We're not hunting animals in these woods," Riina replies, her sharp gaze darting around. "We're being hunted."

Satu and I both go still. "No," she whispers. "No, they mean to make us work—"

"Don't be a fool," Lilja hisses. "They have enough dead to work for them. That's not why we're here. And you heard the witch. Do you know what a kalman väki is, little Satu? It's a death spirit born of rot and decay. It is Kalma's Wrath, and it haunts these woods looking for mortal souls to feast on. And the keijulainen are evil fae that poison your mind with nightmares. If they touch you, they infect your skin with festering boils."

"How do you know all this?" Satu says with a whimper.

"My father is a shaman," Lilja replies. "He follows the old ways."

"I think this might be a game," Riina adds, still glancing around. "The death witches love nothing more than to toy with mortals. The stories say they often set mortals an impossible task. The trial doesn't end until they succeed . . . or die trying."

"I can't eat another bite of that rotten bread," Lilja says. "If I *do* get a clean shot, I'm taking it."

Riina nods. "Vammatar caught me trying to sneak an egg in the courtyard yesterday and gave me this." She holds out her arm and pulls up her sleeve, showing us all a line of thick purple bruises that look like they were made with a rod. Her bruises confirm my suspicions. The other girls aren't being treated as gently as I am. Perhaps this is part of the test. Should I admit it to them? I could sneak food to Riina and Helmi as I pass through the courtyard. This is the first I've seen Lilja since our rotten feast, but surely I could find a way. Where are the others?

I take a step forward. "Listen, there is a raven—"

"Hush," Riina rasps, spinning around to face the darkness.

I hear it, too, the faint rustle of a bush off to the left. Next to me, Satu grabs my hand.

"Let's split up," says Lilja. "No offense, Satu, but you look like you're going to cut your own leg off swinging that axe. Aina, can you hunt?"

I shake my head. "I've always been a better forager."

Riina rolls her eyes. "I'm going this way." She points to the right. "Lilja, go that way and swing back at the river," she adds, nodding to the left.

"You two just keep walking straight ahead," Lilja adds. "With all the noise you make, you'll scare whatever's hiding and send them our way. Agreed?"

"Agreed," Riina says with a nod.

Next to me, Satu gasps. "Wait—if we make noise, won't we lure the ghosts and väki closer?" But the other girls aren't listening. They part ways, disappearing into the darkness. "Don't leave me," Satu begs.

"Come on then."

We begin walking, picking our way over roots and around ferns.

"Do you think there are boars in Tuonela?" she whispers. "A boar killed my uncle. It was a nasty, brutish thing with great, long tusks. It gored my uncle in the groin. He bled out in my father's arms. It was awful."

"Boars are clever," I reply, keeping my voice low. "They'll smell us coming . . . or hear us. We'll do as Lilja says and make some noise. If we can help them make a kill faster, we might all escape this alive."

"But if we make noise, we may lure the walking dead or the sprites or—"

I pull her to a stop. "You don't need to remind me of what may lurk in these dark woods. I'm already so terrified, I can hardly breathe. Let's just be scared together. All right?"

Slowly, Satu nods. I can hardly see her face in this dim light. "All right."

Before we can move, branches snap to our left. Satu spins around with a gasp, swinging her axe. The glint of the blade flashes by my eye as I barely move away in time.

"What is it?" she rasps. "Can you see it?"

Inching closer, I wrap my hand around her wrist. "Here . . . why don't you give me this?" I gently pull the axe from her shaking hands.

"I can't be unarmed—"

"You'll do more harm than good with it, I'm afraid." I tuck it through my belt. "Just stay with me. I may not be as good as Siiri with a hatchet, but I'm not hopeless either."

"Who's Siiri?" she asks as we continue walking forward.

"My friend from home. She's the best with a bow I've ever seen. And she can win a hatchet-throwing contest with her eyes closed. She drives all the young men crazy."

"With her beauty?"

I can't help but laugh. "No, because none of them can best her. I once saw her fell an elk from the other side of . . ." My voice trails off as I spy something lying on the ground, partially concealed behind a fern.

Satu sees it too and goes still. "Is it . . ."

"Dead," I finish for her, stepping around the fern to take in the form of an elderly man lying peacefully on a bed of moss, lost to eternal sleep. Satu holds tighter to my arm, staring down at the dead man with wide eyes. "Come away," I say gently. "He won't hurt us. The sleeping dead are at peace."

"And what of the walking dead?" she whispers.

We step around the dead man, both of us startling when we quickly spy two more bodies lying in the gloom. "It was a meadow," I say, hoping to distract her. "Siiri managed the shot clear across a meadow."

Not far from these bodies lies another, half-hidden in the ferns.

"Gods, she's so young," Satu murmurs. "She looks . . . wait. Aina, *look*."

I notice the differences immediately. All the dead have a look about them. Their color is off, tinged in blues and greys, like they're more shadow than living creature. And they possess a smell of rot. Some smell worse than others, depending on their injury or malady. I have come to the conclusion that we must come to Tuonela frozen in whatever form we took at the moment of our death—headless, fevered, an arrow through the eye.

But this young woman looks different. She looks . . . well, she looks like a freshly dead body in the woods. Her colors are still pinks and whites. She wears a fine dress of spun silver. Her body is arranged as if someone took the time to make her comfortable, crossing her arms over her chest and even placing a flower in her cupped hands. A small stone rests in the middle of her forehead, marked with a rune.

I crouch over, narrowing my eyes in the darkness. I think the carving is of a swan. "A sielulintu," I whisper, dropping to my knees at her side.

"What?"

"A soul bird," I say. "The Swan of Tuoni is a good omen. She guards the river, perfectly balanced between life and death. Someone wanted to help this young woman pass peacefully. They honored her death and the place where she will find eternal rest."

"Why does she look so different from the other dead?" Satu whispers.

I go still, my gaze locked on her fine outfit, so similar to the one I was gifted when I first arrived. Then I take in the wound over her heart. She took an arrow to the chest.

"Aina?"

"Look at her dress," I say, suddenly breathless.

Satu takes in the silvery dress and her colorful slippers, her fox-fur stole.

"Look at *this*," I say, my fingers brushing the wound that no longer bleeds. Shifting her aside reveals an arrow tucked under her. No doubt it was the arrow plucked from her heart.

"Oh gods," Satu whimpers.

"She was one of us. Perhaps of the group stolen before we were taken. She didn't die in the realm of the living. She was brought to these woods and killed. I think she died right here," I add, holding up the arrow. "This is how we look when we die in the kingdom of death."

"We're going to die out here, aren't we? Aina, I don't want to die—"

A bloodcurdling scream tears through the silence of the woods all around us. We both scramble to our feet, following the sound, but Satu turns one way and I turn another.

"Help!"

"Oh no—it's Lilja," I gasp. Pulling free of Satu's hand, I race towards the sound.

"Wait," Satu shrieks. "Aina, wait for me!"

The scream fills the forest again. *"Help! Somebody!"*

I run, passing several more bodies lying prone amongst the ferns. Some are faded and grey, dead long ago, but at least two more are young girls in full color. I don't pause to investigate.

"Aina," Satu calls from behind me, as screams of, *"Oh gods, help us!"* come from Lilja ahead.

"Where are you?" I shout.

"Aina, it could be a ghost sent to trick us," Satu warns, meeting me at my side. "It could be a death sprite or a—"

"It's Lilja," I say, cutting her off.

Satu grabs for my arm. "That's what the witches want you to think—*Aina*—the screams are coming from the other way—"

I jerk free of her grasp at another cry.

"No! Please, Inari, no—"

A low growl raises all the fine hairs on my arms. Heart racing, I stare into the haunted red eyes of Surma. The shaggy black wolf pants, mouth open to reveal his white teeth.

Then the smell hits me. I gag, a hand going reflexively to cover my nose and mouth as I try to hold my breathing. But my chest heaves from my sprint. I need air.

Kalma steps from the shadows at his side, one bony hand tangled in his scruff. The witch appraises me with her black eyes, not unlike the glossy black eye of my raven. Her face is painted with blood that has dried in streaks down her neck. Her horned head tilts, as somewhere near, another scream pierces the silence.

"Please, goddess, just tell me which way," I say, dropping my trembling hand to my side.

Slowly, Kalma raises an arm, her long finger pointing to her right.

I inch away, not daring to turn my back until the shadows of the forest swallow them. Then, turning on my heel, I sprint in the direction Kalma pointed. "Lilja," I call, pushing my way through the brambles.

"Aina," Lilja sobs. "Help me."

Inari lies on the mossy ground between the rocks, her body spreadeagled. An arrow protrudes from her neck. Lilja is doing what she can to tend to the girl, her hands bloody from trying to apply pressure. Her bow lies forgotten on the ground.

"Inari, I'm sorry," Lilja whimpers. "I didn't know. Gods, I swear, I didn't know."

Inari's hand flutters at her side, like she's trying to reach for the arrow to pull it out.

"What happened?" I say, stepping forward.

Lilja's head jerks up, tears streaking down her cheeks flecked with soil and blood. "She was the deer," she shrieks. "I swear by all the gods, I didn't know. It was those bloody fucking witches!"

I drop to my knees on Inari's other side. This is the witches' idea of a game, and it is one they've played many times before, I understand now. They turned some of us into animals and had us hunt each other through the darkness. That's what killed the other girls. The girls like us. The girls who had been taken.

I place my hands over Inari's wound. Immediately, I can feel her weak pulse. The poor girl is dying.

"I didn't know," Lilja sobs. "I just wanted to hunt the deer. I'm so hungry."

My sympathies overflow for Lilja. She doesn't need to be here to watch Inari die. "Riina. You have to go find her, Lilja. You have to warn her, stop her from hurting any of the others."

Lilja looks from me to the dying girl. "But Inari, she needs me—"

"I will do all I can to help her, but you have to save Salla and Helmi. Lilja, *go!*"

Lilja gets to her feet and darts through the trees, calling out Riina's name. From the other direction, Satu comes stumbling into the clearing. "You l-left me," she sobs. "You—"

"Get down here and help me."

She takes in the scene, and her cries are cut short. She stands there, chest heaving, cheeks pink. "What happened?"

"We're not being hunted. We're hunting each other. The other girls are the animals."

Satu drops to her knees. "How cruel." Then she gasps. "Oh, Aina—the other girls, the ones in the woods—"

"Yes," I say, holding both hands over Inari's wound. "They left them where they fell."

Tears slip down Satu's cheeks as she glances down at Inari. I look down too. The poor girl whimpers, blood coating her mouth as she tries to suck in air around the arrow in her throat. Her eyes are wide as they watch me, her pale, white hair stained with her blood. "Hold on," I murmur. "You'll be all right."

"Aina . . ." Satu places a gentle hand on my arm. "You should take your hands away."

I glare at her. "We have to help."

"She's suffering, Aina. Taking your hands away *is* helping her."

My heart clenches in my chest. Satu is right. There will be no saving Inari. Resolved, I take one hand away from Inari's neck and pick up the hatchet I left discarded on the ground. For once, Satu doesn't whimper. She takes Inari's hand and begins to sing in a soft voice:

Beside the stream in the summertime,
Beneath the boughs of a sweeping pine,
My love, I vow I will make you mine,
And we will live in love forever.

Tears falling, I press down with the blade and jerk it across Inari's throat, opening her to death completely. It only takes a moment. Inari gasps and gurgles before she goes still. Her face relaxes as her eyes glaze over. Satu closes her eyes. "There. She's resting now. She's at peace."

I drop the blade with a sob. I spared poor Lilja this, at least. Inari's death is now mine to bear. Satu slips her cloak off her shoulders and drapes it over Inari's body, covering her face. She reaches out to me with a comforting hand, but I jerk away, anger burning inside me.

"Aina, this wasn't your fault—"

"I won't die like this," I say, voice trembling. "We're getting out, do you hear me? I don't know how, but I am not dying here. Ilmatar, mark my words."

"Oh, Aina, please don't try to escape. They'll kill you for sure—"

"Like Inari didn't try to escape? Much good it did her."

"Don't," she says, her bottom lip quivering. "Don't speak ill of the dead where they can hear you."

Hot shame fills me as I gaze down at Inari's form. Satu is right. I lean down, giving Inari's shoulder a gentle squeeze. "I'm so sorry," I whisper. "I'm sorry I couldn't save you. I will do everything in my power to save the others, I swear it."

"Aina, this is Tuonela," Satu says. "What power can a mortal wield against the death gods?"

"They're hunting us for sport," I murmur. "Starving us and tricking us, scaring us half to death. This is not the Tuonela of the songs. Something is wrong here, Satu. Tuonetar's magic has cursed this realm—all the realms. Have you not felt it? For years now, we've suffered—healthy women taken in child-birth, strange accidents, gruesome murders. Awful deaths. Cruel deaths. Meaningless deaths. I thought it was because life was somehow out of balance with death. But now I think death is out of balance with itself."

I pause. "Where is the god of death, Satu? Where is Tuoni, who should sit on the throne?"

Before Satu can reply, we both turn towards the crack of branches.

"Aina!" Lilja reappears, pulling Riina into the clearing behind her. Both girls are winded, dropping to their knees at either side of me. Lilja takes in Inari's shrouded form, her expression changing from one of exhaustion to one of horror. "No—*no*! You said you'd help her," she cries, falling on Inari's body with a sob.

"Where are the others?" Satu asks, glancing behind them as if she expects to see Helmi and Salla stumbling through the ferns.

Riina looks white as death. "I didn't shoot. I saw a deer. I had my bow raised . . . but then I heard Lilja."

"Did you see the other girls?" Satu asks. "The ones from before?"

Riina scowls. "Yes, the goddesses have played this game many times. All women our age, all dead. The foul, rotten witches, may Ukko pound their bones to dust," she curses, spitting on the ground.

"We have to try to find Salla and Helmi," I say, getting to my feet.

"How are we supposed to do that?" asks Lilja. "Inari only changed back when I shot her."

"We can't just leave them trapped out here," I say, wiping my bloody hands on my skirt. "Let's split up. Satu, come with me—"

A chilling laugh from the darkness makes us all jump. "Well, you've made quite a nasty little mess of things. Haven't you, my pets?"

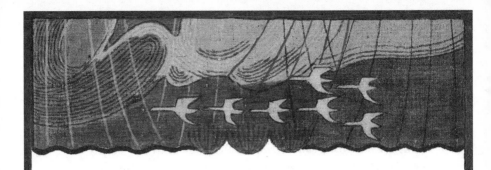

Siiri

I TAKE THE BEST of the trappers' supplies, loading them into Halla's packs. They don't have much beyond some dried venison and a sewing kit. I let the pair of other reindeer loose to make their own way. It took many soothing words to get Halla to walk anywhere near the lumbering bear, but after a few hours of practice, we achieve a good rhythm. He walks to my left, and she walks to my right.

"This is just like Aina," I say, holding one hand against the seeping cut at my throat that won't stop bleeding. "She would put me in this position. She was always getting us into trouble."

Halla glances at me, her soft eyes blinking.

"I told her to run," I say to the bear, knowing Halla has heard it all before. "She just stood there like her feet were made of stone. She let Kalma take her."

The bear grunts, showing me that he's listening.

"Growing up it was just the same." I give Halla's lead a tug. "Let's climb that tree, Siiri," I say in a mockery of Aina's voice. "Oh, we climbed the tree . . . and found two hornets' nests hiding in the branches. We were stung within an inch of our lives. Mummi was putting salve on us for a week."

The bear makes a noise that almost sounds like a laugh.

"Oh, and boat racing. Let's drag the boat to the river, she said. Never mind that the spring thaws mean there may be rapids. The boat tipped, and I nearly drowned dragging her out of the water."

He glances my way, his expression veiled.

"Here I am again, risking life and limb when she's too weak to save herself. I should leave her to her fate!" As soon as the words leave my lips, I regret them. I stop, tears stinging my eyes, as hot bubbling shame burns a hole through my gut. The pain is only matched by the throbbing at my temple from the axe blow and from the wound on my throat. I could swear the bear is frowning at me.

"Fine," I mutter. "It was me. It's always me. I get us into trouble. I fight when I should flee. I leap without thinking. Aina is the only one who follows me. She would follow me to the ends of the earth."

The bear gives me a searching look.

I look away, blinking back my tears. "I may get us into trouble, but I always get us out of it again."

A few hours later, it's nearing dark, and I'm still walking. The bear lumbers on all fours at my side, his back nearly reaching my shoulder. His head alone is huge, made thicker by his full winter coat. Large, fluffy flakes of snow land on his fur and stay there, dusting his broad back and shoulders.

"I think you need a name," I say.

He stiffens.

"What about Valo? It means *light*."

The bear just grunts.

I laugh. "Hmm . . . what about Syksy? No, Kosto. *Vengeance.* That seems fitting."

He sniffs disinterestedly at those names too.

"We go on a journey north to seek out a hero from legend," I muse. "What about Kalev, the great King of Kalevala? He and his sons built castles of ice in winter and stone in summer. I can call you Kal for short."

He leans into my shoulder, looking for an ear scratch, and I take this as assent.

"Kal it is then."

He grunts.

"And you do know where we're going, right?" I ask for the hundredth time. "The goddess said I'm following you."

He's not listening. His golden ears have perked up, his mouth closed as he sniffs the air.

"What is it?" I follow Kal's eyes and peer through the dense evergreens. "Is something out there?"

In answer, a dog barks in the distance. Then another. Multiple dogs mean people, perhaps even a whole village.

"If they live this far north, they must be Sámi."

Father told me many stories of Sámi, our brothers and sisters to the north. They are reindeer herders, following the herds with the changing of the seasons. It's a harsh, nomadic life of constant motion.

I met one once, a young hunter, beardless and handsome. He traveled all the way down to Lake Päijänne. He passed through our village on the way to the southern market. I still remember his bright clothes and his wide smile.

We keep walking, and I look for signs of people—footprints, animal droppings, smoke, tracks. To our left, more barking breaks the silence. Kal pauses, taking a few panting breaths to taste the air.

"You better stay here," I say. "I don't want them to panic. If this is a village, they might be willing to trade. Three people won't make it south without more supplies, and I'm not finding Aina just to lose her again."

He pushes his head against my hip in protest.

"Hey, you're the valuable one. You know the way to Väinämöinen, not me." I tie Halla to the closest branch as Kal glares from my throat to the bruising on my temple. "You think I haven't thought of that?" Opening one of the leather packs, I take out Aksel's old hunting hat, lined with fur. It has two flaps that come down around the ears. Putting it on over my little blue cap, it covers the worst of my bruises. I fasten the top button of my jacket, hiding the bloody bandage at my neck. "I'll call if I need you. Stay hidden. And don't eat her," I add, pointing at the reindeer.

I leave them together, shrugging my bow off my shoulder as I walk, nocking an arrow. My feet crunch on the fresh, powdery snow, my warm breath coming out in white puffs. Using a hunter's trick, I scoop a small handful of the snow, putting it in my mouth to cool my breath. I weave through the dark trees, bow at the ready.

Snap.

I whirl around, pulling back on my bowstring. I'm face to face with a young man with weather-burned cheeks and bright green eyes. He lowers his axe and raises his free hand in a sign of peace, his voice muffled by his scarf.

I lower my bow. "I'm sorry, I don't understand."

He speaks again as he tucks his axe into his belt.

I shake my head. "I don't understand you."

He sighs, glancing around. Then he switches to a language I understand. "You are Finn."

"Yes," I reply. "I'm Finn."

"Come. I take you to Lumi." Without waiting for me, he

turns and walks away. I slip my bow onto my shoulder, tucking my arrow back into the quiver, but I keep my hand on my hatchet as I follow him through the trees. I walk with slim knives in both my boots now, and Kyösti's hunting knife is nestled between my shoulder blades.

I smell the village before their fires appear through the trees. They're smoking meat. My stomach groans, twisted with hunger.

The trees thin and I catch my first glimpse of the huts. Men, women, and children emerge to watch us pass. The young man leads me to a large, conical hut close to the center of the village. Thick layers of peat cover the hut's wooden frame, and the peat is dusted with a layer of snow. Smoke drifts out from the top. The young man gestures with both hands for me to stay put. Then he ducks inside the narrow, hide-covered doorway.

After a few minutes he emerges and points to my bow, then points to the ground. I clench my jaw, knowing what he wants. I peer inside the opening of the hut and see one woman sitting inside. This must be Lumi. Surely, I can handle a single woman alone. I give the young man my quiver and bow. He gestures to my hatchet, and I sigh, handing him that too.

With a nod, he lets me enter. I step inside the hut, mentally counting all the blades I still have hidden on my body. The door rattles shut behind me. A series of long, narrow branches are stacked in parallel to form the conical shape. It looks like I'm inside the rib cage of a forest giant. The floor is padded with a layer of reindeer furs that keep out the cold, save for a space in the middle for a stone-ringed hearth.

"Hello," the woman says. "Won't you sit down?" She flicks her hair back with a casual hand as she hangs a pot of water on a chain over the fire.

She's beautiful, with high cheekbones and thick locks of auburn hair framing her face. Her beauty puts me on edge.

And there's a scent in the air, something sweet and pungent, almost cloying. It smells like fecund earth. It smells like secrets and mysteries and hidden truths.

It smells like magic.

This was a mistake. I should leave. Witch, shamaness, goddess—whatever she is, she's no mere mortal.

"Remove your boots, please. We don't want to track in the mud," she says. "They tell me you're Finn?"

"Yes." I slip out of my boots, leaving the blades concealed within. Then I step on blue-socked feet over the reindeer pelts to where Lumi sits. Slowly, I sit across from her.

"What is your name, child?" she says with a smile. It's her eyes that give her away. She has the glowing golden eyes of a wolf.

"Esteri." I give her my dead mother's name. Aina always says there's power in knowing a name. I don't want this woman to have any more power over me.

She appraises me through dark lashes, those golden eyes flashing. "No, that's not it. But it's fine. You may keep your secrets for now. Who are your people?"

"I'm from the south," I reply.

She laughs softly. "That much is obvious. Everyone who is not Sámi is from the south." She uses a forked stick to take the small pot of boiling water off the fire. "Would you like some tea? It's just dried bilberry leaves and chamomile petals, but the taste is pleasant enough."

I nod. I have no intention of drinking this tea.

The goddess gave me one instruction: don't tarry. Yet here I am, tarrying again. I tarried at the steam and look where that led. I wince, swallowing through the pain in my throat. I should have just listened. I should have kept walking right past this village. But I never listen, and that's my curse. I eye the door as Lumi pours herself a cup of tea. Then she's handing one to me.

"How did you come to live with the Sámi?" I ask, cupping the hot clay cup with both hands.

"You wouldn't believe me if I told you," she replies. "Hungry?"

"No," I say as my stomach growls, giving me away.

She smiles. Slipping her hand inside a basket behind her, she pulls out a chunk of dried reindeer meat. Revealing a knife hidden in the pelts, she begins to cut the steak into bite-sized pieces. "If you reach behind you into the basket, there are some turnips and potatoes. Will you hand me one of each?"

I fish a turnip and a potato out of the woven pine needle basket, setting them on the rock slab before Lumi.

"Why has a young woman, alone and with so few provisions, traveled so far north?"

I raise the cup to my lips, breathing in the tea. It's faintly floral, with a sharp sweetness. "You wouldn't believe me if I told you," I echo her.

The blade of her knife glints in the firelight with each cut she makes through the vegetables. "You conceal your name. Now you conceal your purpose." She pauses, glancing at me across the fire. "You're not interested in being friends, then."

"The less you know, the safer I am."

"Wise words," she admits, returning to her chopping. "And has this philosophy served you well so far?"

I don't answer.

Lumi pauses in her dicing, those glowing golden eyes searching my face. I stiffen, waiting for her to look away. "You've recently taken quite a beating," she says. "The lump on your temple could be from a fall, but the faded bruise at your eye reeks of old magic. You smell like death, Esteri. And your throat . . . that was surely the work of a blade, dealt by a malicious hand. Someone wanted you dead."

I hadn't realized the collar of my jacket had opened enough

to reveal the wound. It pains me awfully, and it's only getting worse.

"It's infected," she says, tipping the chopped vegetables and chunks of reindeer meat into the stew pot. The pot hisses and bubbles. "If left untreated, it will kill you. I know some herbs that will cleanse it, but fire is best."

I set down my cup of tea. "Are you asking my permission to hold a red-hot blade to my throat?"

She lets out a chiming laugh. "I guess that *is* how it sounded. I'm offering to help you, Esteri."

"Are you a wisewoman?"

She stirs the stew. "Of a sort."

I sigh. "Look, witch, I'm not interested in playing this game. I need provisions to finish my journey, and I have goods to trade. Will you deal with me, or shall I move on?"

She just keeps smiling. "The tea will kick in soon. We'll talk again in the morning."

My eyes narrow. "I didn't drink the tea, but I'm glad to know I was right." I get to my feet. "I'm going now. Try to stop me, and I'll kill you where you—" I sway, my vision dancing with white spots. "Wha—what is this?" I lift my hands, blinking through the spots as I feel my arms go heavy. "What's happening?"

"You didn't need to drink the tea for it to work." The witch's voice sounds suddenly very far away. "The fumes have already filled your lungs."

My heart races as panic burns in my gut. "No—"

"Just breathe."

I drop to my knees, my vision going dark. "No—Kal—"

"Rest now," says the witch. "We'll talk in the morning."

I wake to my own screaming. My throat is on fire. There's pain like nothing I've ever known. Surely, my head is being cleaved from my neck. I try to fight off my attacker, but I can't move. Not an inch. Every part of me is secured—my head, my arms, my chest. I blink my tired eyes open to see I'm trapped in a sitting position, my legs stretched out before me. From forehead to waist, I'm strapped to one of the beams of Lumi's hut.

"There, there," Lumi soothes. A Sámi woman moves away behind her, setting a red-hot knife on the edge of the hearth. "We had to bind to you," Lumi explains. "Otherwise, you could have hurt yourself. Fire really was the only way to cleanse that nasty wound. Sleep now."

She brushes a cooling hand across my fevered brow, and I spot a glint of silver peeking at her wrist. My eyes narrow on the braided silver bracelet. Rage burns in my gut as pain burns at my throat. "You—" It's all I can rasp out through the pain.

She lifts a brow in question, following my gaze to her wrist. Then she lets out a soft laugh, brushing her fingers over my grandmother's silver bracelet. The movement shows the second bracelet wrapped around her other wrist. "Consider these payment for services rendered," she says. "Sleep, child. You'll feel better when you wake."

The smell of my own burning flesh hangs in the air, stinging my nostrils. Oh gods, this is it. This is how I'll die, tied inside the hut of this scheming witch. No Aina, no Väinämöinen. Once again, I've failed. I'm not worthy of this task.

My sweet, brave Aina.

A tear slips down my cheek as the darkness takes me. At least, in death, I'll see her again.

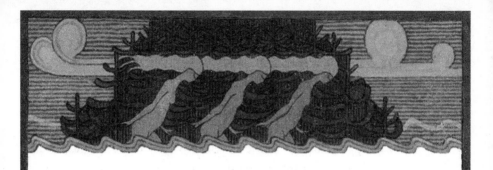

KIVUTAR STEPS INTO THE forest clearing, her sisters trailing in her wake.

"You monsters," Lilja shouts, scrambling to her feet. "You're rotten to the core—*no*—" She struggles as Riina and Satu hold her by the arms, keeping her from lunging at the goddess of suffering. "Get off me—"

"Lilja, please," Satu cries.

The witches laugh. Behind them, Kalma is silent, watching us with those black, unblinking eyes. I think I hate her the most. She's the one who took us all in the first place. I still wear her bruises on my arm. I'm not sure if they'll ever heal.

Vammatar steps past me. With a flick of her hand, she summons a floating ball of light that illuminates the clearing, making us all blink at its brightness. With another flick of her hand, Satu's mantle flutters away, revealing Inari's bloody corpse.

"Don't touch her," Riina snarls. "You have no right, witch."

Vammatar smirks. "I see you've figured out our little magic trick," she says in that simperingly sweet voice. "The other girls remain trapped in this forest. To free them, you'll have to draw their blood."

"We suggest aiming a little lower," Kivutar adds, nudging Inari's body with her toe. "Try hitting something less vital."

I exchange a horrified glance with Satu.

"Free your friends, and you'll all be treated to a magnificent feast," Vammatar declares. She waves her hand once more, and a table appears, nestled in the trees. Lit with two dozen flickering candles, it groans under the weight of a magnificent feast. The smell of roasted meats and vegetable pies wafts tantalizingly close. "Free them . . . or return to your rooms for another feast of bread and water."

I can see the way the others weaken. They're still starving, I remind myself. They don't have the strength to challenge the witches.

"We only have to draw blood?" Riina asks.

Satu grabs at her arm. "Riina, no."

"Silence," the witch commands, slapping Satu with an invisible hand.

The girl whimpers, rubbing the stinging spot on her cheek.

"That's it," Vammatar says with a smile at Riina. "A little blood, one tiny drop, and they'll be—well, they won't be free. None of you are free," she adds, making her sister laugh. "But they'll be human again."

I look to the body on the ground. "What happens to Inari now?" I ask.

"Oh, we'll take care of this one," Vammatar replies. She snaps her fingers, and Kalma steps forward on silent feet, her tattered, soiled robes dragging over the ground as she drops to her knees beside our dead friend.

"No!" Lilja cries.

"Don't touch her," says Riina, still holding on to Lilja's arm.

"Please, haven't you done enough?" Satu says through her tears.

As we watch, Kalma reaches out her skeletal hands, gently cupping Inari's face. Then the witch leans over and exhales into Inari's mouth. The foul smell of her breath makes me gag all over again. I can't imagine tasting her stink in my mouth. In moments, the body twitches. Then Inari's eyes flutter open. They're cloudy and unblinking.

"Gods, help us," I say on a breath.

Kalma leans away and Inari sits up, her head lolling awkwardly on her badly damaged neck. Her animated corpse stands, hands dangling uselessly at her sides. We all take a horrified step back as Inari turns to face Kalma.

"There we are," Vammatar coos. "Good as new."

I search the dead girl's face, looking for some sign of life in her eyes. "Inari?"

"Oh, she's not Inari anymore," says Vammatar. "We'll call her Peuratyttö. Deer girl. It fits, no?"

Kivutar gives a raspy laugh. "Sister, you are too clever."

Vammatar flicks her hair off her shoulder. "Come, Peuratyttö. Your friends have a long night ahead of them. Let's leave them to their happy hunting."

Inari shuffles forward, following the call of Vammatar.

"Wait," I call after them, determined to call the witch's bluff. "You said we could return to our rooms. You said we could choose bread and water."

Slowly, Vammatar turns, glaring at me with narrowed eyes. "You would choose to leave your poor friends out in this dark wood all alone?"

I square my shoulders at her. "Better a deer, free in the forest, than to live as one more captive doll for you to twist and break. I choose to return to my room. I choose bread and water."

Satu takes my hand. "And I. Bread and water."

Vammatar glares at Lilja and Riina. "And you two? Do you choose bread and water?"

Riina's hand tightens on her weapon, and I almost think she means to capitulate to her hunger, but then she tosses it to the ground at Vammatar's feet. "Enough. I choose bread. Just take us back."

Lilja has no choice but to agree. She tosses her bow to the ground. The four of us stand there, waiting for the witch to make her next move.

After a moment, Vammatar sneers. I can see it in her eyes; she doesn't intend to suffer our insolence. Sweeping forward, she descends on me with her hand raised.

"Aina, no," Satu cries.

I lift both my arms and flinch, ready to receive her vicious blow. A sharp caw echoes around the clearing and Vammatar curses, spinning away from me at the last moment. Swaying on my feet, I peek through my raised forearms. There, perched on a low branch, is my Jaako. He takes in the scene, ruffling his feathers and clicking his sharp black beak.

"Have you truly learned nothing?" Vammatar hisses at the raven. "Leave now. Don't come back."

I look back to the branch, heart racing, and Jaako is gone. My shoulders sag in defeat as I wait for Vammatar to turn and strike me down. "Leave the weapons and get back to work," she snarls. "No one rests until you've earned the right, you ungrateful wretches." Her gaze lands on me. "And wash off that blood, before you begin to smell as bad as Peuratyttö."

We drop the rest of our weapons, and Inari leads the way back through the trees. We follow in her silent footsteps, saying nothing as we watch her walk with that odd, shuffling gait.

Ilmatar, hear me, I pray, taking in the looming outline of Tuoni's palace. *Do not let me die in this dark place. Help me. Show me the way.*

Kukka meets me at the garden gate and follows me back to the weaving room. I step past her, moving down the rows of looms towards the back wall. I pass Loviatar too, standing at her loom. "Back so soon?" the goddess says. Is she relieved to know I'm still alive? Does she care at all? It's impossible to tell. Her nose scrunches as I pass. Those sightless, white eyes turn my way. "You smell like blood."

Reaching out with bloodstained hands, I take up a pair of knitting needles and a skein of black yarn. "That's because I'm covered in Inari's blood."

The *clack, clack, clack* of Loviatar's warp weights goes silent. She waits as I cross the room to her side, dropping onto my stool. "Why are you covered in the quiet girl's blood?" she finally asks.

I can't bear to look at her. If I look at her, I fear I'll break, and I refuse to cry in front of this witch. Instead, I feverishly cast the first knots on my knitting needles.

"Why do you wear the girl's blood, Aina?" the witch asks again.

"Because I just killed her," I reply, working my needles over and under, over and under. "Did you know?"

"Did I know what?"

I drop my hands to my lap and glare at the witch. "Did you know, when Vammatar came for me, what they would do to us? Do you help them, Loviatar? Are you part of this violence?"

She turns her attention back to her weaving. "I have nothing to do with my mother's endless games."

"Well, you are fortunate," I reply, still glaring at the back of her head. "How nice for you that you get to sit back as we're forced to hunt each other like animals."

She turns with a scowl. "You think me fortunate?"

"I just opened a girl's throat," I cry. "She died right in front of me. Oh gods—*I* killed her!" I cover my face with my bloodstained hands, holding back a wrenching sob.

"And why did you open her throat? Is it possible she was already injured? Was it a fatal wound?"

My shoulders still, and I drop my hands to my lap. "How did you . . . were you there? Oh gods, were you in the woods? Did you stand back and let it happen—"

"No," she says gently. "It was merely a guess."

We're both quiet for a moment.

"It was awful," I whisper. "Loviatar, I watched the life leave her eyes." I look up, searching her face. "How do you bear it? How can you stand to feel such suffering, to know you are the cause of it?"

"You showed mercy," she replies. "You granted that girl a clean death, a blessed death. It was a noble act."

My heart thrums at her words. Leaning forward, I take a chance. "Tuonela is cursed, isn't it?"

She goes still.

"The Witch Queen has somehow cursed this realm," I go on. "Only her magic thrives, only her chaos and violence. Where is Lord Tuoni?"

She says nothing.

"Is he cursed?" I press. "Can the King of Death die? Is he lost? Tell me, Loviatar."

The witch remains unmoving. She's not answering, but neither has she taken out her wrath on me. Perhaps she doesn't know how to answer?

Getting to my feet, I join her at her loom. "Tell me about your father. Is he the god from the stories and songs?"

"There are many stories," she replies. "You'll have to be more specific."

"Is he truly the god of blessed death? Does he believe in peace and justice? Or does he prefer this wanton violence and destruction?"

The witch remains silent for so long, I fear she doesn't mean to answer me. The moment I'm ready to turn away, she speaks. "My father is an idealist."

"An idealist?"

"A fanciful dreamer, a hopeless romantic," she goes on, her voice dripping with disdain. "He had a vision of what he wanted Tuonela to be. He became obsessed with bringing it about. He pulled us into his schemes, he made us hope . . . made us dream."

"And what was his vision?"

"He would see this realm be a paradise," the witch replies. "To him, Tuonela means peace. It means an end to all suffering, all sorrow and strife. He believes death should be a land of hope, where all souls come to find blessed rest."

"Yes, that is the Tuonela of my mother's stories," I say. "Peace and contentment, eternal rest. What happened to his dream? What happened to Tuonela?"

"Tuonetar happened," the witch replies. "My wretched sisters happened. Witches who cannot share his vision, for they lack all sight." She turns to face me. "I may be blind, Aina, but I was the only one who could see. I saw his vision for our realm. I believed in it. I helped him craft it . . . and it cost me everything."

I search her face, trying to see past her careful veils. "Where is he?"

"My mother and sisters found out about his plans to remake Tuonela. Her vengeance was swift and exacting."

"Why must she seek revenge against him?"

The witch scoffs. "Do you really think there is any place for a witch like Tuonetar in my father's vision of a peaceful Tuonela? She stands against everything he hoped for."

My mind hums. "Wait, was he going to try to banish her? Strip her of her powers?"

Loviatar smirks. "Such a clever little mouse."

"But she got to him first, didn't she? Loviatar, is he dead?"

Her smile falls. "It would stifle my mother's triumph greatly if he were not alive to watch as she remade Tuonela in her own twisted image."

Then he's alive. Somewhere.

"What was his plan? How was he going to supplant her?"

Her fingers brush over her weave, checking the tightness of the knots. "There are many moving pieces in a game of the gods, little mouse."

"Am I one of the pieces?"

She goes still.

I tug on this thread, determined to unravel the truth. "I saw the other girls in the woods tonight. They died here. How many has the Witch Queen dragged below? How many has she tortured and killed? Why does she do it?"

"She is mad, Aina. To try to understand her reasoning is a fool's errand—"

"Don't." I place a hand on her shoulder. "No more games. Not with me. Tell me the truth. Why does she want us to suffer so?"

"It's bold of you to assume she cares about mortal suffering."

"She doesn't, does she?" Hearing it said aloud, I know I'm right. "She's doesn't care about us at all. We are completely expendable to her. This is about Tuoni. It's about making *him* suffer." Another thought comes to me, sending my heart racing anew. I lower my voice, glancing over my shoulder to make sure we're still alone. "Is he out there, Loviatar? Is he trapped in those woods?"

The witch says nothing.

"He is, isn't he? He's being forced to watch as your mother and sisters torture us to death. Over and over, he watches, helpless to stop her."

Loviatar's face is expressionless. "As I said . . . clever mouse."

"But why is it a torture for him? Why does he care if we die? Or perhaps I should ask—what does he stand to gain if we live? What can he mean to do with us?"

The witch remains silent. Perhaps she likes listening to me puzzle it out for myself.

"Only girls are being taken," I continue. "Not princesses or shamanesses, not even goddesses . . . we are all just young, unmarried, common girls—" My words fall silent as the truth hits me. "Oh, Loviatar, he meant to supplant the Witch Queen in all ways, not just stifle her magic. He meant to *replace* her . . . didn't he? Down with the mad queen. He wanted to find someone more aligned with his vision, more willing to help him build the Tuonela of his dreams."

Loviatar smirks. "Who better than a young mortal girl full of bright visions of life and fanciful ideas of death? Together, you could rule this realm and turn it into a beautiful dream." She turns her face, those clouded eyes seeing through me. "The raven was right to bring you to me," she says at last. "You're perfect."

My heart stops. "You know my raven?"

"I know your raven."

"Who is he, Loviatar? He's been protecting me since I arrived. He came for me tonight in the woods. He stopped Vammatar from striking me. Oh gods—" My heart feels fit to burst. I was a fool for not seeing it sooner. "Is *he* Tuoni? Is the death god trapped in the form of a raven—"

Loviatar takes me by the shoulders. "Be calm, Aina."

"No—" I pull away. "I've told the raven too much. I—oh gods—he knows everything about me. Everything—"

"Enough, Aina." Loviatar cups my face with her cold hands, her face inches from mine. "The raven cares for you . . . as I do. We would see you free of this living nightmare. You could free us all if only you have the strength to defy the Witch Queen."

I feel like I'm drowning on dry land. My head is spinning, heart racing. "This will see me dead with my head mounted on a spike in your mother's garden. Loviatar, I'm not ready to meet death as my equal. Gods hear me, I want to live."

She gives my shoulders a squeeze, pressing her forehead to mine. "Listen to me, little mouse. You've been trapped in this nightmare for a few weeks. There are those of us here who've been fighting for a lifetime. We are closer now than we've ever been. *You* are bringing us closer. So, I am going to do something that I haven't done in an age. Are you listening?"

"Yes," I whisper.

"I have decided that I am going to help you."

I lean away, searching her face. "Help me with what?"

"Free my father."

Her words sit heavy between us, pressing like a weight on my chest. "What can I do?"

"Only one person has the power to free him from his prison," she replies. "And freeing him will free us all."

"And you think I am that person?"

"No, you're not," she replies, her fingers brushing down my braid. "Not yet . . . but you *will* be."

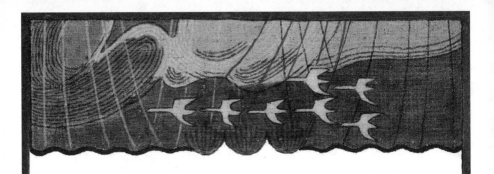

Siiri

SOFT HANDS STROKE MY brow, soon replaced with the sensation of a cool, wet cloth.

"She's burning up," Aina whispers, with fear in her voice.

"A veden väki has taken hold," Mummi replies. "I can't get it out, no matter what I try."

"We should take her to the sauna," comes Milja's voice. "Only a fire spirit can fight water."

I feel a heavy weight lift off the bed as Mummi goes to prepare. On the other side of the bed, Aina still sits, holding my hand and applying wet cloths to my burning forehead. I swallow a moan, feeling the fever race through me like a brush fire.

"Don't you dare die," Aina whispers, my hand gripped tight in hers. "If you die of this fever, you had better be prepared to haunt me, because I'm not living without you, Siiri."

I want to speak. I want to tell her everything I've kept buried in my heart, but my lips don't move.

"Please, don't leave me," Aina begs, her voice breaking as she leans over me, a single tear dropping onto my cheek.

"Come back to me. Siiri, please. Don't leave me here alone. Please, come back."

Those words fill me, warming me, strengthening my will to live.

Come back to me.

Anything for you, Aina.

Come back to me.

Wait for me.

Come back . . .

My throat burns painfully. That's the first clue telling me I'm awake. I don't move, don't open my eyes. I'm not ready to shatter the illusion that Aina is here with me. But that was just a dream, a memory from long ago. Aina is gone, and I'm alone.

Keeping my eyes closed, I use my other senses. They've untied me from the beam, and I lie on my side in Lumi's hut. There's a crackling fire to my left, the feel of fur under my cheek, a cookpot bubbling, the hooting of an owl outside. I'm alive. The witch didn't kill me. How long have I been asleep?

My stomach growls ferociously as I take another deep breath, smelling the savory reindeer stew. I've been starving myself for days, trying to preserve my rations. For every step I take north, I'll have to retread the same steps south with Aina at my side. I will not fight to save her just to lose her again.

"You're awake," Lumi calls. "Good."

I open one eye to see the witch sitting across from me. She watches me with those sharp, wolf-like eyes. I try to roll over and push myself up onto my knees, but my wrists and ankles are still bound. Growling in frustration, I jerk upright, flopping like a fish until I'm sitting up. Then I flash Lumi an accusing glare.

"It was for my protection, I assure you," Lumi says. "Tell

me, why does a weary traveler need all these blades?" She gestures in front of her at the food preparation stone, where all my blades have been collected, including the knives hidden in my boots. My grandmother's silver still glints at her wrists.

"You can never be too careful," I rasp.

"I'm going to ask you some questions now," Lumi says, wrapping a colorful fringed shawl around her shoulders. "Who are you?"

"I told you. I'm from the south, journeying north."

"For what purpose?"

"I'm recovering someone who is lost."

"Lost in the north?" she presses.

"Something like that."

"No, that's not how we'll proceed," she says with a little shake of her head. "I will ask questions, and you will answer. What is your name, girl?"

"How can that possibly matter?" I press my hand to the bandage at my neck. "Ask the question you really want answered."

"That *is* a question I want answered," she counters.

I match her glare for glare. "Listen, witch, I would only tell you my name if I were dispatching you to Kalma in the next breath. Ask me a different question."

She holds my gaze for another moment. "You were attacked yesterday by a pair of trappers. How did you survive?"

"How do you know about that?"

"I'm asking the questions."

"They wanted something from me that I wasn't willing to give," I reply. "So, I killed them."

She raises a brow. "You killed them?"

"Yes."

Lumi doesn't look convinced. "*You* did? This weak, half-starved girl before me with a festering neck wound? You killed two grown men all on your own?"

"You doubt me? Give me back my bow, and I'll show you."

Lumi leans across the fire, her wolfish eyes alight with eagerness. "And where is the bear?"

I blink, heartbeat stuttering. "What bear?"

"Don't play games with me. Some of the men saw you approach our camp in the company of a bear. Where is he?"

A tense moment stretches between us. There's no point in lying to this witch.

"He won't hurt you," I say. "I swear, so long as you don't hurt me, he's no threat to you. Let me go, and we'll both leave you in peace."

Lumi's eyes glitter in anticipation. "You have no idea how long I have waited for that bear. Lead me to him, and I will give you anything you want—food, supplies, weapons."

I consider for a moment. "And if I don't lead you to him, what will you do? Kill me?"

"Not at first," she replies honestly. "Maybe your slow death will lure him in. At this point, I'm willing to try anything."

"What can you possibly want with a bear?"

"You know as well as I that the bear is the key to finding Väinämöinen. I've been trying to follow that bear to him for longer than you've been alive. You have no idea what I've sacrificed . . . what I've lost."

She blinks, her golden eyes refocusing on me. "Now I find that the bear has volunteered to help *you*, a nameless, talentless, mortal girl. Do you have any idea how maddening that is?" The flames dancing in Lumi's eyes give her away.

"Wait . . . did those trappers work for you? Did you send them out to look for the bear? Did they craft that pit too?"

Her eyes widen in surprise. "Ahh, so *you* helped him out of the pit. I'll have you know that was a year's worth of planning, wasted."

"I'm not sorry. May Otso strike you down for hurting his child."

"You don't even know what you tangle with," Lumi hisses. "You've stumbled into a magic you can never understand. Give the bear to me."

I remain unmoved.

She watches me with deep intensity. "Whatever you need, whatever you seek from Väinämöinen, he will not agree. He is selfish and lazy and scared of his own shadow. He will rot before he lifts a finger to help you."

I glare, unwilling to reveal that Tellervo already told me the same thing. "And what makes you think I can ever trust you?"

"I pay my debts," she replies, holding out her hand. "Make a vow with me, and I'll not break it. I will help you to whatever end you seek."

"You're too late."

She frowns in annoyance, hand still extended.

"I honor my debts too. The bear and I share a life debt. I saved his life, he saved mine. We are bonded now. I cannot raise a hand against him or help another do the same."

She drops her hand. Her expression crackles with rage like the logs in the fire.

I lean forward, swallowing against the pain in my throat. "Please, Lumi. Just let us go."

Her lips part to respond, but a cacophony—screams, barking dogs, pounding feet—shatters the silence around us. Then, a thunderous roar—the roar of an angry bear. Kal is coming for me. Lumi's golden eyes change, dancing with magic flame as she launches to her feet, her face splitting into an eager smile. "It appears I no longer need your help."

"No," I cry, raising my bound hands. "Leave him alone!"

"Nothing will stop me from getting to Väinämöinen," she

declares, dropping her shawl from her shoulders. Closing her eyes, the witch reaches out with both hands. A pair of gleaming swords appears. She wears a metal plate on her chest now, over which is crossed the thick black leather of her scabbards. Her hair is hidden under the hood of a snow-white cape lined with fur, trailing to the ground. My grandmother's silver bracelets still encircle her wrists.

"Please, don't do this," I beg.

She looks down at me. "You're a brave girl. I can see why the bear is so fond of you. I will let you live, so long as you stay out of my way. Väinämöinen *will* be mine." With that, she steps past me, disappearing into the night.

As soon as she's gone, I scoot over to the fire's edge and get my knife. I stretch out my bound legs and cut through the rope. My heart races as the screams get louder all around. I think Kal is setting fire to the village. I can smell the smoke and hear flames crackling like a great bonfire. I work quickly, holding the knife between my knees as I saw through the binding at my wrists.

"Come on," I rasp, ignoring the pain in my throat.

The rope frays as I move my wrists back and forth along the edge of the blade.

"Come on, come on—*yes*—"

The bonds break, and I toss them aside, scrambling forward on hands and knees to get my weapons. I stuff my feet into my boots and slide a knife inside each one, keeping my larger hunting knife in hand. I don't wait another second to push open the flap of the hut and rush into the chaos waiting outside.

The sky is filled with smoke. I count at least four huts on fire. At the far end of the camp, men are shouting, running with axes and bows at the ready. Women tug on the hands of crying children. All around us in the forest come the thunder of many hooves. The villagers' panicked reindeer are on the run.

I duck behind Lumi's hut and make for the trees. I nearly crash into a young Sámi man holding the hand of a crying woman. He takes me in with anxious eyes, his hand dropping to the axe at his belt. I move with the speed of a fox, flipping my knife around and slamming the hilt against his temple. The woman screams as I trip him, knocking him onto his back in the snow. She screams again, her hands raised in surrender, crying out in a language I don't understand.

"I'm sorry," I say to them both, wrestling his axe loose from his belt as he weakly tries to fight me off. "I'm so sorry."

I duck away, sprinting for the cover of the trees. Behind me, the village is in chaos. The north end burns, the huts engulfed in flames. Kal is trying to push the Sámi south, clearing the way for me. He roars again in panic.

Lumi stands in the middle of the clearing. One of her swords is sheathed on her back, and she clutches a tall reindeer-herding staff in her free hand. It curves intricately at the top, cradling a glowing white stone. As Lumi holds it high, the stone glows brighter, nearly as bright as a star, illuminating the forest. She's looking for the bear.

In the light of the star staff, I can see across to the other side of the village. There, tied to a high line with several other reindeer, stands Halla. She still wears her packs, shuffling from side to side in a panic, trying to pull herself loose. My heart drops. To reach her, I'd have to get past Lumi.

"I'm so sorry, girl," I whisper. I'm more than sorry. Halla has everything in her packs—my food, my fishing gear, my heavy winter coat. How will I survive in this wilderness without even a coat?

I glance to my left and see a hut with the hides torn loose from the entrance. The family must have fled into the woods by now. Taking a deep breath, I dash out of the trees and inside. I work fast, throwing everything inside the only pack I can find—a cookpot, a bowl, a chunk of dried reindeer meat, and anything else that looks like food. Lastly, I take several reindeer pelts off the floor and roll them up. With the pack on my shoulder and the pelts under my arm, I take my pilfered axe and dash back into the night.

I'm barely past the trees when the snow all around glows golden-white. I turn to see Lumi in the clearing, shouting orders to the Sámi as she slams the end of her staff against the ground. A burst of starlight shoots into the sky, expanding like white flames with a crackle of lightning. It's so bright that night shines like day.

I smile. Kal eludes her still. "Run, you crazy bear," I say, into the trees. "Go north, and I'll find you." I don't wait another moment. I turn and sprint into the darkness.

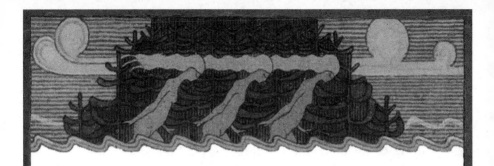

Aina

I SIT ON A STOOL across from Loviatar, noting her stiff posture, her rune-marked hands folded in her lap. My heart hammers in my chest. Some answers at last! She's going to tell me how we free Tuoni from the Witch Queen's curse and restore the Tuonela of the songs.

"Start at the beginning," I say. "Please, Loviatar, leave nothing out."

"You have to understand," she says. "If Tuonetar's sickness is her inclination for chaos, my father's is his dogged belief in justice and order. It leaves him unsuspecting of the machinations of others."

"What machinations? What did they do to him?"

"He believed so fervently in the rightness of his course, this dream of a blessed, peaceful kingdom of death. But he failed to anticipate the way some of my sisters would respond. In the end, it was their doubt, their fear of change, that felled him."

"What did they do?"

"They went behind his back to Tuonetar. They told her of

his plans before he could set them fully in motion. His vision would have taken her power from her, and they told her as much."

I suppress a shiver. "And . . . what did the Witch Queen do when she found out he meant to constrain her?"

"She turned on him with a vengeance," Loviatar replies. "She used the very shackles he had made for her, and she bound him instead. It cost her every bit of magic she wields to overpower him. It costs her still."

"How?" I whisper, praying for some proof of the Witch Queen's weakness.

Loviatar's lips twist. "My mother is a vain woman, Aina. The power it took to curse Tuoni stripped her bare, until the rotten core of her was exposed like a berry in autumn that withers overripe on the vine."

"You're saying her ugliness is part of this curse?"

She nods. "Before, she used her magic to conceal the rottenness within. Now, she cannot hold a simple glamouring spell for more than a few minutes. Truth will always out. Her truth is that her body is as rotten as her soul."

"That first dinner," I say, putting the pieces together. "She cast a spell to conceal the ugliness of the room as well as herself."

Loviatar nods. "Tuonela is a realm where power and magic are made. There is magic in the very walls of this palace. The goblins crafted it with stones hewn from the heart of our mountains. The palace has become a reflection of Tuonetar's madness, her need for violence, her unquenchable thirst for pain. If another were to claim dominion over Tuonela, the palace would reflect *their* nature."

I consider her words. "You're saying if Tuoni returns to power, the palace will change?"

"Everything will change," she replies solemnly.

"You said he's shackled. And the shackles somehow constrain his magic?"

She nods.

"Well, does Tuonetar hold the key? How can we free him?"

Before Loviatar can respond, the door to the weaving room slams open. Snow flurries in as Vammatar appears. She sweeps across the room in a fury, dragging me off my stool by my arm. "Let's go, bonebag. Up. Now."

"Sister, what's happening?" says Loviatar, rising to her feet.

Vammatar's hand around my arm squeezes tight. "The bonebag is coming with me."

Oh gods, not again. I swallow my fear.

"Take one of the others to play your insipid games," Loviatar challenges with an irritated sigh. "This one is useful to me. I'm keeping her."

"No games tonight, sister," Vammatar replies, pulling me forward.

Loviatar goes still. "What happened?"

"What always happens?" Vammatar replies. Something in her tone fills me with dread.

"This one has done nothing," Loviatar says. "She's been with me since you took her to the forest. Whatever you're about to do—"

"Oh, spare me." Vammatar points a rune-marked finger in Loviatar's face. "I warned you, sister. You get too attached to them. It's pathetic. I don't understand why you bother when nothing will ever replace the child you lost."

With a snarl, Loviatar lunges, slapping her sister across the face. Vammatar uses me as an anchor, nearly wrenching my arm from its socket. She rounds on her sister, red scratch marks from Loviatar's sharp nails marring her cheek. "You dare!"

Loviatar doesn't back down. Black mist swirls around

her fingertips as she raises her hands. The tips of each finger elongate with sharp black nails like the talons of a great bird of prey. "Speak of my child again, and I will plague you . . . *sister.*"

I wait with bated breath, glancing between the witches. Vammatar still holds my arm. "Come," she mutters at me, giving my arm another tug.

"Return to me when my sister is finished with you," Loviatar calls. "You still have much work to do."

Vammatar drags me from the weaving room, pulling me through the busy kitchens full of laboring dead. We weave between the back rooms before we enter the grand receiving hall through a side door.

I look at it with new eyes, remembering what Loviatar said about the walls reflecting Tuonetar's inner nature. The room is dark, cold, and uninviting. Only one antler chandelier is lit, barely casting any light, let alone warmth. The walls of twisted skulls are lost to the deep shadow.

"Aina?"

Helmi and Riina stand in the middle of the room beneath the chandelier. Vammatar flings me forward, all but knocking me into Helmi, who embraces me with both arms. She's trembling, little cuts marring her cheeks and hands. Her dress is muddy at the knees, dusted with dirt and pine needles as if she was rolling around on the ground.

"Oh, I'm so happy to see you alive," she whispers, squeezing my hand.

"And I you," I reply.

"I had the strangest dream," she goes on. "Aina, I don't know what's happening. I woke alone in the woods. Where are the others? Inari and Satu?"

Riina and I exchange a glance. "Inari is dead," she replies for me.

Helmi gasps. "What? How?"

"She was hunted," Riina replies.

The doors at the far end of the hall open, and a pair of dead guards drag a whimpering Satu forward. She's shoved towards us, and the guards make their retreat. "Oh, thank the gods," she says to Helmi. "We were worried you'd be a deer forever."

Helmi's eyes go wide. "That was real?"

Riina peers around the room. "Where are Salla and Lilja?"

Another door by the dais slams open, and the Witch Queen sweeps in, golden robes billowing. This time she wears a crown of antlers on her head, their jagged tips casting long shadows. I take in her hideousness, noting the way her face rots off her skull. Her eyes are bloodshot, the right one somewhat foggy. There's no muscle on her bones. Her fingers are like that of a corpse, gnarled and stiff.

Rotten fruit, Loviatar called her.

Vanity explains her beautiful clothes. She can't wrap her body in magic, but she can hide it beneath regal gowns that twinkle like starlight. I now think her beautiful silver tresses must be a wig. If this is her only curse, it's not nearly enough. She has brought so much strife to the world. I want her to rot to dust, and I want it to take a thousand years.

The other girls bunch around me under the circle of light, Helmi and Satu each taking one of my hands. Tuonetar's aura is so ominous that it takes me a moment to realize she's dragging something on the ground behind her.

I go still. "Oh—Ilmatar protect them," I say, breathless with horror. For it's not some*thing* . . . it's some*one.* Two someones. The Witch Queen drags a squirming Lilja and Salla by their long braids, one in each hand.

"No," Riina cries.

Satu and I work quickly to restrain her.

Tuonetar drags the girls right up to the edge of the ring of light, her bony chest heaving as she drops their braids and steps back. Why are they soaking wet?

"Oh gods, no," Riina whispers, all the fight leaving her.

I piece it together too. Fools! What were they thinking?

Salla recovers first, scrambling forward on hands and knees like a frightened dog, as if she means to cower behind us.

"They cannot save you now, measly worm," the Witch Queen shrieks. "Back. All of you, get *back*!" She brandishes her wand at us. We have no choice but to step away, leaving Lilja and Salla exposed on the floor. Vammatar is still in the room, standing by the dais with her arms crossed. I can see the faint red lines on her cheek where Loviatar struck her.

"How *dare* you try to leave my realm," the Witch Queen bellows, drawing my attention and confirming what I already knew. The girls are wet from the river. They tried to cross. They tried to flee Tuonela. Magic magnifies the witch's voice tenfold. She shouts loudly enough to shake the dust from the rafters. "No one leaves Tuonela. *No one!*" Her wand transforms into a whip. It falls with a heavy hand, and the poor girls cower as each strike slices their tender flesh.

I can't bear it; I have to look away. Satu's face is already buried in my shoulder. Next to me, Helmi silently weeps.

"Mother, *enough*."

We all glance over the Witch Queen's shoulder to see a new goddess approach. This is the only daughter I haven't met, but she's just as haunting as her twin. She must be Kiputyttö, the goddess of pain. She has a hunched, haggard appearance like her mother, with large, weepy eyes and curtains of thick black hair that drag along the ground. Crossing the room, she passes Vammatar and takes hold of her mother's bony wrist, staying the whip.

I hold my breath, afraid to move, afraid to even blink. Is

Kiputyttö about to stand up to her mother? Is she about to put the Witch Queen in her place? Oh gods, is the rebellion starting now?

Tuonetar screams a primal scream that raises all the hairs on my arms. Outside in the courtyard, the dogs howl. Next to me, the other girls wince and shiver, hands over ears, trying to block out the sound. I clench my teeth, sagging with relief when she stops on a strangled cry.

"Mother," Kiputyttö coos, her voice now soft and soothing, even as it grates like a boat scraping rocks. "You'll tire yourself out, dearest. There are *other* ways of torturing them."

My blood runs cold. Apparently, this is not the start of a rebellion. The goddess of pain reaches into the deep pocket of her robes and pulls out a small rune stone. She holds it flat in the palm of her gnarled hand and flashes us a cruel smile.

Tuonetar steps back, shoulders heaving. "Yes, daughter," she says through panting breaths. "Always so clever. What a sweet girl. What a loyal child."

"Bring my mother a chair," the pain witch commands.

A dead servant shuffles forward with a stool, placing it before the Queen. Tuonetar sinks onto it regally, conjuring a goblet for herself with her wand. She takes a deep drink of the wine, letting some of the bloodred liquid dribble down her chin. Then she raises the goblet in assent. "Begin, daughter."

The four of us stand there frozen. Next to me, Helmi and Satu squeeze in tighter. Kiputyttö turns slowly to face the girls still lying on the floor. With a menacing smile, she turns the stone over once in her palm. Lilja and Salla cry out, shrieking and writhing on the floor. Their bodies wriggle like fish out of water as the goddess of pain turns her little stone once . . . twice . . . three more times. Their tortured cries burrow into my chest.

Tuonetar watches disinterestedly for a few more moments

before she holds up a hand. Kiputyttö pauses, her fingers closing around the stone in her palm, and Salla and Lilja go limp on the floor, overcome with pain and exhaustion.

"Now, let's take a moment to talk about actions and consequences." Tuonetar speaks to them like they're a pair of naughty children who stole a handful of berries meant for a pie. "What action did you take that displeased me so greatly?"

None of us dares to move.

"I'm speaking to you, you wretched beasts," she screams.

"We—tried—to leave," Salla pants, unable to lift herself up on her shaky hands.

"Yes, you thought you could just swim across my river, and I'd be none the wiser, didn't you?" Her voice drips with disappointment. "You were mistaken, for you are stupid and worthless. *Say it.*"

"We're stupid," Salla blurts as Lilja mumbles something that sounds like the word "worthless."

"*Sit up*," she commands with a wave of her wand. The girls are both yanked into a sitting position as though by an invisible hand. Tuonetar's voice shifts to be all simpering sweetness again. "And why would I be so greatly disappointed by this deep and treacherous betrayal?"

"Because we're your captives," Lilja hisses through clenched teeth.

"You are my *guests*," she corrects. "I have fed you and clothed you. I've provided warm fires and soft feather beds. Just imagine the poor, wretched souls above, trapped in life, toiling in the dirt like so many filthy voles. Here, your every need is met," she says, gesturing around the stark emptiness of her hall, adorned with only the skulls of the dead. "All I have asked from you in return is that you help me without complaint. This was too much for you, apparently. I fear I can expect nothing less from ungrateful worms—"

"You are my *captor*," Lilja shrieks. "You're a monster, and you don't deserve the title of Queen. I will never stop trying to escape. You'll have to kill me, you horrible witch!" With that, she spits on the floor at Tuonetar's feet.

My heart stops.

To my surprise, Tuonetar smiles, her teeth blackened and cracked. "Thank you for your candor. I wanted to know which of you first had the idea to leave, and now I do."

I have to fight to keep my mind from playing tricks on me. Lilja looks so much like my Siiri. The same blonde hair, the same proud spirit, the same defiant will to live. Siiri would never have survived this place. *Blessed Ilmatar, thank you for sparing her this fate.*

"So, now we must turn to consequences," Tuonetar says, a cruel glint in her eyes. "What should the consequence be for two ungrateful worms who so monstrously abuse the hospitality of their beneficent hostess?"

Lilja's shoulders sag in defeat. "You're right. It was my idea. Salla didn't want to do it. She didn't know I was tricking her."

"Tricking her?" The Witch Queen tips her head to the side.

"I planned to use her," Lilja admits. "I knew I could swim faster than her. She was to be my escape."

"You needed bait," Tuonetar clarifies. She turns to Salla. "Do you hear that? You were nothing but bait on a hook. Surely, that kind of treachery must come with some consequence. I'll leave it to you to decide her fate."

Salla looks stricken. "What?"

"She was using you, worm. She admits it," the Queen replies. "Decide how she will be punished."

"Take my life," Lilja pleads, crawling forward on her knees.

I close my eyes, imagining Siiri in the same position, pleading for my life, fighting to the bitter end.

"Please, show Salla mercy," Lilja begs. "Kill me—"

"Lilja, no," Salla cries.

"*Lilja, no,*" Tuonetar echoes in a mocking tone. She turns to Salla. "It appears she wants you to kill her." She flicks her wand, and a sword appears at Salla's feet. "Go on then, do it."

Salla shakes her head, not looking at the blade. "Beat us. Use the lash again, turn the stone, lock us in our rooms and throw away the key, only let us both live. Please, goddess. I want to live."

Her words tear at my heart. Have I not said almost the same words to Jaako night after night? Am I not thinking them now, plotting with Loviatar to end this wretched curse?

Tuonetar puts a thoughtful hand to her chin. "One of you wants to live, and one wants to die? Easy enough. I grant your wish." She turns to Kiputyttö as she stands. "Torture them a while longer, daughter. Then kill the earless one."

"No," Salla sobs.

"No?" Tuonetar sneers. "Very well, then, *you* can be the one to die. I'm afraid I can't keep you both. Who knows how you'll plot and scheme together, and we simply can't have that. Be done with it, daughter," she says with a wave of her hand.

Kiputyttö steps forward, her open palm outstretched.

Lilja and Salla scramble across the floor clinging to each other.

"The rest of you are here to witness," Tuonetar calls to the room. "This is an important lesson that must be learned. I am a benevolent hostess. All I ask is that you treat me with the respect I am due as your Queen."

I don't dare look away as Kiputyttö begins turning her stone, for Tuonetar doesn't watch the girls writhing and screaming on the floor. She watches us. She watches me most of all. I feel her eyes on me, boring into me with concentrated hate. I will myself to make my eyes unfocus. I look through the floor, not at what writhes atop it.

But nothing can block out the screams.

Tuonetar holds up a hand, and her daughter stops turning her stone. The Witch Queen sweeps forward, dropping to her knees, her pristine robes billowing around her. She lowers her face to meet Salla's eyes, stroking her wet hair with a bony, gentle hand. Salla whimpers and flinches at her touch. "You know I never had any intention of letting either of you live," she says, her voice soft. "It's important to me that you understand my nature. You were both dead the moment you crossed my river."

Salla's frail body shakes uncontrollably as she gives the faintest of nods. Then she closes her eyes, ready to succumb. Next to her, Lilja lies still, her breathing ragged.

"Thank you, worms," the Witch Queen coos. "Thank you for seeing me as I am." She stands and places a hand on her daughter's shoulder. "Finish them, daughter. When you're done, feed them to Kalma. She'll find use for their corpses."

With that, the Witch Queen sweeps from the great hall. Vammatar follows her out, leaving us alone with Kiputyttö. The door slams shut behind them.

I clench my jaw, bracing myself for the horror to come. There can be no escape from Tuonela. Many before have tried and failed. Kiputyttö begins her torture again. Each turn of her little stone hardens my resolve. There is only one immortal in this realm with the power to save us, and he's just as trapped as we are.

I have to find him. I have to find Tuoni.

I FLEE LUMI AND the Sámi village, praying Kal will follow. Using the north star as my guide, I run until my lungs burn with fire, until my legs are numb and sweat slicks my tunic to my back. Only when I feel faint do I stop running.

I drop the pack and rolled furs at my feet. I hunch over in the snow, hands on my knees, heaving, but there's nothing in my stomach. Black spots dance at the corners of my vision. The snowy ground around me begins to spin.

How did everything fall so perfectly apart? What am I going to do now? I have no supplies, no guide. How will I find my way to Väinämöinen on my own? He doesn't want to be found. The goddess had said Kal was the key. Without the bear, I have no hope.

Even if Kal finds me, and together we find the shaman, what assurance do I have that he'll help me save Aina? Two goddesses and a witch have now warned me that Väinämöinen will refuse. And why should he help me? Who am I to demand this favor?

I groan, heart racing in my chest. I have nothing left. There is nothing. Even if I somehow reach Aina, how can I bring her home in the dead of winter with no supplies? I would save her from one cruel fate just to deliver her into another. Either way, she ends up in Tuonela.

"No," I pant, clutching my chest. I can't breathe. The cold air feels like knives piercing me. Oh gods, I'm losing her all over again. I'm failing her. I've failed so many times. My mummi was wrong; Milja was wrong. I was never strong enough for this task. I fear the next failure will end with my death.

"Gods, help me," I whisper into the dark.

Silence is the only reply. Silence and loneliness and crippling doubt. They wrap around me like a shroud, suffocating me. I fall to my knees in the snow, the strength leaving my legs.

"Please," I say, not knowing which god will hear my prayers. "Do not abandon me to this despair. Show me the way." Tipping my head back, I gaze up into the starry night sky, looking for a sign.

The darkness erupts with an eerie light. Is this Lumi's magic? I go still, my breath catching in my chest, ready to run again. High above me, off in the distance, a river of green dances its way across the sky. The colors change, flashing in waves of white, purple, and blue. The river flows between the stars, shimmering like water, burning like flame.

"Oh gods . . ." Hands braced behind my head, I watch the lights dance. "Revontulet."

The great foxfires of the north. I've never seen them with my own eyes. They say the colors are made from the flaming tail of a tulikettu, a firefox. The men of the north hunt him, determined to claim the strength of his väki. So, he runs. The firefox runs so fast across the snow that his tail sparks, lighting up the sky.

I smile as peace fills me. This is surely a sign. Väinämöinen is like the great firefox. Many have gone in search of him, and yet he cannot be found. He lives on, lighting up the sky, showing me the way.

"I see you," I whisper to that river of light. A flicker of hope glows in my chest, so weak and precious. Aina is alive. Väinämöinen is alive. He will help me save her. And then, he'll help save us all. "I am coming," I say, tracing the river of light as it dances over the hills. "On my knees, I will crawl to you, oh great Väinämöinen, oldest and wisest of shamans. Revontulet, show me the way."

The river of light elongates, moving in a great dance, blanketing this snowy hillside, which glows blue, purple, and green. A deep grunting sound makes me turn. I jerk my axe free from my belt, heart pounding. Kal snorts in welcome, bounding through the snow to join me at my side.

"Oh, thank the gods," I cry, wrapping my arms around his massive head. His breath is hot, his great mouth open as he pants. I pull back, brushing my fingers over his snout. "Lumi didn't hurt you, did she?"

He grunts, and I step back, looking for injury.

"I'm so sorry, Kal. Gods, I shouldn't have gone in there. It was foolish, but I was desperate. Now, I have nothing left. No food, no shelter. Please tell me we're close. Otherwise, I'm dead."

He grunts again, pushing past me, ready to lead the way.

Tucking my axe in at my belt, I hurry after him. "Kal—wait. Lumi is the one who's after you." I brace my hand at his back as we make our way down the hillside. The foxfires still dance in the sky above us.

"She trapped you in that pit," I go on. "She knows you know the way to Väinämöinen." I pant, my feet slipping in the deep snow. "I've turned it over in my mind, and I think she *let* me go. I think she means to follow us, Kal. In this snow, we can't hide our tracks."

He just grunts, trotting the last distance down the hill. An expanse of flat tundra opens before us, ending in another sloping, forested hill some three hundred yards away.

I pause, taking in the landscape. "We should go around, stick to the trees."

But Kal doesn't listen. He just charges across the open snow, cast in an eerie green by the light above.

"Kal, she'll follow us," I shout, running after him. "We're not safe out here. It's too exposed. Väinämöinen's not safe either. We'll be leading her right to him—"

From behind us, at the top of the hill, wolves howl. The sound raises all the fine hairs on my arms. Their song is a war cry. They're coming for us.

I look to Kal. "Tell me she doesn't have wolves."

He just grunts, his breath coming in a puff of white mist.

The wolves howl again, closer now, moving quickly.

Taking a deep breath, I shoulder my pack. "Kal, *run!*"

We take off at a sprint. All we can do is try to make it to the trees. And I'm so tired, so weak. I want to surrender. I want to sleep for a thousand years. But Kal needs me. Aina needs me. Nothing is finished yet.

Behind us, the wolves break through the trees, yipping and howling with excitement, knowing the hunt is on. Over my shoulder is a haunting sight—Lumi has four of the wolves harnessed to a massive sled. Her staff casts a moon-white glow all around. They're gaining ground. We'll never outrun them.

Lumi is a powerful witch, but she's not powerful enough to find Väinämöinen on her own. If the gods were on her side, would they not help her? Could she not call on them to come to her aid? The thought makes the flame of hope in my chest burn brighter. They don't want to help her. She's not worthy of finding him.

But you are, comes Aina's soft voice in my mind.

You can do anything you set your mind to, says Milja.

You were born to love with your whole heart, Mummi whispers, her hand soft on my brow.

Love guides my steps. Love of my friend, of my family, my people. Lumi wants to find the shaman for herself. Undoubtedly, she means to abuse his power for her own ends. I want to find the shaman for the good of others.

Lumi has prayed for this moment. She's prayed for Väinämöinen to fall within her grasp, but the gods have not seen fit to answer her prayers.

I smile, gazing up at the river of light in the sky.

The gods answer me.

"Ututyttö," I cry out to the night. I cut my palm open on the blade of my axe, spilling my blood onto the white snow. "Maiden of the Mist, I beseech you. Hide us from this witch's eyes. Help us!"

The wolves snarl, calling out as they race behind us.

"I want that bear alive," Lumi calls across the snow.

"Goddess, *please*," I pant, squeezing my bleeding palm. "Help us, or we die."

A boom echoes across the vast open space. Kal slides to a halt, his eyes wide. I do too, swaying on my feet from fatigue. All around us, the snow rises off the tundra, swirling and billowing in the air. The foxfire tints the mist blue-green. We hear the wolves' confused yips as the eerie fog envelops us.

"Ututyttö has listened," I cry. "She's helping us, Kal."

Behind us, Lumi shrieks, pounding her light staff, trying to pierce the fog. A fork of lightning casts a bright light overhead, but it just makes the fog shine greenish white. The fog swirls so thick, I can hardly see my hand before my face.

I grip Kal's fur and climb onto his back. He grunts, lowering himself to the ground to let me on. "Run," I whisper.

He takes off, his massive form bounding across the snow.

I hold on tight, snow whipping at my cheeks as the bear races forward. Behind us, the wolves yip as the witch shouts.

Crack.

The ground beneath Kal's feet rumbles and shakes; I feel it through his body. Deep thunder echoes off the trees. I know this sound like I know the beating of my own heart. "Oh gods, no—"

We're not on a frozen tundra. This is a frozen *lake* and Lumi is breaking the ice with her magic staff.

"You're mine, Väinämöinen," the witch screams. "Show yourself, coward! Save them if you dare!" All around us, the wolves howl, circling closer, tightening their trap.

I lean over to whisper in Kal's ear. "Keep running. We can make it."

But the bear grunts, shrugging his shoulders as if he wants me to get off.

"Kal, no—"

He rises up on his hind legs, and I shriek, falling backwards into the snow. I roll to my feet, hands outstretched towards him. "Kal, come on."

He drops back down and gives me a push with his snout, urging me to keep moving.

"I can't find him without you. Kal, *please*—"

He shoves me once more. Spinning around, he stands up on his back feet. With a mighty roar, he slams his paws down on the ice.

I gasp, feeling it weaken under me. A deep rumble echoes across the ice. "Kal, don't—"

The bear turns his head, his eyes now glowing blue-white, lit from within by a magic that gives him impossible strength. The same light shines from his open mouth. The look on his face is clear.

Run.

He turns away from me and pushes up onto his hind feet again. He towers in the mist, twice as tall as any man. With another roar, he slams his front feet down onto the ice until it splits. From deep in the fog, a wolf yelps, followed by a splash.

I scramble to my feet, inching away from the crack. Kal tries to balance with his front and back paws on different floes, his heavy weight tipping them. His eyes still glow with magic as a wolf leaps from the swirling mist onto his back. Kal roars, twisting around to dislodge it. He and the wolf both cry out in panic, their claws scratching the ice as it tips.

"No!" I scramble backwards, too afraid to stand.

"Take them alive," the witch shrieks. "I need that bear alive, you fools!"

The crack in the ice rumbles beneath me, right between my braced hands. All around, the wolves howl. Lumi's glowing staff signals her approach through the mist.

I flip onto my stomach and push myself up. I have to get off this ice. I have to—

Crack.

The ice splits between my feet. One moment I'm standing on solid ground, the next my axe drops from my hand, and I'm falling backwards, my weight tipping a floe of ice high into the air. My arms windmill uselessly through the air as I crash into the black water. A thousand tiny knives stab me all over, stealing the air from my lungs, as I begin to sink. The shock of the cold water nearly paralyzes me.

Swim, comes that soft, soothing voice. *Fight, Siiri.*

The goddess is here. She's with me. I am not alone. Hope burns in my chest. I'm not ready to die. I'm not ready to give up.

I kick for the surface, fighting the weight of my sodden furs. My feet are useless in these boots. My hands hit ice above, and I scream, bubbles of air erupting from my lips. The floe has righted itself, trapping me. I pound on it with my fists to no avail.

Above me, Kal roars, throwing his weight downward. The ice sheet shifts, and I surface, buffeted by the water as it breaks around the floes. I gasp for air, coughing and sputtering, looking for anything to hold onto. I'm so weak, I can't pull myself out.

Two wolves leap over me out of the mist. With a panicked roar, Kal rolls backwards, and the floe comes crashing down. I barely take a breath before I'm forced beneath the surface again.

Keep fighting, Siiri, the goddess urges.

I fought to the bitter end. When the ferrywoman asks me how I lived and how I died, I can tell her I was a fighter. But there's no fight left in me now. I fought, and now the fight is over.

Come back to me, Aina whispers.

I'm coming, Aina. Wait for me. Beloved, I'm coming.

In the icy depths, I take a deep breath, filling my lungs with cold water, surrendering my life.

Come back . . .

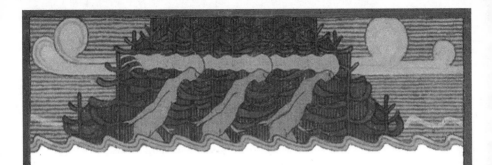

Aina

KUKKA GIVES ME A gentle shove through the door into the weaving room. I'm in a daze. My body feels cold, numb. I can't stop hearing Salla's and Lilja's screams of pain. I watched the life leave their eyes. I watched Kalma drag their bodies away. I can't close my eyes anymore. If I do, I see them all. Pale Inari, dead by my hand. Dead Lilja. Dead Salla. If I push their faces away, more take their place. Dead Siiri. Dead mother. Dead brothers.

So much waste of life. So much pain and suffering. Too much.

It's all too much.

A cool hand on my cheek. Soft words. "Come, little mouse."

I think a part of me might be dead now too. Can one be both alive and dead? I think it must be possible. I think we can die in parts. I died a little the night Kalma took me from Siiri. I felt it. Something escaped me in that moment when the darkness took me. It left and never came back. I am less now. Less Aina.

If I stay here for long enough, I fear the Witch Queen will find a way to take all the best parts of me. That's what she does. Her Beer of Oblivion erases the soul. It leaves you hollow and empty, carved out. Her captivity is a different kind of carving. It will be bloodier and take longer. Gods help me, I think I might beg for her brew before the end.

Hands press on my shoulders, and I sink onto a stool.

"Bring her some water."

A cup is pressed into my hand, but I can't grip it. It slips through my fingers, rattling to the floor, the water spilling.

"That's all right," the witch soothes. "Aina, you're safe now."

I blink, focusing on her face. "Safe?" I hear myself say. "There is no safe. Not in Tuonela."

Loviatar's cool hands cup my face, her white eyes catching the light. "I won't let them take you again."

She shouldn't make promises she can't keep. It's too cruel.

"Aina—listen to me now." Her hands hold my face still, not letting me pull away. "We can stop this—all this pain and suffering, all this mindless death. *You* can stop this. But it's your choice. It has to be your choice."

"How?" I whisper, my trembling hands wrapping around her wrists.

"Tuonetar is overconfident," she replies. "She believes she is untouchable. And she loves nothing more than a game. She's like a cat, Aina, taunting her prey before she eats it, scaring it to death. She wanted to taunt Tuoni, to show him her power. He wanted a wife to share in his vision of a peaceful Tuonela, a true partner and queen, a helpmate, a friend."

"I don't understand—"

"Tuonetar imprisoned him with that promise," Loviatar says over me. "Only his wife can set him free."

I lean away from her touch. "Then . . . surely, only Tuonetar can set him free."

The witch smirks, dropping her hands from my face. "Tuonetar is not his wife."

My heart stops. "What?"

"They are not married."

I don't even realize I'm still shaking my head. "But my mother always said—"

"Has your mother divined the secrets of the dead? Has she crossed the veil in body or soul? Has she sat at our table and heard our stories from our own lips? Who is she, to know our natures?"

I'm unsure of how to respond. In the end, stories are all just stories, I suppose. This wouldn't be the first time someone got the details wrong. "I'm sorry." Reaching out, I take her hand. "I will listen. Loviatar, please tell me your story. Help me understand."

She relaxes. "Tuoni and Tuonetar were made by the will of the All-Mother to fulfill a divine purpose here in death, as we all were. Tuoni was not made a king; he is a god. The title of king is a mortal appellation. But it turns out there is power in your mortal ideas."

"Is he not your father, then? Is Tuonetar not your mother?"

"He is my father by choice only," she explains. "He protects us and tends to us like his own children. In turn, we honor him as our father and our king . . . or we did."

"What happened?"

"Tuonetar became obsessed with being queen," she goes on. "At first it was enough to rule at his side, balancing his inclinations towards peace and mercy. But with her chaos came delusions of grandeur. She wanted to be queen without a king. She wanted all powers of death vested in her. She became impossible, intractable . . . until she had to be stopped. Tuoni was right to try."

"But he failed." I drop my hand from hers.

She nods. "He is broken, Aina, but not beaten. He will fight her, and he will win, but he cannot do it alone. She thought to mock him with her curse, binding him with the promise that only his wife can set him free—when he is not married and has no chance of marriage while bound."

"And then she taunted him," I whisper. "She brought girls from life into death only to kill them in front of him?"

"It is complicated," she replies, her expression veiled. "But yes."

I close my eyes, wincing against the pain of this truth. "All this time . . . all these girls . . . and she's just taunting *him*. We mean nothing. Our lives, our families, all our hopes and dreams, taken from us to feed her need for pain. It's too cruel."

Loviatar grips my shoulders. "Then stop it. The maiden must come willingly, Aina. She must *choose* to marry him. She must choose to be his wife."

"What?"

"Tuonetar believes no mortal would ever choose such a fate," Loviatar explains. "Not if they only see this rotten nightmare, this world she's created."

I pull away. "No, I only ever wanted to *free* him. So that he would free us. If I marry him, I'll be trapped here forever. She'll kill me in the end—"

"No—"

"Yes," I cry, "she *will*. You know she will. She's too powerful."

"Tuoni would protect you."

"As he's protected you?" The words are spoken in haste, and I have no choice but to watch as her mask flickers, revealing her pain and rage.

"I'm still alive," she replies.

I lean forward, searching her face. "And . . . what about your child? The one you lost . . ."

She goes still, only the corner of her mouth twitching. "Careful, little mouse."

"Did he promise to protect them too? Did you watch them die like I watched Lilja and Salla—*ah*—" I'm not prepared for the slap that sends me reeling backwards off my stool. I cry out, hitting my shoulder on a loom, as Loviatar grabs me by my braid and jerks me up to my knees. I wrap my hands around her bony wrist. "Let me go—"

"Listen to me, little mouse," she hisses. "You truly know nothing of us. He is only imprisoned because he helped my child escape. *That* was his great treachery against the Witch Queen. My child is free of this place thanks to his grace."

I gasp, ceasing my struggling. With a final jerk of my scalp, she lets me go. I sink back to the floor.

She angles her face down. "You know nothing of what I have suffered for him, for my children. I would suffer still more. But it is not in my power to protect them now. No, that power is in the hands of a weak little mortal with the soul of a mouse."

I let out a heavy breath, shoulders sagging.

"What will you do, mouse? Will you lie there on the floor and let the foxes and the owls make your life small? Or will you stand up and fight? You could claim a power beyond anything in your wildest mortal imaginings. You could be more to him than a wife, Aina. You could be a queen. You could be a goddess."

I swallow the nerves in my throat, shaking my head. "I don't want to be a queen or a goddess. I'm not even sure I want to be someone's wife," I admit. "It was always just expected of me, and I hate to disappoint." I glance around the confines of the weaving room. "But this place is not my dream. Thanks to the Witch Queen, I fear it can only ever be my nightmare."

Loviatar's expression softens, turning sad. She sinks back down to her stool. "I cannot force your hand," she says at last. "I thought, when I heard of how you sacrificed yourself for your friend, that there was nobility in you, a rare kind of courage."

I go still, heart aching at her mention of Siiri.

"I thought it again when you claimed Inari's life to spare Lilja the pain of the kill," she goes on. "You are generous and kind. You are selfless, Aina. Loyal. Patient. Resilient. Rare qualities in a mortal, even rarer in a god. You would be a queen worthy of a crown."

Before I can reply, the door to the weaving room slams open.

With a scream of rage, Tuonetar sweeps in, wand held aloft. "Daughter," she shrieks, blasting a loom out of her path. It slams into another, and they both splinter. From my place on the floor, I make like a mouse and scamper, ducking behind the looms, staying to the shadows.

Loviatar rises regally to her feet, her black hair unbound, flowing down her back. She folds her hands before her and waits. "Yes, Mother?"

The Witch Queen stalks forward, chest heaving with rage. "Was it you?"

Loviatar doesn't cower. "You'll have to be more specific—"

Tuonetar snatches her daughter by the throat one-handed, lifting her clear off the floor. "Was it *you?*" she says again. "Did you sneak those dead little rats out from under my nose?"

Loviatar dangles in the air by her throat, not struggling. She places a hand over her mother's wrist. "No," she rasps.

I scoot further into the shadows, trying not to make a sound, trying not to even breathe.

Tuonetar drops Loviatar to the floor with a snarl and paces away. Loviatar rolls to her knees, brushing the column of her slender throat with a shaky hand. "You must think you're so clever," the Witch Queen taunts. "I know how you plot and scheme against me. You've *never* been on my side. I told you I wanted to keep them. I had such glorious plans!"

"And they would have been torturously cruel, to be sure," Loviatar replies, still rubbing her neck. "You are singularly talented at brewing despair."

Tuonetar grabs her daughter by the shoulders, her voice dripping with venom. "I will ask you this only once, you faithless maggot. Do you still plot with him against me? Would you see your own darling mother overthrown and cast aside, diminished like the frost gone with a spring that blooms too soon?"

Loviatar raises her chin in defiance. "I learned my lesson. I take no sides. How many times must I say—"

"Your words mean *nothing* to me," the Witch Queen screams, her voice rattling the very walls. "You defied me once, you sightless, mewling monster. You helped that girl escape my clutches, and I will *never* forgive you."

They're speaking of her child, the one Tuoni helped free. A daughter.

A tear slips down Loviatar's cheek. "I'll never forgive myself," she replies. "And that is punishment enough. Believe me, or don't," she adds, setting her shoulders against the witch's wrath. "I will not attempt to persuade you, either way."

With a growl, Tuonetar brandishes her wand again, shooting jets of light across the room that smash looms, turning them to kindling. I hardly have time to roll out of the way before the loom I cower behind bursts apart in a spray of splinters. I crawl on my belly along the wall, seeking safety.

"You have always been my bane." Tuonetar's voice quivers with rage. "I should have let the north wind tear you asunder!"

"I would have let you," Loviatar whispers.

"Keep to your muck, worm. And know that if I scent so

much as a whiff in the air of further treachery, I will rip the beating heart from your chest and eat it with a garnish of lingonberry jam."

Loviatar frowns. "As I said—"

"Shhh." The Witch Queen shushes her, placing a bony finger to her daughter's lips. "No more lies now, dearest. Let them rot and fester deep within your heart. That's a good girl." She brushes Loviatar's cheek with a long finger, wiping her tear away. Bringing it to her cracked lips, she flicks out her tongue, tasting Loviatar's sadness.

"You've always been soft," she says, shaking her head in disappointment. "You're a dreamer, just like him. It's a waste, my darling little parasite. Turn away from him. Turn away from these ideas of order and rules, right and wrong. Embrace chaos as we are all meant to do. Embrace chaos . . . or be consumed by it. For I will *never* give way to him. I'll die first . . . and death cannot die."

With that, the Witch Queen stalks away, rattling the door in its frame when she slams it shut. Only her menacing aura remains, seeping into the shadows of every corner.

Loviatar stands in the shattered mess of the room, back stiff, shoulders straight. "You can come out now, little mouse."

I pick myself up off the floor. "What happened?"

"Mother had plans for the girls she killed today," Loviatar replies flatly.

I step around the mess to her side. "Lilja and Salla? Inari?" The witch nods.

I groan, feeling sick. What tortures did she have planned for their corpses?

"We managed to get them away from her and put them back to rest," Loviatar soothes.

I glance sharply at her. "We?"

Her expression turns veiled, protective. "There are those

who would help us, those who *are* helping us. Powerful forces in Tuonela are ready for a change, Aina. They weren't ready before, but Tuonetar's reign of terror has gone on for long enough. Say the word, and I will rally them to you, to my father. You will not be alone. We *will* protect you. Free him, and we will do everything in our power to keep you safe from Tuonetar."

Tears fill my eyes. Sorrow and fatigue are etched on every line of her face. I think of her long years of suffering. I think of the other girls, the pain they felt when they died, the fear and humiliation. I think of my Siiri, so bold and full of life. She deserves a long life and a blessed death. So many people—mortal and immortal—have suffered under the Witch Queen. I can stop this. I can save them.

All it will cost me is my soul, bound in a loveless marriage to the god of death.

Hail Aina, Queen of Tuonela. Will the bards and minstrels ever know? Will they sing my songs?

I suppose my choice is made regardless. It was made the moment I reached out my hand to Kalma to spare Siiri. It was made again when I first heard the Witch Queen's taunting laughter. It was made thrice over when I dragged a sharp blade across Inari's neck. It was bound in iron when I watched Lilja and Salla writhing on the floor. It was plated in gold just now, when I saw Loviatar dangling from her neck.

"Yes," I say. "I'll do it."

The witch goes still. "Are you sure?"

I don't know how I came to be on this path, but I'll not stray from it now. Stepping closer, I press my forehead to hers, breathing deeply of her comforting smell of juniper and lanolin. She places her hands on my shoulders. "You've put your trust in me," I whisper. "Now I'm trusting you. Take me to your father. Take me to Tuoni, and I will set us all free."

Siiri 4

"GODS, YOU WEIGH A ton," a deep voice grunts.

All around, I hear the excited yips of dogs. There's sloshing and splashing as someone drags me out of the lake. I'm weighed down by my wet furs like a dead fish. Is this death? Have I washed up on Tuoni's shores?

"Cough it up," the voice says. "That's a good lad. Come on, cough it up or die."

My rescuer turns me on my side and pounds my back with a large fist that rattles my ribcage. Retching mightily, I empty my stomach of a lake's worth of freezing water. I'm surprised a whole pike doesn't flop out onto the ice.

Not dead yet. I'm very much still alive . . . and wet . . . and freezing.

"There we go," says the deep voice. "Get it all out."

The feeling of emptiness washes over me. I'm numb—never a good sign. My entire body trembles with the shock of almost drowning in the icy depths of a deep lake. How did I get here?

I shut my eyes tight. I was running through the snow across a frozen lake. I called upon the mist maiden to hide us from view. Lumi—the wolves—the ice breaking beneath my feet . . .

"Kal," I rasp with my damaged throat. I roll onto my face, trying to sit up.

"Take your time," the deep voice says. "That bear nearly got you. Fate intervened in its own way. Nearly killed by a bear, nearly killed by the ice. Death has your name, lad."

I look up sharply at him, a scowl on my face.

"You're a girl," the man says with a surprised laugh, his voice deep, muffled behind a thick cowl.

"Y-yes," I say through chattering teeth. "I-I am."

The man is wrapped from head to toe in thick furs. All I can see are his deeply weathered cheeks, well-lined from years of toil in this harsh landscape. His eyes are bright blue, sharp and penetrating. Behind him, up in the night sky, the lights of the foxfires still dance.

"You need to get out of those wet clothes, or you'll freeze to death." He picks me up with ease, setting me on the back of his sled. Then he wraps me in a fur. It smells like smoke and pipe tobacco. All around us, his dogs bark excitedly, waiting for him to take his place on the runners of the sled. They dance in place, the sled already shifting forward.

His feet touch the rails, and the dogs burst into action, racing across the snow. I blink against the bitter cold, trying to control the shaking of my limbs. The curled tops of pine trees flash by, weighed down by the snow, illuminated by the foxfires overhead.

Before long, the sled slows to a stop. The man picks me up, furs and all, and pushes his way through the door of a large, blissfully warm hut. It's cozy, with the thick scent of pine logs. He sets me down on a bed of soft reindeer furs by the fire.

"Take those clothes off, girl. You can wrap up in this for now." He tosses a heavy pelt next to me. "Better naked than dead," he adds with a grunt. "I'll go tend to the dogs." With a snap of the door, he's gone.

I strip off my sodden mittens first, placing them on the warm stones by the fire. They instantly begin to steam. With frozen, fumbling fingers, I shed myself of all my layers. In minutes, they all lay in a pile by the fire. My hands shake as I wrap the bear pelt around my weak frame and edge closer to the flickering flames, moaning with relief as the heat gradually thaws out my frozen body.

As soon as the fire restores enough of my wits, I peer about the hut. It's large, more than twice the size of Lumi's. In the center is a ring of stones forming the hearth. To my left, a thick pile of furs serves as a bed. To my right, a rickety set of low shelves contains an assortment of cups, bowls, and utensils. A pair of antlers hanging by the door have been repurposed as hooks to hold snares, rope, and a fishing net. Everything is simple, rough-hewn wood and natural stone. Everything except the drum in the corner—and the kantele by the bed.

My breath freezes in my throat as my eyes lock on the kantele. Before I can crawl over to inspect it, the door rattles open. The man closes it with a thud and secures it with a crossbeam to protect against harsh winter winds.

"Still alive then?" he calls to me, dumping an armful of kindling by the fire.

"Yes," I reply, taking in his features in this brighter light.

The man is tall, taller even than my father. Taller than Onni. He unwraps the cowl from his face. He has a long, flowing white beard. And yet, time hasn't bent his back or weakened his shoulders. He still has the body of a strong man, one who doesn't merely survive in the wilderness but thrives in it. He pulls off his hat, uncovering a snarled mess of long white hair that matches his beard. Then he slips off his large mittens. His hands are as weathered as his face . . . and covered in rune tattoos like the ones on Kalma's hands.

I suck in a breath, my initial fearful reaction giving way to determination. The tattoos must mean something important. Regardless, I know who he is. "Väinämöinen," I whisper.

He stiffens.

"You are Väinämöinen," I repeat, more loudly.

He faces me across the fire, holding a knife in his hand. "Did you come all this way to try to kill me, girl?"

"What? No," I cry, sitting up. "Do many people travel this far north intent on killing you?"

He shrugs, dropping to his knees on the other side of the fire. "Some, not many. Not anymore." He prods at the fire with a stick, making it hiss. "Most people think I died, lost to the stories and songs. Sometimes I doubt it myself," he adds with a soft chuckle.

"You doubt that you live?"

"Life is nothing but a long dying," he replies. "I get the feeling you are well familiar with the sensation of dying to live."

I nod, swallowing against the pain in my throat.

His blue eyes watch me, gleaming in the firelight. He huffs, his white mustache twitching. "If you're unfortunate enough to reach my age, you'll find yourself living to die. At this point, I would welcome death. I'm ready for a good long sleep."

"Oh, great Väinämöinen, oldest and wisest of shamans, you can't die," I say, gazing up at him. "Please, I need your help. I come to you in my darkest hour, seeking your guidance—"

"Don't even think about it." He raises a large hand in protest.

I blink. "What? But I need your help—"

"What you *need* is food, girl. You need sleep. And from the looks of that nasty cut on your throat, you need a poultice and a healing song. I can smell the infection from here," he adds, crinkling his nose.

"I don't have time for food and sleep." I clutch the bear pelt tighter as I lean forward, the fire warming my face. "My dearest friend was taken from me, and I need you to help me get her back—"

"Are you the greatest shaman of the ages?" he bellows. The fire's crackling quiets. Even the beams of the hut seem to quake with fear.

"No."

"No, you are *not* the shaman. You're a half-dead girl who, at this moment, is more mackerel than mortal. You can't help anyone in your condition. At this point, I doubt you could even stand on your own two legs."

They warned me he wouldn't help, but I'm not ready to give up. Indignation surges through me. Ignoring the screaming pain throughout my body, I meet the shaman glare for glare. I rise shakily to my feet, ignoring that I'm naked and half-frozen beneath the heavy bear pelt. "I'm tougher than I look," I declare, chin raised in defiance.

Across the fire, the shaman smirks, the end of his white mustache twitching again. "Five . . . four . . . three . . ."

I narrow my eyes at him. "Why are you counting?"

"Two . . . one . . ."

My shaking legs give out, and I flop down onto the soft bed of pelts with a gasp.

"See? You're so weak, you've got fins for feet."

My cheeks burn. I'm embarrassed to let him see me so helpless. But he's right. In this state, I'm no better than a fish out of water.

"Food and rest," he says again, more gently this time. "That's what I will offer you, for that is what you need. And once you've had food and rest, you will return south. There is nothing for you here. I am not the shaman you seek."

"But you are Väinämöinen."

"I *was* Väinämöinen," he corrects. "Now I'm just a tired old man with too many yesterdays and an endless sea of empty tomorrows."

Cowed into silence, I watch as the shaman prepares a small cookpot. He tosses a few ingredients into it, including something that looks like meat, from inside his vest pocket. He pours water into the pot and hangs it on the hook over the fire. Soon, the smell of soup fills the hut, making my stomach groan. As he stirs the soup, a lone wolf howls in the distance.

We both go still, our eyes meeting over the flames.

"I fear I must tell you something," I say.

He says nothing, waiting for me to speak.

Fatigue pulls at me as I sit up. "A witch named Lumi followed me north. The wolf is likely hers. I couldn't lose them in the snow. I'm sorry, Väinämöinen. The bear and I, we led her right to you. I think she means to kill you—"

"I'm well aware of what that silly witch wants," he replies, stirring the soup again. "I'm more curious to hear about this bear. He was trying to drown you."

"He was trying to *save* me," I correct. "He broke the ice with his paws to give me an escape, but the ice cracked and pulled me under too. Please, can you tell me if he survived? Did he make it off the ice?"

"That I don't know. The fog was quite thick."

I sigh, resting my chin on my knees. "I suppose that too is my fault."

He glances curiously over at me. "You control the fog then?"

"No, but I called on the help of Ututyttö. The mist maiden hid us from Lumi and the wolves."

He smirks. "You called on a goddess, and she answered you?"

I nod.

Those blue eyes narrow again. "How did you call her?"

I slip my hand out between the edges of the bear pelt, flashing him the stark red line cutting across my palm.

He grunts, dropping his gaze back to his cookpot. "Blood magic is not for the faint of heart, girl. Who are you, that you can wield it with such ease? And why would a bear risk his life for you?"

"I don't know."

He looks across the fire at me again. "You're not a witch?"

I shake my head.

"A väki then? A long-lost daughter of a lesser god?"

"No, I'm just plain Siiri. I journeyed north from Lake Päijänne in search of you. The bear and I crossed paths when I found him in a pit, where Lumi had trapped him. I set him free and continued north. I met a goddess in a sacred grove, and she told me to follow the bear, that he would lead me to you. When my need was greatest, he returned to me. He saved my life. We fought off Lumi and the wolves, and now I'm here," I finish, gesturing around us. "The bear kept his word and led me to you. Now I must keep *my* word and beg for your help. I will not leave until you agree."

Väinämöinen hums, ladling soup into a wooden bowl. "Well, it sounds like you've had quite the adventure." He reaches around the flames, holding the bowl out to me.

I make no move to take it. "You don't believe me. And you have no intention of helping me."

"Oh, I believe you." He places the bowl on the warm stones and ladles a second bowl for himself. Then he settles cross-legged before the fire. "Who am I to doubt the word of a mortal girl who claims to see goddesses and thinks a magic bear is her guide on a quest to track down a dead shaman?"

"You're not dead yet, old man," I mutter.

"As to my helping you, I'm already doing far more than I ought," he goes on, sipping his soup with loud slurps. "You've put me in a precarious position. To pull you from that ice, I had to lower my wards—which is no easy feat, I assure you. The magic that has kept me safe is now shattered."

"I'm sorry, Väinämöinen. I didn't want her to track me, I swear it."

"It's not your fault. Lumi knows me too well. You're wrong to think she followed you north. She *drove* you here."

I swallow my sip of hot broth. "What do you mean?"

"She forced you into my path, knowing my damned curious nature would lure me out." He lets out a dry laugh. "I may possess all the wisdom of the ages, but I still walked right into her trap like a day-old fawn."

My heart races as another wolf howls in the distance. "Can't you just fix the wards?"

"You think a magic as deep as my wards can be rewoven overnight?" He snorts. "You think I can snap my fingers and charm the väki of the earth, the trees, and the very air to carry my spells of concealment? Those wardings took me months to weave. It takes patience, and no small amount of skill. It also takes a forest disposed to bend to my will—easier to do in summer when the trees are warmed by the sun, eager to sing with me."

"But . . . you are Väinämöinen," I say helplessly.

"True enough." He heaves a sigh. "But I am not the shaman I once was, and time is not on my side. Lumi will come for me. Even now, she gathers herself. She makes ready for the fight she feels she must win."

"You could run," I say, abandoning my soup. "Like a fire-fox, you could flee her pursuit. I'll help you—"

"I thought I was the one meant to be helping *you*," he shouts. "I pulled you from that ice, and now I'm feeding you. I'll give you shelter for the night. I may even grant you some provisions to last you a journey south again. But as to any other favors you may be about to ask me, my answer is and must be no—"

"You don't even know what I'm going to ask," I cry, pushing up to sit on my knees.

"It doesn't matter what you ask, for I cannot do it." He rises to his feet. "Whatever feat of daring you expect from me, you must look elsewhere. The time of Väinämöinen is gone. I am all that is left of him, and I promise you, I won't be enough."

"Fine." I reach for my bowl, holding it one-handed. "Then you must teach me."

He raises a white brow, his mustache twitching. "Teach you what?"

"My dearest friend was taken by Kalma and brought to Tuonela. I came here because you are the only shaman to ever enter into death and return alive. Teach me how to cross over. Teach me how to get to Tuonela."

Väinämöinen stares down at me, his expression unveiling his rage and pain, his terrible, aching loss. "You want a lesson from the great Väinämöinen on how to get to Tuonela?" He jerks a large hunting knife free from his thick leather belt and drops it on the pelts beside me. "There," he says, pointing at the blade. "Take that and stab it through your heart. When the ferrywoman asks you how you came to stand at Tuoni's shores, tell her you died a fool's death. For you are a fool to attempt to thwart the Witch Queen." With that, he marches over to the door.

"So you won't help me? You'll just leave my friend to die in that place?"

"I *am* helping you!" He shoves his fur hat down on his head. "Food and water and rest. You leave in the morning, before you call any more calamity down on my head."

"But my friend—"

"Mark me, Siiri. If your friend is in Tuonela, then she's already worse than dead."

"Väinämöinen, please—"

The shaman stomps out into the cold winter night, slamming the door behind him.

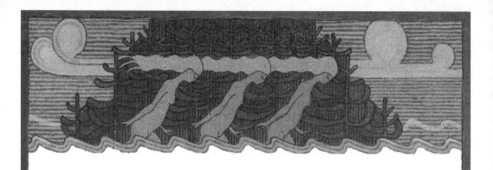

Aina 25

"ARE YOU SURE?" LOVIATAR repeats.

I search the death goddess's face, heart racing. "On the life of your daughter, swear to me that you'll keep me safe from Tuonetar."

Loviatar places a hand over my heart, her rune-marked fingers splayed. "I swear," she intones.

My heart beats a little easier, and I lift the folds of my cowl to cover my head. "Take me to him."

"I cannot go with you."

I still. "But you just said—"

"For me to hold to my oath, you must take these next steps alone." She lowers her voice, inching closer. "As you go to him, I must go to the others. We are hunting a dangerous fox, Aina. If even one of us is out of position, she'll slip our net, and then we're all at risk."

"Tell me what to do."

She moves past me, stepping over the broken pieces of the

looms littering the floor. I follow, thinking we're headed for the door, but she stops before one of the only undamaged looms in the room. "We must move it," she says.

"Move it?"

Loviatar nods, already reaching for the loom. I ask no questions, helping her shove the empty frame across the wood floor. It screeches and groans, the noise loud enough to wake the dead.

I look down and gasp. "There's a door."

"And there's a tunnel underneath," she explains. "It leads to the base of a wooded hill. The river lies just beyond. No one else knows of this. Not the Witch Queen. Not even him. This is mine alone."

I glance up. Taking in the deep lines of sadness on her face, I know the truth. "Yours and your daughter's," I whisper, reaching forward to squeeze her hand. "You sent her down this tunnel once too . . . didn't you?"

She drops to her knees and pulls open the trap door with a loud creak, exposing a set of narrow stairs. "There's another door at the tunnel's end. My father is bound in the woods. You will find him. The raven will show you the way."

"How will I free him?"

She conjures a silver knife and hands it out to me by the hilt. "Use this."

"But what do I—"

"You will know what to do."

I take the knife from her, tucking it into my belt. Bracing my hands on either side of the floor, I prepare to lower myself down onto the steps. "Loviatar, wait—" I search her clouded eyes. "What if—suppose he will not have me . . ."

She smiles, cupping my cheek. "He's waited a lifetime for you, Aina. Besides, if you were not worthy of him, I would have killed you myself . . . if only to spare myself the misery of your slow knitting."

I lean away, glaring at her. "You're all monsters."

"We are as the All-Mother made us," she replies. "Now, Aina, go."

I drop through the trap door and land on the top stair. From this angle, I find myself peering under the hem of Loviatar's long dress. She wears stout reindeer-fur slippers . . . and a pair of my knitted socks. I smile, lowering myself down another step. I nearly slip, catching myself before I reach the bottom. "Wait—Loviatar, I have no light!"

"Mice see just fine in the dark," she calls down. With that, she shuts the trap door.

"No, wait—"

Above me, Loviatar moves the loom back overtop the trap door. I feel dust slipping down through the cracks, landing on my hood, tickling my nose. I step out from under the door, trying to force my eyes to see through this darkness, but it's impossible.

"Ilmatar, guide my steps," I whisper, moving on soft feet.

The smell of damp earth surrounds me, settling in my nose. I can't see, but I can feel the closeness of the tunnel's sides. I reach out with both hands, brushing them with my fingers. Each step is cautious as I test the ground. After several long minutes, I stifle a shriek when my toes hit something hard. I reach out, fumbling forward until I touch a second set of wooden steps. I crawl up them, feeling for the outline of the trap door. Putting an ear to it, I wait and listen for sound.

There is nothing. No birdsong, no wind in the trees.

Using my shoulder, I push against the door. It takes a couple attempts before the hinges creak and the wood gives way. A dusting of dirt and snow fall in on me, making me gasp. I push the door all the way open and crawl out on hands and knees. I scramble to my feet and dust off my dress, peering around. The snow seems to glow the softest white, as if it's reflecting light from an unseen moon and stars. It's a beautiful kind of magic, and it's more than enough to guide my steps.

If only I knew where I was going . . .

The trees are thick here—birch and aspen, dotted with spruce and pine. I hate the way the knots of the birch trees always watch me with unblinking eyes. I do another slow spin, clutching my hood, pulling it tighter against the chill. Peering through the dark, I can see the outline of a wooden hill. Loviatar promises that beyond the hill lies the river of death. In all my time in Tuonela, I have yet to see it.

My heart sinks. Now I have nothing but time, for I'm about to make a bargain with death that will trap me here forever. My life for their lives—Siiri and Helmi, Riina, Satu, all the girls who may ever face Kalma's wrath. But I think that's the difference between the Witch Queen and me. Tuonetar thinks all death must be chaos. In her mind, death is merely a means for *her* to claim more power.

I disagree. Death can be meaningful. Death can be a choice. We can choose to die as we live. There is power in that choice, power in death that Tuonetar in her cruelty can never understand, for she has never truly lived. I am choosing to thwart her, knowing I may die. But I will die knowing there are things worth dying for, and she cannot take that power from me.

The trees stand quiet, unmoved by wind. Snow clings to their bare branches. I take a few steps forward, letting fate guide me. "Tuoni?" I whisper his name, feeling a sort of power pass over my lips. "Tuoni . . . my lord . . . I come of my own free will."

Behind me, a shadow swoops out of the darkness, and I

duck. Something large flies over me, stirring the air with its wings. Swallowing my scream, I cover my head with my hands just as a loud caw breaks the silence. I look up to see my raven perched on the low bough of a pine tree. "Jaako," I say, breathless with relief. "Oh, thank the gods. Show me the way."

He ruffles his feathers and swoops away through the trees. Holding up the bottom of my woolen dress, I run after him. I trip over roots and rocks hidden by the snow, doing my best to keep up. He caws softly, encouraging me to follow.

"How much farther, Jaako," I pant. "How much—"

There, not fifteen feet from me, stands a lonely alder tree, its base lit by the soft, undisturbed snow. I narrow my eyes, inching closer as I take in the strangeness of its trunk. A man stands in the shadow of it. No, he's not in front of the tree. He's *part* of it. Over time, the tree has grown around him, rooting him in place.

"Ilmatar, give me strength," I whisper to the dark.

I know well the stories of the alder tree. Some people call it the "death tree." It has deep ties to Tuonela. My father often carves sielulintu from a piece of alder that we bury with the village dead. The birds carved from alder branches make good guides as souls pass through the realms.

As I stand before the tree, I know with all certainty that I'm standing before the god of death. This tree is his prison.

Behind me, Jaako emits another caw. Swooping past me, he flies towards the tree. Just before he reaches it, he disappears, falling in a flurry of black feathers to the snow.

"Jaako, no—" I rush forward. Dropping to my knees, I pick up a feather. "No, please. I need you." I peer all around, searching for the raven in the trees. "Jaako—"

Before me, the alder tree groans. I scramble back to my feet and step closer, taking in the ghastly sight of the god trapped in the tree. The alder's bark has all but swallowed him. His arms look like they've been chained above his head. The rest of the tree grows around his head and shoulders, locking his jaw shut. "Gods . . ." I inch closer. "How long have you been trapped here, my lord?"

He cannot move. He can't speak. But he can see. The god of death gazes down at me. My free hand trembles as I brush my fingers across his furrowed brow. One eye is dark as night, the other clouded and pearly white. A thick, pronged scar crosses the white eye from cheek to brow, leaving it sightless. He has a proud nose, a bearded face, hair black as a raven's wing. The tree is claiming that too. His skin is dusted with lichen. Our eyes lock, and bone-deep knowledge shivers through me.

"Jaako?" I whisper, awed by the truth. My raven isn't a messenger for the god of death. Somehow, he *is* the god of death. "Tuoni." I say the god's name, watching as his eyes shut tight. He's suffering, his face pained. I brush my fingers over his brow again. "Look at me, my lord."

The intensity of his dark eye is fathomless, like Tuonela's sky, while the cloudy one is as radiant as a full moon.

"I'm going to free you," I say, heart racing. "But the only way I know how to do that is if I marry you."

His jaw clenches tight as he grunts, fighting his cage. He doesn't want this. He doesn't want me.

"We neither of us have a choice," I say, my shame rising. "You know as well as I that the only way Tuonetar can be stopped is if we break her curse."

The tree creaks as he struggles.

"I won't pretend to know all of what has happened here," I go on. "But I know enough to know I trust Loviatar . . . and she trusts you." This stills him. "Let me help free you, so you can free us. Are we agreed?"

His gaze softens, and I have the feeling he's trying to nod his assent.

Taking a few steps back, I circle the tree, considering my options. Then I search his face. Jaako is so readable—his expressions, his mood. Is Tuoni the same? It's so hard to see the man for the tree. "I will marry you, my lord. I will bind myself to you, soul to soul. And in so doing, I will free you . . . but I have conditions you must agree to first. Blink once if you consent to hear my terms."

Slowly, he blinks.

Taking a deep breath, I stand at my full height, daring to bargain with the god of death. "First, you must let the others go," I declare, my voice sounding much stronger than I feel. "Riina, Satu, and Helmi—you must return them to the realm of the living. And you will vow *never* to take another girl in this way again." I level a finger at his face.

He blinks once, agreeing to my first condition.

"So, then, my second condition . . ." I pace away in the snow, trying to think of the words to use to extract his oath. "I told you many things as the raven . . . about my family, my friends. You must swear never to raise a hand to them. You will never harm them or send another to act in your stead. As you are the god of blessed death, you will bless their deaths. Siiri, my mother, my father, and brothers—you will protect them from Tuonetar's wrath. Swear it, or I take my chances and try to swim to freedom here and now."

This is an expression I can read—the tilt of his dark brows, the set of his jaw. He's affronted. I imagine he's not used to being given a list of demands from a mortal girl. Narrowing his eyes, he blinks.

"My third condition . . ." Here I pause, fighting a blush that has nothing to do with the cold. I adjust the cowl over my hair. "If I am to be a wife to you . . . I would ask that you be kind. I don't—" Gods, this feels too unnatural to speak aloud before any man, let alone a god. Steeling myself, I say the words sitting like a block of ice in my heart. "I would ask that you not hurt me, my lord . . . or take what I do not want to give. I know the duties of a wife, and I will fulfill them. I only ask . . . please be kind."

I fall into awkward silence, too embarrassed to look him in the eye. But his eyes are the only way he can respond. Swallowing my nerves, I glance up. The god is surveying me with that black eye. He looks so much like my raven. He holds my gaze and blinks.

I sigh with relief, giving him a little nod. "Thank you, my lord. I think I only have one more condition." I curl my hands into fists at my side, feeling the bite of my nails against my palms as I step closer to him. "You must swear to me that you will do all in your power to protect me from Tuonetar. And if you cannot protect me . . ." I pause as a tear slips down my cheek. I wipe it quickly away. "If you cannot protect me, my lord, I beg that *you* be the one to kill me."

He grunts, his face a mask of rage as he fights the tree harder than ever.

"Give me a clean death, my lord. Kill me quickly and lay me to rest. Swear it to me." I frame his face with both hands, all but sharing breath with the death god. I need to see his face, his eyes. I need to know he'll hold himself to this last oath. "I'm not afraid of death," I whisper. "I'm afraid of how she'll make me die. Swear you'll be merciful, my lord. Swear it, or I make for the river and leave you to your fate."

Tears well in his good eye as he looks down at me in agony. Slowly, he blinks.

A breath of relief leaves me, my shoulders sagging. Suddenly, I feel the cold again. I sense eyes on us, and I doubt they are the knotted eyes of the trees. Someone watches me. Some *thing*. I'm terrified to turn around. I must hurry. The trouble is that I'm unsure of what to do next. Loviatar was certain I would know how to free him.

With trembling hands, I pull out the silver knife she gave me. It's a lovely thing with a sharp blade and a polished reindeer-horn handle. Runes I can't read are etched down the thin blade. I turn the knife over in my hands, gazing upon the bark of the alder tree. "If I was meant to cut you out, I imagine Loviatar would have given me an axe," I muse.

Tuoni watches me, unable to assist. This is my puzzle to solve.

"I cannot possibly carve you away from the tree," I go on. "Can your magic free you?"

He blinks.

"Then I must marry you here and now to free you to use your magic and—" I gasp, looking down at the knife in my hands. I know why Loviatar gave it to me. I've heard of wise-women using blood magic in their binding rituals. But blood rituals are said to be a deep magic, an old and dangerous magic—powerful when performed correctly, disastrous when done wrong.

"Once, all marriages were sealed in blood," I say, holding up the knife. "Palm to palm, the two lovers pledged their lives to one another under the boughs of the oak tree." I glance around the dark clearing and feel a flutter of sadness. "I always imagined my wedding day a little differently from this. My in-tended would ask for my hand. Is that not how all the ballads go? He recites poetry or a song of love that makes me feel more beautiful than the moon goddess." I frown, gazing up at Tuoni, studying his lichen-dusted face. "But now I stand before my bridegroom who is as silent as the grave . . . for he is death."

Tuoni waits with a somber look in his eye.

"There is no oak tree lit with candles. No drumming in the

woods as you seek me out, the bridegroom on his last hunt. No wisewoman is here to witness the binding oath. And my family, my—" I bite back the words, closing my eyes against the pain of not having Siiri and my mother here. A bride is supposed to have her loved ones close as she makes this step, leaving the comfort of her house to begin a new life. A bride is supposed to be in love with her new husband too. So much about this moment is not what I would have wished, but I must take my fate in my own hands. I gaze up at the god of death. "My lord, do you consent to be my husband? Will you take me for a wife, forsaking all others?"

Slowly, Tuoni blinks. He has no choice. This is a marriage of desperation for us both. He doesn't love me. If he could choose another, I'm sure he would.

I step closer, raising the blade. "I'm sorry for this, but I know no other way." I slice open his cheek, watching as red blood drips down the knife. Lifting my hand, I wince, dragging the blade across my palm to spill my blood too. Tucking the knife in at my belt, I place my bleeding hand against his cheek. He closes his eyes at my touch.

"I'm not a wisewoman to know the right words," I whisper. "But by my blood, I bind myself to you as your wife. No other may claim me. By your blood, you must offer me your protection . . . and I think the wisewomen usually say something about hearths, but I can't remember. Your hearth fire burns, or I make a place for you at mine. Whatever the right words are, let's agree they've been spoken." I gaze up at Tuoni's weathered face and wait for something to change. Am I supposed to feel different?

"I don't know if it worked," I admit, my hope dwindling. "Maybe it can't work unless you make the vow too. I—*ahh*—" I cry out in pain as a heat like fire courses through my hand where I'm touching the death god's face. I try to pull away, but I can't. The alder tree is burning from the inside out. No—wait—the tree isn't on fire. The *god* is on fire. I whimper, tears stinging my eyes as his skin turns molten. Flames dance in his dark eye as the tree around him begins to melt away.

Oh gods, it's working. He's breaking free.

I stumble back as a flaming hand wraps itself around my wrist, steadying me. The flames warm me, but they don't burn. A thick metal chain dangles from the death god's wrist, proof of his long captivity. I turn my wrist in his grasp, marveling as I take hold of his hand. It's strong as iron, unyielding.

Holding tight to my husband, I pull him from the tree. The god of death steps forward, towering head and shoulders over me. He sheds his cloak of fire, leaving it burning in the trunk of the ruined alder. I cough from the smoke as the tree crackles and snaps.

"Aina," he says with a deep, rasping voice.

I'm rooted to the spot. The raven couldn't speak to me, but the god can.

Fire gives way to smoke and shadow as he changes before my eyes, burning away all remnants of his alder cage. I blink, taking in the face of a hunter. He's not quite handsome . . . or is he? There's an ageless quality to his features. He looks at once wise and ancient, virile and strong. His black hair is long, falling past his shoulders. It's unkempt, dusted with soot that falls from the burning tree like snow. He's clad in dark breeches and boots, a thick, black wool jerkin, a woven leather belt. He carries an axe at his hip, etched to match the knife at my hip. A wolf pelt rests on his shoulders over a long black cloak, making him appear even larger as he stands before me.

He looks . . . mortal. All except for those eyes. They contain such depth—ice and darkness, spirit and shadow. These are no mortal eyes. But this could all be a trick. Tuonetar likes to change appearance to lure her victims in. I suppose I expected Tuoni to match her in hideousness, or perhaps paint himself with blood and wear horns like Kalma.

In the angle of his cheeks and the arch of his nose, I see only the raven. I see my friend. "Tuoni . . ." Lifting my bleeding hand, I trace the cut on his cheek that has already healed. The only proof of our marriage is a faint white scar.

Taking my hand in both of his, he turns it over, exposing my cut. "My Aina," he says, stroking a finger over the wound.

A chill colder than ice seeps through my skin, making me shiver. When I look down, the cut is healed. I, too, bear only a thin, white scar as proof of my marriage to the god of death.

"Now we are one," he intones, his voice weaving through the very fabric of my soul, burrowing itself into the core of me. He raises my hand to his lips, pressing a soft kiss to my knuckles. "I wanted it to be you." He meets my gaze, the intensity of those mismatched eyes holding me captive. "From this moment, there is only you."

Part Three

Come with me, thou lovely virgin,
Be my bride and life-companion,
Share with me my joys and sorrows,
Be my honored wife hereafter.

—Rune 18. *The Kalevala*

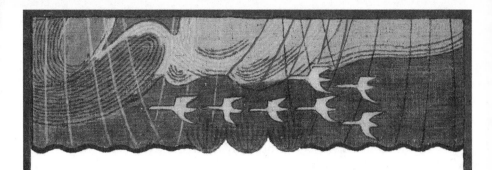

Siiri

A NOISE STIRS ME from my sleep. I open one eye to find myself passed out on the floor of Väinämöinen's hut. I nearly forget I'm naked under this heavy bear pelt when I sit up. It slips from my shoulders, but I catch it just in time.

Väinämöinen crouches by the fire across from me, stacking it with kindling and fresh wood.

"How long was I asleep?" I say, trying to suck on my tongue to bring a little moisture back to my mouth. It feels dry as bark.

"Two days." He drops down to his hands, lowering his face to the fire. He puffs out his cheeks and blows, his mustache fluttering as he gives the fire new life.

So, he already bent his iron rules for me. He said he wanted me gone by morning. That was two days ago. I smile. *Maybe there's a chance . . .*

I pull my warm, dry clothes under the pelt and shimmy into them. "I've lost two days," I say, sitting up. "We need to get started."

"Good idea. I packed for you. There's enough food to see you south." He points over his shoulder to where a leather pack waits by the door. "The weather should stay clear. You'll likely have Revontulet's light to guide your way."

"I'm not leaving." I tie back my mess of unevenly chopped hair. "We need to start my training."

Väinämöinen pauses, eyeing me across the fire. "I thought I already told you, *no*."

I groan as I get to my feet, testing my balance and my strength. "Look, old man, I'm not asking you to go to Tuonela. I'm asking you to show me how to get there. The risk I take will be all my own."

"You have no idea what you risk." Pushing off the ground, he moves away from the fire, leaning against the pinewood wall of the hut. "You say you met Kalma?"

"I fought her with my bare hands. She gave me this," I add, pointing to the scar on my brow.

"How do you know it was Kalma?"

I cross my arms. "Shall I describe her to you?"

He says nothing, waiting.

"Kalma is tall," I begin. "As tall as you. She wears tattered black robes and paints her face with blood. Her eyes are two dark orbs, like looking into a bottomless well. And her hands . . ." I glance down at his hands folded over his lap. "They're like yours . . . with those tattoos."

He grunts, stuffing his hands in his pockets.

"Plus, there's the smell," I go on. "Gather every dead animal and every pile of dung you can find, and it still wouldn't match her awful stench."

He shrugs. "Fine. You met Kalma. And which goddess gave you that one?" he says, pointing to the bruise on my other temple.

I ghost a finger over it. "This wasn't a goddess's work. It

was from a pair of Lumi's trappers in the south. They wanted something from me I wasn't willing to give. They're dead now. And Lumi will join them if she stands in my way."

"You're not afraid of her either, then, I suppose," he says, lips pursed in mild amusement.

"Should I be?"

His mustache twitches, and he ignores my question. "Now, about this bear . . ."

"I told you, he's my friend. He's no threat to me."

"But is he a threat to *me*?"

"Why would a bear be a threat to you?"

He huffs, pulling a pipe from his pocket. "You really know nothing about magic, do you?"

"What do you mean?"

"I'm not concerned about the bear," he says, stuffing the pipe with a bit of smoking leaf. Returning to the hearth, he lights it at the fire. "I'm concerned about who's *inside* the bear." A haze of white smoke wafts my way, sweet with notes of vanilla, cardamom, and raspberry.

"What do you mean?" I ask again.

"In my experience, bears care more about finding berries and succulent fish. This close to winter, they look for a den to sleep through the long night. But your bear fights witches and breaks ice. More to the point, he knows how to find me, a shaman who chooses to be lost. Do you see why that might be concerning?"

I've had my suspicions, but I didn't have time to stop and consider. Everything happened so quickly. "You believe someone might be inside Kal? Who?"

"How am I to know without questioning the bear?" He takes another long drag from his pipe. "If the bear died a watery death in that lake, whoever was inside him will have either perished with him or lost their host."

I drop back down to the pelts, crossing my legs. "Their host?"

"Certain väki require a host, meaning they cannot take physical form," he explains. "But they can possess another's body—human, animal, tree."

His words stir up a memory that's plagued me of late, a memory of Aina holding my hand, begging me to come back to her. "I was once taken ill by a veden väki," I say.

He relaxes back against the pinewood once more, pipe clenched between his teeth. "A water spirit? Nasty little sprites. How did you banish it?"

"My mummi used fire. She says only fire can fight water. She took me to the sauna and left me there for a half a day while the väki battled inside me."

He considers me, his eyes narrowing. "It takes a strong constitution to survive a water väki without the aid of a shaman's spell . . . and an even stronger spirit to host a fire väki. You say you had both in you at once?"

I hold his gaze. "Give me a chance, Väinämöinen. You'll see I'm more than strong enough for this task. I promise I won't be a burden. I'll hunt my own food, melt my own water. I'll gather and split wood, even heat water for your baths if you wish. I'll do anything except lie with you and—"

He lifts a hand in protest. "Lie with me? You're little more than a child."

"That hasn't stopped others from trying." I peel down the edge of my bandaged throat to show him my wound. "And I'm not a child. I may be younger than you, but isn't everyone?"

He snorts despite himself. "Call me 'old' again, and see what happens."

I ignore his threat. "Teach me how to get someone out of Tuonela alive."

He just shakes his head, that same shadow of fear flickering in his deep blue eyes. "What you ask is impossible."

I smile. "Fighting Kalma was impossible too. Escaping Lumi and her wolves was impossible. Finding a shaman who doesn't want to be found was impossible. And yet, here I am. I don't doubt that I can do the impossible. Why do you?"

He sighs again, stretching out his long legs before the fire. "I shared your faith once. I thought there was nothing I couldn't do."

"What happened?"

He holds my gaze through the flames, his eyes taking on a hollowness as he searches my face. "I survived the impossible too," he replies, his voice haunted but sincere. "Surviving it too many times is a fate worse than death. I don't want this life for you. Please don't ask me to help you."

"I have no choice." I shrug. "Help me, Väinämöinen."

He grunts. "Gods, you're relentless. You're worse than a horsefly. Who is this person for whom you would risk so much?"

I've had a long time to consider what I might say, how I might persuade him. In all the stories and songs of his great adventures, Väinämöinen was only ever motivated by one thing. I watch the shadows cast by flames over his face. "You had a great love once . . . a love you lost."

He goes still.

"I've heard all your songs. You wanted to marry the fair sister of your rival, Joukahainen. You asked for her hand, but her brother forced you to win her in a contest of strength. He lost, but she chose to die rather than betray him. Your story ends in sorrow." The age lines around his eyes crease. "You couldn't be with your beloved Aino—"

"I know my own damn songs," he mutters, blowing out a cloud of smoke.

"Well, I'm still writing mine." I crawl around the hearth to take his tattooed hand, holding it in both of my own. "My Aina chose to die to *save* me. That's the depth of the love we share. She didn't think twice. She let Kalma take her to spare me. You ask who she is? Let me tell you our stories, and you can decide for yourself if I am right to save her at any cost."

Tears well in his blue eyes. "Her name is Aina?"

I nod, giving his hand a squeeze. "Let me tell you *our* story. Let me tell you about my dearest friend."

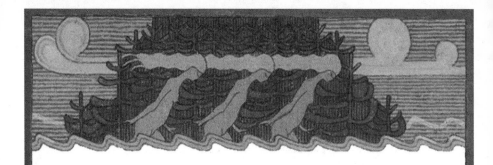

Aina

27

I'M STANDING IN THE dark of the forest, snow on the ground, a tree burning to ash before my eyes, and I'm not alone. I stand in my husband's embrace. The word sounds so strange to me, even unspoken. Husband. *My* husband. I take in the features of his bearded face—the tilt of his lips, the wild tangle of his black hair, the way the scar over his eye creases as he gazes down at me. I shift my hold on him, hands trembling as I run my palms over his forearms.

"We must finish the ceremony," he says in that deep voice. It's rich and melodic yet edged in iron. He's not asking me. His hands are firm against my hips, keeping me close.

I nod, heart in my throat. "Yes, I—tell me what to do."

His mismatched eyes watch me, so like my raven. All this time, he was Jaako? In the hours of my long confinement, he was always there. I whispered my secrets to him in the dark, all my heart's desires. He knows everything about me. But I know nothing of him, at least nothing real. I don't know the limits of his magic. He can become a raven, control fire and the dead, change his appearance at will. What else can he do? How does his magic compare to the Witch Queen's? Can he truly protect me from her?

"Aina," he says again, his hand brushing under my chin. "We must finish the ceremony."

"How do we . . ." As soon as the words leave my mouth, I pull away from him. "Oh—my lord, but I—I've never—"

"I will not hurt you," he soothes, bringing his lips towards mine. "I vowed kindness, remember? It's only a kiss."

But it's not only a kiss to me. I've never kissed a man before. A few boys in the village have asked. Two even tried without asking. Siiri took care of one. The lad couldn't sit for a week. Her brothers took care of the other. Now my new husband wants to kiss me. He wants to bind me to him, blood with blood, soul with soul. The curse is not broken until our marriage is sealed. His face inches closer, one calloused hand cupping my cheek. I hold still, knowing Tuoni is about to kiss me.

Tuoni.

Recalling his name, the dream of standing with a handsome stranger in the dark snaps with the violence of a tree crashing to earth. Tuoni, god of death, holds me in his arms. Death wears many faces for me now—Kalma the destroyer, Tuonetar the deceiver. His face overwhelms me—the intensity in his iron gaze, the determined set of his jaw. I see the truth in his eyes: He wants me. He *craves* me. He means to claim me for his own.

"Wait." I step back, tripping on the hem of my dress. My cowl slips from my hair, falling around my shoulders.

He glances around the dark wood, seeing things I can't. "Aina, we have little time." He holds out a hand to me, the chains of his long confinement still dangling from his wrist.

"Come, my love. The coup has begun, but my curse is not yet fully broken—"

"Wait," I say again, clutching at my chest. My heart feels like it's beating more quickly than a bee's wings. "All this time—all these deaths—and now you're here. You're . . . *you*."

He lowers his hand back to his side, his dark brow furrowed. "I am me, yes." He tips his head slightly to the side, so like the raven. "I fail to understand why you hesitate. A moment ago, you were so sure—"

"A moment ago, you were a tree!" I drag both hands through my hair. "Before that you were a raven. Oh gods, this is madness. This can't be real. No, no, no—"

"Aina . . ." He approaches as if I'm a startled doe. He's so tall, his shoulders broad, even under the thickness of the wolf pelt. His aura pulls at me, luring me closer. My very blood hums as I feel a kind of need, an ache to be closer to him. Stepping away makes the humming louder.

"What is this?" I whisper, one hand over my heart. "This humming. This feeling."

"I can't be sure," he replies. "I think it must be our blood bond."

My brows lift in surprise. "You feel it too?"

He nods, pressing a large hand over his chest. "I feel you here, my love. I feel your fear, your hesitancy. It coils under my ribs like a basket of eels. It is . . . strange," he adds with a smile.

"And I feel your surety," I say, awed by the realization. His confidence sits like a stone in my chest, leaving less space for my doubt. He fears nothing. Why would he? I feel more too—his curiosity, his eagerness, his barely contained rage. He wants to kiss me nearly as badly as he wants to rip Tuonetar from her throne and cast her into a fiery pit.

"You're afraid of me," he murmurs.

I can feel him tugging at the threads of our strange new bond. Weighted warps tie us together. Like a weaver, he reaches out, plucking at each thread, testing it, learning how it fits within the tapestry of us.

"You fear I mean to trick you as Tuonetar did," he says, so easily unraveling me. "You fear more cruelty, more violence."

"Of course I do. How can I not in this dark place?"

"Tuonela is a peaceful realm—"

"You have been absent for a long time, my lord," I say over him. "The Tuonela I know is a land of unspeakable cruelty, a land of senseless death, panic, and festering hopelessness. Even your daughters are sick with it."

"Tuonetar is a curse on this realm," he growls. "She infects everything with her poison. The Tuonela you know is diseased, Aina. It reflects her chaos." He holds out his hand again. "Together, you and I will set it right."

I feel him inside my chest, pulling at me through the blood bond. "Did you know this would happen? Did you know the marriage would bind us in this way?"

He's quiet for a moment. "I hoped," he admits.

I search his face, determined to understand. "Explain."

"Others among the gods have completed the ritual of marriage in the old way," he replies. "Tapio and Mielikki, Ahti and Vellamo—they are joined in all ways. They have children of their blood. So I knew what to anticipate. But as you are mortal, I expected it to feel more . . . muted. I am quite pleased at your vibrancy," he adds, rubbing at his chest again. "The fragility of your life is like a tender flower blooming too early in a bed of snow. You're so scared of death. It fascinates me—"

"I told you, my lord, I'm not afraid of death," I counter. "I'm afraid of *dying*. I'm afraid of how the Witch Queen will torment me." Tears sting my eyes as I glance around. "This all feels like one more trick. And I still don't understand—why did you *do* this? To what possible end could you have need of a mortal bride?"

"Why does anyone marry? Is it not the condition of life to find someone to pass through it at your side? A partner and helpmate? Someone to share with you in all your burdens and triumphs?" He pauses, his expression veiled. "But all mortals come to me already dead. Can't you understand? I seek the joy and wonder of watching a mortal live. I want to see it for myself. I want to hold your mortality in my hands and marvel at it, for you are so beautifully made. Do you not see how rare you are in this realm? How precious—"

"If you wanted to see how mortals live, then go to the realm of the living," I cry. "Do not drag us down here to rot in the dark. You are utterly selfish, my lord. If you truly cared for mortals as you claim, you would never have done this to me, to any of us. You would seek us out in the light of day—"

"I cannot leave this place." He speaks softly, his words swollen with sadness.

I go still, chest heaving. "No—I—Kalma, she came for us. And Loviatar said—"

"My daughters may leave Tuonela. They come and go at will. But I am bound to this place. I *am* Tuonela, and it is me. I cannot leave." He steps closer, taking me by the shoulders. "And I *never* wanted this, I swear it on my undying life. I never meant to hurt any of you. But Tuonetar has always wanted to rule on her own. She saw an opening, and she took it. I intend to repay her duplicity tenfold. I will take everything from her, and you will help me."

"What can you possibly expect me to do beyond freeing you?"

"You are my wife, bonded to me by blood," he declares. "Seal this marriage, and Tuonela shall be yours. Together, we will cleanse it of Tuonetar's fetid magic. We will make it beautiful again, peaceful and pure."

"Do I have a choice?"

He smiles softly. "Aina, you've chosen this every step of the way."

My hands wrap around his wrists, my fingers brushing the cold metal of his chains. "What choices have I made, my lord?"

"You chose to save your Siiri," he replies. "You had a choice to open your window to me as the raven. You had a choice to show me kindness, to share what little you had with me. I will tell you now that the others were not so kind. Most of the maidens never opened their windows, too afraid even to look out. Those who did never shared food with me. Some even fought to make *me* their next meal."

I fight a sad smile, thinking of Lilja. No doubt she would have cooked him in a pot if he had been too slow to get away.

"But you gave everything away," he goes on, pride in his voice. "You shared your food and your fire, your stories, your laughter. Even when you were scared, even when you felt hopeless, you always had a smile for me, your raven."

This is impossible. I can't think with him this close. Can't breathe.

His thumbs brush the tears from my cheeks as he lowers his face towards mine. "You had so little to give, yet still you shared more. You shared your bed and your warmth. You shared the comfort of your touch. Even trapped as I was as the raven, you came to need me . . . as I needed you. I need you still. I ache with it, my love."

My cheeks warm at his words, even more so at the memory of stroking his feathered back in the dark of my room, seeking out his comfort. I cannot lie to him, not with this surge of feeling humming along the threads of our blood bond. But I try anyway. "That's not fair, my lord. I didn't know who you really were—"

"But you knew the raven was more than he seemed. You knew, Aina. You're far too clever to have doubted who and what I was. The moment you saw me in the tree, you became resolved. I saw it in your eyes. You could have walked away, but you stood before the alder tree as my equal, a queen before her king. Will you now deny what we both know hides in the center of your tender, beating heart?"

My heart dares try to stop. "What do we know?"

A smile curves his mouth as he brushes a thumb over my parted lips. "We know you want to kiss me. You've had a taste of power, and now you want more. You're desperate for it—"

I slap his hand away. "I have no power, my lord. I have nothing."

"Is that really what you think?" He looks almost amused. It riles me still further.

"You say I gave you everything, and it's true," I reply. "I gave the raven every story, every hope and fear, every dream. I kept nothing for myself. There is nowhere left to hide. You have all you need to destroy me, and I am powerless to stop you."

"You're wrong." He takes me by the wrist, turning my hand palm up. "You want to know your power, wife?" Slowly, he traces a finger over the faint white scar on my palm. "You have the god of death in the palm of your hand."

I shiver, too enraptured to pull away.

He lowers his forehead until it's all but touching mine. "Mortals pray for rain and a good harvest. They worship Ukko and Tapio. The others are honored with festivals and sacrifices. Meanwhile, I am feared. Only feared. My name is whispered in the dark. My world is the setting of your nightmares. No one can escape me, mortal or immortal. Yes, I am all power and control . . . and I am yours."

Holding tight to my wrist, he lifts my hand, pressing it flat against the thick wool of his tunic, just over his heart. "You need no weapons nor secret magic to destroy me, wife. Just keep recoiling from my touch. Deny me your love. Break me open with your indifference. You will devastate me."

His words leave me breathless. The surety of them is reinforced through our bond. He is stone wrapped in iron, unyielding, steadfast. "You deserve a wife of your choosing—"

"I *have* chosen," he counters. "I choose the mortal who clings to fragile hope like dew on the grass. I choose the mortal who resolutely sees the good in everyone. You saw it in me as the raven. You see it in the dead, in your fellow captives, even in my wretched daughters, so undeserving of the name. You are a light in the darkness that is my world of unending night."

I tremble as his words bloom in my chest, spreading heat down to my very core.

He inches closer, his hand splaying protectively over mine on his chest. "In all my years of undying, I have never felt the warmth of the sun on my face . . . until *you* looked at me. You say you are powerless, but it is the sun that feeds the grain. My goddess, my queen, I am at your mercy."

I gasp, torn between pulling away and leaning closer. Tuoni stands before me, offering me everything—his home, his heart, a piece of his crown. This is dangerous. *He* is dangerous. Gods, but this pull between us is so strong. I feel it down to my bones. In a fit of abandon, I lift up on my toes. Clutching his tunic with both hands, I tip my chin. He's right, I have to know what it feels like, what it tastes like . . . just once.

Quivering with nerves, blood on fire, I kiss the god of death.

For the briefest of moments, I know I've caught him by surprise. He goes still, his lips unmoving against mine. Has he ever kissed a woman before? I feel his curiosity, his excitement and desire. Suddenly, his arms are around me. His lips are warm, and his beard bristles against my lips. Then he's kissing me back, his mouth slanting open. It feels strange, even as the rightness of it coils deep inside me, fusing around my very bones.

My hands brush up his chest to grip his shoulders as his strong arms wrap around my waist, nearly lifting me off the ground. I open my mouth to him, deepening our kiss. I drink of him, taking every drop of passion and need he offers me. We're both hungry and desperate, eager for more. But a snapping of branches has me breaking our kiss.

Tuoni holds tight to me. "Be at ease," he soothes. "The curse is broken. They will not harm you."

I press my back to his chest as I peer through the night. Trees loom all around. He wraps a protective arm across my chest, his hand at my shoulder. My free hand drops instinctively to the little knife at my hip.

"You won't need that." His fingers brush over mine wrapped around the knife hilt. "They're just curious."

"What's out there?" I whisper. "I can't see."

"Come," he calls out in his deep voice. "Come, meet my wife."

All around us, shadows move. On silent feet, a horde of the waking dead come stumbling forward. Dozens. More than I've ever seen at once. Many are armed soldiers bearing swords and shields, bows and arrows, great, menacing axes. Women too—old women, hunched and ragged, emaciated women sick with fevers, young women carrying dead infants in their arms.

The god of death keeps me close, his hold on me relaxed as he lets the dead step towards us. "Welcome, friends," he calls out. "Meet your new queen."

"Queen?" I whisper.

"Our kiss sealed your fate," he replies, brushing his lips to the back of my head. "My power is in you now. The dead are yours to command."

I go still, unable to stop the fear from creeping in. "It's not possible."

"Give them an order," he says, his voice low in my ear. "Prove your power."

Heart in my throat, I watch as the dead approach. More are coming through the dark. Leaning against Tuoni's firm shoulder, I call out in a trembling voice. "Please . . . don't come any closer."

As one, the dead stop at my command.

Tuoni laughs, his exuberance barreling towards me through the bond. He leans down, brushing his lips against my temple. "Come, wife. This is a new beginning. Let me show you all that Tuonela can be."

I flinch as he lets out a shrill whistle, his arm dropping away from me. An unearthly howl echoes through the trees to my left. Tuoni takes my hand, leading me forward through the snow. The sound of pounding hooves has me turning. I watch in awe as a mighty horse comes bursting through the trees. His eyes glow red as coals. Deep inside the belly of the beast are the flames of an iron furnace. His metal sides creak as he pants, tossing his head.

I clutch Tuoni as he leads me forward. He speaks to the horse in a language I don't understand. The horse snorts, his breath a billowing cloud of steam. He turns his coal-red eyes on me. "What is it?" I whisper, holding Tuoni's hand in both of my own like a scared child.

"Hiiden hevonen," he replies, giving the horse's head another pat. "A gift from the goblins, and my old friend. He's born of the mountain, forged in her unquenchable fires."

"He's fearsome," I admit. Tuoni leads me closer, his hands

lowering to my hips, and I know instantly his intention. "Oh, my lord, you cannot mean for me to ride him."

He laughs. "What better way to make an entrance?"

"An entrance where? My lord, where are we going?"

"A queen needs a throne, does she not? A witch now blights yours. But fear not, my love. You will root her out."

"Me? Tuoni, I can't—*ah*—"

The death god takes me by the hips and lifts me, placing me on the back of the great iron horse. The beast tosses his head, and I tangle my fingers in his coarse black mane.

Tuoni climbs atop the horse behind me, his arms wrapping around me to reach for the thick leather reins. The strength of his will echoes down the bond. "Tuonetar's reign of chaos is at an end. Tuonela has a new queen."

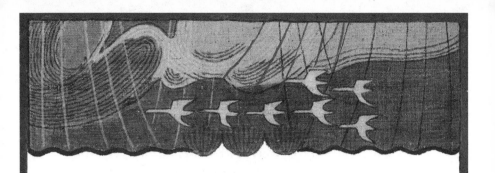

Siiri

DAY TURNS TO NIGHT, and Väinämöinen and I don't leave the hut. We sit around the fire, and I tell the greatest shaman of the ages my stories of Aina—foraging adventures in the woods, quiet nights laughing by the fire, dancing under a full moon and begging the goddess to turn us into stars. I talk until my stomach growls with hunger.

Helping myself to his stores of food, I begin preparing us an evening meal. I chop carrots and onions and a chunk of dried caribou meat for soup, thickening it with reindeer milk and seasoning it with salt and dill. Using his barley flour, I make small, unleavened rieska loaves, leaving them to cook on the hot stones of the hearth.

All the while, Väinämöinen sits with his arms crossed. The air is thick with the cloying scent of his pipe smoke. "Your Aina sounds like a rare beauty," he muses, accepting a wooden bowl of steaming soup with both hands.

My cheeks warm at the memory of her laugh—her head

tipped back, the arch of her neck, the music of her joy. "She's undeniable," I say, unable to think of a better word.

I pull my hands away and ladle a second portion of soup for myself. "She's the best person I know. She is kind where I am callous. She's caring where I'm selfish. She puts everyone else first, even to her own detriment. It's maddening."

"You love her," he says with a chuckle, accepting the rieska loaf I offer him. "First loves always cut the deepest, leaving the greatest scars."

"Of course I love her. She's my dearest friend. She's closer to me than my own sister. It's like . . ." I pause, struggling to find the words. "It's like she holds a piece of my very soul."

Across the fire, the shaman goes still.

"She was taken from me, and in that moment, something inside me snapped—something *here*." I press my hand over my gut, just beneath my ribs. As I push on the ache, a log on the fire snaps, sending up a spray of hissing sparks.

The shaman watches me with haunted eyes.

Blinking back my tears, I shrug. "Don't ask me to explain it any better. I just know I have to get her back. I can't live like this." I pluck the other rieska loaves from the hearthstone before they burn. "I feel like I'm dying. Without her, I feel dead. That's our story." I glance across the fire at him. "Does it compel you to help me?"

Without answering me, Väinämöinen tastes the soup. He takes a few slurping bites, groaning with delight. "I never figured you for the cooking type."

"My mummi taught me well. Even if I prefer to hunt and fish like my brothers."

He nods, dipping his rieska loaf into the soup and tearing into it with his teeth. Soup dribbles down his bearded chin. "You've told me of your Aina's beauty and her cleverness, her unfailing kindness. But answer me this: What is she worth to you?"

I gaze across the fire at him, studying the lines of his ancient face. "Is that not yet obvious? More than my own life."

His bright blue eyes twinkle in the firelight. "And what are you willing to risk to get her back?"

I square my shoulders, my meal forgotten. "My very life."

He nods again, his focus back on his soup. "Good. It will likely cost you that and more by the end."

"Does that mean you will help me?"

He eyes me warily. "And how do I know you won't use this knowledge for ill? Many before you have sought me out, desperate to learn the secrets of the shamans, only to use my gifts for wicked and destructive ends."

"Nothing I can do or say will convince you of the honesty of my intentions," I reply. "You must accept that there may still be some good in the world." I lean forward, elbows on my knees. "Now, tell me about the shamans."

"I am the first shaman," he replies. "From me was born the magic of combining wisdom and song. With my kantele and my drum, I sang pieces of myself across the realms, across time itself. I learned the secrets of nature and the gods. I traveled the world and heard all the stories, learned all the songs . . . and made up a few of my own along the way," he adds with a smirk. "All the magic of the shamans was born out of me."

I search his weathered face. "How old are you?"

He shrugs, draining his drinking horn of milk. He wipes the back of his hand across his mustache, smacking his lips. "I don't know anymore . . . maybe I never knew."

"But you're immortal?"

He considers my question for a moment. "I think once

I was immortal. Now, I'm not so sure. My immortality has changed. There are . . . conditions."

"What kind of conditions?"

He glares at me. "You've been here for all of two days, and you want me to trust you with my most intimate secrets? Trust is earned, Siiri."

I cross my arms, glaring right back.

"You're a brave girl, I'll give you that. And not unclever. The gods have surely blessed you, but some of your survival must be down to your own skill. And your intentions towards your friend seem true enough."

I brighten a little. "So, you'll help me? You'll teach me the ways of the shamans?"

He frowns, his blue eyes piercing as they study me. "Don't get too excited. I've told you, girl, I'm not the shaman I once was. We may both find I'm not enough."

"You'll have to be enough," I declare. "Väinämöinen, you're all I have."

An hour later, we sit side by side at a fishing hole at the edge of the frozen lake behind his hut. No foxfires light the sky tonight. Heavy clouds hang low; a winter storm is coming. The only light comes from a lantern Väinämöinen hung on a pole he wedged into the ice. We each have a fishing line in the water, fluttering our fingers so the bait appears to move.

"What do you know of shamans?" he asks, his voice muffled by the cowl wrapped around his face.

"My mummi says shamans hold the secrets of medicine and healing," I reply, through my own cowl. "They also divine the weather and make the crops grow."

He snorts. "We do nothing of the kind. To claim we hold

knowledge in secret is an affront to a shaman. This will be your first lesson: knowledge is power. That power is always meant to be shared."

Before I can respond, there's a tug on my line. I gasp, gripping it tighter.

"Hook it, girl," the shaman grunts.

I jerk the line sharply, twice, and it gives a mighty tug back. "Got him." I wrestle it for a minute, reeling and tugging, before I pull a slippery trout from the black water. Väinämöinen lifts the lid from the basket between us, and I place the fish inside. "You were saying? Knowledge is power, and power should be shared . . ."

He mutters under his breath, something about being bested by a girl. Then he gives his own line a few irritated tugs.

"Väinämöinen?"

"Yes, knowledge is power," he repeats. "We don't hold our knowledge in secret. We learn, we explore, and we share our knowledge for the good of others. And we don't divine the weather or make crops grow. We use a stout knowledge of the natural world to inform our predictions." He points to the dark sky. "Take this weather today. What do you predict?"

I look up. "It will storm, likely within the hour."

"Yes, precisely. But how do you *know* it will storm? Does every low-hanging cloud lead to a snowstorm?"

"No, of course not."

"So, why can you look at this winter sky and tell me it will storm within the hour?"

I glance all around. "You can smell it in the air, I suppose. It smells like a storm. And the clouds are thick and low to the ground. They swell heavy with snow."

"What else?"

I watch the clouds move. "There's a stillness too, a quiet in the trees."

"What else?"

Something moving through the dark trees near the barn catches my eye. Light pools from a pair of lanterns hanging by the open doors. "The reindeer are moving back towards the barn," I say. "They know it's coming too."

"Good. A shaman collects all these pieces of knowledge and uses them to improve people's lives. This is where your mummi gets her ideas about secret medicine and magic crops." He chuckles. "The great truth is that shamans aren't more magical than everybody else, just cleverer. And they put that cleverness to use to help people, never to harm them," he adds, pointing a gloved finger in my face. "That's important, Siiri. If a shaman uses their knowledge to cause undue harm, it can lead to grave consequences."

I nod, feeling suddenly nervous.

"Now, not all shamans can turn their wisdom into magic," he goes on, tugging lightly on his line. "For a rare few, as our knowledge grows, so too can our ability to cast spells, influence väki, and even travel the realms in different forms."

My mind races with the possibilities. "What knowledge must I gain to get to Aina? How will I know if I can turn my knowledge into magic?"

He lets out a little laugh, but then he shakes his head. "So young . . . so foolish . . . so eager to put your neck in a noose."

"You won't dissuade me, old man. I've come all this way. I've battled men and monsters. I've fought and starved and nearly died." I pause, giving him the truth I only half revealed earlier. "I've killed, Väinämöinen. Men have died by my hand on this quest. And now I have no time left to waste. Aina needs me, so test me. See if I have what it takes."

Slowly, he nods. "I will test you."

I can't help the smile that lights my face.

The shaman just chuckles, giving his fishing line another pull. "You may come to regret asking."

"Again," Väinämöinen barks.

"Let me catch my breath," I pant. The air is sharp in my lungs, cold enough to burn when I wheeze. I clutch my side, arms trembling with fatigue. It's been three days, and this shaman is relentless.

"Do you think Lumi will let you catch your breath? Or Kalma? Or the Witch Queen herself? Master the sword; master your fatigue. They do not control you, Siiri. You control them. Again."

With a growl of frustration, I take up my stance in the snow, gripping the shaman's longsword with both hands. We've been at this for hours today. Väinämöinen is putting me through my paces with every weapon he owns. He says he won't know where to begin with my training until he learns where my knowledge ends.

Before weapons training, he dragged me through the woods all around his hut, asking me a thousand and one questions, watching as I proved the strength of my foraging and trapping skills. *How do reindeer find food in winter? Where are the best places to look for mushrooms? How do you stop bleeding? Wood from what trees is best for crafting bows and arrows? How do you cure a fever?* If I didn't know the answer, Väinämöinen instructed me. Then he drilled me throughout the day, making sure I remembered his long-winded answers.

I raise my sword and duck left as he comes in swinging, growling like a bear. He fights like one too, with wide movements and sheer brute force. I'm faster, but he's so much taller, and the arc of his blade is deadly. Metal clangs, echoing around the trees as I parry a blow. I grit my teeth, the shock of that blow radiating down my elbow and up into my shoulder.

"You fight like a stone giant," I mutter, darting away as he takes another swing at me. He's skillful enough not to cut me, but each strike with the blade's broad side still hurts.

"Have you ever met a stone giant, fool girl? They don't bother with metal blades. They crush you with their bare hands. A stone giant would pop your skull with a pinch of their fingers, like squeezing an overripe berry."

I grimace at the gruesome image. "And what does all this mean—swinging a sword and foraging for winter moss? Will it help me save Aina?"

"You've never been to Tuonela," he challenges. "How will you find your way through a dark forest? There will be no stars or moon to guide your way. But knowing how moss grows on trees will provide you direction. And Tuoni's guards are all swordsmen. They will hunt you to the river's edge. They will not be complacent, so neither can you be."

With a scowl, I redouble my efforts, swinging low and fast. Väinämöinen ducks at the last second, but it's a close escape. I grip the blade tighter and lunge again, determined to make him bleed. He parries me easily, laughing as he dances away.

"You're too strong," I pant, rolling my shoulder with a wince. "Each blow feels like it will break my arm."

"You're too weak," he counters, letting his own weapon fall to his side. "I can't teach you all I know about wielding a sword in an afternoon. We'll have to rely on your skills with a bow."

Defeat surges through me, making my eyes sting with tears of frustration. "I can do it. I can fight."

"I don't doubt that," he says, crossing through the snow to my side. "You have the heart of a bear and the sharp claws of an eagle. Your spirit is strong, Siiri. That will count for a lot."

He gives my shoulder a squeeze. "Come inside. You need food and rest."

For the first time in days, he helps me cook a meal. Together, we grill a few fish we caught in the lake. He's acquired a taste for my rieska loaves, so I leave a few of those to bake on the hearthstone. We boil the winter mushrooms and tubers I foraged this morning in a pot.

"You're a bright girl," he begrudgingly admits as we lounge around the fire after our meal. "And I'd like to meet this mummi of yours."

I smile. I've taken to telling him Mummi's stories at night. That's how he's gauging my knowledge of the gods. I don't tell the stories as well as Mummi, but I still get a few laughs and appreciative smiles. "And this will help?" I ask again. "Knowing all this will help me save Aina?"

"It certainly can't hurt," he replies. "Crossing the realms is no easy thing, Siiri. Plenty of shamans could never manage it. The only chance of succeeding is if your heart *and* your head are in the right place." He gives me a level look, his mustache twitching. "You seem to have the cleverness. And you have more than enough heart."

I bloom under his praise, sitting up straighter. As he searches his pockets for his pipe, I glance around the hut, settling on the kantele in the corner. It's a beautiful, hand-crafted zither. It hasn't escaped my notice that in our short time together, his eye never seems to land on it. "Will you play something for me?"

He stuffs some loose leaf into his pipe, not looking up. "What?"

"In all the stories, you're playing the kantele. I can't play, so you'll have to teach me."

"You don't need to play the kantele to be a shaman," he says quickly.

Setting my bowl of soup aside, I search his face. "Väinämöinen . . . are you afraid of it?"

"Don't be ridiculous." He makes a fuss of lighting his pipe and taking a long drag, blowing sweet smoke into the air.

From his reaction, I know I should let this lie. But that's just not in my nature. "You never play it," I press. "You never even look at it. Why?"

He makes a grand gesture of slowly turning his head to gaze in the direction of the zither. He puffs out another cloud of pipe smoke. "I don't play anymore. I can't. Not since . . ."

I wait for him to finish the thought, watching his face change from frustration to sadness to deep longing.

He clears his throat. "To make a kantele really sing, you've got to put your whole heart and soul into it . . . and mine's been missing for a very long time."

"Your heart?"

He turns away from the instrument, wiping a tear from his eye. "No . . . my soul."

"What happened to you?" I whisper.

"You wouldn't understand."

"Say that again, and I'll burn this hut down around your ears."

He puffs on his pipe, blowing smoke my way.

I search his face, desperate to know the truth. "When I first arrived, you asked if I meant to kill you. Many have tried, you said. Lumi certainly wants you dead, though it seems important that she do the deed herself. Why? What did you do? Why would people hunt you?"

"You don't get to know everything just because you're curious," he mutters. "My secrets are my own."

"I thought shamans don't keep secrets," I challenge. "You said your wisdom belongs to the people. There is knowledge you possess, and I'm asking for it. You are bound as a shaman to share what you know. Now, what happened to Väinämöinen?"

He holds my gaze. After a moment, his mustache twitches. "You are prodigiously clever. I think I'd rather hear you say what you think happened."

I close my eyes, imagining my mummi singing his farewell song. I recite the words, my voice soft, "Let time pass, let days go by . . . needed will I be again. Longed for, looked for . . . I will bring a new day."

He stills, his blue eyes piercing me.

"I don't think you left as the songs tell us," I say. "As *your* song tells us."

"Oh, no?"

"No, it wasn't some magnanimous gesture. It wasn't prophecy. You were on the run . . . weren't you?"

He says nothing.

"You disappeared without a trace, gone forever from the lands of Kalevala with promises to return. But that was just the song *you* sang. You never actually intended to return, did you? Why? What happened to you? What has you running scared, old man?"

Slowly, he turns his pipe in his hands, his face wearing all the lines of his age. The fire dances, casting him in shadows. "I told you," he says, voice low. "I endured the impossible. This is how I survive. If I let the witches find me, I'll be hunted. I'm too old to fight them as I once I did, Siiri. Too weak and too tired, body and soul. This time, I'll certainly be killed . . . and Tuonetar will win."

"Tuonetar? What does the Witch Queen have to do with this?"

His own gaze takes on a haunting look of sadness. "Everything."

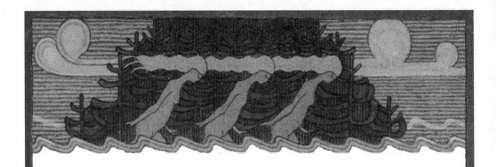

Aina

THE IRON HORSE RACES through the dark woods of Tuonela. Tuoni's arms hold me fast as I hold on for dear life, my fingers tangled in the horse's mane. We crest a hill, breaking through the trees. All across the frozen clearing, the dead wait for us, forming a kind of processional line that leads up the hill. Tuoni's palace looms in the dark, lit by a thousand flaming torches, so much brighter and more welcoming than before. The two stone towers spiral into the sky to north and south, separated in the middle by the grand receiving hall.

The horse slows to a trot as trumpets blast in welcome from the walls of the palace. More dead swarm the field, raising banners and slamming their swords and axes against their shields, welcoming the lord of death home. As we approach the palace gates, they swing open to admit us, revealing a dark courtyard.

Foreboding sinks deep in my chest. The echo of my husband's hesitation down the bond leaves me feeling sick. "Why is she not resisting us?"

He doesn't answer, and the sick feeling grows.

The horse sweeps into the dark courtyard, his hooves clattering on the stones.

"Guards!" Tuoni shouts.

Feet stomp in thick boots. Swords rattle. In moments, a troop of soldiers files in from behind us. They flood the courtyard, every fifth one armed with a torch that casts brilliant light.

I blink, raising a hand to shield my eyes. This courtyard is the one I passed through every morning on my way to the weaving room. The walled garden is to the right, the bustling kitchen courtyard to the left.

Tuoni presses against my back, bending me forward as he slips off the giant horse and drops to the ground. Then he reaches both hands up for me, waiting. I slide off the iron horse's back and Tuoni catches me easily. He sets me on my feet, his strong hands at my waist. "Look at me," he says, his voice soft.

I lift my chin to meet his mismatched gaze.

"You are queen now." He places a hand over my heart, his large fingers splayed. "Take your power, Aina. You fought for this moment—for yourself, for me, for all the maidens past and future who might be abused by the Witch Queen. I go with you, but it will be for you to finish what you started. Are you ready?"

Overthrow the Witch Queen. How can anyone be ready for such a task? My mind flashes with images of great heroes who journeyed to Tuonela to perform feats of daring. Never mind that most of those heroes died a fool's death. I have no sword or kantele. I have no warrior's heart. My weapon is the knitting needle. My power, according to Tuoni, is the ability to see the good in people. But what good is there in such a twisted witch?

"Aina . . ." Tuoni cups my cheek. The chain of his confinement still hangs from his wrist. Feeling the sting of that cold metal against my skin, my resolve hardens.

"I'm ready."

With a nod, he offers his hand, a gallant lord to his lady. Taking a deep breath, I place my hand atop his. Not waiting another moment, he strides on, his dead guard making way for us. They stomp their feet in time to our steps, rattling their swords against their shields as we walk. Tuoni strides with purpose. All doors open to him. Torches flare to life as he passes. I glance around, gasping in surprise as each room we enter changes. Loviatar warned me this would happen. The magic of the palace is responding to his presence; the very walls are welcoming him home.

Cold and dark are swept away with warm golden light. Spiders skitter down into cracks; walls of twisted skulls are transformed. No more, the anguished faces of the tortured. Now there are thick tapestries depicting scenes of nature and the gods. The stone floors are covered in fragrant rush mats that keep away the cold. It's beautiful to behold. Tuonetar's magic is nothing to Tuoni's. This thought fills me with confidence as we reach the receiving room, the room where I first met the other girls.

"Stay close to me," I whisper, weaving my fingers through Tuoni's.

He lowers our hands between us and nods at the guards to the left and right of the doors. A trumpet sounds from within, and the guards push the doors open. Our retinue floods in first, their flaming torches warming me as they pass.

Tuoni squeezes my hand. "Come, wife." He leads me forward, sweeping into the throne room. The moment he enters, a flurry of magic bursts around the room, banishing Tuonetar's darkness. All six of the hearths blaze to life, as does the trio of great antler chandeliers. The walls now resemble the hunting lodge Tuonetar magicked on my first night in this room. Swords and shields hang between still more tapestries.

The tables are cleared away, leaving the space empty as we move towards the dais. The dead flock in behind us.

One look at Tuonetar's throne, and my heart stops. There the Witch Queen sits, the nails of her hands digging into the skulls that adorn her armrests. Only her throne resists Tuoni's magic. Everything else has succumbed to his will. His own throne is now a resplendent golden chair. No more bones, no more shadows.

But I can't look at his throne. I can't look to the other chairs where I know his daughters sit and wait for us. I can't focus on anything but the Witch Queen . . . and the skeletal hand gripping her throat. I follow the bones of that hand up a robe-clad arm. I take in Kalma standing at her mother's side, holding her mother fast. The Witch Queen doesn't move, her neck stretched to accommodate Kalma's grip.

"Lord Tuoni," the Witch Queen calls. "Back from your exile at last. Such a pity. I'll always prefer you in chains."

I glance to Tuoni, but he doesn't look my way. His eyes are locked on Tuonetar. Slowly, he smiles. "I would say I'm pleased to see you again," he calls out, his voice echoing around the hall, "but that would be a lie. I've had decades to think of how I would punish you."

Tuonetar hisses. I follow her gaze to the floor of the dais, where her willow wand rests, just out of reach. Kalma squeezes, her claws digging into Tuonetar's throat. The Witch Queen has no choice but to hold still, her bloodshot gaze shifting between us. "The sight of her on your arm is punishment enough." She turns her gaze on me. "I am going to tear you apart. But first you will watch as I make the other mortals dance, starting with the weepy one."

A soft whimper draws my attention. To the right, I see Riina, Satu, and Helmi huddled together just off the dais. Loviatar stands sentinel at their side. She looks haunting, her magic coursing through her with her a vengeance. Dark circles frame her glowing white eyes. Her blood flows black in her veins, just visible beneath her pale skin. The black lines zig and zag across her chest and up her neck like forked lightning. My gaze drops to her hands, now tipped with sharp black talons. She looks fearsome . . . and furious.

What happened while I was in the woods?

Tuonetar locks eyes with Tuoni. "You should have stayed gone, oh great crownless king. My pets and I were having such a wonderful time here without you."

I feel his rage simmering. "Tuonetar, you're a tiresome bore. Your madness has grown tedious, your threats empty. And now you're finished. I come at last to reclaim what is mine."

She leans into the grip of Kalma's hand, grinning as Kalma's talons dig deep enough to draw blood. "Tell me, my king, how did it feel, watching me take everything from you? Did you enjoy your view, powerless to stop me as I snuffed the life out of all those maidens? What delicious mischief I've wrought. What glorious fun."

His hand goes stiff in mine, his fury pounding in my chest like the beat of a hammer to an anvil. "You are right," he replies. "It was not in my power to stop you. My task was to watch and wait . . . wait until your own schemes backed you into a corner, wait until even our most wretched of daughters grew sick of your twisted games, wait until one would come along worthy enough to fight you and win."

Her gaze darts to me. "If that squirming worm thinks to take my crown, she'll have to fight me for it. I am not so easy to usurp as you—"

"Enough!" Tuoni's rage boils over. "Great Mother hear me, I will rip you from that chair and rend you to pieces." Shadows pool out at his feet, creeping towards the Witch Queen. Her face lights with excitement, pleased to get a rise out of him. She wants to bait him into action. She wants him to lower his guard and distract Kalma. Oh gods, she wants her wand . . . and then she'll kill us all.

"Tuoni, stop," I call out, finding my voice at last.

He pauses, glancing over his shoulder at me.

I step forward. "This is my fight, remember? I started this, and I will finish it."

"Yes, let the creeping creature come," Tuonetar sneers. "Let's watch her wriggle and writhe as I take off her fingers one by one." Her grin spreads, flashing her mouth of cracked and blackened teeth.

Tuoni turns. "If you touch her—"

"My lord, *please*," I beg, my hand brushing his shoulder. I tug at the threads of our bond, seeking out the cords of trust and patience. Whatever happens, I have to stop him from dueling her. It's what she wants. I can't let her win again.

He stiffens, eyes still locked on the Witch Queen.

I walk past him, stopping at the foot of the dais. Ignoring the Witch Queen's seething glare, I stoop and pick up her wand.

"You *dare*—" Kalma's grip chokes back her words, and she hisses and spits like an angry cat.

In my hand, the wand quivers like an animal that doesn't want to be touched. I pinch it between two fingers, holding it away from myself. To think of the pain and suffering it has created makes me ill. "Someone please take this away," I call to the room.

A dead guard appears at my side, hands outstretched. I deposit the wand into his care, and he backs away, head bowed in deference. The Witch Queen watches, eyes wide with horror, as the dead do my bidding.

I glance from Kalma to her sisters. Vammatar sits still as a statue in her chair, flanked on either side by a sullen Kivutar and a bored Kiputyttö. Kiputyttö plays with the small stone in her hand. I can only guess what Tuonetar had her do to the other girls before we arrived. I let my gaze return to the Witch Queen, the goddess I am to usurp. I have no sword and shield. I have no strength of arm. I am Aina the nervous and scared, Aina who likes a good fire and a warm pair of socks. They don't write stories about weak little mice like me. I'll have to write my own. How shall Tuonela remember me?

I take a deep breath, finding myself in my truth: Aina the Kind, Aina the Merciful. I look past the Witch Queen, dismissing her taunting glare. I look instead to Kalma. The witch watches me with those unblinking eyes. The horns are crooked on her head, her dark hair matted, flecked with debris. I can smell her from here, her stench enough to make me gag.

It makes no sense. Why is she suddenly helping Tuoni, after serving the Witch Queen so faithfully for so long? Looking past the hideousness of her chosen appearance, I focus instead on the line of her jaw, her slender nose, her slanted cheeks. I trace the ridges of her bony chest, marked with more tattoos. One tattoo catches my eye: a raven in flight, the wingtips brushing over her heart.

The raven.

It all comes back to him.

Suddenly, I see the truth so clearly. All this time, she's been helping Tuoni. She kept bringing us here in the hopes that one of us would finally free her father. In her chaos, I suppose Tuonetar chose to see only what she wanted to see. She saw Kalma aiding her in torturing him. What fun they had together, scaring us, hurting us, killing us.

But it was Kalma in the forest who directed me to Lilja and Inari. It was Kalma who raised Inari from the dead. Kalma dragged the girls away. Did she hide them? Did she put them to rest? Her methods were cruel and misguided, but whatever kind of monster Kalma is, she's loyal to her father. She loves him in her way. For now, that's enough.

I offer her a soft smile. "Thank you, Kalma. You've made your father very happy. Would you now be so kind as to remove Tuonetar from my chair?"

"You little witch," Tuonetar shrieks, her fingers clawing at Kalma's bony hand. "You will not command *my* daughter. You—" She sputters and chokes as Kalma squeezes tighter, lifting her by the throat. "I'll kill you—wretched snake in my garden—"

Kalma lifts the Witch Queen off her throne. Tuonetar's feet dangle in the air, kicking helplessly as she tries to gain purchase. Her beautiful copper robes trail along the floor as Kalma steps back. As soon as Tuonetar is lifted away, the throne transforms. The skulls and bones are replaced with ornate silver.

"No—unhand me—" Tuonetar struggles and shrieks, fighting Kalma's iron grip as the death witch drags her back, pulling her into the shadows of the room.

Tuoni steps up behind me, placing a firm hand on my shoulder. "Come, wife."

Hearing that word, the other girls gasp. "Wife?" Riina whispers. "Did he just call her wife?" They look to me with wide eyes, shocked and confused.

Tuoni offers his hand, and I take it, letting him guide me up onto the dais. It's a surreal moment, watched by every-one—living and dead—as I take a seat on my silver throne. Beside me, Tuoni sits, taking my hand in his own. We face an odd crowd of assembled dead, the death witches, and three terrified mortal women.

"All here now must bear witness," he calls to the room. "Tuonetar is forthwith stripped of her titles and power in this realm." Turning to me, he smiles. "You will show all due deference to my wife. Kneel before Aina, Queen of Tuonela!"

As one, the dead in the room drop to one knee, their heads bowed. I fight my own trembling as I glance to where Tuoni's daughters sit. Vammatar stiffly inclines her head, a deep scowl on her face, but the twins do nothing.

"Bring forth Tuonetar," Tuoni calls with a raise of his hand.

I hold to the arms of my silver chair as Kalma sweeps out of the shadows, dragging a struggling Tuonetar along with her.

"You're all a bunch of faithless—" Tuonetar shrieks as Kalma's other hand rises to cover her mouth. She kicks and squirms, biting at her daughter's bony hand. Blood drips between Kalma's fingers, but her hand remains still, stopping the Witch Queen's poisonous words.

Tuoni rises from his golden chair. All light in the room seems to dim. I fight the urge to lean away as shadows creep outward from him. Flames flicker on his tongue as he speaks, his words laced with deep magic. "Tuonetar, I remove you from your seat of power and banish you from this court." He holds out his hands, showing the broken, dangling chains on his wrists. "These chains were once my prison. At long last, they shall be yours."

I gasp, leaning back in my throne, as the chains disappear. In another moment, Tuonetar shrieks and wails behind her gag, her body going limp in Kalma's arms. The chains are now on her wrists.

"I sentence you to a life without magic," Tuoni declares. "The chains that held me so well shall now hold you. From this day, you shall not conjure so much as a drop of jam for your porridge."

Kalma drops her mother to the floor. Tuonetar sinks like a stone to her knees, the chains rattling on the floor as she scrambles forward like a panicked spider. "My lord, no," she begs. "Anything but this—"

But Tuoni is unyielding. "A life without magic seems a fair trade for the chaos you've wrought, the mortal lives you've destroyed, the horrors you've unleashed!"

Tuonetar pushes up off the floor, her shackled hands shaking. Her body goes still, her eyes shut tight. I lean away, heart racing, as she tries to spin her magic. Then the Witch Queen screams, her body convulsing as the manacles creak and tighten. Blood like thick, black tar drips from her wrists. "Noooo," she wails. Falling forward, she pounds her fists on the stone floor, the chains rattling. She looks up, panting like a dog, her eyes locked on the king. "Do not take my magic. I will do anything, my lord. Anything you ask of me—"

Down the bond, I feel Tuoni's rage surge and break upon the rocks. He sweeps forward off the dais, the fires surging higher. They blaze with the heat of a thousand suns. I wince, blinking back tears of pain. He grabs the Witch Queen by the throat. "I asked for nothing but your fealty!" he bellows, his face inches from hers. "I have always given you a long leash, Tuonetar, but then you *choked* me with it!" He lowers his voice. "I will never take you at your word again. All friendship between us is now severed. All love, all loyalty. Was it worth it, Queen of the Ashes? Shall you now be content to rule over the worms?"

Her manacled hands wrap around his wrist as she gazes up at him with those bloodshot eyes. The blazing fires twist both their faces with flickering shadows. "Give me the chance to prove myself—"

He shoves her away in disgust. "You had a thousand chances. You've left me no choice, Tuonetar. Your chaos must now be contained."

"My chaos is the only worth I have to you," she cries from her knees. "For what am I if not a foil for your obstinate, ludicrous notions of a peaceful death?"

"You take your chaos too far," he counters, turning back towards his throne. "You always have. There must be order! This is something you could never understand."

"You're a fanciful child," she hisses, crawling after him. "There must be more to death than this tedious fade to nothing. There must be games and intrigue, surprises and shocks. For what is life without the dreadful threat of an unexpected death? You need me! You *all* need me!"

Tuoni sighs. I can feel the weariness in him. Slowly, he turns, peering down at the witch. "Why do you think I'm letting you live?"

She blinks up at him, holding out her hands. "Take off these chains. I swear I'll do better. Tuoni, my old friend, *please*—"

He holds her gaze. "Fear not, Tuonetar. You will still be a goddess. Your continued existence guarantees that at least a little chaos shall remain in death. But at long last, it will be tempered by order and justice." After a moment, he waves a tired hand. "Guards, take her."

Tuonetar shrinks back, shaking her head. "Don't do this. Tuoni, don't—"

"Secure Tuonetar in the north tower," he commands. "Her exile begins now. She shall have an armed guard night and day. No one shall be permitted in or out. Let her madness be her only companion."

"No—"

Kalma steps aside as two dead guards sweep forward. Grabbing Tuonetar under the arms, they pull her to her feet. A third guard steps to Tuoni's side and holds out the witch's willow wand. Tuoni takes it with a grimace, slipping it inside his cloak.

"Daughters," Tuonetar wails. "My darling girls, help me. I am still your mother. Don't let him lock me away!"

I glance to Loviatar. Her face is turned, not towards the Witch Queen, but towards me. She waits for me to act. My eyes grow wide as Vammatar does the same, a deep scowl marring the lines of her beautiful face. To either side of her, the twins of pain and suffering scowl, arms crossed. Even Kalma watches me. The unspoken language I share with Siiri speaks to me from all sides now. They whisper the same thing.

Do something.

"Wait." Pushing out of my chair, I stand. "My lord husband, wait."

Tuoni glares over his shoulder. "Stay out of this."

His dismissal burns in my gut. I turn instead to the guards. "Stop!" I call out.

To my continued surprise, the dead guards stop. Out of the corner of my eye, I see Vammatar smirk.

Tuoni rounds on me. "You will not interfere in this, wife. I will have justice!"

"And your justice will be tempered by *my* mercy," I counter, holding my ground.

"You cannot show Tuonetar mercy! She doesn't understand it. She will only see it as weakness."

"I do not seek mercy for Tuonetar," I counter. "I seek it for your daughters."

"None of my daughters are on trial." Glaring at them he adds an ominous, "Yet."

Taking a breath, I try to slow the beating of my heart. "I cannot pretend to know the nature of a god," I continue. "But I *do* know the nature of a daughter. I am a daughter too, my lord, and I love my mother. To banish Tuonetar is to punish your daughters. Whatever else she has done, she loves them in her way. As they love her."

His frustration with me threatens to boil over. "What is it that you want, wife?"

I glance quickly around, thinking through my options. I can't possibly let her roam free. And I won't dare remove her shackles. He's right, she'll kill me without a second thought. My gaze alights on the row of tables stacked against the far wall, and I speak before I realize I've even spoken. "Supper, my lord."

"What?"

I take a hesitant step forward. "Tuonetar will be confined to the north tower. She will wear your chains and practice no magic . . . but she will join us for supper."

He huffs a mirthless laugh. "You cannot be serious."

"Every night, she will be brought down to dine with us and your daughters," I go on. "Mercy, my lord. If not for Tuonetar, then for your children who love their mother."

"I would rather starve than break bread with you, *worm*," Tuonetar snarls.

I turn to face her. "No one said you had to eat. But you will sit at my table all the same. I've had quite enough of separating daughters from their mothers."

She scoffs. "You think you can win them over with kindness? Fool girl! They are *my* creatures. I raised them in the dark. I as good as suckled them at my breast. My chaos is theirs now. It runs like a poison in their veins. You cannot root me out."

"I would never dare try to replace you in their cold, unfeeling hearts," I reply sweetly. "You are their mother, Tuonetar. I am just their queen."

She snarls, lunging for me. The dead guards hold her back. I wave my hand in dismissal, and they drag her kicking and screaming away. As the doors slam shut, Tuoni turns to me, his hand cupping my face. "You are formidable, wife. Iron mercy suits you."

I find him a smile too, even as my heart races. Holding on to my faith, I make yet another rash decision. My left hand rises, covering his on my cheek. As I step in, I drop my right down to my belt and jerk my knife free. I angle the tip at his throat and press in with the blade hard enough to draw a drop of his immortal blood.

Tuoni goes still as stone, his dark eye glittering. The tension in the room pulls tighter than a bowstring as the remaining witches and the dead follow the line of my knife to the death god's throat.

Slowly, Tuoni presses in against the blade. "Do it, wife. Show me your violence."

"My conditions in the woods were nonnegotiable," I say. "I want to hear you say the words. Swear it to me now, before all assembled here. Swear you'll release the others and never take another mortal from the realm of the living. Swear that everyone I love is beyond the reach of your reprisal. You will never raise a hand against them or send another to do the same."

"Or what?" he taunts. "Will you cut my throat with that little knife? You'll have to be more creative than that to kill me."

In a flash, I step away, turning the knife on myself. I hold the cold metal to my own throat. "Swear your oaths aloud, or I'll open myself at your feet."

"Aina, no," one of the girls cries from the corner.

His smile falls. "Put the knife down."

I press in and wince, the cold metal cutting my tender flesh. "Swear it, my lord."

At sight of my blood, Tuoni growls, panic shivering down the bond. He lifts out his hand towards me. "Aina, don't—"

"If I cannot trust you to keep your first three promises to me, you surely won't keep the last. So, I will end it here and now, and you will have a corpse for a wife."

His eyes blaze with heat as he takes me in, his gaze settling on the knife at my throat. "Kiss me."

I blink, leaning away. "What?"

He closes the distance between us, desire for me thrumming down the bond. "Before all these witnesses, you will kiss me again. Kiss me, and I'll do as you say. I'll set them free. Now. I'll vow never to take another. But first, I want to taste your righteous fury." He leans closer, sharing my air. He overwhelms me with his closeness. "I want to see your fires lit, Aina. You're far more fearsome than you know. Show me, and I'll give you anything. Show me, and I'll give you everything."

My hand slackens on the blade. He wants my rage, and I feel I have it overflowing. It's such a strange feeling. This isn't me. I'm not a cruel or a violent person. But here in this room, where I've watched so much violence unfold, I feel I am not myself. I am something different now, something . . . *more.*

I close my eyes and think of Lilja and Salla writhing on the floor not feet from where I stand. I picture Inari in the woods, her throat cut. I think of all the death I've seen in my short life—mothers in their birthing beds, old men in their sleep, a child drowned in the stream just last spring.

Senseless deaths, sad deaths, deaths come too soon.

Now I stand before the god of death. I am his bride. I never have to watch another soul die, for I will never leave this realm again. For me, there is only death. There is only him. Like Kalma, to the raven I am bound. He looks down at me, waiting, willing me to act.

In this moment, I don't want to be the scared little mouse. I want to be a creature worthy of Tuonela, a beast of shadow and flame. Fearsome, he called me. Aina the Formidable, a mortal queen in a realm of monsters.

And I mean to survive them.

Gripping his tunic, I pull my raven closer. Blade still at my throat, I arch up on my toes and press my lips to his. He's ready this time, groaning out his need as he wraps his arms around me, holding me against him. His breath is warm against my lips, his arms like bands of iron. I can still smell the smoke of the burning alder tree on his skin. Ashes dust his hair.

His mouth opens, and I feel the flick of his tongue against my teeth. I gasp, my lips parting in surprise. He tastes like salt and cool shadow, a sharp forest wind. His embrace feels like a winter's night, my front warmed by the fire while my back prickles with the sharp chill of the frost. There is safety in his arms . . . danger too. My husband. My raven.

The blade clatters to the floor as I reach for him with both hands. He holds me tight, giving me everything. I weave my fingers into his long, black hair, and my mouth slants over his, deepening our kiss. My skin feels afire. A deep burning cores out my insides, leaving me empty and aching. I want more. More—

But I cannot forget myself.

With the same hands that pulled him closer, I push him forcefully away. He lets himself be pushed, his chest heaving out a shaky breath. I'm no less affected. I lift my trembling hands up to my face, feeling the heat of my cheeks. Not a soul in the great hall moves or breathes. A hundred sets of living and dead eyes are locked on us.

"Keep your word, husband. Bind yourself to me."

"I swear," he replies without hesitation, his hungry gaze focused on me. "I am bound to you, wife. Blood and soul."

I sigh with relief, knowing the others are free of this place, knowing Siiri, too, is safe. My father and mother, my brothers, all those I love are now under the death god's protection. My nerves return as I feel the press of eyes on me. Dropping down to one knee, I pick up the little silver knife and hold it out.

Tuoni makes no move to take it from me. "Keep it," he says, curling my fingers gently around the blade. "You never know when you might need it again."

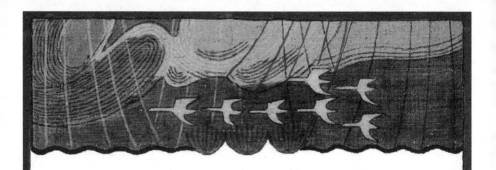

Siiri

I SIT ACROSS THE fire from Väinämöinen as he puffs on his pipe. "Tell me what happened," I repeat. "What did the Witch Queen do to you?"

He breathes out a cloud of smoke, filling the hut with the smell of sweet grass and raspberries. "It's true, I was immortal once. But then I crossed into Tuonela."

"And crossing into Tuonela drained your immortality?" Dread sinks into my chest. If the journey could take so much from one as strong as him, what might it take from me?

"No, it wasn't the crossing that did me in," he explains. "It was the Witch Queen. Tuonetar cursed me. Her wretched curse changed my immortality."

"Changed it? How?"

Leaning away, he taps the burning leaf inside his pipe out onto the hearthstone. With a sweep of his tattooed hand, he scatters the smoldering ashes. "She's a devious witch, Siiri, not one to be crossed. She was furious at me for sneaking into her realm."

"I've heard this story," I whisper. "You went to find Antero Vipunen, the great giant."

He nods. "Yes, Vipunen was a shaman . . . and my friend. He was powerful. When he died, he took his wisdom with him to Tuonela. They buried him there, body and soul. I had no choice, Siiri. I had to find him. I had to retrieve the lost spells he carried into death."

"The stories say you found him."

He nods again. "I did . . . but not before the death gods found me first. Siiri, I learned more than I wanted." He looks at me across the fire.

"I saw death with new eyes. I thwarted the Witch Queen's attempts to detain me. I found Vipunen. He was almost too far gone. It took all my cunning to wrest the lost spells from him. And then, I'm afraid, I did something reckless."

I lean forward, elbows on the table. "What did you do?"

He holds my gaze, the flames dancing in his eyes. "I stole something from the Witch Queen. I took it right out from under her nose. Then, I escaped like a thief in the night.

"Oh, she tried her hardest to stop me. In the end, I had to transform myself into a slippery snake and wriggle my way through her nets. But I made it. I returned to life."

"What did you take?" I whisper, unable to keep my eyes from darting looks around the hut in search of some magic sword or amulet.

Before the shaman can reply, a thundering roar echoes across the clearing outside.

"Was that—"

"Shhh. Wait."

We sit quiet, unmoving. Our gazes lock as we wait to hear it again. I silently pray, hoping beyond hope that my senses didn't deceive me. The shaman heard it too. Surely that must mean . . .

A second roar, weaker this time.

"It's Kal," I cry, leaping to my feet.

Väinämöinen taps out his pipe on the hearthstone. "I think your bear is back. Now we shall see who hides inside."

We collect our boots and coats from around the hut.

He grunts as I reach for the door, pulling me back. "You're waiting here."

"Not a chance." I plop his large fur hat on my own head.

"Siiri, I can't protect you and fight the väki at the same time—"

"I don't need your protection. I told you, Kal's my friend."

He grabs his axe. "Don't be a fool. At best, the väki is using you to get to me. At worst, that bear is injured, and the väki now searches for a new vessel. What better vessel than a girl with more strength than sense?"

"I'm going."

"You'll get yourself killed."

"Then I'll get to Tuonela either way. Now *move*, old man." I jerk open the door, buffeted by a burst of frigid winter air. I hurry out into the dark, my feet crunching in the deep snow.

"Siiri—godsdamn it—wait!" Väinämöinen calls after me, slamming the door shut.

Snow falls light and quiet. From the shadowy woods at the other end of the clearing, the massive form of the bear emerges. When he spots me, Kal lets out another weak cry. Väinämöinen steps in front of me, holding his axe in both hands.

Kal stumbles forward across the snow, his gait slow. Behind him, the snow is dark, stained with his blood.

"He's hurt," I cry, trying to dart around the shaman.

One tattooed hand clamps down on my shoulder. "Stay."

I wrestle against his grip. "Let me go—"

"Wait." His eyes are locked on the bear as Kal weaves his

way across the clearing. In the barn beyond the hut, the dogs yip, desperate to be set loose. They scratch at the wood of the door, growling and barking in alarm. As we watch, Kal takes one more lumbering step. He grunts, falling into the snow.

"Kal!" I jerk free of Väinämöinen and rush forward, falling to my knees at the bear's side.

"Be careful, Siiri."

I inspect Kal's injuries, and tears fill my eyes. "Oh no," I murmur. They look bad. The wolves have torn his flesh, nearly opening his side with their sharp teeth. The muscles are shredded so deeply, I can see bone. There are similar wounds at his scruff and along his haunch.

"How did he ever make it to me?"

"Magic," says the shaman, now standing at my side. "This bear should have been dead days ago. Whatever possesses him is powerful indeed."

I place both hands on the rough fur of Kal's shoulder. "You have to help him, Väinämöinen. *Please*. Save him."

The shaman crouches down. "It will be easier to extract the soul within if we let the bear die—"

"Let this bear die, and I'll kill you. Otso hear me, you will save him."

He huffs. "Call on Otso all you want, girl. That scoundrel still owes me for all the times I pulled his feet from the flames of trouble."

I feel Kal's labored breathing slow. "Please, help him."

With a muttered curse, Väinämöinen drops to his knees at my side, his axe falling into the snow. Reaching out with his weathered hands, he inspects the bear's wounds. "He knocks at death's door," he surmises with a grim frown.

"Surely there must be something you can do. You mentioned a healing song, before. You must know dozens of those. Try one now."

He shakes his head, his beard and hair dusted with falling snow. "No, he's too far gone."

"*Look* at him! Look how he still breathes. He's alive, Väinämöinen. How can you act as though he's already dead?"

"I'm sorry, I can't—"

"Don't give up so easily. *Please*, Väinämöinen, where is your heart?"

With a grunt, he grabs me by the shoulder, pulling me back. "Gods, fine. Out of the way, girl. Stand back, or I'll open him up with my axe here and now."

I scramble to my feet, taking two steps back.

"This is madness." The shaman's hands do a walking dance over the bear's form, his fingers tapping the shredded sinew and flexing over the exposed bone. "Utter madness. Doesn't understand the complexities of healing magic . . ."

"Just try. I owe him that much."

"Yes, but I owe him nothing. And this will cost me more than you know."

I wait, watching the shaman work. In moments, his shoulders go still, his hands splayed over the bear's motionless form.

"Do not stop me once I've started," he intones, his voice somehow deeper, laced with a power that has me trembling more than the winter cold.

"I won't."

"Take up my axe," he adds without turning around. "If anything comes out of this bear, kill it. Do you understand? If anything pulls me into the bear, run. Back to the hut, and bar the door."

Dropping to one knee, I pick up the shaman's axe, my cold fingers wrapping around the worn wooden shaft. "I'm ready."

The shaman places his hands directly on the worst of the bear's wounds and begins to sway from his shoulders. A low hum emanates from deep in his chest. The sound builds, flowing out of him like water from a spring. As Väinämöinen's hands move, the song changes. Words chime out, ringing with magic, their power filling the air.

The fine hairs on my arms prickle under my coat. My breath catches in my chest as I inch around the shaman's back, stepping closer to Kal's head. A blue-white light glows in the shaman's eyes. He's lost in the trance of his song as his hands move in their dance.

In moments, his palms, too, begin to glow, as he pushes his healing magic out through his hands into the bear. The light curls in wisps and smoky tendrils, seeking entry into Kal through his many wounds. A tear slips down my cheek as the muscles and sinew stitch themselves back together with threads of blue-white light.

Väinämöinen's song grows louder. The dogs in the barn fall silent. Nothing moves. Even the snow seems to wait as the shaman's haunting music fills the air. At the first sign of the bear stirring, the song stops. Kal lifts his head with a soft grunt. Then he blinks his eyes open, eyes that glow with the same light reflected in Väinämöinen. "Oh . . ." the shaman says. The light fades from his eyes with a blink, and his crystalline blue gaze is now cloudy with tears. "All this time, you were with her?"

"Is Kal all right?" I whisper, looking from the shaman to the bear.

Väinämöinen leans forward, brushing the soft fur of the bear's cheek with a shaking hand. "Old friend . . . it took you long enough to find me again."

"You know who's inside?"

"Oh yes, I know him as well as I know myself."

"Who is it?"

Väinämöinen lets out a barking laugh. "You wouldn't believe me if I told you."

I huff, offering him his axe. "I'm weary with wondering. Please, just tell me."

He gets to his feet with a tired groan, taking the axe. "Oh, we can do much better than that. I will *show* you."

My heart skips with relief as Kal stands up too, weak and heavily scarred, but alive. "You can extract the soul with Kal still alive?"

"It's easy now that I know he wants to come out. You *do* want to come, right?" he adds at the bear. Kal heaves an irritated grunt. Väinämöinen chuckles, tucking his axe into his belt. "Right, then. Siiri, would you like to meet the crafty scoundrel who led you north on an impossible quest to find the greatest hero of the ages?"

"Just work your magic, old man," I say excitedly.

"Do you see what I've had to put up with?" he says to the bear, jabbing a thumb my direction. "How you didn't leave her beneath the ice, I'll never know."

I smile despite myself at Kal's indignant growl. "He seems to like me more than you do."

"He's always had terrible taste in women," the shaman replies. Turning his back to me, he faces the bear directly. "Up you get then. You've been trapped in there for long enough."

I take a step back as Kal pushes off the ground with his massive front paws. He brings himself to his full height, towering over me and the shaman.

"This shouldn't hurt him," Väinämöinen says. "Either of them. But it may be a bit unpleasant to watch."

"What are you going to—*argh*—" I cry out, falling on my backside into the snow. One arm covers my eyes as white light blasts from Väinämöinen's glowing hands and slams into the bear's massive chest. Kal is tossed backwards, landing in a heap in the snow.

"What did you do? If you hurt him—"

"Wait," the shaman rasps. He looks like he's aged a hundred more years. The magic clearly took its toll on him. If Lumi came out of the woods now, she could knock him down as easily as plucking a tulip by the root.

I offer him my arm for support. "Are you well? Can I fetch you some water or—"

"Just *wait*. Watch. He's coming out now."

Holding the tired shaman up with both hands, I turn to look. The bear stirs, but Kal doesn't rise. Something rises *from* him—a man, dressed head to toe in trapper's furs. He appears solid in form, and yet he stands inside the bear. The trapper lifts his hands, inspecting them in the moonlight, as if surprised to see that they're truly his.

Väinämöinen's hand on my arm tightens as he chokes back a sob. "Come on out, you old fool."

Slowly, the trapper steps fully out of the bear.

I gasp, taking in his bearded face, the lines creasing the corners of his eyes, already so well known to me.

"Good to see you again," he calls. "You look like death, old man."

"You've kept me waiting so long," Väinämöinen replies. "Come." He holds out a trembling hand. "Come to me now."

The other Väinämöinen walks on swift feet, glancing from the shaman to me. Holding my gaze, he smiles. "Hello again, Siiri."

"If you're Väinämöinen," I say to the shaman to my right, "Then who is this?"

"I'm Väinämöinen," the bear spirit replies.

I blink, trying to puzzle this together. It makes my head hurt. "I don't understand."

"We don't often understand it ourselves," Bear Väinämöinen says with a smile. "Soul magic is so old, it's all but forgotten. We've never claimed to know how all of it works."

"Hence, how we found ourselves in this little conundrum." My Väinämöinen gestures between them.

"How shall we do this?" says Bear Väinämöinen. "It's too late to recall me in the usual way."

"I tried that for years, and you never returned," Väinämöinen replies with a scowl.

"I couldn't hear you, old friend."

"I've been alone for so long. I had all but given up hope."

"There is always hope," Bear Väinämöinen replies. "We made sure of that. Whatever else comes our way, hope will remain."

Väinämöinen offers a tattooed hand. "No more waiting. Take my hand. We will be one again."

Bear Väinämöinen nods, stepping forward. The moment they touch, the same blue-white light bursts from their joined hands. I'm rocked off my feet again, landing in the snow several feet back. I squint into the blinding light as the two Väinämöinens become one.

As soon as it begins, it's over. I wince, blinking in the dark and shading my eyes from the afterimage, to find only one Väinämöinen standing before me. He takes deep breaths, his eyes still glowing as he pats his arms, his chest. He flexes the strong, tattooed fingers of his hands.

I scramble back onto my feet. "Väinämöinen?" I venture.

An incandescent smile lights his face. He's looking at me with new eyes. Gone are his suspicion and resentment. Gone are his anger and frustration. The haunted look I've seen him wear so often is replaced with something softer. Now, I see love. It overflows from him. *Protection. Contentment. Pride.*

"Siiri." He says my name like a song. Stepping forward, he wraps me in a tight embrace, laughing and crying. I don't understand, but I let him hold me until he's ready to break away.

I take in the set of his shoulders, the faint glowing light in his eyes. "Are you—you're you again? You're whole?"

He nods, still smiling. "I am whole, thank Ilmatar."

A grunt behind him has us both turning. Across the snow, the bear is stirring.

"Kal—"

"Siiri, no." The shaman holds tight to my wrist. "You need to leave him now."

"But he might still be hurt," I protest.

"He's fine. He is only a bear now. He'll be scared and confused. We have to let him go."

Kal takes deep, panting breaths, taking in his surroundings. He looks at us. The light in his eyes is gone. He's just a bear.

Reaching for the knife at his belt, Väinämöinen cuts his palm, squeezing a few drops of his blood onto the snow. "Otso, brother of the forest, I thank you for your shared fellowship these long months. I return your servant to you. Go in peace, friend."

I hold out my hand, and he drags the blade across my palm too. I wince, squeezing a few drops of my own blood to the snow. "Thank you for seeing me safely to Väinämöinen."

The bear grunts. Far off in the distance, a pair of wolves howl. Turning, the bear trots off, disappearing into the shadows of the forest.

"Lumi is coming," I whisper, listening to the wolves. "Väinämöinen, we're running out of time."

"I know," he replies, sheathing his knife at his hip. "Kal was a vessel used by Lumi to keep my soul contained. She preferred to contend with an angry bear over an angry shaman."

I bristle with anger at hearing her name. "What do you intend to do now?"

"We have little enough time," he says, jerking open the door of his hut. "Lumi is on her way north. She's recruiting wolves to fight for her as we speak. When she thinks she has the numbers, she'll come for me."

"How do you know?"

"I saw her," he replies. "As the bear, I heard her plans. She won't come until she's sure of her victory. We have only days now."

I follow him into the warmth of the hut. "But—why does she want to find you so badly? Is this to do with your curse?"

"Yes. Fetch me that drum."

I grab the painted drum while he settles himself at his low worktable. "What happened to you? What did you take from Tuonetar, and why do so many people now want you dead?"

He sighs, taking up the drum I offer him. "That's just the thing. I can't die, Siiri."

I let myself fall into the pile of furs on the other side of the table. "What?"

"I can't die," he repeats. "That's my wretched curse."

I search his face. "I don't understand."

"I can only be killed," he continues. "And whoever kills me will claim my magic."

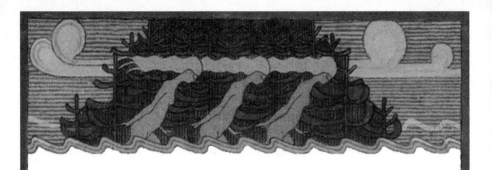

Aina

"AINA?"

"Oh gods, what's happening?"

I stand on the banks of the black river encircling Tuonela. Behind me, far in the distance, Tuoni's palace looms, casting light in all directions like a beacon in the darkness. Before me, a boat waits at the dock, its high prow bobbing on still waters. A haggard old woman stands in the back of the boat, clutching a long wooden pole. She is Tuonen tytti, the ferrywoman. She's short and bent, with white hair sticking out stiffly, like straw, from under her cap. She watches me with dark eyes set in a skull-like face.

To either side of me, the other girls huddle close, trembling. Satu and Helmi clutch at my hands, while Riina stands tall, her gaze darting to where my new husband waits. Kalma and a troop of dead soldiers flank him.

"Aina, what have you done?" Riina whispers.

"Come," I say, leading the girls down the dock. "We haven't much time. You must cross."

"Cross where?" says Helmi. "What's happening?"

"Did you marry him?" Riina presses.

I nod, glancing over my shoulder. "It was the only way to break the curse and set you all free."

"Set *us* free," says Satu. "You're coming with us. Aina, we're leaving together. All of us."

I smile and kiss her forehead. "I made a bargain with Tuoni to spare your lives—"

Riina flinches away as Helmi stifles a cry.

"This isn't a trick," I say, cupping her cheek. "He has promised to protect me from the witches. I will be safe here."

"You will be hunted and despised, and you will die a fool's death," Riina replies.

"Then I die at peace knowing others I love will live."

"Could you not ask him now to free you too?" Satu whispers.

As she speaks, I feel his fingers pluck at the threads of our blood bond, reminding me of how completely I am bound. "My place is here now. Oh, do not weep for me," I add, wiping Satu's cheek. "I'll be happy in the knowledge that you're safe. But there is something you must do for me."

"What?" asks Satu.

"I want my family to know I'm alive. I need you to find them for me. They live on the southwest shore of Lake Päijänne. My mother is the wisewoman of our village. Her name is Milja. My father is Taavi; he's a woodworker. And my best friend, Siiri. You must find them and tell them what happened to us here. Tell them—tell Siiri—" I wipe away my tears with a sniff, my heart breaking as I picture her anguished face. "Tell her I love her. Tell her this wasn't her fault. Tell her I am at peace. You tell her that."

Satu and Helmi nod.

"I'll find them or die trying," Riina says, her hand on my shoulder.

"It is time," Tuoni calls from behind us.

The other girls jump, their gazes darting over my shoulders to the death god striding towards us. His thick boots thunk on the boards of the dock. He sweeps to my side, his black cloak trailing on the ground. The girls shrink back as he places an arm around my shoulders.

"I am bound by sacred oath to my wife to return you to the land of the living," he declares.

Satu and Helmi flinch again at hearing his voice, spoken directly to them. I feel so small, tucked in at his side, my shoulders fitting under the spread of his arm, a great black raven guarding over his little dove.

"W-we thank you, my lord," Satu murmurs.

Trembling like a leaf, Helmi dares to step forward. "Could you not find it in your heart to release Aina as well?"

Tuoni's arm stiffens around me. "The Queen of Tuonela belongs in Tuonela," he replies tonelessly.

Helmi and Satu cry anew. Riina simply shakes her head. But I don't let myself feel despair at his response. I never expected he would set me free. Our bargain is struck, my fate sealed.

"You should know that no oath was required," Tuoni goes on, surprising us all. "You have suffered enough under Tuonetar's schemes. You go now under my protection, and with my blessing. The hand of Tuoni shall be a guide upon your heart. Where it is in my power, I shall bless you with long lives and peaceful, painless deaths."

I breathe a sigh of relief.

"As a token of my goodwill, you shall take these with you." With a wave of his hand, three horses appear in the boat. Their saddles are strapped with large packs. The contents rattle and clank as the horses toss their heads and paw their hooves. "Each horse carries gold and silver that equals you in weight," Tuoni explains. "You also have a sack of barley grain blessed by Päivätär herself. So long as you pray to her daily, it will never empty."

The girls exchange surprised glances, and my heart races. Päivätär, goddess of the sun. He is giving them each a dowry fit for a queen.

Tuoni gives my shoulder a squeeze. "Say your last farewells, wife. They must go."

Stepping out of his embrace, I cross the few short steps to their sides and wrap my arms around Satu again. Helmi steps in too. "You saved us," she whispers.

"You would have done the same," I reply.

"Come with us," Satu pleads again.

I pull away, cupping first her cheek, then Helmi's. "Find my family. Find my mother and Siiri. You tell them where I am," I say, looking to Riina. "You tell them not to worry. Tell them I love them, and I would be with them if I could."

Riina nods, a look of determination set on her face.

Four dead guards step forward, flanking us on the dock.

"It is time," Tuoni calls.

"No," Helmi whimpers, holding to me.

My heart drops, even as I try to keep smiling. This is what I wanted. This is what I fought for. This is the bargain I made. The dead step closer, ready to force the girls into the waiting boat.

Satu peers around me, her hands gripping me more tightly. "Please, my lord," she cries. "Make a bargain with me. My gold for Aina's life. Take it all, only give me Aina."

"And mine too," says Helmi. "Please, my lord. We offer you everything—"

"Enough." Tuoni reaches out, his hands like iron banding over my shoulders. He pulls me back, breaking Satu and Helmi's hold on me. "Do not insult me with such an offer again."

The girls cower and back away.

"You cannot so carelessly return a gift once given," he intones, his words laced with shadow and fire. "And my wife cannot be bought or traded for mere sacks of gold. She is priceless to me. You dishonor her sacrifice by daring to change the terms of her bargain. Take the blessing of life I offer you and leave my realm in peace."

Riina steps behind the girls. "Come away," she says softly. "Girls, come."

Helmi and Satu let Riina walk them backwards, the dead pressing in as they're forced to step into the boat. The horses snort as the boat rocks. "Don't forget us," Satu cries out at me.

"Never," I call back. "Do not forget me. And do not break your word."

"We will not fail you!"

Tuoni holds me fast as we watch the ferrywoman push off with her pole, guiding the boat away from the dock.

"Aina," Helmi cries, reaching out a helpless hand.

The ferry moves away across the dark water, separating me from the last three living mortal souls left in this realm. I pull away from the death god, running to the end of the dock. The dead to either side cross their pikes, creating a barrier I cannot cross. I lift a hand, waving to the girls in parting, until I lose sight of them to the darkness.

Tuoni steps in behind me, his hand returning to my shoulder. "Come, wife."

"Tell me this is no trick," I whisper. "Tell me they're safe. Tell me they will feel the sun on their faces again."

With gentle hands, he lifts my cowl, covering my hair against the winter chill. "I gave you my word," he replies solemnly. "They will step through the veil and ride a dangerous road. They must cross over marsh and mead, through fen and forest, before they pass through the gates of the North, returning to the land of the living."

"A dangerous road? But you gave them no weapons."

"They do not go alone," he replies. "Kalma shall be their guide."

I glance over his shoulder to where Kalma had been standing moments before. Now, there is nothing but shadow. "All this time she was fighting to free you?"

He nods, tucking a lock of my hair behind my ear.

I bite my lip, holding back the question I know I must ask, fearful of his response. Finally, I say, "Did you ask her to bring the girls into death? Was she acting on your orders?"

His brows lower and his jaw clenches. I've seen the same look on the raven. He's affronted I even asked. "No," he replies. "In fact, I ordered her to leave me to my fate. Many times, I ordered her to stop." His tone is shadowed by anger and resentment.

I peer up at him, studying his mismatched eyes. "She was willing to kill as many women as it took to set you free . . . because she loves you."

He nods.

"I understand your relief. You would still be bound to that tree if not for her . . . but if not for her, so many girls would still be alive," I add, trying to stop my voice from breaking.

"I know you fear Kalma, my love. I saw it as the raven. Now I can *feel* it." He presses a hand to his chest, giving me a somber look. "She has been the source of so many of your nightmares. In your heart, you hate her."

"It's complicated," I admit.

"Her loyalty to me can only be a comfort to you now. Kalma is *mine*." He cups my cheek. "As she protects me, she will protect my wife."

I fight a shiver, whether from the cold or this feeling of dread I cannot shake.

"Come," Tuoni says, offering me his hand. "The hour is

late, and you are tired. Let us return home and get you warm by the fire."

Home.

I glance over his shoulder once to the beacon that is his palace on the hill. Tuonela. My home. There can be no going back now. I made this bargain. All that remains is for me to survive it. Taking my husband's hand, I let him lead me away from the dock, away from the land of the living, deeper into the Kingdom of Death.

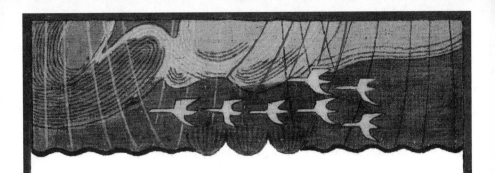

Siiri

VÄINÄMÖINEN SITS ACROSS FROM me at the table, his drum balanced on his knee. The runes dotting the hide are almost identical to the faded markings on the shaman's hands. "Make us some tea."

"Tell me about your curse," I counter without moving. "What do you mean you can't die? What did Tuonetar do to you?"

He sighs, setting the drum on the table with a soft rattle. "It was my punishment for thwarting her, for stealing from her. She called on her coven of forest witches to curse me. Ajatar led the coven, Lumi's mother."

I gasp. "Ajatar is Lumi's mother?" I know the name of this witch well. Mothers teach their children to fear her. For a moment in the sacred grove, I thought Tellervo might be Ajatar, the forest witch who hunts the hunters. She curses lonely foragers with her nightmares. She climbs onto your chest while you sleep, stealing your air and breaking your bones.

Väinämöinen takes in my look of horror and scoffs. "I take it you know Ajatar?"

Slowly, I nod.

"A nastier witch has never drawn breath on this side of the veil," he mutters. "She was all too eager to help Tuonetar curse me. I think she only agreed because she expects Lumi to be the one to fulfill the curse and claim my magic. And poor Lumi thinks claiming it will fix what's broken inside her," he adds. "She thinks my magic can make her worthy in her wretched mother's eyes. She has no idea what this will cost her. To possess the knowledge I do . . . to hold it in my head and my heart . . . it's not a gift, Siiri. It's an awesome and terrible burden."

I hold his gaze. "A burden it may be, but it is your duty to give your wisdom to the people, and you left."

He goes still, his blue eyes searching my face. "Siiri—"

"You left your people when we needed you most," I shout over him, my frustration rising. "You've spent all these years hiding in this godsforsaken wilderness while your people suffered. We're *suffering*, Väinämöinen."

"That's not my fault—"

"When you left, the stories stopped," I say over him. "No new wisdom. No songs. Your leaving was like the first fall of snow. The other gods grew silent too . . . then they grew distant. We were left freezing in the winter of your indifference. Then foreigners swept up from the south with stories and songs of a new god, bloodthirsty and vengeful. They're taking everything from us. And we've been too broken to notice, too alone and scared to fight back."

His face looks haunted. "Siiri, please—"

"You left us to save yourself. You say a shaman can't use knowledge for selfish acts, but that's exactly what *you* did.

Your wisdom is meant to be shared, but you used it to hide yourself away up here—"

"I had no choice!"

I rise to my feet. "There is *always* a choice! Look at me," I cry, raising my arms out to the side. "Look at Aina. Look at how we've fought for each other, how we're ready to *die* for each other before ever giving up. Finding you was never just about saving her. I meant to bring you south with us. I meant to bring you *home*. You belong with your people, Väinämöinen, as Aina belongs with me. Your magic belongs to the people. It is not yours to hide away. It never was."

A tear slips down his weathered cheek as he gazes up at me. "Help me, Siiri. Save me from myself."

After a long moment, I nod. Sinking to my knees, I face him across the table. "I will help you. Gods as my witness, Väinämöinen, I will fight for you. If it comes to it, I will die for you. You are my shaman, the son of the blessed All-Mother."

He reaches a rune-marked hand across the table, and I take it, holding it tight.

"You need never be alone again," I assure him. "I am here now, and I will never leave you again. I didn't leave you as the bear, and I will not leave you as the man. All I ask is that you fight for me as I fight for you."

Slowly, he nods.

"Help me rescue Aina, and then I'm bringing you *both* home where you belong."

We sit in silence, the crackling of the fire the only sound between us.

After a few moments, he smiles, that blue twinkle returning to his watery eyes. "Tell me, Siiri, what do you know about soul magic?"

Once we're settled at the table with cups of yarrow root tea and a fresh loaf of rieska, Väinämöinen reaches for his pipe again. After he lights it, he picks up the drum with both hands, his pipe clenched between his teeth. "To cross over into Tuonela as a shaman, you need to understand the power of soul magic."

I gaze at him warily. "Isn't that how a piece of you got trapped in the bear?"

He huffs. "Well, that was a bit of soul magic gone awry, but yes. The kantele is used to work with väki—useful in spellcasting, necromancy, healing, and the like. The drum is the key to crossing the realms. Do you understand? Without the drumming, you can't release the pieces of your soul to go awandering."

I nod as if this makes sense to me.

He gives me a wry look before continuing, puffing on his pipe as he talks. "Each rune on this drum signifies some-thing important to the drummer. You can learn much about a shaman and their power from the drum they play." He points to the central rune, a double-lined rhombus. "This is the sun. It marks the center of our world. Most shamans will play a simple drum designed for use in this realm only. The runes will flow naturally outward from the sun."

"What kind of runes?" I say, my eyes fixed on the drum.

"All kinds," he replies. "Reindeer, cattle, fish. There are runes for hunting and gathering, runes for weather and the seasons, the gods, love and death." His hand dances around the surface of his drum as he points to the different runes. Then he glances up. "You mentioned feeling like a piece of your soul was with Aina. You said you feel its loss?"

I scrunch my brow. "I . . . it felt like I was being torn

apart, yes." I rub at my chest with a grimace. "It felt like being stabbed . . . or like I was being stretched. It was . . . unpleasant."

"And you feel it still?"

"No," I say aloud for the first time. "No, it faded. I don't—I can't feel her anymore." I'm quiet for a moment, letting myself sit with her loss. "Did she take a piece of my soul? Is it gone forever? Is it in Tuonela? Is that why I can't feel it?"

He raises a hand. "Peace, girl. Let me explain. Unless you're the most powerful *and* the most careless shaman of a generation, I doubt very much you managed to place a piece of your soul into Aina without knowing it. But the sensations you describe are not dissimilar from the pain inflicted by a soul-rending."

"How many pieces of soul are there?"

"Three," he replies, setting the drum aside. "The very life of you is called your henki. When your henki leaves your body, you die."

"I know this word," I say, leaning forward. "Aina's father is a woodworker. He makes sielulintu. He says the soul birds guide your henki to Tuonela when you die."

Väinämöinen nods. "He's right. Now, your second piece of soul is called the luonto. All luonto take the form of birds, much like a sielulintu. The luonto is your guardian."

"What form does yours take?"

Holding out his right hand, he traces his left thumb over the largest tattoo. "I'm a white-tailed eagle."

I smile, thinking of the stories Mummi tells of Väinämöinen and the Eagle. "How do I decide what form my luonto should take?"

He chuckles, puffing on the stem of his pipe. "You don't decide anything. Your luonto was born inside you. It already has a form. All you must do is let it take flight."

I press a hand to my chest, imagining I can feel the fluttering of wings deep inside me.

The shaman watches me with a smile. "Yes, your luonto is strong, Siiri. Sometimes I can almost see it looking out through your eyes."

My smile widens.

He goes on, "Now, when your luonto travels, it will always be in the form of a bird. This limits the interactions you can have. Do you understand? If you're an owl or an eagle, you can't talk to people or be understood. But you can see, you can hear, you can *learn*. You can gather intimate and secret knowledge. And knowledge is—"

"Power," I finish for him. "Yes, I understand."

He eyes me for a moment, his mustache twitching. "The last piece of your soul is called your itse. It's your essence, your mirrored self. It can leave your body and travel for you. What's more, it will *be* you. So, you can walk and talk, think and feel. Others can see you and communicate with you."

It all falls into place. "He was your itse. The Väinämöinen trapped inside Kal. That was your itse, wasn't it?"

He smirks. "Now you see."

"You said he was gone a long time. What happened?"

He sighs, setting aside his spent pipe. "You have to understand that the soul does not want to be split apart. Sending out a smaller piece like your luonto is harmless enough. But using your itse can be dangerous, Siiri. The more often you send it out, the longer it stays out, the harder it gets to come back to yourself. Once an itse is lost, it becomes all but impossible to retrieve."

My heart flickers. "Oh, Väinämöinen . . ." Reaching forward, I take his hand in mine. "The lost shaman," I whisper. "You've been lost in more ways than one, haven't you? Lost to the world, hiding up here all alone. Lost to yourself, your itse wandering the woods without you, unable to return. What happened? When did you let it go?"

"I was careless and overconfident. I thought I could survive this life of isolation with ease. How could I not when the world could still be mine? If I was careful, in my itse I could walk the forests and fields where I had my greatest adventures. I was selfish, Siiri . . . and I paid the price."

"How do you live with only two pieces of your soul intact?"

"You don't." His words settle between us like a thick mantle. "It will kill you in the end . . . and it will be slow and painful. The 'long dying,' they call it. I once met a man afflicted with a loss of itse." His face takes on that haunted look I've come to know so well. "I don't wish it on anyone, Siiri."

I search his face. "How long did you live without yours?"

"Too long."

"But Tuonetar's curse tied you to life . . . you couldn't die."

He nods again.

I give his hand a squeeze. "And now?"

"Now I'm whole," he replies. "As whole as I'll ever be. But Siiri, death has taken root in me. The withering of my other souls has eaten at me like a cancer. My luonto is weak, my henki even weaker. I cannot risk separating from my itse again, do you understand? Whether I want to or not, I *cannot* go with you to Tuonela. I cannot survive another rending."

"I understand," I say. "So, it is my itse we will send to retrieve Aina?"

"Yes."

I brush my thumb over the marks on the back of his hand. "What do the tattoos mean? Kalma has them too. And the goddess in the woods, the one who gave me supplies and told me to follow the bear."

He glances at his hands, flexing his fingers. "They're meant to be a safeguard against losing your itse. You mark your hands with the same patterns that are on your drum. They are a tether as you wander between the realms, guiding the pieces of your soul back to where your body waits."

I look down at our hands. Mine are pale and unblemished. "So, if I am to cross over into Tuonela, I must anchor the pieces of my soul?" My heart sinks a little in my chest. "I must wear the marks of Kalma?"

"Do not think of them as Kalma's marks," he says gently. "Think of them as the marks of a shaman. That's all the tattoos are meant to indicate: a shaman or deity capable of soul-rending and crossing the realms. Some gods don't even bother with such tethering. They believe their souls are powerful enough not to get lost."

I gasp, squeezing his hand. "That's why I couldn't kill her."

"What?"

"I stabbed Kalma in the heart, and it did nothing. In her itse form, I may as well have been stabbing at the rain to kill a storm."

He nods. "Yes, you cannot kill someone in their itse form. But you can untether their itse. An untethered itse may struggle to return to its body, which can lead to the long dying."

"How do you untether it?"

He frowns. "You're clever, Siiri. Be clever."

I furrow my brow as I piece it together. "Oh gods . . ." I whisper, meeting his gaze. "Sever the itse's hands. Break the bond between the shaman and their drum."

He gives me a solemn nod. "So, do you understand the risk? When you let your itse roam free, you must do all you can to protect your hands. If you become untethered, it's possible you may never return to your body again. And you mustn't separate the pieces of your soul for long. A soul too long out of its body will lose itself."

"Lumi was using your itse to find your body, wasn't she? She wanted to make you whole again." I sit back on my heels, cursing under my breath. "She was never going to kill him so long as your itse was trapped inside. She wants you whole so she can kill you herself and take your magic."

"Now you understand."

"I'm sorry I helped her. I gave her a path to follow that led her straight to you. This is my fault—"

"No," he says, voice firm. "Lumi has been on this path for too long to stray from it now. If she hadn't used you, she would have found another way."

"Then she has to die," I say grimly. "I'll not let her harm you, Väinämöinen. And I'll certainly not let her take your magic."

He smiles, his mustache twitching.

I raise a brow at him. "What? Why do you smile?"

"I am once again struck by the curiosity of life. The threads of fate weave an interesting tapestry."

"What do you mean?"

"I thought my story was coming to an end," he replies. "But then a fierce girl leaned over the edge of a pit, calling down to me."

"You remember that? Or do you speak of Kal's memories?"

"They are one and the same, for he is me. As soon as we rejoined, I reclaimed myself."

I can't help but laugh. "All those days, I searched and searched for you, but you were by my side all along." I hold his gaze, my mood sobering. "You saved me then, Väinämöinen. In helping me rescue Aina, you'll save me again. How can I ever repay you for what you've done, for what you will do?"

He grunts dismissively, but there is mist in his eyes. "When it comes to saving maidens, it seems I can't help trying to play the hero." He picks up his drum, smoothing a weathered hand over the surface of the runes. "You call me a great shaman, but the title is undeserved. In the end, I couldn't save any of the people I loved. I've failed so many times, Siiri. Sometimes it feels that all I do is fail."

"You will not fail this time," I say, praying my determination is enough to sustain us both.

He hands the drum over to me. "Let's hope you're right. Regardless, all the pieces of my soul seem to agree that we'll save your Aina . . . or die trying."

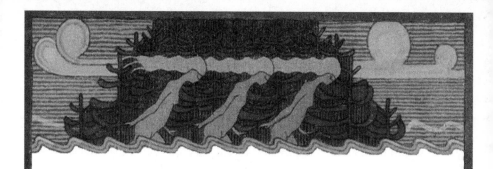

Aina

I CLUTCH TUONI'S HAND as he leads me through the palace gardens. Away from my room. "Where are we going?"

"A queen deserves a chamber befitting her status."

I peer up at the north tower, Tuonetar's new prison. The shadow of her tower looms over the palace, a constant reminder of how close I remain to danger. And I'm the one who decided to bring her out each night to sit at my supper table. If Siiri were here, she'd kick me in the shins and call me a fool. In this moment, I think I'd let her.

Guards swing open a stout wooden door at the base of the south tower, and Tuoni steps through into the stairwell. Taking a torch, he leads the way up the spiraling steps. I lift the sodden hem of my dress with my free hand, following him as we climb. We pass two landings with closed doors, climbing higher. I nearly lose my footing as he stops on the last landing before yet another closed door. With a creak, the heavy wooden door swings inward to reveal a large, circular room. Tuoni drops my hand to secure the torch in a bracket on the wall.

I step past, glancing around. The first thing I notice is the delicious smell—rosemary and mulled wine, roasted duck with stuffing, winter squash soup, fresh-baked pulla bread, buttery jam tarts. The evening meal is set on a table before the hearth, which burns with a happy fire. I walk past the chairs, my fingers fluttering over the soft furs on the four-poster bed. Thinking of the man standing behind me, and the purpose of this bed, I drop my hand to my side, heat blooming in my cheeks.

An ornate wooden cabinet stands in the corner. Opening the doors, I smile, brushing my fingers down the sleeve of a finely embroidered gown. One of many. If Loviatar had any say in their selection, I'm sure they're all exquisite.

I glance to my right. A polished mirror is affixed above a dressing table. The table contains boxes and vials for cosmetics and jewels. A boar-bristle hairbrush rests next to a pair of golden hair clips. Catching Tuoni's gaze in the mirror, I blush anew. I've never been alone in a room with any man except my father and brothers.

"The door locks from the inside," he says, swinging it shut. The latch clicks with such finality, I feel it in my bones. I do my best not to tremble as he steps fully into the room. "And you have a much better view now."

Taking any distraction, I step over to the closest window and unlatch the shutter. A gust of wintry air sweeps in as I take in my view of the garden and the sloping hills beyond. Tuonetar liked the palace to feel dark and dank. Tuoni clearly prefers warmth and light, even knowing the sun will never shine. I peer down into the walled garden. The trees and flowering beds lay concealed beneath a thin layer of fresh snow.

"How do the plants grow?"

Tuoni joins me at the window. "With soil and water and light, same as in the realm of the living."

"But there is no light here, my lord."

"Is there not?"

I turn, one hand clutching to the cold sill. "I've never seen a sun rise, nor any glimpse of moon or star."

"Do you have to see a thing to know it's there, to feel its presence?"

"Well, I suppose . . ."

"Turn around."

I go still.

"Turn, wife." He takes me by the shoulders, pressing against me as I face out the window. I don't look down as his hands cover mine on the sill. "Close your eyes," he says, leaning down, his breath warm against my ear.

Heart fluttering, I close my eyes.

He presses in until my hips are against the sill, his body firm behind me. "Now . . . tilt your face towards the sky. Keep your eyes closed. It is still night. The moon is waxing. Search for its light. Feel it touching your face, soft as a lover's breath on your cheek."

I tip my face up. I feel the cold, to be sure. The chill of winter has set in so quickly, hardly a week wasted on autumn. There is no wind. No birdsong. But there is . . . something. A feeling. A deep kind of knowing. It doesn't put me in mind of a cool breath on my cheek. Instead, it feels like the eyes of Kuutar watch me from the sky, warm and inviting.

"Where is the moon?" he says in my ear.

With my eyes shut tight, I smile and lift my hand, pointing up and to the left.

"Good," he says behind me, his hands dropping to my hips. "You will come to feel the sun as well. In time, you'll hardly notice the darkness." He steps away, leaving me craving the warmth of his closeness.

"It's beautiful magic, my lord. Truly." I rest my hip against the sill as he sheds his cloak. "Whose is it?"

"Tuonetar's," he replies, tugging the axe loose. "For all her violence and madness, she has a deep love of flowers and growing things." He sets the axe down with a clatter and helps himself to a cup of wine.

With his back to me, and his cloak shed, I admire the shape of his shoulders, the set of his hips, the length and strength of his long legs. All the other gods of the underworld are haunting in their strangeness. He looks so . . . normal. How can it be that his broad hunter's shoulders and raven-dark hair cause me as much disquiet as Tuonetar's cracked teeth or Kalma's skeletal hands?

"You watch me, wife."

I jump, my eyes darting away from him to look instead at the rug on the floor.

"What are you looking for in me?" Slowly, he turns, offering me a cup of wine. "I disappoint you in this form?"

"No," I say, quickly, accepting the wine. I step away and his frown deepens.

"I frighten you."

I take a nervous sip of wine. It's delicious—rich and red, with fine notes of sweet plum. "'Fear' is not the proper word, I think."

"Which word suits better, wife?"

I take another sip, stepping to the right to put the table between us. "You intimidate me, my lord."

"Are they not one and the same?"

I place a hand down on the wood of the table, taking solace in something solid. "Fear implies a risk of pain. It assumes you are a danger to me. It assumes I will act against my will or character to avoid such threat of pain."

"You do not fear pain by my hand?"

Feeling no need to lie, I say, "I believe you would cut off any hand that caused me pain . . . even if it be your own."

A darkness flashes in his eyes at the mere thought. Behind him, the fire sparks. He sets his cup down, making no move to step closer to me. "I would do that and more, wife."

I drop my gaze away from him. "You keep using that word."

"Which word now offends?"

"Wife."

"You *are* my wife. There is nothing wrong in me calling you what you are."

"It is your very use of the word that intimidates me," I admit.

"And why does my calling you 'wife' intimidate you?"

I swallow my nerves, looking for the right words to explain. "I have been afraid all my life. The sensation is known to me, as known as my name. When you call me 'wife,' when you show me kindness, when you look at me as you are looking at me now . . ."

"How am I looking at you?"

I shake my head, not daring to raise my eyes.

"Aina . . . look at me."

I close my eyes, denying him what he wants. "I cannot," I whisper.

"Why?"

"Because in your face, I see the raven who loves me. In your body, I see the man who hungers for me. But in your eyes . . ." I glance up at last, holding his mismatched gaze. "In your eyes, I see the god who owns me . . . and I am intimidated."

"If I own you, then you own me. Ought I to feel intimidated too?"

"We are bound together. From the moment our blood joined, I've felt you pressing in at me," I say, placing a hand over my heart. "I feel you *here*, seeking and pulling. Wanting, needing, aching. I think you mean to unravel me. You mean to take every knot in my tapestry and untie it, binding it into yours until we are no longer two people but one."

"And should I not want this from my wife?" he says, his frustration rising as he steps closer. "Should I not want to shelter and adore you? Carve out half of me to make a place for you?"

"You take the words of marriage too literally, my lord. I must remain my own person. I must be free to choose you, to . . . to want you."

"And do you?"

I go still, my gaze now locked on the candle. Tuoni waits, unmoving, his good eye watching me as I watch the flame. "I do not know you," I say at last.

"You know the raven—"

"You are not the raven," I cry. "For weeks I lived with him, sharing my every thought and dream. He knows me so well—*you* know me so well." I shake my head. "But you are now a man, and I don't know you beyond the stories and songs meant to frighten me. A god calls me 'wife,' and he is a stranger to me. So yes, I am intimidated."

He glances around, settling his gaze on the feast. "Dine with me."

I let out a little laugh. "What?"

"You're hungry. I can hear the way your stomach groans. A feast stands ready for us," he adds, gesturing to the table. "Dine with me and ask me any question. You say you do not know me. Now is your chance, wife. Dine with your husband and get to know him."

My laughter grows. I see it upsets him, and I try to stop, covering my mouth with my hand.

"What is funny?" he mutters, his frustration rising.

"I just—" I shake my head again, stifling this laughter that has quickly turned to nervous trembling. "The god of death wants me to dine with him." I choke on another laugh as I imagine saying the words out loud to Siiri. I picture the horrified look on her face. "The god of death is my husband and—oh gods—I am now the Queen of Tuonela." I clutch at my side, sucking in a sharp breath. With my free hand, I reach out, frantically grasping for the back of the chair to steady myself. "I am—I married you, my lord. Your spurned queen now haunts the opposite tower, casting a pall over my life. And not an hour ago, the only three mortal souls left in this realm sailed away from me. I am truly alone now." I can't catch my breath. Nothing about this is funny anymore. "Oh gods, I am—I'm alone—"

He takes me by the shoulders, helping me into the chair. Soothing me with soft words and touches, he drops down to one knee. The god of death deigns to comfort me, his weak mortal wife. "You are not alone, Aina. You shall never fear loneliness again. I am here."

"I miss my family," I whisper, my trembling hands holding tight to his strong arms. "I miss my mother. I miss Siiri."

He stiffens, sinking back on his heels. "Always Siiri. Your thoughts never seem to turn from her."

I go still, not daring to look up. I can feel his jealousy through our bond. "She is my friend—"

"Don't lie to me. You can lie to yourself, but not to me. As the raven, I listened to endless stories of your exploits together. You held me as you cried for her. I stayed by your side as you dreamed of her. Your fondness for her is a thorn in my side."

"What other stories can I share when it is she who has been more constant in my life than the sun itself—" I gasp as he presses against me, his hips between my legs, his large hand cupping the back of my head as he pulls me closer, stealing all my air with the violence of his expression.

"I don't want to hear another word about Siiri Jarintyttär."

I look at his eyes, from light to dark. "What use is jealousy when you know I will never see her again? How can you deny me even my memories—"

With a growl, he cups my face with both hands, his grip tight, his lips all but brushing mine. "I will not share you with another. You are *my* wife, Aina. Not hers. I will carve a place for myself in your heart, I swear it. I will be first in your affections."

I stiffen in his embrace, feeling the chaos and confusion of his thoughts down the bond. He's panicking. Gods help me, I think he's scared. He's just as unsure of this new bond as I am. He doesn't know what it means to be a husband. I'm not sure he even knows how to be a friend. Slowly, I lift a hand, brushing the wool of his tunic. "You cannot force affection, my lord. Think of the raven."

His dark eye fixes on me, his mouth set in a grim line as he sinks back, giving me room to breathe. I look for my Jaako in the slant of his cheekbones, the arch of his nose. Gently, I lift my hand and cup his face, my thumb brushing the softness of his wiry black beard. "A caged bird will only beat at its bars. Once the cage opens, it is sure to fly away . . . never to return."

Shifting my hand, I brush my thumb over his lips. They part for me, and I feel his warm breath on my skin. "But a bird fed from an open hand will return to you." He leans into my touch, his lips forming the echo of a kiss against my thumb. "Open your hand, my lord. Give me leave to love you in my time and in my way. And please, if you care for me at all, let me keep my memories."

Slowly, he nods, his shoulders relaxing as I let him have my willing touch. I brush my hands over his scarred cheeks, across his brow, down his beard. He sinks against me. His hands drop to rest on my knees, gentle but claiming as they graze up my thighs. He lowers his head to my shoulder, content to breathe me in.

There is nothing sensual in our touch. He is a man, and I am his wife, but this feels altogether innocent. In this moment, we are two souls bound by some strange iron thread, seeking shelter in each other as the darkness presses in. He's part of me now. Tuonela is part of me. I feel him in me, his blood, a whisper of his magic. There is a taste on my tongue, a taste of iron and salt.

It's the tang of the death.

The death god is in me as much as he kneels before me. I know with a knowing marrow-deep that I can never root him out. Swallowing my fear, I lift my trembling hands and brush my fingers through his hair. Flecks of ash from the alder tree flutter loose, landing on his shoulders. I freed him from that prison. I bound him to me with blood and oath, pulling him from the fires of Tuonetar's broken curse.

The awesome truth hits me as he leans away, his gaze full of longing as he looks in my eyes. The death god is in me. I am his. But this was binding magic. Two souls were required. If he is in me, then I am in him. If I am his, then Tuoni is *mine*.

Heart racing, I cup his bearded face, smiling down at my raven. "I want to know you. I want to know Tuonela. Show me everything."

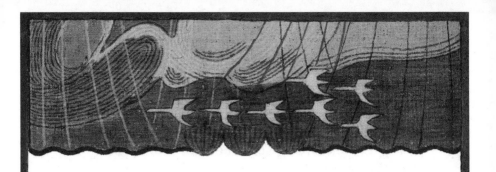

Siiri

54

"WHAT IS THIS?" I say, pointing to a freshly painted rune on the face of Väinämöinen's drum.

"That's you." He winces as he folds his knees under himself by the fire.

The new rune looks like the figure of a person riding a bear. I smile, remembering our escape on the frozen lake. "Why did you add me to your drum?"

The shaman makes a frustrated sound. "Because if I'm forced to follow you, reckless fool girl, I need something to guide my way. I suggest you add me to yours as well."

I look down at my new drum. Väinämöinen made it for me over the last two days. He watched, carefully instructing me, as I mixed wood ash and animal fat to make ink to paint the head. Then he walked me through the precise placement of each rune as I painted it.

A line across the middle of the drumhead separates the realm of the living from that of the dead. The center line is broken in the middle by the sun. "Will you add my rune to your hand?"

He grunts in assent. "The tethering must be completed. You'll have to do the same."

My skin prickles at the thought of the needle piercing my skin. As often as I am injured, I don't enjoy pain. "Will we do it now?"

"No, we work with only the luonto today. That's the easiest piece of one's soul to master. You have to prove you can rend yourself at all before we attempt to set your itse free. And there's no need to be tethered when you use your luonto. As you'll see, you won't lose your sense of self in quite the same way."

"Why not?"

He considers for a moment. "The bird embodies only the strongest pieces of your personality. The rest of you remains with your body. You'll feel its tether, even if you cross realms—even if you cross time."

I go still. "I can cross time? Now?"

He glares at me. "Focus, Siiri. Aina is not lost in time, she's lost in death. Your task is already insurmountable."

I nod, looking down at my drum again. Nervous excitement flutters in my gut. "What if—" I swallow the rest of my question.

He grunts in frustration. "Gods, help me. Speak, girl."

"What if I can't do it?" I say before I can stop myself.

"What?"

"What if I can't release my luonto?"

He glares at me, mustache twitching. "Have you been poisoned?"

I blink. "What? No."

"You didn't eat any questionable mushrooms for breakfast?"

"No—"

"Did you take a great fall? Hit your head, perhaps? Lose consciousness?"

"No," I say again.

"Then I don't understand your question," he replies, still glaring at me.

I glance around, my hands clutching to the drum. "I just . . . what if I can't do this? What happens then?"

With a huff, he shakes his head. "You've been a pain in my side from the moment we met. Your unflinching godsdamn self-assurance drives me to the very edge of madness. I have never met someone more confident in her own strength—and now you ask me this? I must assume you suffer the effects of eating a bad mushroom cap."

My lips twitch as I fight a smile. "So, you think I *can* do it . . ."

His eyes flash as he points with his mallet. "Pick up that godsdamn drum, and do as I do. We'll discuss whether or not you can do it after we've done it."

I smile now, taking up my drum, and mirror his seated stance. The fire crackles, warming our faces. Next to me, Väinämöinen begins muttering under his breath. Then he takes handfuls of the smoke, wafting it over his face and down his arms in a cleansing ritual I've seen even the Christian priest perform. "What are you doing?"

"Smoke purifies the body and awakens the luonto," he says.

As I waft the smoke over myself, trying not to cough, he grips his drum by the stout wooden frame and begins to tilt the face of it in towards the fire in a rhythmic motion. His whole body sways.

"You need to warm the head," he explains, his eyes growing distant and unfocused. "Otherwise, the hide may crack in the cold when you strike it."

I mimic his gestures exactly, angling the head of my drum towards the flame.

He shifts his hold on his mallet. "Follow my lead. We aim to release the luonto here, in this clearing. I want you to think of all the strongest parts of you—your determination, your cleverness. Let all the best of you fill you. Imagine a light glowing inside you *here*." He points to his chest. "Push all those aspects of yourself into the light. The pulsing of the drum, the rhythm of your movements, they'll help you. Let them take over. And when you're ready—your luonto will know the moment—release the light. You're not forcing it out but willing it to go. This is important."

"I'm ready." I nod, picking up my mallet.

"Use only the runes representing life," he cautions, gesturing to the center of his drum. "We want our birds to take flight, so focus on the trees, the snow, the lake beyond the hut. It wants to come out of you, Siiri. It's curious. It wants to fly."

My excitement grows as I grip tighter to my drum and mallet.

"Don't venture below the line, do you understand?" he adds, pointing at my drum. "Be measured. You mustn't cross over."

I scan the surface of my drum. There are marks denoting Tuonela across the bottom: the river, the dead, Kalma and Surma, the Witch Queen, even a small figure for Aina. "I can do it," I say.

Väinämöinen tilts the head of his drum once more towards the fire. "Then we begin."

I do my best to watch him as he makes the first stroke, the drumbeat echoing through the hut. With a rush of nerves, I tap my own mallet against the head of my drum. My hand vibrates as the warm tone hums.

We start slowly. Each time he drums, I echo his movement. The sound changes depending on where I strike. In the center, near the sun and moon, the pitch is lowest. It rattles low in my chest. Near the edges, the pitch is higher. *Rap, tap, tap.*

We slowly pick up speed. I strike the rune for the trees, the fish, the stars, the moon. I let my mallet move in aimless patterns.

Boom . . . boom, tap, tap. Rap tap. Boom.

I close my eyes and imagine that light inside me, filling my chest with heat. I fought Kalma. I am strong.

Boom.

I traveled north, battling the elements, the forces of magic, the evils of men. I am tenacious. I am brave.

Boom.

I risked it all for love. *Not for me, Aina. For you. This is all for you.* I am loyal. I am steadfast.

Boom.

The light inside me glows brighter, warmer, spreading until it burns in my chest. When the heat feels like it might turn my ribs to ash, I gasp and then suck in a quick breath. Head tipped back, I drum furiously, my body rocking as I lose myself to the sound and motion.

Boom. Boom. Boom.

The forest, the fields, the stars, the sky.

I call out to my luonto, *Be free, my friend.*

Stillness washes over me. Arching my shoulders back, I breathe deeply, opening my chest wide. The light wants to be free, and I want nothing more than to free it. On a deep exhale, I let go, one word fluttering in my mind: *Fly.*

My heart races, an odd buzzing in my chest. I feel dizzy and disoriented. The last thing I remember is sitting on the floor of Väinämöinen's hut. I remember the drum. The sound still echoes in my ears. I was trying to release my luonto. Did it work?

As I open my eyes, I'm suddenly bobbed up and down. I grip the branch beneath me, holding on for dear life. My body feels strange—light as air, but strong. I flit left, then right, testing the strength of my wings.

I have wings.

Exuberance bubbles out of me as I flap them again.

The hut is right below me. Light glows from the smoke hole as white smoke rises in a steady stream. At the far end of my branch, close to the trunk, a white-tailed eagle watches me. He has a curved yellow beak ending in a deadly point. His eyes gleam in the dawn light.

How do I communicate to him that I'm well and un-harmed—that I'm me?

I hop up and down, flapping my wings and clicking my beak.

With a nod, the eagle pushes off the branch and launches into the sky. His massive wings unfurl, and he flies upwards, following the spiral of the smoke.

There is no time for doubt. If I'm a bird, I can fly too. I must trust in the strength of my luonto. Opening my wings, I take a leap of faith, launching myself into the air. With a thrill, I feel myself rising, not falling.

I'm flying.

As soon as I feel the first cold rush of the air against my wings, I'm free. I climb higher, chasing after the soaring eagle. With the last of the night's stars above us and a blanket of snow below, we fly off beyond the hut towards the frozen lake. The eagle swoops suddenly downward, pulling its wings in tight to plummet towards the ground. As he nears the frozen surface of the lake, he stretches out his wings and soars along the ice. Crystals of fresh, powdery snow stir under his wingtips.

I don't know how long we ride the current, darting between the trees. But all too soon, Väinämöinen lands atop a towering pine. My heart drops, even as I follow. I don't want this magic to end. For the first time, I feel unburdened, truly wild. A secret part of me wants to stay as a bird forever. But the stoic eagle catches my eye. His curved beak clicks, his chest feathers ruffle, and I can almost hear the old man's voice.

Watch me.

A white light begins to glow at the center of his chest. With a faint pop, he disappears in a puff of feathers. My body goes rigid as I feel a sensation like someone gripping my shoulder.

Come back, a deep voice whispers in my ear. *Return your light.*

I puzzle out his meaning, remembering how it felt to release the light to free my luonto. Closing my eyes, I concentrate on willing all the pieces of myself I set free to coalesce into a ball of light. The more I feed of myself into the light, the more the sensation of being a bird fades. For a frantic moment, my luonto clings to freedom. I understand the impulse well. But my will prevails as I turn inward, following the light home.

"Come on." Väinämöinen's voice is soft, muffled. "Come back now, girl. First time is always the hardest."

I'm lying flat on my back, my face turned to the side. Soft reindeer fur tickles my nose. Blinking my eyes open, I sit up quickly, rubbing my arms and chest. My forgotten drum clatters to the floor as a sheen of sweat breaks out across my forehead. I feel dizzy.

"Easy, there. Take it slow."

Too late. I sway, feeling the churning of my gut. Väinämöinen is ready. He sets a bucket between my knees with a chuckle, just in time for me to double over and empty myself of my breakfast.

"The first time is always disorienting," he soothes. "You did well. You're a natural. I've had students spread their wings only to crash right back down to earth."

Heaving a deep breath, I groan, lifting my head out of the bucket. "What was I?"

"Here." He ignores my question, pressing something into my hand. "Nettle and willow bark. Chew it. The nausea will soon ease."

I pop the small wad in my mouth. My teeth release the juices of the nettle. The bark is hard, soaked in something to give it a little sweetness. In a moment, the waves of nausea buffeting me like water against rocks begin to recede. I push the bucket away, rubbing a shaky hand over my face. "It all felt so real."

"It *was* real," the shaman says with a laugh. "You were the bird, and you were also in here. Both happened."

"What was I?" I ask again.

Väinämöinen smiles, his blue eyes twinkling. "Your luonto is a woodpecker."

I frown. "A woodpecker?" I can't deny feeling a little crestfallen. I was hoping to be a bird of prey. If not an eagle, perhaps an owl or a hawk.

The shaman senses my thoughts. "The luonto is never wrong. It suits you perfectly. What do we know of our friend the white-backed woodpecker?"

I chew on my wad of sweetly sour bark. "They're bloody annoying."

Väinämöinen blinks twice, then roars with laughter, the sound deep and musical. He slaps his leg. "I was going to make that joke if you didn't get there yourself." He wipes a tear of mirth from his eye. "You're quite right. Like you, the woodpecker is bloody annoying."

I scowl at him, but his smile has already fallen, his tone more somber.

"And clever, resourceful. Highly industrious. You'll never find a more hardworking, tenacious little bird. They like to stay close to home, but they're not averse to traveling long distances if the need arises." He pauses, raising a thick white brow as he offers me a knowing smile. "And they mate for life."

I spit the wad of bark into my hand. "Fine, I'm a woodpecker."

"Too right," he replies, hiding his smile.

"So, I did it. I released my luonto. That means my itse is next, right? Am I ready?"

"You can't release your itse until you are properly tethered. Your drum is done. All that remains is your hands."

I swallow my excitement as he moves around the hut, rattling things about. He means to do this now.

Slowly, he turns. "Are you ready?"

I nod, determination filling me. "Yes."

"Why do you do this?"

"For Aina," I reply.

He nods. "For Aina."

I place my hands flat on the table. "Do it, old man. I'm ready."

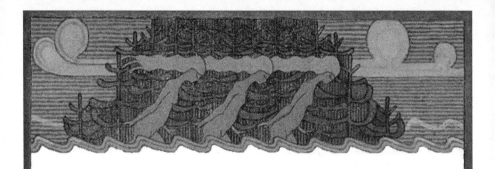

Aina

5

"TELL ME ABOUT JAAKO," I say, helping myself to a second jam tart.

Across the table, the god of death sits, sharing a meal with me. He glances over the flickering candles, the light playing off his white and black eyes. When he tilts his head in that way, dark brows lowered, shadows dancing on his face, I can almost see the raven inside him.

"What do you wish to know?" he asks.

"Where is he?"

"He is here." Tuoni taps a finger to his chest.

"He's inside you?"

"He *is* me, wife."

I set my tart aside, sucking the jam off my thumb. "I don't understand. How did the curse work? Tuonetar shackled you with goblin-forged chains that limited your magic. How could you then visit me as the raven?"

He's quiet for a moment. "I'd need a shaman to confirm my theory, but I think soul magic cannot be contained. She could have my body, she could have my ability to make fire, manipulate shadow, control the dead. But she couldn't have my soul. That part of me will always be free. I am no shaman, so it took some time for me to work out how, but I found a way to release my luonto."

"Your luonto?"

He gives me a patient smile. "The piece of my soul that takes the form of a raven."

"Can I ask another question?"

"Ask me any question, wife. I will answer."

I reach for the tart again. "You know, you may call me 'Aina.'"

"I prefer 'wife.'"

I sigh, taking another bite of the berry tart. Across the table, Tuoni seems oddly at ease sitting in this silence, while I feel like I have a hive of bees buzzing inside me. As the raven, he listened to me prattle on for hours every night. It should be easier to speak to him, now that he can respond. But what could I say that a god would possibly want to hear? He sits there, black-bearded and fearsome, a complete mystery to me.

"What do you like, my lord?"

He's still looking at me. He hasn't stopped since I pulled him from the tree. He never stopped as the raven either. "What?"

"You can't possibly do the duties of a king at all hours of the day and night," I stammer on like a nervous fool. "So . . . what do you do with all your time?"

He narrows his eyes, the motion crinkling the jagged scar on his cheek. "Why do you ask such a question?"

"Because I seek to know you, my lord. Do you like cloud-berries, for instance?" I gesture to the little plate of them sitting on the table. "Not everyone likes berries. It's the seeds, I think."

He glances at the small dish of berries by his hand. "I like cloudberries."

"And?" I smile in encouragement. "What else, my lord?"

"Are we still talking of my food preferences?"

"Why not?" I say with a nervous laugh. "Do you prefer to hunt, forage, or fish?"

"Hunt."

"I like to forage," I offer. "Alone in the woods, the feel of the sun on my skin, the search for rare herbs and flowers, the thrill when I find that which evades me. It's how I prefer to hunt."

"You should never be alone in the woods," he warns. "And foraging isn't hunting."

"It is to me," I reply. "It's far superior to a hunt. Nothing bleeds when you forage. Nothing dies."

He holds my gaze, missing nothing of my meaning. "I like to read."

I lean forward, genuinely curious. "You can read, my lord?"

His head tilts in confusion. "Of course I can read."

"Who taught you?"

He considers with a frown. "You know, I have no idea. Perhaps I've always known."

"And do your daughters read?"

"Of course. Everyone can read," he says dismissively.

"By 'everyone,' I assume you mean gods. Certainly you can't mean mere mortals."

Understanding dawns on him and he sighs, setting his cup aside. "You can't read."

"I'm hardly alone, my lord. Only the priests for the foreign god can read."

"Well, if you'd like, I can teach you," he offers.

My breath catches. "You would teach me to read?"

"If you wish. In which language?"

I laugh. "I only speak the one, my lord."

"Well, we can work on that too."

I've always longed to read. It feels so isolating to know there might be a world of knowledge hidden away inside those inked pages. "Thank you, my lord."

He pops a few of the cloudberries into his mouth. "And I like to ride."

I smile, taking a sip of my wine. "A fitting kingly pursuit, I think."

He narrows his eyes at me again. "You can't ride either."

"Your new queen is just a poor woodworker's daughter, my lord. Your fire-sided stallion was the first horse I ever rode."

The chair scrapes back as he stands, holding out a hand. "Come."

I rise. "Where are we going?"

He smiles. Unlike the wretched Witch Queen, it meets his eyes. "I can't teach you to read in a day, but I can certainly teach you to ride."

The dead servants scurry with excitement as Tuoni and I stride into the stable courtyard. He's dressed all in black, the heavy wolf pelt back on his shoulders. I walk at his side, dressed in thick, reindeer-fur boots, a cream woolen dress, and a blue hooded mantle trimmed with white rabbit fur.

The fur tickles my chin as I peer around, noting the way the dead fawn over us. No longer do they slink away like dogs waiting to be kicked. A child bounds forward. A young woman approaches with a tray, offering me a steaming cup of mint tea. This is Tuonela under Tuoni, relaxed and free.

It makes me ache . . . it makes me hope.

Tuoni steps away, giving orders to the guards in the stable. In moments, the servants lead two horses to us. The first is a menacing dapple-grey charger. The other horse is smaller in frame, more docile, its coat a sleek, snowy white.

Tuoni takes the reins of the smaller horse. "He's a calm fellow."

Handing my cup of tea back to the maid, I approach the horse. I let him sniff me, his whiskers tickling my palm. "Hello," I coo, giving his face a pat. "You're a pretty thing."

Tuoni stands by the animal's shoulder. "Come. Give me your foot."

Humming with excitement, I step around behind him and grip the supple leather frame of the saddle. Tuoni gives me a boost, helping me settle. He slips my foot into the stirrup. "Keep your heels down, and gather your reins like this." He shows me the proper hold. "Horses are sensitive. You don't need a heavy hand or leg to get your way."

I nod, and he steps away, leaving me on my mount. The snow-white horse stands calm and patient.

Tuoni swings up into his saddle. "Let the horse do the work," he says over his shoulder, leading the way through the pair of double doors.

"Wait," I call. "You can't mean for us to go out there?"

Tuoni just laughs, continuing through the entry courtyard and out through the wide-open palace doors. Sitting atop his horse, the god of death rides boldly into the endless night. Feeling a surge of excitement, I give my mount a little nudge to follow.

We ride for what feels like hours, weaving along the edge of the forest and across meadows. Before long, my mount is cantering over a snowy hill, Tuoni's charger snorting at my side. The snow crunches under my horse's hooves as the cold wind blows my hood back. I feel the chill of it on my cheeks. I thought Tuonela was a realm of darkness, but Tuoni is right, there is light if you know where to look. The moon must be full, so the snow glows a little brighter. The light from the palace shines like another kind of sun.

As we ride, we pass many sleeping and wandering dead. There are creatures here too. Eager to greet Tuoni, they approach. A swarm of keijulainen follow us through the trees. They look like little birds made of flame. They flutter around us, teasing and swift. We pass a wolf mother and her cubs. Like Hiiden hevonen, their sides are made of iron, and they have fire in their eyes.

Tuoni slows his horse to a trot as we move into the shadow of a looming hill, and the keijulainen flit away. "Are you well?" he asks, searching my face. "You look cold. Do you wish to return?"

I smile. For the first time since I arrived in Tuonela, I feel free. I feel like the Aina before Kalma, before lonely nights and cursed bread, before Witch Queens and blood oaths. "I am well, my lord. Only thirsty."

Without hesitation, he swings out of his saddle, tying his horse to a low-hanging branch. I slide off too, gasping in pain as my cold feet hit the ground. Tuoni is under his horse's neck and at my side, hands on my shoulders. "Are you hurt?"

I smile, wiggling my toes in my boots, feeling them come back to life. "I'm fine."

He lifts my hood, covering my hair against the cold, his fingers brushing along my jaw.

Reaching out, I press a hand to his chest. "Truly, my lord. I suffer from nothing but thirst."

With a reassured nod, he ties my horse to the tree. Then he offers his hand. "Come."

We weave a short distance through the snow-covered trees.

"Where are we?" I whisper, feeling an odd sort of chill that has nothing to do with the cold.

"We're near the alder tree," he says. "That hill is the Kipumäki. The river lies just beyond."

I pause, letting him pull at my hand. Kipumäki, the hill of pain, where Kivutar stirs the suffering of the world in a great pot and Kiputyttö mines rock to polish into stones of pain. So much evil and cruelty. So much anguish. No wonder the very air seems to tremble with fear.

"What is it?" Tuoni asks, squeezing my hand.

My breath feels tight in my chest as I trace the shadows of the hill. "I can't—I don't want to see it. Please, don't take me up the hill."

"We're not going up the hill," he replies. "We're going *under* it."

I let myself be led forward until we reach an odd sight. There's a round wooden door set directly into the side of the hill. "What is this place?"

"There's fresh water inside," is his only reply. He sets a palm flat on the door. He mutters a few words in a language I don't understand, something deep and guttural. Once the words are spoken, the door glows along the edges and rattles in its frame. He swings the door open and turns. "Best not tell Loviatar I've brought you here. I don't think she would like it."

"Why—"

"Just trust me," he presses.

He's so tall that he has to duck to get inside. With a wave of his hand, he sets a fire crackling to life in the hearth. I look around the room, taking in the comforts of this small underhill home. There's a table and chairs, a sitting area, and a bed in the corner. The room has a distinctly feminine feel—dried flowers in a vase on the table, a knitting basket by the fire, a standing loom in the corner with unfinished cloth upon it.

"Who lives here?"

"No one," he replies. "Not for a very long time." He rattles around, finding two cups. Then he disappears through a doorway, returning with the cups full of water. "A freshwater spring runs beneath the hill," he explains, handing me one.

"Thank you," I murmur, watching him.

He takes a turn about the room, lost in memories, his hand brushing over the back of a chair. Whoever lived here, they obviously meant a great deal to him. Strange that my first reaction is jealousy. I swallow it back with the water, clearing my throat.

"It's peaceful here," I say. This little house has all the comfort of my own home. Thinking of it makes me miss my family, and I can't bear to think of them now.

"You're sad."

I go still, looking at the fire. "I'm fine."

He steps around the table to my side. "I know your face, wife. And your thoughts. I feel you here," he adds, pressing his hand to his chest. "You're thinking of your family."

I nod.

He places a hand on my shoulder. "It's good that you miss them. The love of family is a rare gift. To be loved in return is . . ." He falls into silence, but I feel him. He holds such deep longing. Gods, he's so lonely.

Reaching out, I cup his bearded cheek. "This place holds painful memories for you. We can go—"

"No."

I drop my hand away. We stand there, not speaking. I can tell he needs comfort, but I'm not sure how to approach him. As the raven, touch felt safe. As the man . . .

"I lost someone very precious to me once," he admits. "I've never come back to this place. I don't know why I'm here now." He glances around.

I set my cup down and step in closer. "What can I do, my lord?"

To my surprise, he laughs. The sound is full of bitterness. "You seek to help with my grief? You who've endured so much. This realm, my curse . . . it took everything from you. You are blameless, wife. How can you offer help to one so broken as me? How can you even bear to be near me?"

I search his face. I see the pain there, the vulnerability. I know in his eyes, I'm perfect. Siiri has always been just the same, measuring all her own faults against what she perceives as my perfection. It's a heavy crown for anyone to wear.

"I stole something once," I whisper.

He raises a dark brow. "What?"

"Siiri's mummi makes the most delicious blackberry pies. Once, when she was busy in the garden, I stole one right off her table. I didn't even share it with Siiri. Her brother Onni caught me. I had to kiss his cheek so he wouldn't tell Siiri or their mummi what I'd done."

He blinks.

"So . . . I'm a thief," I say with a shrug. "I'm a thief and a liar, and I permitted a boy to kiss me so he would keep my secrets. Nobody's perfect, my lord."

Slowly, his mouth tips into a grin. Then he barks out a laugh so loud it makes me jump.

"It wasn't meant to be funny," I mutter, embarrassment rising.

His laughter dies and he holds out his hand. "Come here."

Hesitant, I step forward, taking his hand. He pulls me in, wrapping his arms around me. With his chin resting against my temple, I can still feel the laughter he holds in his chest.

"So, this young man took advantage of you? Do you want me to kill him?"

"No," I cry, pulling away. I'm mortified until he smirks. "It's not funny," I say, slapping his chest. "Kaisa was furious, and Siiri took the blame. She was splitting firewood for a week. I've never told anyone. Only Onni knows."

He laughs again, smoothing my hair back from my face. "Listen to me, you wild and dangerous creature. You will never have to resort to stealing pies again. And as your husband," he adds, the growl in the word making my stomach flip, "if I ever hear of you being forced to trade romantic favors with a man so he'll keep your secrets, I'll find the brigand and string him up by the ears on my palace walls."

I purse my lips. "That won't be necessary, my lord."

His smile falls as he lets himself look at me with the same unabashed curiosity as the raven. I hold still as he lifts a hand, brushing his thumb over my lips. "Call me by my name."

The thought of saying his name excites me as much as it makes me nervous. Since I pulled him from the tree, I've been playing a careful game of pretending he's someone else. But he can't be a handsome man from a neighboring village with a name that strikes fear into the hearts of all Finns.

He leans closer, our foreheads almost touching. "Say it."

Heart in my throat, I whisper his name. "Tuoni."

His control snaps, and I'm in his arms. Our lips meet in a pressing kiss. Gods, I want to sink into this feeling. I want to feel safe. I want to feel cherished, protected. His hand slips beneath the edge of my fur-lined cloak, his fingertips grazing the bare skin exposed in the V of my woolen dress.

I hiss and pull back, pushing on his shoulders with both hands. "Stop."

Cool air rushes between us, and I take a halting step backwards. My heart is beating so loudly in my chest, I'm sure he can hear it. He's looking at me. He's always looking at me. I close my eyes, shaking my head. "I need . . . this is . . ."

He takes a step closer, his hands brushing down my arms as if to comfort me. "This is madness," I murmur. "I still don't know you. I don't know anything about you, and I've never—" I blush, letting my truth fall unspoken.

He doesn't advance, but neither does he step away.

My eyes flutter open to see him still looking at me.

"You said you weren't afraid of me," he challenges.

"I'm not."

"Do you now believe I mean to harm you, wife?"

"No."

"And do you believe I would ever allow another to do you harm?"

"You did," I cry, pulling away. "These witches have done nothing but scare me and torture me, starve me—"

"I was bound," he replies. "I did everything I could to protect you, to protect all the girls, even in my cursed state. I risked everything to curtail Tuonetar's power. For the longest time, I *lost* everything. There are things that cannot be recovered, Aina. Wounds that cannot heal, lives that can never be made whole again."

I close my eyes against the pain in his voice.

He steps closer, and I let him. "From the moment I met you, I knew you could be my redemption, my light in the dark. You stood before me and declared yourself mine. You freed me, Aina. I am myself again, and I *will* protect you."

"I'm yours?" I repeat. "Your property, my lord?"

"No."

"Your servant?"

He takes me by the shoulders. "You are my wife and my queen. Gods hear me, you'll be my lover too. Mother of my children, mate of my soul." His grip softens, even as he holds fast to me. "But I vowed kindness. I will never force you, Aina. You will come to me willingly, or not at all."

"You would force me without meaning to," I reply, fighting the urge to tremble. "You're doing it now. This bond in my chest pulls at me. And then you look at me. *Please*—will you just stop looking at me? You did it as the raven and now as the man—I feel like I can't breathe with you always looking at me!"

He smirks, not looking away. "Shall I close my eyes and feel my way out of the room? You may have to help me mount my horse."

I bristle. "And now you're laughing at me."

His smile falls. "I told you, wife. You have all the power here. I don't think I've ever been so completely unveiled before another soul." He rubs absently at his chest. "This bond is a curious surprise." He glances back at me, dropping his hand to his side. "I will wait for you."

My heart squeezes tight. "I don't want you to wait for me. Don't you understand? I know what I promised at the alder tree, but I *can't* give in to this, my lord. I can't give you children. Not in this place. I can't—I can't pretend Tuonetar doesn't live in my house. I can't forget that your daughters who betrayed you and sold you out to the Witch Queen still eat at my table."

"They are being dealt with," he replies. "They are not a threat to you. Aina, please—"

I shake my head, tears welling. Behind his calm demeanor, buried deep within the bond, I feel his anguish, his fear and loneliness. My threats are breaking him. Ilmatar help me, I think the god of death is in love with me. My voice is hesitant as I say, "How long will you wait for me?"

He takes my question as an invitation and steps forward. Cupping my face, he presses his lips to my forehead. "Until day is night and night is day," he vows. "Until snow falls from the earth and birds fly north for winter. Is that what you want to hear?" His thumb slides against the coolness of my cheek. "I know you, Aina. I *see* you. Tuoni, god of death, doesn't frighten you. I don't even think you're afraid of Tuonela. Not anymore. Not in my arms. You're afraid to give yourself to me . . . afraid to *lose* yourself to me."

I swallow my frustration, hating how easy it is for him to read me.

"I will come to you as a poet if that is what you wish," he goes on. "I'll whisper honeyed words and make you feel like the queen of the forest. I will play the eager bridegroom. I will court you with flowers and songs. If that's what you need, I will do it. But know this, wife: all words are hollow in the end. No words I speak will lead you to love me. You will love me for my actions."

"Tuoni—"

He steps away, placing a chaste kiss on my hand. "Take all the time you want. Deny me for a hundred years if you wish. Mortal men may lack the strength to stand before your radiance, but I am not mortal . . . and I'm not going anywhere."

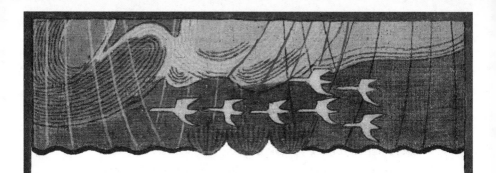

Siiri

I SIT AT VÄINÄMÖINEN'S low table. A bucket of fresh ice thaws by the hearth. The scraps from our shared meal still litter the table. I give the clear liquor in my cup a wary sniff. "What did you say this is?"

Väinämöinen chuckles, dropping to his knees at the table and picking up his own cup. He takes a contented sip, smacking his lips. "It's a barley mash. I sweeten it with juniper berries. Try it, girl."

He rifles through a basket as I take a small sip. The liquor stings like fire all the way down my throat. "*Poison*," I rasp, setting the cup aside.

He barks out another laugh. "Keep drinking. This will hurt. My mash will help numb the pain."

Aside from the crumbs of our meal, the table is now scattered with Väinämöinen's tattooing tools. I grimace at the set of small fishbone needles tucked inside a strip of leather.

"I've been saving this for something special," he says, taking something from his vest pocket.

"Saving what?"

He dangles a little leather pouch in his outstretched hand. "Do you know what this is?"

"How can I possibly know?"

He hands it over. "Look inside."

I untie the worn leather strings. Working the top open with two fingers, I dip one inside. Fine black dust coats my skin. "It's ash."

"It's not just any ash, fool girl." He takes the bag holding it reverently, his eyes misting. "It's oak ash, taken from the first oak tree."

I go still, heart racing. "You can't mean . . . the oak you planted with Sampsa Pellervoinen?" I can hardly believe it. How many times has Mummi told me stories of Väinämöinen and that first oak tree?

"The very same," he says, smiling.

"The oak that grew so tall it blotted out the sun, moon, and stars?"

He chuckles as he mixes a pinch of the ash into a bowl with water. "It was tall, yes. The songs may exaggerate it a bit, though."

I frown at him. "You wrote the songs."

He laughs again, that mustache twitching.

"The oak tree was cut down by the Copper Man, yes? They say he was as tall as the tree."

"When I first met him, he was so small he could fit in my pocket," Väinämöinen replies. "I thought it was a trick when he emerged from the water in his little copper suit saying he was sent to fell the tree. But then, my mother always liked a good joke."

"Your mother," I murmur. Sometimes I forget where I am. I sit before Väinämöinen, greatest of all shamans, and the All-Mother is his mother.

He hums, focused on his work as he turns the ash to ink. "Take the other leather pouch out of that box." He directs me with a nod towards the small box on the table.

I flip the lid, curious to see what other treasures he keeps. Inside are a few trinkets: a fine-toothed comb, a jeweled brooch, a lock of black hair tied with a white string, and the pouch. I run my finger over the tines of the ornate bone comb. "These look like they belonged to a lady."

"They did . . . they do," he corrects.

"Who?" I say, plucking out the pouch.

"A friend," he replies. "She left it with me for safekeeping."

"What's in this pouch?"

"Open it and see."

I wrinkle my nose as I inspect the soil pinched between my fingers. "Is it dirt?"

He hums again. "Grave dirt. From Tuonela."

I scowl down at the bag.

"Give us a pinch, then," he says, stirring the ink with a thin twig.

My hand tightens on the pouch. "You'll mix grave dirt into the ink? You're asking me to wear Tuonela under my skin?"

Slowly, he looks up, his eyes somber and knowing. "Life and death, Siiri. A shaman must seek to understand, respect, and *appreciate* both. You don't fear death any more than I do; you harbor hatred of the death gods, which is itself your great grief at the loss of your beloved Aina. If you are to become any kind of shaman at all, you must be willing to *understand* Tuonela and her gods. They are part of the great balance." He holds out the little bowl of ink, waiting.

With a huff, I work a pinch of the black soil between my fingers, sprinkling it atop the wet ink. "Life and death," I echo, watching as he stirs it in. I take a swig of his terrible barley mash, coughing as it burns its way down my throat.

Slowly, he reaches across the table for my hand.

Clutching the cup in my right hand, I extend my left. "Väinämöinen?"

He bends his head over my hand as he gently washes it. "Hmm?"

"Who was she?"

"Who was who?" he replies, not looking up.

"The girl who gave you that box," I say. "The girl you stole out of Tuonela."

He goes still. "What do you mean?"

"You say you took something from Tuonela," I press. "I thought it might be some deep magic, another spell . . ."

"But?"

"But others before and after you stole spells from Tuonela— or so the stories say," I continue. "I believe you took something else. The gods fought you to keep it. Once you were free of them, they continued to hunt you. They never forgave you. They can never forget. All these long years later, the Witch Queen still wreaks her vengeance on you. Few emotions have the power to create such enmity."

"And which emotions are those?"

I know he's testing me. I know he wants to see if I can puzzle this out on my own. We'll call it more shaman training. "Jealousy is a powerful emotion. It tends to linger. It makes us irrational. Grief, too . . . but grief often fades with time, thank the gods," I add, thinking of the scar in my heart where my mother once lived.

"Are those the only two motivations for the Witch Queen's enmity?"

"Love," I whisper, my gaze locked on our joined hands.

"Love?"

I look up. "You say that to be a shaman, I must understand and respect the death gods. Well, I think the Witch

Queen and I have something in common. I understand her rage, her resolute determination."

"Oh?"

I nod. "She fights with the same fire of will I now wield to free Aina. You took someone from her . . . didn't you? It must be someone dear to her, someone important. A child, perhaps?"

His mustache twitches as he holds my gaze. "Your passion does you credit."

"An answer that is no answer at all."

"Knowledge is power," he intones.

"Meaning you still don't trust me with your secrets. What must I do to prove myself?"

"Continue your training," he replies gently. "Master your itse, and I will tell you all I know of Tuonela. I will tell you who I met there . . . and what I took." He picks up a sharp fish bone, dipping it in the black ink. "But first, we must get you tethered." He taps the table with a tattooed finger.

Flexing my fingers flat on the cool wood, I relax, willing him to begin.

Väinämöinen proves to have gentle hands, but there is no ignoring that he's piercing my skin over and over. Using a damp rag, he wipes away my blood along with the excess ink. He's methodical, completing each rune and pausing to admire his work.

I spend most of the day gazing at the crown of his head. He stays hunched over my hand, humming quietly as he works. The rune of the bear-riding girl is followed by ones for the sun, a lake, reindeer and a hut, a bow and arrow, and two hunters denoting my brothers. Like the shaman, I now have runes going up my fingers as well, covering the first and second knuckles—runes for strength and joy, one for time, one for love, one for power.

"This hand represents life," he says, putting the finishing touches on the rune for my shaman drum on the first knuckle of my thumb. "Your other hand will represent Tuonela."

"Will I go there tonight? Am I ready?"

He snorts. "A girl with fresh tattoos who only just learned how to free her luonto? I'll not send you through the veil until we're sure you can inhabit your itse and recall it again."

"We don't have time to practice," I counter. "The death witches could be working all manner of pain and suffering upon Aina. She could be injured. She could be—" I swallow the words, refusing to say them aloud, even if they burn in the quiet darkness of my heart.

Slowly, Väinämöinen gazes up at me. "Go on, girl. Say it."

I shake my head.

"*Say* it," he barks. "Speak aloud that which you fear."

A moment stretches between us; only the fire crackles.

"She could be dead," I whisper.

He nods. "And is that your worst fear, Siiri Jarintyttär?"

My gaze drops to my hand.

"Ah, I strike the proper chord at last."

I jerk my hand away, and he lets me go, the tattoos now finished.

"You don't fear your own death. You fear *her* death," he goes on, his words like a knife to my heart. "You are right to fear it. For Tuonetar is unequaled in the skills of torture and bloodletting. If she stole all those maidens as you say, and if her design is merely to play her wicked games, then your Aina is surely dead."

I raise my gaze to his and hold it.

He nods. "Yes . . . you have doubts too. You question the

death gods' motives. Why did Kalma take her? On whose orders? With whom does Aina now spend her endless nights?"

"What is your own theory?" I ask, afraid to hear the answer.

He clears away the mess on the table before us, wringing out the rag in the bucket of fresh lake water. Then he holds out his hand and waits. With a sigh, I extend my right hand, bracing myself for the next round of pain.

"This hand will represent Tuonela," he says, brushing a calloused thumb over my skin. "The first rune I shall mark on you is the raven. Do you know who that is?"

I nod.

"Say his name."

"Tuoni," I whisper. As I do, the fire behind him sputters and hisses, moved on an unseen wind. I fight a shiver. "You met him in Tuonela."

He nods. "He's an interesting immortal. Not at all what I was expecting. I think you might actually like him. You'd surely respect his plight."

"His plight?"

"When I was first captured, it was Tuoni who sheltered me, much to the dismay of the Witch Queen. We spent many long nights together, drinking and talking. He asked me many questions about the realm of the living. And he answered my questions about death in return."

I wince as he makes the first stab into my skin. "What do you make of his character? Is he a cruel god? Would he hurt Aina?"

He's quiet, focused on his work. "The Tuoni I knew was a lonely man," he replies. "We had much in common. He told me of his dreams, his hope for the future of his realm. His hope for his own future . . . his legacy. Lonely men can do desperate things, Siiri."

A feeling of dread creeps down my spine. Did Aina not say

the same thing to me on the day she was taken? "Why do you say such things?"

He glances up over my splayed hand. "Because a girl as clever as you has surely thought about this puzzle from all sides. Why would the death gods take mortals to the underworld? According to you, they are all young women, all unmarried . . ."

"Please just speak your mind, old man," I beg, too tired to keep puzzling this through on my own.

He sets aside his tools, holding my gaze. "I will, my stubborn little woodpecker. The Witch Queen has no fondness for mortals. She has no fondness for anyone except her daughters, and then only when they're behaving monstrously. Her only interest in mortals would be in watching them suffer and die. So, if your dear Aina is still alive, someone is *keeping* her alive. Do you understand me?"

My dread grows, even as my voice remains calm. "You believe, if she's still alive, Aina is being sheltered by another immortal?" My mind races as I consider the possibilities. "Only one other death god has the power to protect Aina from the bloodthirsty Witch Queen . . . right?"

"Only one," Väinämöinen echoes with a nod.

"Tuoni," I say again. "The stories tell of death's maidens, but I always thought they were meant to be his daughters, not his captives."

"Or his lovers . . ."

"One cannot call one's captive a lover," I snap. "And my Aina would never let any man use her in such a way. Not even an immortal."

"You don't know what's at stake," he replies solemnly. "I have seen people do wild and dangerous things, Siiri." He pauses for a moment, his thumb brushing over the inkless skin of my right hand. "I know a woman who chose to drown herself rather than become a god's prize."

I stare at the top of his white head. He's speaking of Aino, the fair sister of Joukahainen that was meant to be his bride. It wasn't enough for her that she chose death over becoming his wife. In death she taunted him, appearing to him in the form of fish, only to transform and swim away, forcing him to catch her and lose her all over again.

"Väinämöinen . . ." I turn my palm in his grip, giving his hand a squeeze. "That wasn't your fault. She made her choice—"

"As your Aina will make hers," he replies. "You must prepare yourself, Siiri."

"Prepare myself?"

"You fight to save a friend you believe wants to be saved. In your heart, you cling to the hope that she *can* be saved. But Tuonela is a realm of magic and monsters. It is a realm built from your darkest nightmares. There is no telling what your Aina has done to survive. The Aina who left you on the shores of your lakeside home may not be the same Aina you find once you cross the river. You must decide now whether she is truly worth the risk."

"Of course she is," I say without hesitation. "There is nothing she could do that would turn me from her."

He nods. "Cling to that, then . . . and forgive her, Siiri."

"Forgive her?"

"Accept her for who she is now, not who you wish she could still be. And if she declines your offer of escape—"

"She would never do that—"

"*If* she declines," he continues over me, "you must be ready to let her go and return empty-handed."

I shake my head, pushing those fears down into the deepest, darkest parts of my being. "Aina will always choose to come home, and that home is with me. She would never betray me. And you will never deter me, old man. I'm rescuing Aina, and I'm taking you *both* home."

He turns his attention back to his work, stabbing the rune of the raven into my skin. "I know where you must go to practice with your itse."

"Where?"

"The first time you send your itse out, it needs to be to a place you know in body and soul," he explains. "You should know it better than the backs of these hands I now tether. It will make it easier to navigate your way there and back." He glances up with a twinkle in his eye. "Do you know of such a place?"

A smile quirks my lips. "You want me to return to Lake Päijänne."

He nods, dipping the fishbone needle back into the ink. "We'll try it tonight."

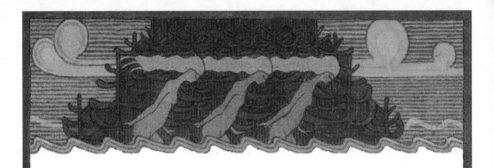

Aina

37

I WAKE DISORIENTED IN a new room. The curtains around the bed are pulled shut, wrapping me in warmth. I blink a few times in the welcoming darkness. Yesterday, I woke in the room Tuonetar designed to be my cage. This morning, I wake in the queen's suite.

And I wake alone.

After our late-night ride, Tuoni returned me to this room without crossing the threshold. He stood on the dark landing and bid me goodnight. No chaste touches, no searing kisses. Nothing. Is he really so committed to waiting? His only request was that I not leave the room until morning. Feeling safe for the first time since arriving in Tuonela, sleep came easy.

Now, I'm awake.

I sit up, my unbound hair spilling down my back. As I pull back the curtain, there comes a knock at the door. A fire burns high in the hearth, and candles glow along the mantle. More candles light the table where breakfast is laid.

My gaze darts to the locked door. "Who is it?"

"It's me."

Me. The god of death has no need for further identification.

"Coming." I slip out of bed in nothing but a thin shift and wool socks. I wrap my robe around my shivering shoulders and hurry over to the door, pulling it open.

Tuoni stands on my doorstep. He looks different from last night, and just the same. He has bathed. The ash that greyed his hair is gone. Now he is the sleek, black raven. His hair is tied back, changing the shape of his face. Otherwise, he still wears the clothes of a hunter—dark breeches and boots, a thick wool tunic, a cowl.

He looks me over from my unbound hair to my socked feet. "You slept well?"

"Yes, my lord. Thank you." At his annoyed look, I smile. "Yes, Tuoni."

"I have some things to attend to today outside the palace," he says. "I'll ask that if you leave this room, you bring a maid. You had one from before. Is she still acceptable to you?"

I blink in confusion. "A maid? Do you mean Kukka?"

"Who?"

"The dead maid Vammatar assigned to me."

He nods.

"Yes, she's acceptable."

He snaps his fingers, and Kukka appears in a swirl of shadow. "Serve your mistress," he commands.

Kukka bows her head, hurrying over to the table to prepare my tea.

"I can leave the room?" I ask, watching her work with her odd, broken fingers.

He frowns, one brow raised. "You're not my prisoner. You're my wife and my queen. Soon we'll have you crowned, and all the gods in all the realms will honor you." With that, he turns to leave.

"Wait," I call out.

He pauses, his hand on the door, not turning around.

"Will I see you later?"

He turns, his face unreadable. He's quiet down the bond too. "Is that what you want?"

Slowly, I nod.

His mouth twitches with a smile. "Then I will come to you later."

The thought of freedom is too delicious to ignore. I finish breakfast and dress, tucking my marriage knife at my hip. With Kukka at my side, I journey down the spiraling stone steps in search of my first adventure alone as Queen of Tuonela.

I start in the garden, collecting roots, flowers, and stems to dry for teas. Before long, I find my way to the bustling kitchen courtyard. Kukka holds my foraging basket as all the dead hurry to accommodate me, offering me slices of fresh buttered bread and sweet treats. It feels strange not to see the other girls, but I'm relieved to know they're safe from Tuonetar's wickedness.

The others would still be here if not for Loviatar. Two days ago, the blind weaver was my friend, my only ally in this dark place. Now, everything is different. I know more. I *see* more.

And I have questions.

Steeling myself, I march across to the weaving room. Kukka hurries around me, opening it before I can reach out. Once inside, I breathe deeply of the familiar scents of wood and lanolin. Then I hear the *clack, clack, clack.*

"She returns," Loviatar calls without pausing in her work.

I move down the row to where she works alone. "May I sit with you?"

"Sit, don't sit. You outrank me now . . . my *queen*."

I sink onto the stool she left beside her loom. "I've come to ask you something."

"I am at your disposal, my queen."

I purse my lips, sensing the teasing in her tone. "Are you quite finished?"

Her hands pause in their work. "Ask."

"Does Tuonela have a sauna?"

She sighs in annoyance, setting her shuttle down. "We're not animals, Aina. Of course we have a sauna."

"Wonderful. Meet me after supper, and you can show me the way."

At first sight of the sauna, I groan with longing. It's a small wooden hut, nestled at the edge of the snowy wood, perched beside a dark pool. A narrow dock extends several feet over the water. Beyond the pool, thick pines ring the shore, making the space feel intimate and peaceful. The sauna and the dock are lit with torches, casting a golden glow. Behind me, high on the hill, the palace glows even brighter.

Loviatar walks silently at my side. Kukka walks at my other side, holding a torch aloft. In the golden light, I take her in. She's still the same Kukka, with her fumbling gait, vacant expression, and broken fingers. But her thin hair is brushed. Her clothes are clean: a white wool dress layered under a grey woolen overdress. Across her chest is embroidered the sign of the black raven, its wings spread wide. From the raven's head, three lines extend like a sun's rays.

"I've never seen such a sigil before," I say as we walk.

"Tuonetar banned all signs or mention of the king,"

Loviatar replies, her clouded eyes unblinking as she moves unhurriedly to the edge of the pool.

"This is the king's sigil?" I glance over my shoulder to the pair of dead guards behind us. The sigil on their chests is different. It is still a raven, but instead of a sun's rays, their ravens wear crowns.

"The maid wears your sign," Loviatar clarifies.

"My sign?"

"They're calling it the Sun Raven. The Queen's Raven."

I smile, empowered by the idea. A mortal queen that shines with the light of the rising sun. The dark and the light. Death and life. Immortality and mortality.

Loviatar quietly sheds her clothing until she stands naked, her long, black hair plaited down her back. She doesn't shiver in the winter cold. Ignoring me, she walks right into the frigid pool. Her pale skin is cast into even brighter effect by the darkness of the water. Slowly, she turns, now waist deep. Her chest is marred by thick, raised scars. Down her arms I see evidence of still more pain and suffering. She lifts her tattooed hands from the water, tucking her hair behind her ears. "Do you not wish to bathe, my queen?"

I shed my clothes, handing off each layer to Kukka. The winter chill burns my skin as I hurry over to the pool's edge. The water is deep and cold. It will sting like a thousand slaps from a nettle. With a squeal, I dive in, letting it claim every inch of my skin. I break the surface with a sharp gasp. "Gods' blood, it's f-freezing."

Loviatar turns with a frown. "You do realize the goddess of illness stands at your side?"

"I do," I reply, treading water to keep my muscles from turning to ice.

"Do you fear no sickness then?"

I splash her, laughing as she hisses like an angry cat. "Should I be pleased that you're worried?"

"Do not flatter yourself, little mouse."

"You said you sometimes go to the realm of the living," I say, floating away.

"I used to," she replies. "That was long ago."

Finding the pebbly bottom, I stand in the water. "You don't go anymore?"

She glares. "You are too curious for your own good. Ask a question of a witch, and she may decide to answer."

"You know, the stories and songs paint you as unfeeling and vicious. Some call you even more monstrous than Tuonetar. Some give you another name: Louhi, Witch of the Northland. They tell tales of your children, sent forth as plagues upon the world of men."

Her hands brushes down the scars on her arms. "Do not speak of my children."

"So, it's true? Your sons are the nine plagues of men?"

She purses her lips.

"And what of your nameless daughter? The one you helped to escape—"

"You will not speak of her," she hisses, turning my way at last.

I cross to her side. "You saved your father. You saved me. You saved the other girls—"

"Because I am selfish and manipulative. Do not paint me as your champion, Aina. I am Loviatar and Louhi, black of heart, old and wicked, worst of all the death-land women. Yes, I know all your wretched songs."

"I believe them," I say. "I believe the songs. I believe you are wicked and self-serving. I believe you connive to get your way." I reach out a hand to her. "But I believe you are more—"

"Don't. Believe nothing good of me, Aina." She wades out of the water towards the sauna.

"For weeks, I've tried to make sense of all this," I say, following after her. "Why was I taken? What purpose did I serve? Kalma finally makes sense. She was playing Tuonetar the whole time. Her loyalty to Tuoni is unyielding. She was ready to kill a hundred mortal girls so long as she found the one who could break his curse. She's a monster. She's utterly unforgivable and yet I understand her."

Loviatar scoffs. "She'll be thrilled to hear it."

"What I didn't understand was you," I call after her. "Why did you shelter me in your hand? Why did you help me get to Tuoni? What did you stand to gain with his freedom and Tuonetar's fall? Now I know!"

She keeps walking. Wrenching the door of the sauna open, she disappears.

I join her inside. The heat is enough to take my breath away, my senses filling with the smell of warm pine. I blink in the darkness, looking to where the witch already sits, fanning herself with a birch vihta. "I believe you love your children," I say, closing the door behind me. "You love your daughter. And I believe she was once here in Tuonela. She was the girl you set free."

Loviatar stills.

"Tuoni took me under the hill last night. I saw, Loviatar. I saw where she lived. Was that place her home . . . or her prison?"

"He had no right to take you there," she hisses.

"He grieves her too. His grief is enough to drown him. I feel it through our bond. He loves her, as he loves you—"

"I *hate* him!" She leaps to her feet, tossing the vihta aside. "How can I not, when loving him has cost me everything?"

"Tell me."

She growls low in her throat, the sound a mix of anger and pain. "I was on his side from the beginning. I heard all his beautiful dreams. I wanted that Tuonela for myself, for my children. My daughter wanted to help us. We were ready to fight against Tuonetar, ready to make my sisters see reason but we failed. Tuoni is not the only one the Witch Queen punished."

"What happened?"

Loviatar's eyes gleam in the dark, as if her memories are a form of vision. "She took her from me. Tuonetar hid her away. For years, I couldn't find her. I didn't know whether she was dead or alive. It took a shaman to find her buried under that hill. And it took everything we had to get her out."

"And under Tuonetar's rule, she could never safely come back to Tuonela," I guess. "And you could never leave."

Slowly, the witch sinks back down onto the wooden bench. "Yes."

"You helped Tuoni, and it cost you your daughter. So you used Tuonetar's curse and Kalma's zeal to find Tuoni a bride that could break his curse. For, only when his curse broke, and he reclaimed Tuonela, could you be free to reunite with your lost daughter."

A smile quirks her lips as she reaches out and cups my face. "Such a clever girl."

I brush her hand away. "You never cared about me. You're just like the others. You sank your claws into me, manipulated me, and served me up to your father as a prize. You won, Loviatar. I am bound to him and to this realm, a life of endless night. And now you're free. You can leave Tuonela, never to think of me again."

She picks up the vihta and fans herself. "You've been doing so well, little mouse. Don't disappoint me now by weeping and saying you'll never forgive me. It's far too trite, too human."

"I do," I say quickly. "I forgive you, Loviatar."

The witch stills, the birch bundle clutched in her tattooed hand.

"A mother's love holds fast and forever. If I ever become a mother, I imagine there is nothing I won't do to keep my children safe. I can forgive you without forgetting. And mark me, witch, I will *never* forget what you did to me."

She flutters the vihta again, a proud smile back on her face. "And how shall you punish me, my queen?"

I take in the lines of her face, the fall of her raven-black hair. "I won't."

"Aina, you *must* punish those who wrong you. It's foolish not to. It's weak."

"You would take punishment as absolution," I reply. "This isn't about winning and losing for me, Loviatar. This is about my life and having a choice in how I live it. You took that from me as surely as Kalma did. Was it in your power to help me escape this whole time? Could you have saved me, even while Tuoni was bound?"

The witch says nothing.

I sigh. "You chose to help me only as it suited your own gain. To reunite with your daughter, I was the necessary sacrifice. You owe me, Loviatar. Give me her name."

"Ask me anything else."

"My mother says names hold deep magic," I reply. "There is power in knowing a name, and you have kept your daughter's name from the stories and songs for generations. I was under your power, and now I will have you under mine. Tell me your daughter's name."

The witch is quiet for a moment. "You're right, Aina. A mother's love is as fierce as a winter storm. I have spent a lifetime protecting my child. I fear my voice can no longer speak her name."

Setting my anger aside, I place my hand on hers. "This is not a punishment, Loviatar. I vow to you: I will not hurt her or you. This is *trust*. My trust with you is broken. *You* broke it. If you ever want to repair it, you know the road."

Slowly, she nods.

Feeling overheated and overwhelmed, I rise to my feet. "If you demand a punishment, let it be this: You will not leave this realm in search of your daughter before I hear her name from your lips."

"Aina, no—"

"As Queen of Tuonela, that is my command."

Loviatar leans back against the wooden wall with a softly muttered curse, her eyes shut in frustration.

Nursing my own pain, I leave her there. Stepping back outside, I hurry through the snow on bare feet, not even feeling the cold as I run naked to the end of the wooden dock. My skin prickles with the cold as I peer into the black water. A shadow of my reflection looks up at me. I frown at her. I hardly recognize myself. Aina Taavintyttär is sweet and kind. A summer berry, Siiri calls me. To her, I am a paragon of goodness and gentleness. I am peaceful and even-tempered. That's what men like in a wife, and a wife is all I was ever raised to be.

Now I am someone's wife, and my every feeling revolts at becoming more like that girl in the water. What did goodness and kindness earn me in this dark place? I have been abused, neglected, tricked, manipulated. My peaceful nature meant I rolled over and watched as others around me fought and died for their freedom. Used by the Witch Queen to torture Tuoni. Used by Kalma to free her father. Used by Loviatar to reunite with her daughter. Used by the others for cruel entertainment. And here I stand, too scared to fight, too timid to demand justice, too shy to admit even to myself the way my body betrays me at Tuoni's every look and touch.

Rage boils inside me. It has to come out, this hate, this fear, this agonizing feeling of betrayal. Stretching my arms out wide, cold air brushing my naked skin, I let out a feral scream. It echoes out across the water, rippling my reflection. I inch my toes to the edge of the dock, ready to leap—

Clang.

My dead guards stand at the other end of the dock. They slam their swords against the metal of their shields, making that awful noise again. "What are you doing?"

Clang. Clang.

"Stop it," I cry. The sound sets my teeth on edge.

Kukka slips past them, stumbling forward. Her dead eyes are wide, making the first true expression I've ever seen: fear.

A chill slithers down my spine, coiling around my gut. "Kukka, what's wrong—"

Kukka points over my shoulder.

As I stand there on the dock, cold toes curling around the edge of the wood, something creeps across the dark surface of the water. "Oh gods . . ."

The shadow creature elongates, taking form, rising up off the water until it steps onto the end of the dock. It looks like shadows stitched into the form of a man, but the proportions are all wrong. It's impossibly tall, with narrow shoulders and lanky arms. The legs are uneven. It walks with a halting gait, making no noise as it moves. Its eyes are white, blinking like two stars.

I hurry back to Kukka's side. The dead maid takes my hand in hers, pulling me between the two guards. They square off against the shadow monster, their swords held at the ready. I give the maid's clammy hand a squeeze. "Go," I say on a breath. "Fetch Loviatar."

Kukka hesitates, torn between defending me and following my order.

"Go," I hiss.

Kukka hurries off towards the sauna. I stand in the snow, naked as a babe, watching as the shadow lets out a bone-chilling screech. It grows to twice its size, its hands lengthening into talon-like claws. It strikes out at the guards, those talons scraping across the metal of their shields. The guards parry, but the blades of their swords simply pass through its body.

"Help me," I whisper to the dark.

The creature makes quick work of the guards, smashing them to the ground with a few strikes of its powerful hands.

Behind me, the door of the sauna blasts open. Loviatar strides out, an open robe around her naked shoulders. "Kalma," she shouts, her voice laced with the magic of summoning. "Aina, get back," she adds at me.

A jet of light whirls through the air, passing right over my shoulder. It's a flaming torch, thrown by Loviatar. The torch passes through the shadow with a grotesque crackling sound. It clatters down to the dock before tumbling off the side, the flame extinguished in a hiss of steam by the dark water. The monster shrieks, its shadowy center reforming, the embers sewing themselves back together.

All the creature's attention is now on the goddess. It creeps forward on silent feet. Gods, it smells like death. It smells like Kalma.

"You ought to be asleep," Loviatar calls to it. "You dare come here seeking to feed? Away with you!" She swings with her open hand as if to slap the shadow. It recoils, clearly afraid of her touch. But then it takes a step closer.

Kukka presses in at my back, her hand wrapping around my upper arm. She pulls me away, trying to keep me from danger. With her free hand, she presses something into my palm. My fingers wrap around the hilt of my little silver knife.

"Aina, go," Loviatar calls. "Run!"

My first instinct is to obey her, but then she stumbles back, her hands seeking purchase on that which she cannot see. Loviatar is naked and unarmed . . . and blind. The shadow will soon have her pinned against the sauna. She needs me. She needs my eyes. I jerk away from Kukka's grip and step forward. "Loviatar!"

The witch goes still, her face turned towards me, pale eyes catching the light of the only remaining torch.

"Use the knife!" I say a little prayer and throw it just like Siiri taught me. It spins through the air, landing with a thud in the wood of the sauna wall not two inches from the witch's ear.

Loviatar grabs it and slices at the shadow. "You have no power here, Formless One. Go back to your grave and sleep."

The shadow shrieks, the sound like a thousand blades dragging across stone.

"Aina, you must run! Back to the palace!" Loivatar swings again, the little knife slicing through the shadowy flesh of the creature's arm. It lets out a furious noise and lunges for her.

"No," I cry, watching as Loviatar is backhanded and sent flying through the air. The goddess slams into a tree and crumples to the ground in the deep snow.

The shadow rounds on me. Its hulking form moves haltingly across the clearing. Those white eyes lock onto me, and I feel frozen. I've been here once before. A monster in the woods that stinks of death, fear sitting like ice in my gut, no weapon in my hand, my only savior wounded. I survived this once. I will survive it again. "I am powerful," I whisper to the dark. "I am queen."

Kukka grabs at my arm, frantically pulling me towards the trees.

"Run, Aina!" The witch's voice echoes across the clearing as she fights to stand. "You must run!"

No. No more running. Raising a shaking hand, I face down the shadow. "As Queen of Tuonela, I order you to stop!"

The shadow stills, its hulking form towering over me. My breath catches as it looks at me with those haunting eyes, its head tipped to the side like a bird of prey.

"Aina, *no—*"

I have no time to react. The shadow lunges forward, clawed hand reaching. Kukka leaps in front of me, but it takes nothing for the shadow to bat her away. Its claws grip my shoulder, talons of smoke piercing deep into my skin. I gasp, breathless, as pain lances across my chest. A scream splits the air, and I realize it's coming from me.

"Aina!"

The shadow squeezes, and the bones in my shoulder splinter like shards of ice. The pain of it tears me apart. And then I'm flung to the side as the shadow screeches, turning to fight the goddess, who is now back on her feet.

I whimper like a wounded animal as I drop to the ground, landing on my shattered shoulder. "Tuoni," I moan, rolling to my side. "My lord . . ." I tug hard on every thread of our blood bond, begging him to feel me, to know I'm in danger.

Darkness closes in at the corners of my vision. One thought fills me: I am going to die.

"Tuoni," I whisper, eyes fluttering shut. "Help me."

Siiri

"TRY AGAIN," VÄINÄMÖINEN COMMANDS.

I groan, holding my drum with aching hands. The tattoos are fresh, the skin swollen. The shaman used a salve of beeswax and tallow to seal them; the backs of my hands shine with grease. "We've been at this for hours." I can't keep the dejection from my voice.

Väinämöinen has talked me through freeing my itse several times. He has shown me how to breathe, how to turn inward, how to create a picture in my mind of where I want to be. I understand, but, for the first time in my life, throwing myself at a task is not enough for me to master it. We've tried twice now, the shaman watching as I drum over the runes that best remind me of Lake Päijänne. Twice now, I've let myself sink into a trance, and twice I've woken up with a pounding headache, my soul still intact.

"I can't do it," I say, defeated.

He glares at me. "What did you just say?"

"I said I can't—*ouch*—" I shriek, my drum tumbling off my lap, as Väinämöinen lunges at me, whacking me on the shoulder with his mallet. "What was that for?" I rub the new spot of pain.

"Don't you *dare* say those words again," he bellows, pointing a rune-marked finger in my face. "Your precious Aina doesn't have the time, and I don't have the patience." He's thoughtful for a moment, surveying me with those sharp blue eyes. "Painting pictures in your mind clearly doesn't work for you," he says at last. "And frankly, I'm not all that surprised."

"You're not?"

"No. You're not a thinker."

I square my shoulders at him. "And just what is *that* supposed to mean—"

"I'm not saying you're not clever," he corrects with a raised hand, stopping my tirade in its tracks. "You're as bright as they come, Siiri."

I settle with a frown, still feeling like a failure.

"Perhaps we must let your luonto be our guide," he muses. "A woodpecker doesn't waste time picturing the pretty places it would like to visit. It doesn't lose itself to sentiment. It doesn't idle. Like you, Siiri. You don't rest, you don't wait. You just *do*."

"So, to release my itse I should . . ."

"You should just do it," he says with a shrug.

"That doesn't make sense."

He chuckles. "Why does it not? You have a task ahead of you that must be done. So, do it." He points to the instrument in my lap. "Pick up that drum. Don't waste another moment thinking about it. And don't do it my way. Do it *your* way."

Hesitantly, I reach for the drum. "Don't think," I mutter, brushing my calloused fingers over the runes for the lake and the hunters. I call the larger one Onni. I smile, feeling the warmth of his laugh in my chest. I close my eyes tight. "Don't think."

"Go and come back," Väinämöinen warns. "If you're gone too long, I'll send my luonto after you. When you see the eagle, follow your tethered hands. Let them be your guide."

I nod, keeping my eyes closed.

Don't think . . . don't think . . . don't think . . .

All I can do is think . . . and I think this is madness. I sit on the floor of Väinämöinen's hut, tattoos fresh on my hands, willing half my soul to split itself away from my body and travel a vast distance across the wintry woodlands back to my lakeside home. I do this as practice so that I can send it out again, next time through the veil of death itself.

This is all utter madness.

This is a dream.

This is impossible.

"To be a shaman is to embrace the impossible," comes the shaman's voice, the hint of a smile in his tone, and I know I must have said that last bit out loud.

I flex my fingers around my drum mallet. This *is* impossible. And yet I've been doing the impossible every day since the moment Aina disappeared. Nothing is impossible.

Lifting my mallet, I strike my drum.

I groan, rolling onto my back as something cold and feathery tickles my nose. It makes me want to sneeze. I hold it in, blinking my eyes open to find that I'm lying on the forest floor. A canopy of snowy trees overhead all but hides the moon and stars. The air is cold, but I'm bundled up, warm. I feel it only on my cheeks and the tip of my nose.

I sit up, glancing around the snowy clearing. I'm fully dressed in thick reindeer-fur boots, wool socks, elk-hide breeches, and a fur coat. My neck is wrapped up in a scarf to conceal the scabs that will one day soon fade to scars, and a fur hat sits low on my forehead, covering my ears. Lastly, I raise my hands, wriggling my fingers in thick rabbit-fur-lined mittens. Inside the mittens, my hands sting. I scramble to my feet and pull the mitten off my right hand, revealing the spray of black runes tattooed on my skin.

"I did it," I whisper to the trees. I'm standing in my itse. I drummed it free. And if I did it right, that should mean . . .

I stomp off through the trees. Väinämöinen was right; even in the dark, I know my way. My breath comes out in little puffs as I near the lights of my homestead. I walk around the trees beside the barn, eager to see my family again. I miss them all so greatly—even Liisa, who before was only ever a nuisance.

But she was *my* nuisance. We looked out for each other. We love each other. I'll be glad to see her again.

I hurry around the side of the house, my boots crunching in the snow. Slipping my other mitten off, I tuck them in at my belt. Then I rap twice on the door and wait.

Nothing.

No sounds from within, no scuffling of chairs dragged across the wooden floor.

"Odd," I mutter.

I knock once more. Before my frustration can grow, a sound has me turning around on the top step. I listen for the sound again.

Drumming.

Something is happening on the other side of the village. The drumming grows louder, echoing through the quiet of the forest. It's a celebratory sound, the rhythm fast and jubilant.

Hopping off the steps, I jog across the clearing, leaving my family home behind me. I pat down my body as I jog, noting the knife on my hip. If I'm not mistaken, there's another tucked into my boot. Väinämöinen had assured me that my itse would arm itself. Clothing and weapons can change to fit the needs of the itse.

The forest before me is aglow with the light of two dozen torches. As I move closer, I frown. I think I know what has drawn the people out on this dark winter night. I hide behind the trunk of an oak a few feet removed from the edge of the clearing. Peering around, I look above the heads of the revelers to the massive bear head perched atop a pinewood pole in the middle of the clearing.

This is a peijaiset, a bear funeral.

Whoever was forced to kill the bear now hosts a funeral in its honor. To appease Otso, we don't mourn a bear's death; we only celebrate its life. A fallow deer roasts on a spit over a large fire turned by two men. Women stand before more cookfires, readying the soups and other savory dishes that will accompany the venison. Drummers drum and dancers dance around the pole, singing songs that will help the bear's spirit find its way out of the forest and into the stars.

My heart stops at the smiling, pink-cheeked face of my sister, who twirls around with ribbons clutched in her hand. She dances with the other girls, their feet stomping in the snow. I inch to the right, staying to the shadows as I survey the crowd, my eyes not resting until I find her. "Mummi," I whisper.

Her blue cap is pulled over her grey hair, her thick braids falling on either side of her breasts as she stirs one of the cookpots. Her friends stand to either side, the three of them lost in conversation. She looks good, healthy and whole. I lean further around the tree to get a better look. I can't just march out into the middle of this crowd. It would raise too many suspicions. They'll ask too many questions. No, I have to get her alone—

Snap.

I glance over my shoulder, ducking to better hide myself in the underbrush.

A shadow moves through the dark, trying to walk stealthily. Like me, they don't want to be discovered. Firelight from the clearing flashes on their face as they duck between the trees.

It's Brother Abbiørn. The hood of his habit is pulled up over his head, but the gold cross around his neck glints in the light. Why does he not join the villagers by the fires?

Oh gods . . .

He's holding a large stick with both hands, gripping it like a club. He means to stop the funeral. Why? Because the people dare to celebrate and worship Otso?

My blood that ran cold begins to boil. I will kill him first. Now is my moment. I could drag him off and sink him to the bottom of the lake. They would never find him.

I pull my knife from my belt and push off the trunk of the oak, ready to circle behind my prey. But I've barely taken two steps before a new sound has me turning. Someone else is creeping in the dark. Behind me, a low whistle sounds. It's Brother Abbiørn, calling out his position. Not ten feet in front of me, a large shadow moves and whistles back. The fine hairs on my neck bristle. I know that whistle. How many times have I heard it in these woods?

One look at those big shoulders, and I know I'm right. Ignoring the priest, I move towards my brother. Onni wears the same brown cloak as the priest, the sign of the foreign god around his neck. Forgetting myself, I whisper, "Onni, what are you doing?"

He jumps with fright. "Siiri? What are you doing here? We thought you were dead. We buried you!"

"What? No, I told Mummi—"

"You said you'd be gone a few days. We followed you north to the hiisi. We looked everywhere for you. But the winter storms blew in, and father was sure your provisions had run out."

"I got more. Onni, why are you dressed like the priest?"

He glances around again. "You shouldn't be here. Go home. Wait for the others there."

My sense of foreboding grows as my gaze settles on the club balanced in his giant hands. "What are you going to do? Are you going to attack your own people because that creeping creature told you to?"

"Brother Abbiørn only wants to help us—"

"He wants to *control* us," I hiss. "Father didn't raise you to be a fool."

"This is the only way," he replies. "This is the Way. The people will see in time. We must tear down all the false idols."

"Onni, *please*." I hold out my hand to him. "Please, brother. Come away. Come home with me."

He stills, eyes narrowed on my outstretched hand. "What are you?"

"What?"

He grabs my wrist and turns my hand over, his thumb brushing over the tattoos for Tuonela. "What did you do? What dark magic infests you, sister?"

I groan. Did I not think the same thing when I first saw the tattoos on Väinämöinen's hands? "It's not what you think. I'll explain if you'll just come home with me—"

He drops my hand as if burned, his shoulders tensing. "This is a test of my faith. You're not really here, are you?" He glances around wildly, clutching his club tighter. "She's not here. The Lord is testing me with visions. He means to trick me into confessing my doubts—"

"Confess them," I cry. "How can you believe in this foreign god when you saw Kalma for yourself? And I tell you now, all the others are real too—"

"Liar," he growls, taking a swing of his club.

I shriek, dropping to my knees to avoid the impact that nearly takes off my head. "Onni, are you crazy?" I scramble to my feet. "I'm not dead, you fool. I'm Siiri, and I'm alive. I'm with Väinämöinen. We're trying to save Aina—"

Onni's eyes flash with anger. "Aina was a heretic, the daughter of a witch. There was no hope for her. The Devil took her."

"Kalma took her, you complete horse's ass! And she was your friend as well as mine. I'll prove it to you. I'll prove to you all that she still lives. Just give me time—"

A shrill whistle from our left has the rest of my plea falling from my lips. Brother Abbiørn and Onni aren't the only zealots in the woods tonight. Turning from me, Onni walks towards the clearing. I duck around him, darting between the trees with the speed of a rabbit.

"Siiri, stop!"

Onni chases me, but I'm faster. I burst through the trees into the clearing. "The Christians are coming! Everyone, run!"

Those closest to me shriek. My name spreads like wildfire.

"Siiri?"

"Is that Siiri Jarintyttär?"

"Kalma, protect us from the dead that rise," an old man intones.

"She's a ghost come to haunt us!" a woman shrieks, clutching at her child.

"I'm not dead," I shout. "But you may soon be! You must leave this place—"

Before I can finish my warning, the shouts of men fill the clearing. From all sides, men in habits matching the priest's come marching through the dark, clubs at the ready.

"Turn away from these acts of false idolatry!"

"Repent of your pasts and live in the Light of His Way!"

Screaming erupts all around me. I don't know where to look as the priests start smashing whatever they can reach, determined to stop our heathen celebration. Feast tables and chairs, baskets of food. Cookpots are tipped into the fires until the air is filled with hissing and the smell of burning food.

"This woman is Satan's child!"

Turning around, I see Brother Abbiørn. The hood of his habit is thrown back and he points a finger at me. His cronies continue to smash things, setting fire to the bear's feast, dashing it into the mud and snow. All around us, women and children scatter. Some of the men are fighting back. Neighbor turns against neighbor as scuffles erupt. A few priests are dragged to the ground.

"Repent, all ye who sin!" one shouts.

"Turn to the Light!" calls another.

"There is nothing to repent," I cry. "Do not listen to them! You've done nothing wrong! Aina did nothing wrong!"

"The Word of God is clear and true," Abbiørn calls over me. "Thou shalt not suffer a witch to live. Seize her!"

"Siiri, no!" Those two words, called out in my grandmother's panicked voice, are like a bucket of ice water poured over my heart. Gods, what am I doing? How did I get here? I can't be here now. I can't save them, not like this. Aina is the one who needs me. And I need her. Our people need her. She will be proof of the gods' power. Our gods took her, and our gods helped restore her. Our gods live.

Ilmatar hear me, Aina has to live too.

"Seize the witch," Abbiørn shouts, spittle flying from his lips. "She means to blight us with her magic words."

"Siiri, *run*," Mummi calls.

I spin on my heel and sprint away from the priest.

"Don't let her get away!"

I shriek as a pair of hands lifts me off my feet. "Put me down!"

Onni holds me tight. He hauls me kicking and screaming over to the pinewood pole. I look up, heart racing. The face of Otso looks down at me, his jaws open, his blood dripping down the pole "Please," I call out to my people. "Please, hear me! Väinämöinen is returning—*ah*—"

Abbiørn strikes my face. "Be silent, witch." He turns to face the crowd. "People of Päijänne, hear me! Neither seek shamans nor allow them to defile you. This is the Word of the Lord! Says the Lord, your God, do not dabble in the occult, or you shall pollute your souls!"

"You're a madman," I cry, my chest heaving with my rage.

"Bind the witch to the pole," he orders.

"Onni, you fool, let her go," Mummi shouts. Father and Aksel hold her back, their faces stricken with fear. "That's my granddaughter. She's not a witch!"

Brother Abbiørn turns on her. "She speaks of a shaman's return. There is only one return you need concern yourselves with, and that is the second coming of Jesus Christ, Son of the Living God."

"Väinämöinen *will* return, and I will be at his side when he does," I shout. "Please don't lose faith!"

"But how can you know?" someone calls from the crowd.

"Yes, what proof do you have?"

Before I can reply, a piercing cry fills the clearing. I gasp, looking up, to see the massive shadow of a bird in flight pass over me. Väinämöinen has arrived in his luonto. The eagle swoops low, attacking Onni's hands as he tries to tie me to the stake.

I jerk away, stepping free. "He's here," I shout, pointing to the dark sky. "Look to the eagle. It is Väinämöinen. He comes for me now, but we *will* return," I say, my gaze leveling on my mummi's face. "I will save Aina from the depths of Tuonela, and we will *all* return to you."

Tears fall down her face as she nods.

"Burn this witch," the priest orders. "Her ashes will simmer in the fires of deepest Hell."

With another screech, Väinämöinen lands on my outstretched arm.

Those closest to us step back, in awe of the eagle and what he represents. Hope burns in my chest. Our stories and songs aren't dead yet. If I have my way, they will soon be given new life. Holding my ground, I face the priest. "Abbiørn, you are powerless here. Take your unwanted god and return south with all haste. Never darken our forests again."

He meets me stare for stare. "I'm not afraid of you, girl."

I stroke the eagle's feathered head, flashing the priest my new shaman tattoos. "You should be."

Eyes wide, he leans away. "Devil take you."

I smile in the face of his disgust. "Trust me, priest. She'll take you first."

With that, I pull on every fiber of my being, willing myself to fold inward. I follow the tattoos, desperate to return through the tether. Aina is out of time, and clearly so, too, are our families. We cannot delay another minute.

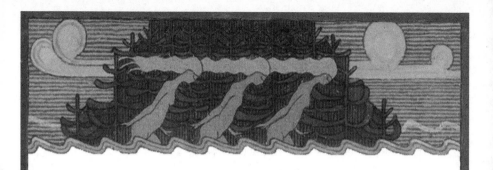

Aina

FIRE. I'M ON FIRE. A burning heat courses through my body as smoke fills my lungs. I try to cough, but the pain of doing so nearly makes me faint. Oh gods, I'm broken. This is it. Only death remains.

"Aina," a frantic voice calls. "Aina, no!" Rough hands touch me, moving my broken body. I moan, unable to form words. "Kalma!" the deep voice bellows.

I open my eyes to see the death god looming over me. Raising his hand, he forms an orb of fire in his palm and lobs it through the darkness. An unearthly screech, followed by a sharp sizzling sound, tells me he hit his target.

The shadow creature advances on Tuoni with a snarl. The god of death places himself between me and the beast. With a downward pull of his hands through the air, he fashions himself a sword of flame. He grips it one-handed, forming a shield in his other hand. "You will never breathe the free air again, Foul One!"

The creature hisses, growing in size as if it means to intimidate the death god. But Tuoni holds his ground. I can only watch, broken and naked in the snow, as Tuoni battles, swinging that sword to hack the creature at shoulder and neck. It lets out a squeal as the fire burns through its smoky flesh.

"Get your monster under control," Tuoni shouts.

Out of the corner of my eye, someone sweeps through the darkness. A choking, noxious smell sinks into my nose, burning away all the fine hairs. Oh gods, I'd know that stench anywhere. The monster's stench is but an echo of hers. The goddess of decay stands behind the shadow. Reaching out her claw-like hand, Kalma grabs the creature, her fingers constricting around the back of its neck. Like a dog snagged by the scruff, the shadow whimpers. In moments, it shrinks down to the size of a man.

"Bury it," Tuoni calls over to her. "We must remake the bonds." He drops to his knees in the snow at my side, his flaming sword and shield vanishing from his hands. "Aina, look at me," he urges, touching my face.

I hiss, trying to pull away from the heat of his hands. I'm in so much pain. I can't move anything below my neck.

"Stay with me." Tuoni puts his hands on my shattered shoulder.

"You—promised," I pant.

"What?"

"Kill me," I beg, fluttering my eyes open. "You promised—"

"No," he growls. "I can fix this. Don't move."

I gasp, unable to draw a proper breath as a new kind of fire sinks through my skin. Tuoni has both hands on me, his lips moving as he chants. He sings the words low, his body swaying. His dark eye goes white, glowing an almost blueish color. It matches his cloudy eye. He sings his song over me, the pressure of his hands making me want to faint.

"Ahhh—" I cry out as the bones of my shoulder snap back into place. Taking another gasping breath, I fill my lungs with air. I feel the muscles of my shoulder sewing themselves back together beneath my skin. My hands rise up out of the snow as I clutch at the god, clinging to him. He keeps singing his mournful song until the pressure eases, and I feel whole again.

Tuoni lifts his shaking hands away from me. He blinks twice, the blue-white light fading from his dark eye.

"Wha-what was that?" I say through chattering teeth. Now that my body isn't broken, I feel the cold of the snow.

"A healing song," he replies. "You're not yet dead," he adds with a soft smile. "No need to fulfill any oaths."

But I was as good as dead. I could feel the life fading from me. And yet, I am healed. The god of death healed me. "How d-did you learn to heal l-like that?" I cover my breasts with my snow-dusted arms, too cold to blush at my nakedness.

"Väinämöinen taught me," the god replies, helping me sit up. He undoes the clasp of his cloak, removing it and wrapping it around my shoulders. He pulls up the hood, covering my wet hair. I gasp as he pulls me into his lap. In one movement, he's standing, my naked, trembling body cradled in his arms.

"Lovi-atar," I pant.

"She's fine," he replies. "See for yourself."

He turns so I can peek around the edge of my hood. Loviatar is on the far side of the clearing being helped to her feet by Kukka. Just beyond the witch, Kalma still clings to the scruff of the shadow. At her side, the great wolf Surma growls, its glistening teeth bared.

"I'm taking Aina back," Tuoni calls to the others. "Prepare the grave. We must seal it with all haste." Not waiting for a response, he takes off through the darkness with me bundled in his arms.

Tuoni sets me down in a chair by the fire in the south tower.

"Thank you," I murmur, settling myself against the soft cushions.

He waves his hand, and the fire roars twice as high. The god drops to one knee at my side, frost dusting the fringe of his night-dark beard. He cups my cheek with a trembling hand. "You're freezing."

"I'm f-fine." I reach for his hand, but he's already moving away. He returns with a thick fur, which he drapes over my lap.

"Will you allow me to look at your shoulder?"

I nod, and help him undo the clasp at my neck, unwrapping his cloak enough to peel the thick wool away from my shoulder. His warm fingers move over my icy, pale skin. "No pain?"

I lean into the warmth of his touch. "No pain."

He pulls away so quickly it nearly topples me over. "I must go."

"Wait," I cry. "What was that, my lord?"

"A kalman väki," he replies, tossing two more logs onto my fire.

Fear shoots through me. A kalman väki, a death spirit. "Wait—did Kalma—"

"No," the god says quickly. "If Kalma wanted you dead, she wouldn't have come when I called her."

"You really trust her?"

"I do. She is mine."

I fight a shiver but nod. *Trust.* I have to trust these witches. I have to trust Tuoni. Without trust, I'm all alone. I lean forward, holding more tightly to his cloak. "If not Kalma, then who? Tuonetar is still without her magic, yes? She remains locked in the north tower?"

"I must go," is all he says as he moves towards the door. "The väki must be reburied. We cannot delay."

"My lord—"

His hand is on the door. "I will return, wife." With that, he leaves.

I'm left waiting what feels like an age. As soon as my body is warm enough, I'm up out of the chair. I set Tuoni's cloak aside, opting instead for a simple white woolen dress. I pick up a wolf pelt and wrap it around my shoulders. All fatigue I might have felt is replaced with frustration and anger—at this situation, at the death goddesses, and most of all at myself.

I almost died tonight. *Again.* Tuoni was nearly too late. Anger at Tuoni simmers too. He promised me I'd be safe. He promised no harm would come to me. Either he lied, or he made a promise he knows he can't keep.

Which is worse?

My anger at myself burns brightest. Loviatar made me believe I could be more. She made me feel like I was clever and resourceful, the mouse who outwits and outlasts. But maybe I'm not meant to survive this place. Maybe my story is already written. Tuoni's curiosity at having a mortal for a wife will put me in jeopardy again and again. It's only a matter of time before this mouse succumbs to the will of the monsters. Fate or no, this mouse wants to fight. Tonight has reinforced this simple truth: I want to live.

A knock at my door makes me jump.

"Aina, it's me," the death god's voice calls through the door.

I hurry over to the door and pull back the bolt, letting Tuoni enter. He steps into the room, snow dusting his boots. A gust of winter chill sweeps in after him. I shut the door and latch it, leaning against the heavy wood. Tuoni crosses the room. He reaches for the carafe of wine. "Don't," I hear myself call.

His hand stills.

"I want you sober, my lord. I have questions."

He drops his hand back to his side. Slowly, he turns, eyes locked on me. I find I want to run my fingers down his scar. Who hurt him? How did it happen? Was there no healing song to sing for him then? "What happened?" I say instead. "Where did you go?"

He sighs, leaning against the table with his hip. "The väki is bound and reburied."

"Bound?"

He nods. "Kalman väki feed on mortal souls. When you all began arriving in Tuonela, Kalma had to bury them and bind them with spells. Someone let one loose."

"And . . . was I the target?"

He crosses his arms over his broad chest. "You are the only living mortal in Tuonela."

I hold his gaze. "Who did it?"

He turns away.

"Was it Vammatar?" I call, following him. "She hates me. She's just like her mother. She hates all who stand between her and more power."

"It was not Vammatar," he replies, filling a cup with wine despite my request. "She just helped us bind the väki—and at great personal risk, I might add."

"So, it wasn't Kalma . . . and it wasn't Vammatar. The Witch Queen remains locked in her tower," I summarize, ticking off each name on my fingers. "That only leaves . . ." I glance up to see the look of deep disappointment flutter across his face. "It was the twins, wasn't it? Kivutar and Kiputyttö, they've chosen their side already?"

He drains the cup of wine and slams it down. "We searched

the Kipumäki. They've disappeared, taking all their mischief with them."

"But . . . surely, you can find them. You can reason with them—"

He spins around, glaring at me. "There is no reasoning with Tuonetar's creatures. There can be no mercy. They don't understand it. They only understand power."

"What will you do?"

"I've had to triple the guards on all the buried väki," he replies, refilling his cup. "There's no telling where the twins might go or what they might do. They could make deals behind my back with the goblins or the other witches. They will continue to sow trouble. And if they get their hands on you, wife, they'll no doubt ransom you for their mother's freedom. Which, of course, I cannot allow."

"And when you find them?"

"I will have no choice but to bind them in iron and sink them into the bog."

"And will that . . . does that kill them?"

"No," he mutters. "I will strip them of their magic, as I did their mother, but I need them alive. Their powers are important. They help us achieve the great balance. They know how they are needed. They know how they now bind my hands."

"Kalma should have just let the väki take me," I whisper. "I would be less of a burden to you dead—"

"*No.*" He crosses the room in three strides, cupping my face with both hands. "Do not say that again. Those words are forbidden between us, do you understand?"

"Why do they want me dead so badly?"

He considers for a moment, lowering his hands to my shoulders. "This wasn't about killing you. It was about testing their sisters. They had to be sure who was loyal to me . . . who they could trust."

"What do you mean?"

"They saw Kalma's actions in the throne room as a great treachery. She played her part too well, feeding Tuonetar's need for chaos for far too long. All the while, she was scheming in the dark, plotting to set me free. Kalma surprised her sisters with her loyalty to me. She confused them. She scared them, Aina. And there is nothing more dangerous in Tuonela than a scared witch."

"She scared me too," I admit. "I had no idea she was so powerful. She held the Witch Queen's throat as if Tuonetar was a mere rag doll."

"Kalma is indeed powerful. In some ways, she holds more power than I."

"In what ways?"

He frowns, dropping his hands away from me. "Well, for one thing, only Kalma can control a kalman väki."

This truth reveals so much more about the politics of Tuonela. The twins forced Kalma to choose publicly yet again. Would she save her father's new wife? Or would she let her väki devour my soul as it was made to do?

It was a test for Loviatar too. Would she fight a kalman väki for me, even knowing she would lose? I let out a shaky breath, relieved to have the answer for myself. Maybe I was wrong about the witch. She loves her daughter, but Loviatar would clearly fight death itself to save me too.

This is a night of revelations for us all.

"And Vammatar?" I say, glancing at Tuoni.

He frowns. "She goes wherever the wind blows. Such has always been her nature."

"So . . . she helped you tonight only because she believes you're winning against the Witch Queen? Can we expect her to turn on us both with the first changing of the wind?"

He holds my gaze. "I will protect you, Aina."

Frustration and sadness are etched on his face. I feel them echoing down the bond. Stepping closer, I place a hand over his heart, my fingers brushing the soft wool of his tunic. "My presence is tearing your realm apart."

His hand lifts to cover mine. "You deserve neither credit nor blame. My realm was in pieces long before you arrived."

"But the fact remains that I am a liability to you. You can't spend the rest of your days fighting to keep me alive in a realm where I am meant to be dead."

He closes his eyes, that scar over his clouded eye crinkling. "I said don't speak of it. I cannot bear it."

I trace the scar lightly with my finger. "The god of death . . . afraid to speak of dying?"

"Afraid to speak of your death."

"But I *will* die here," I press. "You cannot keep me safe—"

"I can," he bellows, pulling away from me.

"You shouldn't have to, and that's the point," I call after him. "Wanting me shouldn't cost you everything. It shouldn't cost you your crown, the love of your daughters, the peace of your realm."

He broods, face cast in shadow by the fire behind him. "And what would you have me do?"

"Sometimes . . ." I follow him to the fire's side, trying to control the racing of my heart. Surely, he can feel it down the bond. I smooth both hands over his chest. "Sometimes, my lord, when we love a thing . . . when we *truly* love it . . . the only way to love it is to let it go."

He stiffens, his hands raising to grasp my wrists. "*Never.* You bound yourself to me, Aina. You're mine in life and death, body and soul."

I defiantly hold his gaze. I never expected him to agree to

releasing me. He has his claws in me now. There will be no escaping Tuonela. But that doesn't mean I have to keep living as a mouse. "You would lose your family all for the sake of me?"

"Any witch of my realm who would raise a hand against you does not deserve to call me 'Father,'" he replies solemnly.

"You would lose your crown for me?"

"Let them try to take it," he growls, eyes flashing with fire. "I will burn them down." His voice rasps with ash and flame.

"You would make me your queen?"

"You *are* my queen," he corrects, his hands dropping to my waist. "And come tomorrow evening, you shall be celebrated at a grand coronation feast. All the gods shall watch as I place you on the throne at my side."

My heart races. But I don't just want his attention, I want his power too. I want the feeling of control he gives me. In his arms, I feel strong. In his arms, I feel like a goddess. I *want* to be his goddess.

I tip up my chin. "I married you in the woods for the good of others. I married you to break the curse and spare countless mortal lives that would have otherwise been wrapped up in Tuonetar's schemes. Whether you like hearing it or not, I married you for Siiri. I married you to keep her safe."

He grimaces, his hands dropping away from me.

I give chase, my hands pulling at his arms. "I bound myself to you by blood, my lord. I know there is no escape. I will live in Tuonela; I will die in Tuonela." I run my hands up his chest, settling them back at his shoulders. The motion drops the fur from my shoulders, leaving me in nothing but my simple white dress.

He takes me in, the want open in his heated gaze. I feel my body respond to his closeness. I swallow, holding his odd gaze. "But there is something I realized tonight as I was lying there, pulling on every thread of our bond, calling you to me."

He winces. The memory of my broken body lying in the snow will haunt him. "What did you realize, wife?"

"As I am bound to you, you are bound to me. I called, and you came. I'm sure if I pulled on this bond hard enough, I could rip the heart from your chest." I brush my fingers over his scarred brow. "You death gods like doing that to people, don't you?"

He sighs. "Aina—"

"Don't call me that," I say, cutting him off. "You don't get to call me that ever again. That's what I realized, lying broken in the snow."

His scarred brow raises in curiosity. "What shall I call you then, wife?"

I take a deep breath, holding it in my chest. "If I am to survive this place, I must become something more than Aina, the meek little mortal. I must be seen as your equal in all ways. Loviatar says this is a realm where power is claimed. So, I claim a little for myself now. I claim a new name."

He smiles, the heat in his gaze enough to set me on fire. "Say it, wife."

"I am Ainatar."

He drops his face closer, making me shiver as he traces the tip of his nose along my jaw. "Ainatar . . ." He tests the syllables, tasting them. "My queen . . . my goddess . . . I know what is in your heart." He places a hand over my chest, fingers splayed. "You told the raven all your hopes and dreams, remember? You told me again under the hill. You want a good man, a kind and beautiful man, strong as the sunrise. A man who will recite poetry and make love to you under the summer sun in a field of wildflowers."

"Aina wanted that man," I correct, placing my hand over his, entwining our fingers together. "But I am not Aina anymore. I stopped being Aina the moment our blood bonded us. I am something different now . . . something more. I feel Ainatar stirring inside me. I feel *you*, Tuoni. I feel your want and your passion, your raw, aching need."

He tries to pull away. "I am a creature of darkness—"

"You are *my* creature now," I counter, holding him to me. "I married you for others, it's true. But I claim you now for myself. Ainatar doesn't want a weak, mortal man. A mortal man would see her dead in this place, buried in a shallow grave. I want *you*, husband. I want your fires and your shadows, all your simmering strength. I want the raven's kindness . . . the man's hunger . . . the god's power."

He closes his eyes as if my words cause him physical pain. But I can feel down the bond that this pain is caused by restraint. "Do not open this door unless you wish me to walk through it," he warns.

"A mortal man was enough for Aina. Only a god will suit Ainatar. I will have you in all forms. You call me 'goddess'? I mean to have you worship me."

He groans, dropping his forehead to my now-healed shoulder, his hands stroking up my back, hungrily.

"Mortals fear you and seek your favor," I whisper, digging my fingers into his hair. "As I am your queen, you shall seek only mine. Please me, Tuoni. Please your goddess and earn my favor—"

Before I finish the words, he claims my mouth in a kiss. I sink against him, savoring the feel of his strong arms wrapped around my waist. There is nothing sweet or gentle about this kiss, nothing like that first kiss we shared in the forest. Even the kiss in the throne room felt like a controlled burn.

This kiss is an inferno. It consumes me from the tips of my toes, reforming as a searing ache deep in my core. His lips are seeking, demanding. He pours all of himself into me, opening me up in ways I didn't know were possible. At the taste of his tongue against mine, sweet with red wine, I sigh. His fingers weave into my hair, jerking my head back. He breaks our kiss, leaving me breathless, as his mouth drops lower, grazing down my neck, sending flames dancing across my skin. I hold tight to his tunic with both hands as he grips my hips, walking me backwards towards the bed.

"Tell me again how much you want this," he says, his voice like warm honey against my ear. He pulls back, eyes narrowed as he searches my face. "Tell me, wife."

Trembling with nerves, I reach out a hand and stroke the scar across his face. "How did you get this?"

"Väinämöinen."

"The shaman hurt you?" I whisper.

"We hurt each other," he admits. "It was long ago."

Taking his face in my hands, I pull it down. Smoothing his raven-black hair behind his ears, I kiss the edge of that long scar. "The next person who thinks to harm you will have to go through me." The words are so ridiculous, so extraordinary, that we both can't help but let out a laugh. He relaxes in my arms, and I pull him closer, kissing his lips. "I want this."

He stills.

I kiss him again, slow but pleading. "Bind me to you in all ways."

He answers me with action. Jerking his axe loose from the back of his belt, he rattles it down on the table. His thick leather belt comes off next. I'm not sure if I'm meant to help him, so I watch, taking in each of his deliberate movements as he sheds his many layers. He tugs his thick wool tunic off over his head, leaving his chest bare. In the light of the fire, I try to memorize him. His skin is so pale from a lifetime of night. Scars big and small crisscross his arms, his abdomen. A dusting of dark hair trails from his chest down to his navel.

I settle on a tattoo of a raven in flight over his heart. It's a mirror of the one Kalma wears, though twice the size. I stroke the lines of the raven's sharp face with my fingernail. Beneath my hand, the god of death trembles. I meet his gaze again, feeling the coiling and uncoiling of a great beast in my gut. Ainatar seeks to wake and claim our prize.

"You are mine, Tuoni. My raven, my husband."

"I'm yours," he repeats. "Leave your mark on me. Claim me, wife."

I put my hands on his chest and breathe in his woodsy scent, but he lowers himself away from me, sinking down onto the bed. It's the work of moments for him to shed his boots and wool socks. He stands, towering over me again as he drops his hands to the top of his elk-skin breeches. He works the leather ties, his eyes taking their fill of me.

My breath catches as he drops his breeches to the floor. He stands confidently before me wearing nothing but a twisted copper band on his wrist. His desire for me is on full display. I've seen naked men all my life—swimming in the lake, enjoying sauna. But I've never touched one.

Swallowing my fears, I reach for the fabric of my shift and tug it over my head. I drop it to the floor atop his discarded tunic. I stand naked before him, my hair unbound around my shoulders, trailing down my back.

Tuoni stands back, eager to look at me. His dark eye glints in the firelight as it moves, tracing the soft curves of my body. The odd thing is that he's seen me naked before as the raven. Just tonight he found me naked in the snow. In all those times, I never felt what I feel now—pure, unbridled want.

He comes to me, his hands warm on my skin as I tremble against him. "Please," he whispers. "I promised you kindness, and I will obey. I want you, wife. May I have you?"

Heart in my throat, I nod.

With a groan, he sweeps me into his arms and places me

on the soft furs of the bed. They tickle my arms as I scoot back against the pillows. Then he's on the bed too, kneeling over me. A sound escapes my throat as his hand trails up my thigh and between my legs. He watches me with those mismatched eyes as he moves his fingers over me in slow circles.

I arch towards his hand, biting my lip to stifle my moan. I feel like I can't breathe, even as my lungs fill with air. I raise my arms over my head. When he slides a finger inside me, I gasp. He catches the sound with his mouth, his beard tickling as his tongue teases. I open to him, and he drops to his elbows, his weight pressing heavy against my stomach, pinning me down. He pants, his breath warm on my cheek. "Do you trust me?"

He asks me the question I've been asking myself for days. Can I trust him? Can I trust anyone? I have to. In this dark place, I trust him, or I die. "I trust you," I whisper, praying to the All-Mother that my trust is not misplaced.

He claims my mouth again as he enters me. It hurts for only a moment, the sensation strange. I wince, shifting my hips until he presses in deeper, his hips resting in the cradle of my legs. The pain stops and I feel only fullness. "You feel so fragile," he pants, one hand cupping my cheek as he moves on top of me. "I don't want to hurt you."

I arch back, trying to move with him. "I feel no pain."

"But do you feel pleasure?"

"I feel . . ." The truth is I don't know. I feel . . . *everything*. When he drops a hand between us, his fingers find a spot that makes me tremble. My hands move on their own, trying to pull him closer. How do lovers do this as two bodies? I want him inside me, wrapped in me. Down the bond and through my body, I open myself to this pleasure. "Don't stop," I plead. "Don't—gods, don't stop—"

He laughs, changing his angle as he wraps an iron hand

around my thigh. "There are no more gods for you, wife. Only one. Only me. Say it."

"Only one," I pant.

"Say it."

"Only you."

"Who am I?"

I open my eyes, gazing up at the bold features of his face. I see the complexity in him—the curious raven, the heartsick man, the dangerous immortal. He is all three. Is it possible for me to be more than Aina? Do I dare embrace this power I feel waking inside me? Can I really become Ainatar?

Grabbing him by the shoulders, I roll us over. He barks out a laugh. Throwing his head back, he grabs my hips, letting me sink down on him once more. I cry out, trembling at the way he fills me. I drop my hands to his chest. I never want this feeling to end. I'm flying and falling. I'm lost to myself. I am whatever *we* are.

"Who am I, wife?" he says again.

"Mine," I pant, dropping forward to claim his lips. "You're Tuoni, and you're mine."

The need to shatter overwhelms me. Heat shivers down my legs, all the way to my toes. I feel it vibrating across my chest as I pull him to me, wanting all of him. With the god of death around me and inside me, we burn together as a joined fire, our flames scorching the other's skin, before we both crumble to ash.

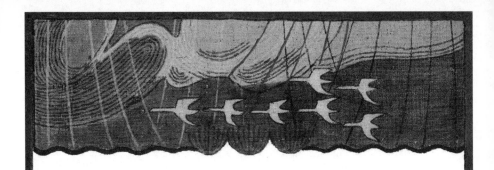

Siiri

"EASY, GIRL. THAT'S IT. Get yourself up now." Väinämöinen's voice calls to me, luring me back to consciousness.

I gasp, jolting upright in panic, clutching at my chest.

"Whoa, whoa. First time is always hard. Worse than the luonto, eh?"

As if on cue, the nausea hits. I groan, body swaying. "I think I'm gonna—"

I shriek, my body going rigid as the chill of ice presses against the back of my neck. The infuriating curmudgeon dropped a piece of ice inside my tunic! It slides down my spine, making me wriggle and wince. I fight to undo my belt and let the ice fall to the floor.

"You—weasel," I shout, unable to think of a better insult.

"But you're not nauseated anymore, are you?" he says with a barking laugh.

I scowl at him.

His smile falls as he glares right back. "Now, what in the name of Ilmatar's fuzzy woolen mittens did you do?"

"Nothing!"

"Oh, 'Nothing,' she says. I found them tying you to a stake, ready to burn you as a witch!"

"It wasn't me. It was that rotten priest—"

"You looked like you were giving as good as you got," he counters, leveling a finger in my face. "I told you to lay low."

"I did," I say, slapping his hand away.

"I said you could pop in on your mummi and tell her you're alive. I didn't tell you to start a godsdamn rebellion."

"I didn't—"

"You told a whole village full of people that Väinämöinen is returning, and then you threatened a priest of the new god. If you think he'll turn tail and run south, you're a fool, Siiri Jarintyttär. He will bring down the hammer and crush your little village into dust."

"I'm going back," I say, reaching for my discarded drum. "I have to go back—"

"No, you don't." He tugs my drum from my hands.

"Give it back! My family—I have to warn them. I have to help them fight—"

"Who are you here to save, Siiri? Will you save your Aina, or will you save your village?"

"I can save both! I'll go now and come back. Then I'll go for Aina."

He shakes his head. "Even a girl as brave as you cannot fight two gods at once. Fight the death gods and save Aina. Or fight the new god and save your village. You must decide which path you will take."

I take in the shaman's lined face. "Oh gods . . . you knew, didn't you?"

He huffs and stomps away, taking my drum with him.

"You've known all along about the Swedes," I call after him. "Of course you do. Your itse has been running loose around the south for ages. You watched it all happen and did nothing to stop it. You're a coward!"

He slams down the drum and turns around. "Do not dare presume to know what is in my heart," he bellows. "I sacrificed *everything* to give the people what they need!" In two strides he crosses the hut, grabbing me by the shoulders. "I risked life and limb to bring her to you. I am now cursed for all eternity, hunted instead of thanked. You have all you need to stamp out the threat of the Swedish invaders and their tyrannical god. You're all just too stupid and selfish to see it, too unwilling to open your hearts to her power."

"Who?" I wrap my tattooed hands around his wrists. The knowledge sinks in my chest. "Oh gods . . . Väinämöinen, who did you take from Tuonela?"

He shoves me away. "Even you, bright as you are, cannot see it. You don't believe, so how can you ever understand?"

"Tell me!"

He spins around. "You met her already, fool girl. You described her to me, remember?"

I furrow my brow, trying to remember. "The woman in the woods. Black of hair, with a child-like face. She came to me twice. She helped me to my feet after Kalma took Aina. Then she appeared in the alder grove. She gave me provisions for my journey north. She told me to trust the bear . . . to trust *you*. Who is she?"

"You already know," he replies. "Use that clever mind and puzzle it out."

I close my eyes, trying to remember what I felt when she was near. She came to me in a time of need, a time when my spirits were low, and I was ready to give up. When I thought all doors were closed to me, she appeared through an open window and offered me her hand.

"Hope," I whisper, blinking open my eyes. "She is hope."

Slowly, the shaman nods.

"But *who* is she?" I say, dropping to my knees by the fire. "Is she Tuonetar's daughter?"

"Her granddaughter," he replies, taking his place at the other side of the fire. "That selfish witch kept her locked away, determined to keep her magic from the world. Not even the gods knew she lived."

I continue to try to puzzle it all together. "I thought you said you went to Tuonela seeking Antero Vipunen? You wanted secrets to use in your spellcasting."

"And what secrets do you think he told me?"

My eyes go wide. "He knew about the goddess? He knew she was being kept hidden?"

"More than that, he knew *where* she was hidden. There is a secret house under the Kipumäki. Tuonetar kept it concealed, but a few secret words could unlock the door. Vipunen learned those words. He shared them with me."

"And Tuoni? He didn't stop you from taking her?"

He laughs. "Stop me? He helped me get her out. He wanted her gone."

"Why?"

"Because she's his only hope too."

I search his face. "His only hope of what?"

Väinämöinen shrugs. "Winning back his realm, putting Tuonetar back in her place, restoring Tuonela to the glory of the time of the first songs."

The heavy weight of this truth sinks like a rock in my chest. "All this death and violence over these long years, it's the Witch Queen's doing? And what of the girl's mother? Who is she?"

The shaman sighs, taking his pipe from his vest pocket. "Her mother is the only reason we escaped."

I narrow my eyes. "Her own mother wanted her gone?"

"She wanted her *free*," he corrects. "She'd been looking

for the girl in secret, planning for them to escape Tuonela together. In the end, we had to abandon our plans. I escaped with her daughter alone."

"It doesn't make sense. What death witch would care so much about the fate of their spawn? I didn't think they had mothering instincts."

"Careful, Siiri," he warns, lighting his pipe. "In my experience, it is the monstrous mothers who love hardest . . . and grieve longest."

"Oh gods . . ." My mind has latched on to something, like fingers scrabbling in the dark. "Loviatar," I whisper. "She's her mother, isn't she?"

He purses his lips around his pipe, smoke spiraling into the air. "And how do you know?"

"Because Loviatar had a daughter. More than that, the name of her child has been concealed from all the stories and songs. I can only imagine that was your doing too? You helped the witch hide her daughter's identity. If she were named, it might be easier for Tuonetar to track her down and capture her again . . . Am I right?"

"You know you are," he replies. "Surely you don't need me to pat you on the head."

"So, what's her name?" I say, leaning forward.

He scoffs, blowing out a cloud of smoke. "If she did not see fit to tell you herself, I surely won't."

I curse under my breath. "Stubborn old fool. I thought shamans don't keep secrets?"

"She will tell you when she's ready," he replies.

"So, what happens now? You see what the Swedes are planning. They want to stamp out all the old ways. You say they mean to crush my village to dust."

He puffs on his pipe, blowing that sweet-smelling smoke towards the fire. "They will crush any and all dissent, yes.

Turning many gods into one can only be done through violence, Siiri. And their politics will come with their religion. New rules for a new god. 'Twas ever thus."

"I will not leave my family to face that threat alone."

He nods again. "You see now how the larger story weaves itself around us all."

"What story?"

He holds my gaze. "You thought you were just a girl in search of her lost friend, but the threads around you are much more complex. I've known that from almost the moment we met in the woods all those weeks ago."

"What did you know?"

"You've been chosen by the gods," he replies. "You are fated for greatness, Siiri Jarintyttär."

My heart stops. "Where is that story written?"

His mustache twitches with half a smile. "You are writing it now, fool girl."

"And how can you be sure this is my fate?"

"I'm not," he replies with another shrug, sucking on the end of his pipe. "But, like you, I have hope. Now, fetch me that rolled hide there, and light a few tallow candles for the table. These old eyes need more light."

I follow his instructions. "Why do you need more light?"

He takes the hide from me and unrolls it, tucking his feet under the low table. "I'm going to sketch a map of Tuonela. Now, getting in is the easy part. Getting out again is harder. It's the mess in the middle that may prove to be nigh impossible."

"What mess?"

He chuckles, dipping the tip of a tattoo needle in what's left of the ink. "Finding Aina, of course. You don't think the death gods will have her perched on the river's edge holding a lantern and a plate of sweet cakes, do you?"

"No, of course not."

"Of course not," he echoes. "So, you'll need to know the lay of the land." Head bent over the hide, he begins to scratch with the needle. "Listen closely now, Siiri. Commit everything I say to memory. It could mean the difference between taking a leisurely stroll through Tuoni's back garden . . . or rotting in his dungeon."

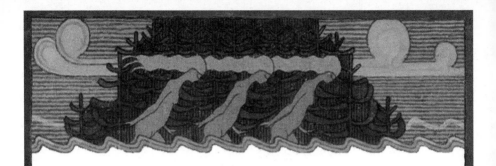

Aina

"MY LORD," I GASP, swatting at his hand as he works it under my dress. "Someone will see us."

"Let them see," he growls, pressing his lips to mine. "I want them all to see the way I hunger for you. And call me by my name. *Say* it."

"*Ah*—Tuoni," I cry.

He presses me against the tree with his hips. Behind him in the darkness, the horses snort, pawing the ground. We're meant to be riding again. It was my request. But Tuoni clearly has other ideas. After showing me the fallow fields and the hot springs, he pulled me from my horse and walked me into the shadows of the trees.

I cry out as he claims me.

"This is all I want," he pants, his face dropping to the curve of my neck. "I want to feel you like this, bury myself inside you, taste the sweetness of your mortality pulsing here at your throat."

I arch my neck for him, and he groans, dragging his teeth over my pulse, as though trying to pull my essence through my skin. It was like this all night. He woke me twice to have me again. By morning, we were slicked with sweat and sated.

"More," I pant against his mouth. "Give me more."

"Everything," he groans. "Anything. It's yours."

We finish, and I fight the heat in my cheeks as I search for my discarded clothes—my mittens, my hat. I like this new intimacy we share. He's attentive, like my raven, but unrelenting, which I can only assume is the god.

I glance around as Tuoni leads me back over to our horses. In this darkness, endless threats loom—spirits that want to eat me, witches who would see me dead, creatures that don't trust me. With the other girls gone, I'm alone.

He cups my cheek. "What's wrong, wife?"

I find him a smile, knowing it doesn't meet my eyes. "Tell me about tonight," I say, looking for any distraction.

He laughs, helping me back into my saddle. "About your coronation? When all shall bow and call you Queen of the Dead?"

"I'm not sure now is the right moment to announce my new status—"

"It is exactly the right moment," he counters, swinging up into his saddle. "There can be no delay. If the other gods sense continued discord in Tuonela, we will all be vulnerable."

"But there *is* discord," I press, urging my little grey mare into a trot. "Surely, inviting a host of immortals into the palace to witness it for themselves will do nothing to shore up our vulnerabilities."

"Ahh, but that is where you underestimate my daughters," he replies, glancing over his shoulder at me.

"Underestimate them how?"

"There is nothing more abominable to them than appearing weak before the other gods. They will do everything in their power to present a united front."

I smile, feeling his hope fluttering down the bond. "And you think that if tonight goes well, we can keep the charade going even when the others leave?"

"All will be well," is his only reply. "Now come, wife. We must return and prepare."

A few hours later, I sit at my dressing table, fine-toothed comb in hand, working it through my unbound hair from roots to ends. Tuoni is gone, overseeing preparations in the hall below. Kukka is my only companion. The dead maid lays out my coronation dress on the bed. It's a beautiful gown of rich green velvet, trimmed in red fox fur at the collar and cuffs. The bodice is embroidered in a scrolling vine pattern. It must have taken Loviatar ages to complete.

A knock at the door has the maid turning from her work. She moves silently across the room and opens the door, admitting the witch. Loviatar is flanked by a pair of maids, each carrying a wooden box. She herself wears robes of white trimmed in fur over a raven-black gown. Silver adorns her ears, while more silver encircles her wrists and neck. "You are recovered from the events of last night?" she asks.

Setting the comb aside, I turn on my stool to face her. "I am. Your father healed me. And you?"

"As you see," she replies.

I narrow my eyes at her. "You are angry with me."

She folds her arms across her middle. "I told you to run. You were a fool not to listen."

"I was trying to save you—"

"You're a fool! You know nothing. Only Kalma can control her väki."

"Yes, I know that now. Tuoni told me."

"When a witch tells you what to do, you do it."

I turn away from her. "That implies trust first, does it not?"

"You still do not trust me?"

"You know I don't. Even as you care for me, you have still manipulated me at every turn."

She gestures to the maids behind her. "Then let these be a gesture of my goodwill."

The first maid steps forward and opens the lid of her box. Inside are two stacks of gold bangles and a necklace set with green gems.

"They're beautiful," I murmur, my fingers brushing over the necklace.

"They're mine," Loviatar replies. "Now they are yours. Perhaps, one day, you will pass them down to a daughter of your own."

I go still as ice floods my veins. A daughter of my own? Gods forbid. I would never seek to bring a child into this darkness. I close my eyes, thinking of the husband who cannot keep his hands off me. I've already put myself at too great a risk. I may be a novice in the ways of love, but my mother is a wisewoman. I know well what lovemaking can lead to. Tonight, after the feast, I will go to the kitchens and gather what I need to make a tonic to stop a child from coming. Wild carrot and rue mixed with honey, ground lily root. I must start taking it daily—

"Aina?" The witch waits for me to speak.

Not looking her way, I pluck the bangles from the box. "Thank you."

She gestures to the other box. "This is a gift from my father."

I watch as the maid steps forward and opens the larger box. "Oh . . ."

It's a crown. *My* crown. It rests on a velvet cushion, a delicate thing of pale white wood. The points where the wood meet are soldered with melted gold. At the front of the crown, a large amber stone sits nestled in more gold.

"It's driftwood," the witch explains. "From the river. It is steeped in the magic of this realm. Only a queen may wear it. The crown knows the difference."

I'm suddenly nervous, gazing down at the twisted wood. "What will it do to the one who dares to wear it without being queen?"

"A sticky-fingered goblin once thought to take it," the witch replies. "The crown grew large enough to drop over the goblin's head to her shoulders. Then the crown grew smaller . . . and smaller . . . and smaller, until—"

"Yes, I can imagine the rest," I say, snapping the lid shut.

Loviatar smiles down at me, or at least her version of a smile. It's little more than a pursing of her thin lips.

"You're lying to me. You just made that up."

"Of course I did," she teases, waving the maids away. "You're too gullible, Aina. Perhaps that is why we all find it so easy to manipulate you."

"That you all seek to manipulate me is why I can never trust you," I retort. "And without trust, there can be no love."

She's quiet for a moment, considering my words. "And how am I to win your trust, my queen?" She takes the comb from my dressing table. I hold still as she drags the teeth through my long, unbound hair. Her touch is gentle . . . motherly.

"You know how," I whisper. "Tell me her name."

The witch's hand stills.

"Tell me her name, Loviatar. I'll trust you only when you prove you trust me."

"Trust no one tonight," she says, determined to keep her secrets. "They will ask you questions. It is a mistake to think they seek to know you. They seek to know only your weaknesses. Give them none."

With that, the witch leaves me alone with the maids. It takes a moment for me to realize she left with my crown.

An hour later, I stand in the receiving hall in my new gown. It fits me perfectly. The skirt falls in folds to the floor, while the white cape at my shoulders trails behind me. Kukka arranged my hair in artful braids that frame my face. I lift a hand, the bangles on my wrist jangling softly as I brush my fingers over the necklace at my throat. I've never worn so much ornamentation before. It feels strange . . . and heavy.

Perhaps I merely feel the weight of this moment.

Kukka is joined by three more dead maids who wear the sigil of the Sun Raven on their chests. They flank me, ready to help me take my next steps. At least I won't be alone. I glance around this room that now holds so many memories for me. I think of the night I met the other girls. We were huddled here in this spot, with tears in our eyes we were too afraid to let fall. Now it glows with the warmth of two dozen candles.

Beyond the doors, a feast—laughter and cheers, the rattle of plates, the stomp of feet. And music, joyous, riotous music—drumming and flutes. Two dead guards step past me, taking up their place at the double doors. Turning as one, they raise their fists and knock. The music changes as the doors swing open from the inside.

I'm greeted with a swirl of color and sound. The hall is full of long tables set with a great feast. All those within stop and turn, eager to watch as I enter the room. It feels eerily similar to the first time. That story ended with bruised shins and my dinner hopping out of my hand, overturning a tray of maggots.

"This is a new story," I whisper to myself.

To either side of the door, the guards nod.

"Be upstanding," a voice calls from inside the room. "Come forth, Ainatar, Bride of Tuoni!"

Hearing my new regnal name gives me strength. Holding my head up high, I sweep into the hall. All eyes watch me as I make my way down the open central aisle. I focus my gaze ahead, looking only to the dais where Tuoni waits for me. He sits on his golden throne, a simple iron circlet on his head. Next to him is an empty chair of silver.

My chair.

My throne.

He smiles at me as I approach, holding out his hand. As he stands, the rest of the hall drops to their knees. I fight my trembling as I finish my walk, pausing at the steps of the dais.

Along the top table, his daughters sit. Loviatar waits to my immediate right, with Kalma seated on the end beside her. Vammatar sits to her father's left and—

Oh gods.

Tuonetar is here. She's dressed in her finest robes, her magnificent silver hair piled high on her head. But she looks as haggard in face as ever . . . and she wears no crown. Her robes are artfully draped to conceal the manacles on her wrists. She clutches her goblet, giving me a look like she hopes I sink into the floor.

Tuoni steps forward, coming to the edge of the dais, his hand still outstretched. Lifting the bottom of my heavy dress with one hand, I ascend the steps, reaching for him with my other hand. His fingers clasp possessively around mine and he reels me in, placing a chaste kiss on my forehead.

"You look beautiful, wife," he says under his breath.

I'm too nervous to reply as he steps back, gesturing for me to kneel. Everyone watches as I sink to my knees before Tuoni. Loviatar appears at his shoulder, my crown in her hands. Tuoni opens the box. Reaching in, he lifts out the driftwood crown, holding it aloft before the assembly.

I can feel every eye in the room. I feel Tuonetar most of all. I don't dare glance to my left to see her glare as Tuoni slowly lowers his hands, placing the driftwood crown upon my head. For a moment, I wait for the crown to declare me unworthy and slip down around my neck, but it doesn't. I gaze up, trying not to move my head.

Tuoni smiles down at me, his mismatched eyes radiant with pride. Then he looks to the crowd, hands splayed wide, and intones in his deep voice, "From the Manala underground, from underneath the blackest soil, rises one of peace and beauty, fairest of the death-land maidens. Behold, Ainatar, Queen of Tuonela!"

"We behold," chants the room.

Chills run down my spine as a kind of claiming magic simmers in the air, settling around my shoulders.

"Rise," says Tuoni, holding out his hand.

I place my hand in his and let him lift me from the floor.

"That is the last time you ever bow to me," he says for only my ears. "A queen does not bow, even to her king."

He leads me back the three steps to our chairs. Slowly, we turn. Following his lead, I sit when he sits. From around the room, all our guests call out, "All hail King Tuoni! All hail Queen Ainatar!"

Goblets rattle and fists pound the tables as everyone cheers. But as I gaze out upon the glittering assemblage, I see more than one unsmiling face. I may not be fully accepted, even now.

In moments, the music crescendos and all our guests resume their feasting. I let go of Tuoni's hand as dead servants come bustling up the dais, balancing a wooden table. They place it before us. I hardly have time to blink before more servants have piled the table with candles and golden plates, jeweled goblets for wine, polished wooden bowls for stew. Then the food arrives—roasted duck, a haunch of pork, blood sausages, root vegetables mashed with butter, wild mushroom stuffing seasoned with pepper and thyme, lingonberry tarts.

But I can't eat a thing. I'm too anxious. I still feel half the eyes of the room on me. Loviatar's warning sits fresh in my mind. They're all looking for weaknesses, waiting for me to make a mistake. I lift my goblet and an attendant rushes forward to fill it. I take a sip of the sweet wine, but even that makes my stomach churn.

"You should eat something," Loviatar mutters. "It will help."

"It won't help when I lose my meal all over this table." Regardless, I transfer a few of the delicacies to my plate. "This is no magic trick? They're all really here?"

"Yes."

"Where did they come from?"

"From the realm of the living," she replies. "A few are from our realm. Father likes to entertain. Now that he has regained his throne, you can expect many more feasts."

I set my wine aside. Not for the first time, I've had to work to reconcile these different versions of Tuonela in my mind. There was the Witch Queen's version, where every waking moment threatened pain and death. Then there is Tuoni's Tuonela. It's clear he's trying to make me fall in love with his realm as much as with him. He wants me to be happy here. He banishes the darkness with firelight. He fills his hall with laughter and music and glittering gods. Why would a woodworker's daughter go back to her simple life on the lakeshore when she could be a queen?

I offer him a nervous smile. He takes my hand and brushes

his lips against my knuckles, gaze drifting up my face to my crown. The look he gives me is enough to melt me inside. Damn him, but he's playing this game to win.

A flash in the corner catches my attention. I turn to see a woman flick a long sheet of white-blonde hair over her shoulder. It almost seems to glow in the candlelight. The woman turns fully, and I stifle my gasp. She's the most beautiful woman I've ever seen: fair brows and wide, dark eyes, soft lips stretched into a smile.

"Who is that?" I whisper.

Loviatar sniffs, setting aside her wine. "I'm sure you don't mean to always be so insensitive . . ."

I blush, realizing my mistake. "She's beautiful," I explain, and try to find the right words to conjure her appearance. "Her hair glows with the light of a star—"

"Say no more." The witch frowns in annoyance. "She is Kuutar."

Kuutar, goddess of the moon. I sigh, taking in the glistening gold of her dress. In all my mother's stories, Kuutar sits at her wheel, spinning golden thread from the light of the moon. The goddess notices my attention. She inclines her head, offering me a smile.

"Oh gods," I gasp, looking down at my plate. "She noticed me looking."

"You're an oddity," Loviatar mutters. "You can be sure they're all looking."

"Loviatar," I hiss. "She's *still* looking."

"She cannot approach you," she replies, amused by my discomfort. "You're a queen. She is not."

"She is *Kuutar*."

"And you are Ainatar, Queen of Tuonela. You outrank her. In this room, in this realm, you outrank everyone. If you want the little fool's attention, beckon her forward."

There's clearly no love lost between the goddesses, but I am not a goddess. "I can't beckon her to me," I say, aghast. "I'd die of embarrassment to say I called the moon goddess to me like a dog."

"Then acknowledge her and turn away."

I do as the witch says. Kuutar looks a little crestfallen, her smile faltering, but with a flick of her long hair, she turns her attention to the handsome man sitting to her left.

Over the rest of the meal, I let my gaze wander the room, trying to guess my guests' identities. It makes me miss Siiri all over again. What a game she would make of it. She'd have no problem calling Kuutar forward with a wave of her hand or challenging Ahti to an arm wrestling match.

"Something amuses you," Loviatar says at my side.

I turn, curious to see if the witch will play my game. Before I can ask, a man charges forward, cap in hand, bowing before Tuoni with a flourish. He's frightfully handsome, tall and lean, with sharp blue eyes and tousled blond hair. "My lord," he calls out in a deep voice. "Now that the feasting is done, is it not time for a dance?"

I can feel Tuoni tense through our bond, but he inclines his head and the room cheers. A great scraping sound fills the air as chairs and benches are pushed back. Across the room, several people stand, eager to join in.

The handsome man turns to face me. "Should not our new queen have the first dance?"

"You're as transparent as ever, nephew," Tuoni replies, his annoyance barely veiled. "If you wish to dance with my wife, ask her yourself."

I fight my look of surprise as the handsome man flashes me his most charming smile. "Will you dance, my queen?"

I glance to Tuoni. He's frowning, but he nods. I can all but hear his voice spoken through our bond. *Be careful with that one.* I try to match the young man's smile. "I would be delighted."

"Excellent," the man calls. "We must have music!" He spins away with a clap of his hands, eager to clear a space at the front of the room.

"I thought you said no one could approach me," I rasp in Loviatar's ear the moment he turns away.

"Nyyrikki has never been one for following the rules," the witch replies.

I go still as I take in the man's tall form, his lean body and beautiful face.

"You'll need to stand now, my queen," Loviatar teases. "They wait for you to lead the set."

I rise unsteadily to my feet as I commit Nyyrikki to memory. The god of the hunt has just asked me to dance, and Siiri isn't here to witness it. My heart breaks a little, even as I try to find another smile for my husband. "You don't mind, my lord?"

"Go," he replies. "I'll cut in when his hands start to rove."

Kukka helps me with the clasp of my cloak. Then I float as gracefully as I can manage around the top table. Several other couples are already in the middle of the floor.

Nyyrikki prances forward and offers me his hand. "You honor me, majesty," he says with another smile. He's almost too confident. Siiri would drop his hat in the jam bowl before the night ends. With that image in my head, I laugh and smile, giving the god of the hunt my hand.

A troupe of musicians begins plucking the strings of their kanteles and blowing into wooden flutes. The dancers take up their positions in a set of two squares, with the women on the inside, facing out. Nyyrikki stands across from me in the set, holding my hand.

Just as we make our first bow, an ominous knock at the

massive doors echoes through the hall. Tuoni waves the musicians to silence, and the doors swing inward. The crowd is too thick for me to see over all their heads, but the ripple that cascades across the room tells me someone important has entered.

Nyyrikki peers over the crowd towards the door. "Oh, excellent. She came."

"Who came?" I say, still holding his hand.

"My mother."

I have the faintest idea that I'm still standing. As I turn, heart pounding, the crowds part. Tuoni sweeps across the room in his robes of black, the image of a raven in a field of spring flowers. In moments, he's leading a woman of enchanting beauty towards me.

This is Mielikki, goddess of the forests. The goddess I have prayed to every night since I was old enough to speak. She wears robes of earthen brown, dusted with lichen and moss. The robes are belted at her waist with a jeweled sash. The songs say her golden hair is so thick and long that it trails the ground behind her, and that four maidens travel with her through the forest, holding it aloft so it doesn't snag on roots and brambles. Now she wears it braided in two thick plaits over either shoulder. Each hangs well past her knees. On her head is a crown of winter greens.

Tuoni leads the goddess forward on his arm, walking straight to where I stand, clutching the hand of her son.

Nyyrikki is all smiles. "Mother dearest, you came."

"I said I would," the goddess replies. Her voice is low and musical, like a dove's soft cooing.

"Sister, may I present my wife, Ainatar," says Tuoni. "My love, this is Mielikki, Queen of the Forests."

His smile is gentle. He knows exactly what this moment means to me. How many times did I mention her to the raven? Now, he gives me an encouraging nod. Holding my breath, I bow my head. He said I'm not supposed to bow to anyone, but this is Mielikki. "I am deeply honored to meet you, my lady."

The goddess surveys me with her stone-grey eyes. Her face has the same ageless quality as Tuoni's, old and young at once. In truth, she is ageless. They all are. It strikes me all over again that I am the only creature in this room who will age and die.

"She's a rare beauty," Mielikki announces. "But I think this winter chill does not suit her. She is forlorn, a tree without its blossoms." With a flick of her wrist, I feel something flutter around my head like the whisper of a butterfly's wings.

Those closest to us sigh in appreciation. I can't see the changes, but I smell them—strong notes of starflower, sprigs of cowslip, wood sorrel. Mielikki has adorned my driftwood crown with a spray of flowers. "Life and death," the goddess intones. "We must have balance in all things, my young queen."

I nod to her, still trying to control my hammering heart.

"I have a gift for the new bride," she goes on, reaching inside her robes.

I hold out my hand, and she places the heavy item on my palm. As our fingers brush, the goddess goes still. Her eyes roll back in her head. Around the room, the candles flicker. A few people cry out. Still others press closer.

The goddess's hand shifts in mine and the gift between us drops to the floor, shattering at our feet. Mielikki grips my hand, her eyes opening once more. They now glow white. Her mouth opens in a soundless scream, her body rigid, as the white light glows inside her mouth.

I pull away, but the goddess holds me fast.

"Don't fight her," Tuoni says, from somewhere to my right.

"Forest Mother speaks," someone shouts.

A dark sense of foreboding seeps through my veins as the goddess takes a deep, rattling breath. Her voice comes out like a rasping chant, her glowing white eyes locked on me:

The son of Death comes on Raven's swiftest wings.
Born of life, born of death, he shall master both.
He shall be the Light of Louhi, Manala's Son.
Look for him with the Raven and the Bear.
Look for him in fire and water.
Look for him in iron and blood.
He comes . . .
He comes . . .
All Death shall be powerless in his hands.

Mielikki's hand slackens in mine. Her eyelids flutter, the white light fading, before she drops like a stone to the floor. A few maidens shriek, stumbling back. All eyes in the room shift from the goddess to me.

"Well, this is just perfect," comes Vammatar's droll voice. "Don't tell us the little maggot is already pregnant."

I barely have time to turn to Tuoni before all the lights go out. I panic, heart racing, as I blink in the dark. From the corner of the room, a shrill cackle rends the air. "And now the games can really begin."

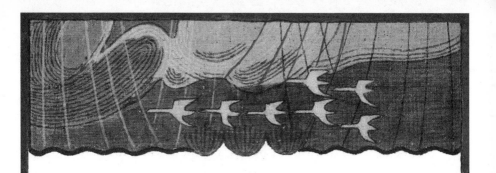

Siiri

42

STANDING IN THE MIDDLE of Väinämöinen's hut in my itse form, I peer down at where my body lays sprawled out by the fire, drum on my chest, mallet still in hand. "Is this really necessary?"

"This is your last lesson, Siiri. You need to know this before you go to Tuonela," the shaman replies. "How do you feel?"

"I feel fine," I reply. "It's just a little odd. I look dead." I nudge my body with my toe.

"Can you feel any consciousness here?" he asks, gesturing to the Siiri on the floor.

I close my eyes, willing myself to feel my body the way I did with my luonto. No matter how good it felt to be the bird, I was always aware that I was also Siiri. I focus on my tattoos, flexing my hands. Perhaps the prickling, itching pain of them might spark some familiarity. With a huff, I open my eyes. "I can't feel a thing."

"So, you see the danger," he says solemnly. "You are utterly cut off from your body, Siiri. The only sensation you can feel through the tether is mortal peril. Your unconscious self at least affords you that protection."

"Mortal peril?"

Väinämöinen drops to his knees at my body's side. Reaching out with both hands, he chokes me, his hands squeezing tight around my neck.

"Hey—what do you think you're doing?"

"Stay back," he commands. "Tell me when you feel it."

To my horror, the old shaman chokes the life out of my unconscious body. In moments, it begins to squirm. My arms flutter as my legs spasm. The first sensation I feel is a sharp pain in my tattoos. I rub the rune of the bear-riding girl. Then my own throat constricts, and I gasp. I clutch my throat as the shaman continues to squeeze. "Stop," I pant. "Gods—*enough*—"

I aim a kick his way. He grunts, but he doesn't let go. I feel dizzy. Black spots dance in my vision. Is he trying to kill me? Unable to do anything else, I fold myself inwards, chasing my tether back into my body. I wake to find myself lying on the floor of the hut, gazing up at the slanting ceiling. I groan, sitting up, my hand rubbing at my neck. Väinämöinen crouches at my side, gazing down at me with those deep blue eyes. It takes me a minute to remember how I got here. My gaze drops to his weathered hands, and I glare. "That's a morbid little trick."

"Where did you feel it first?"

"In my tattoos." I rub my hands together, soothing the aching marks. "Down the tether."

"And that is all the warning you may get."

I nod.

"If someone really wanted you dead, you'd be dead," he warns. "That's why it's always safest to use your itse when there is someone you trust to watch over you as you sleep."

"Is that what happened to you? You used your itse alone—but wait." I chew on the problem a moment. "If your itse got up and walked away . . . how were you awake all these years? Don't we stay asleep if our itse fails to return?"

He shakes his head. "It is precisely because my itse *chose* to stay away that I was able to wake. In choosing not to return, it severed its connection with me. I woke in excruciating pain. I've lived with the pain of that loss every day, unable to die from it because Tuonetar's curse kept me tethered to life."

It really is a fate worse than death. "If I meet the witch, I'll give her a kick in the teeth for you, shall I?"

"Pray you don't. If you're close enough to the Witch Queen to kick her teeth, you're already as good as dead." He sits at the table with his pipe. He's been smoking it nonstop all day. "I'm giving you six hours to find Aina. If you don't bring her out—"

"I know." I pick up my discarded drum. "You'll come down there and drag me out. I'm more concerned about you. If Lumi comes while I'm gone—"

"Forget the witch," he says with a wave of his hand. "I won't have you distracted. Lumi will come when she comes, and I'll deal with her when she does. Your only concern is getting to Aina and getting out safely."

That's easy for him to say. We've both heard the howling of the wolves closing in. They're rallying, drawn by Lumi's magic. She knows where we are, and she doesn't mean to let the old man slip her nets again. I meant what I said; I'll die before I let her hurt him. He's suffered this curse for long enough.

He folds up the map and hands it to me. "Here, take off your vest," he adds. "You'll need to put this on." He rifles around in one of the larger baskets in the back corner of the hut. When he turns, he's cradling an old, worn coat in his hands.

I glance from my fox-fur vest to the heavy winter coat. "I'm not cold. My itse will dress itself—"

"Just put it on," he growls, foisting the coat at me.

I grumble my way out of my vest, tossing it aside, before shrugging into the overlarge trapper's coat and tucking the map inside it. Once it's on my shoulders, I grimace. "Väinämöinen . . . it stinks."

"Well, it's had a dead man in it," he replies with a shrug.

"What?" I squawk, trying to shrug it off.

"Keep the damn coat, girl. You need it. It's part of the crossing magic. That coat has been where you're trying to go. Let it help guide you and grant you safe passage."

I settle before the fire in the smelly coat, picking up my mallet and drum.

"Now, listen to me, girl. If you are caught—"

"I said I'll be careful—"

"Just *listen*." His piercing blue eyes silence my retort. "If you're captured, you will request a prisoner exchange."

"Prisoner exchange?"

"Yes, a life for your lives," he goes on. "You are to offer the Witch Queen my life for your lives—"

"No. Väinämöinen—"

"You don't get to tell me no, girl. I'm allowed to decide my own fate. If you're caught, you will offer the exchange. And not just my itse. I will go to Tuonela, body and soul. I will submit myself to their justice in exchange for both your lives."

"You're mad," I whisper, searching his face. "You cannot waste your life like that, not when we still have such great need of you."

He smiles. "I think we both know my time has come and passed. They have no more need of me. How could they, when they have you?"

"I cannot possibly lead the Finns," I cry. "I wear these

tattoos, but I am not a shaman yet. There is still so much for me to learn, a lifetime's worth of knowledge I don't yet have. You are the shaman of the ages. Yours is the return that was promised. The people need *you*."

"I do not wish for this end," he says gently. "I am selfish and vain. I seek to live forever and a day. I merely offer this as an alternative to your painful demise at the hands of the Witch Queen. I offer my life for your lives."

"She will stretch your death to last a hundred years," I warn.

"I'd bet it lasts a thousand years, knowing how much she dislikes me." He shuffles around under the table, placing a small wooden box between us. He doesn't need to open it for me to know it contains the personal effects of the goddess of hope. "Take this with you. The witches will require an assurance from me."

"All of this is unnecessary, because I will return with Aina," I reply. "No one is dying, old man. And when I get back, we're dealing with Lumi. Once that witch is in the ground, you're coming south with us." I tuck the box in the front of the dead man's coat with the map. "Now that I've found you, I'll not leave you again. Well . . . except now," I add with a smile.

I move over by the fire's edge and begin my smoke ablutions. I turn my attention to my drum, placing it on the edge of my knee. I take a deep breath, letting it out, seeking out that place of calm at the center of me. "I'm going now—"

"Wait," the old man barks. "Siiri, wait." He gets to his feet, his hands clenching and unclenching at his sides. His mouth moves like a fish out of water. All the words he wants to say remain silent and unspoken.

I smile up at him. "Don't worry. You gave me everything I need. I'm ready."

"Gah, you're worse than a woodpecker," he barks, pacing

around to his side of the fire. "You've pecked, pecked, pecked inside my head." He emphasizes each word by jabbing his finger at his temple. "I can't get you out."

"You know you love me."

"You're bloody insufferable!"

My smile falls as he paces. All Väinämöinen's stories contain adventure and heroics, but they tell of something else too: surviving unimaginable loneliness. This old shaman has searched all his life for a place to belong, a people to call his family. Thwarted at every turn, he has never had his love returned. He is alone in the world—utterly alone.

Until he pulled me from the ice.

"Väinämöinen," I say, my voice gentle.

The shaman stops his pacing with a huff.

"You know you love me," I say again.

He sighs, shoulders sagging in defeat. "To know you is to love you, Siiri Jarintyttär."

I smile. "I love you, too, old man."

He goes still, my words swallowed by the silence of the hut, broken only by the soft crackle of the fire. He glares at me. "I'll never forgive you if you die."

"Then we are agreed. No one is dying tonight."

"And nothing too heroic," he warns. "Get your girl and get back here. Understand?"

I nod, his face the last thing I see as I close my eyes and begin to drum. The runes for Tuonela call to me: the raven, the wolf, the moon, the river. It's time to cross over. It's time to rescue my friend.

Hold on, Aina. I'm coming.

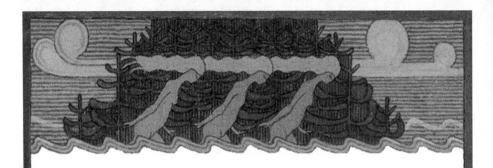

Aina

43

ALL AROUND ME, GODS and goddesses scream, pushing against each other, desperate to escape the room. Darkness creeps in, and with it an unnatural cold. All I hear is crashing, smashing, breaking . . . and that laugh. Tuonetar's feral laugh.

"Tuoni," I cry out.

"Aina!"

I feel him pulling at the threads of our bond, and then a ball of flame bursts to life in his palm. His face is a mask of rage as he draws me to him with his free hand. Around the room, other immortals use their magic to create light. Kuutar's hair shines like a star, rippling down her back as she runs for the door. Nyyrikki's cape is alight with glowing toadstools. He bends protectively over his mother, helping her to her feet.

"Secure Tuonetar," Tuoni bellows. "Protect your queen!" He lobs the fire in his hand up towards the antler chandelier. The candles magically relight, still leaving half the room in darkness.

Loviatar appears at my left, her hand on my arm.

"Take her to the tower," Tuoni commands.

"No, do not leave me," I cry, clinging to him.

He turns, cupping my face with both hands. "I must secure Tuonetar. Go with Loviatar." He kisses my forehead. "Go. I will follow."

"Come," Loviatar commands. "Aina, come."

Tuoni barrels his way through the crowd, magicking a rope of fire. I gasp, pulling Loviatar to a halt. The Witch Queen sits in my silver chair. The twins of pain and suffering stand to either side of their mother. In Kivutar's hand, there is a slender wand.

"No," I cry out.

"What is happening?" Loviatar hisses, her nails digging into my arm. "*Tell* me."

"Kivutar has the wand. Your mother sits on the throne."

As Loviatar pulls at me again, Tuonetar's voice echoes over the chaos. "And so, the great silent hope is now a spoken prophecy. Death shall be powerless in his hands? *I* am death, and I shall *never* be powerless!" She holds out her arms, the chains of her manacles dangling from her robes.

With a flick of her wrist, Kivutar waves the wand over them. Like Ukko's mighty hammer hitting an anvil, red sparks erupt from the wand's tip. The Witch Queen shrieks, black blood dripping as she fights the cuffs, which hold her fast.

"Again," she hisses at her daughter.

Kivutar raises the wand.

"No," Tuoni bellows. He crashes onto the dais, tackling Kivutar to the ground.

The Witch Queen shrieks again and squeals like an animal caught in a trap, still scraping at the manacle. "Get it off," she screams. "Take this foul thing off!"

Kiputyttö grabs it with her bony claws. Tuoni fights his way to his feet, the witch's wand now clutched in his hand. At the same moment he points the wand at the Witch Queen, the bones of her hand crack and splinter, squeezed tight in her daughter's fist, and the manacle slides off and drops to the floor with a clank. Tuonetar slashes her broken hand towards Tuoni, blasting him back, the wand flying from his hand.

"Tuoni," I scream.

Loviatar and I are buffeted by the other gods still scrambling for the doors. "Come," the witch commands. "You are not safe here."

"We're not safe anywhere," I sob, holding to her arm with both hands.

The Witch Queen snarls, leaping from my throne with her broken hand clutched against her chest. She stalks towards me like a wolf, her bloodshot eyes locked on me. The room clears around her as all the other gods dodge from her path. "I told him I would never yield to a mortal's brat," she snarls. "I told him no death magic would ever eclipse me! I will rip the whelp from your womb with my teeth!"

"Protect your queen," Tuoni shouts from his knees, blood dripping down his face.

Loviatar drags me behind her, squaring off against the Witch Queen.

"Your death is mine, Aina, Queen of Tuonela," the Witch Queen screams. "The prophecy cannot come to pass. Step aside, Loviatar."

"I shall never step aside," Loviatar replies, her hands raised. "The prophecy must hold."

"You would have us stripped of our power?" she shrieks.

"I would have us be made whole," the blind witch replies.

"She will ruin us all!"

Loviatar tips her head back, smiling. "She will free us."

"Move, or I kill you," Tuonetar snarls.

Loviatar remains still. "Do your worst."

With a snarl, the Witch Queen lunges. Before she can

reach either of us, a dark shadow descends. I cry out, nearly stumbling to the floor as Kalma shoves herself between Loviatar and the Witch Queen.

"Move, you dog," Tuonetar shrieks.

"Kalma, protect your queen," Tuoni shouts. Wand back in hand, he moves towards us, dragging a struggling Kivutar behind him. The witch writhes and screams, trying to free herself. A dozen dead soldiers march behind him, weapons drawn.

"Don't listen to him. You are *my* creature," Tuonetar calls out to the death witch. "You know this must be done. There is no other way! Help me, daughter. Set us all free. His dreams of a peaceful Tuonela will only ever be a fantasy. *This* is what we are. This is what the All-Mother made us to be. Embrace your chaos, my sweet nightmare. Embrace your nature and kill the mortal wretch."

Kalma raises her arms. Loviatar spins to face me, wrapping her arms around me, nestling me into her chest. "Avert your eyes," is her only warning before Kalma unleashes her fury. The death witch takes a deep, rattling breath. Opening her mouth wide, she releases a torrent of ash from her lips at Tuonetar. It spews forth, filling the air, choking us all. The heat is enough to singe me as I cling to Loviatar.

"No," Tuonetar shrieks, her voice muffled by the ash. "Kalma—faithless dog—"

"Come," Loviatar says, pulling me away. "Now."

I let Loviatar pull me out of the hall as Kalma continues to battle their mother, blinding the Witch Queen in her cloud of noxious ash. The dead guards surround Kiputyttö, who fights ferociously with sword and flail.

Vammatar is nowhere to be seen.

"Come," Loviatar says again, her voice urgent in my ear.

The door to my tower room slams shut, and Loviatar throws the bolt, locking us inside. I pant, chest heaving, ash dusting my coronation gown. Once I catch my breath, I glance around. Everything looks so peaceful. The covers have been turned down on the bed, a happy fire burns in the hearth, buttery rolls wait on a tray by a carafe of wine.

"This is madness." Taking my crown off, I toss it on the bed. "Loviatar, what happened down there?"

The witch doesn't turn from the door. She has her hands out, her eyes closed as she whispers a chant.

"Loviatar," I say again, crossing the room to her side. "Mielikki's prophecy. Why did it seem like the Witch Queen had already heard it?"

She doesn't answer. Her tattooed fingers flex as she mutters low in her throat. Her eyes glow white, brighter than their usual cloudiness, as the sun shines through a fogbank.

"Loviatar!" I grab her wrist, turning her to face me. "As I am your queen, you will answer me."

She twists free of my hold. "It is not for me to speak of it."

"Do not keep me in the dark any longer. I cannot bear it. Mielikki's prophecy spoke of a child, born of life and death. It spoke of Tuoni's son. Am I his mother? Gods, it's been but a few days. Is it already too late? Am I already pregnant?"

She stills. "Too late? You do not want to experience the joys of motherhood?"

"How can you think I would ever wish to bring a child into this darkness? If I were thinking with the head my mother gave me, there would be no question in my mind. I would already be taking the tonic."

"Tonic?"

"As it is, I cannot be sure," I admit. "But it's not too late to stop it. And I will—"

Loviatar's hand flies to my throat. Her nails pierce my skin as she squeezes. "You shall not squander this gift," she hisses. "To be the mother of an immortal is a blessing. You have been chosen, Aina. Whether in one year or ten, you will bear the son of Tuoni. You will bring forth the Light of Louhi. And your son will save us all."

Before I can reply, there comes a heavy pounding at the door.

"Let me in, wife."

I suck in a breath as Loviatar drops her hand away from my throat. She moves to the door, pulling back the latch. While she's distracted, I look desperately around. Moving over to the table, I tuck a knife up my sleeve.

The door swings open, and Tuoni enters. His clothes are dusted in ash. Blood stains his cheek and hands. His tunic is torn, his crown missing. "Tuonetar is secured in the tower," he says. "We prepare the chains for your sisters now. I intend to sink them in the bog. Will you help me, Loviatar?"

Loviatar is quiet for a moment. "I will help Kalma prepare." She steps around Tuoni towards the door. "Be warned, father. Your little mouse has a knife hidden up her sleeve." With that, she leaves.

Tuoni faces me. "Is Loviatar right? Do you conceal a blade from me? Do you now fear I mean to hurt you?"

"I am not afraid. I'm furious."

He takes a step closer. "What angers you, wife?"

I square my shoulders at him, taking strength from the knife blade tucked against my forearm. "You knew, didn't you? This was your true design all along."

His gaze darkens. "I am a god, wife. I know many things. Be more specific when you level an accusation at me."

"The prophecy," I cry, letting the knife slip down my forearm until I'm gripping the handle. "Mielikki's words spoken just now from beyond the veil of life and death. Those words came from the All-Mother herself. I felt it, I *know* it. And you've heard them before . . . haven't you?"

"A prophecy is only told once," he replies. "None had ever heard the Forest Queen's words before she spoke them below."

"Then why did you show no surprise at her words? I saw your face, my lord. I felt you through our bond. There was only hunger, anticipation . . . relief."

He takes a step closer, his hand raised. "Aina—"

"I thought Kalma was bringing us down here merely to find the one to free you. But you *wanted* us brought to you, didn't you? You wanted to fulfill this prophecy. You weren't looking for a mortal wife with whom to pass your days. All this time, you were looking for the one who would bear your child, your son. A true heir for death at last. That is all you want. I am nothing to you—"

He closes the distance between us, grabbing my shoulders. "Do not speak those foul words again."

"Let me go—"

In his frustration and anger, his mortal mask slips. Beneath the beauty, a glimmer of eyes that burn like embers. I feel the iron of his hands as he clings to me. He almost seems to stretch, the darkness of the room pulling at him, making him taller as he towers over me. "Do not doubt me again," he declares, smoke lacing his words.

I lean away, suddenly afraid of my god-husband.

He feels it through the bond, his hands softening, even as his mask flickers again. Life and death. Beauty and power. Control. Always control. "Aina, I *love* you—"

"You don't know the meaning of the word!"

He lets me go.

"And how could you, trapped as you are in this foul place?" I go on. "You speak of the love you share with your daughters. But it is not love. They plot and scheme against you. They dismiss you and deny you. They only serve your wishes when it suits them. That is not love, my lord. They have all the loyalty of a skulk of foxes. You call it love because you are no better. You know no better. You plot and scheme too. You lie. You manipulate." I step back, shaking my head. "In truth, you all deserve each other. You deserve to make each other miserable forever!"

"Are you finished?" he growls. "May I now speak?"

I back away from him until I hit the table's edge with my hip. "I fear your words," I admit. "I fear there will be no truth in them . . . and I fear I won't know it."

"I have told you the truth from the moment you freed me in the woods," he replies, his voice soft and angry. "I don't want you for the children you will give me. I wouldn't care if you were barren. I was ready to risk it for your sake. I want *you*, my beautiful wife. You're the light in my darkness—"

"Stop," I cry, spinning away. "Stop saying that!"

"It's true."

"You say prophecies are heard only once. But you *knew* what she would say. You were not surprised! So, what prophecy did you hear, husband? Tell me. Trust me with the truth."

He frowns, hands clenched at his sides. He's quiet for a moment, searching my face. "It was not a prophecy."

"What was it?"

A long moment of quiet stretches between us. "I think you know," he says at last. "You know part of it, at least. You know of Loviatar's daughter."

I nod.

"She was dear to me, Aina," he goes on. "As dear as a child ever could be. Her power was unlike anything this realm had ever seen. There was no darkness in it . . . no pain, no suffering. She was hope, pure and unbridled. She showed me what Tuonela could be. My dreams came from her. It was she who encouraged me to make this realm a better place. I would purge it of Tuonetar's madness, of the twins and their pain and suffering, of Vammatar's duplicitous evil. I would bring order to death, mercy and justice, peace and eternal rest."

Though our bond, I can feel his emotions. Speaking of Loviatar's daughter brings him such joy . . . and sorrow. He grieves her loss deeply. "She was helping you, wasn't she? That's why Tuonetar took her and hid her beneath the Kipumäki."

He nods. "Yes, Vammatar told her of our plans, and Tuonetar struck first. Tuonetar used the manacles I made to contain her and bound me in them instead, stifling my power. I couldn't stop her from taking the child and hiding her away. Loviatar and I thought her dead. Loviatar grieved . . . and she hated me. I had to make it right. I could not live with the suffering I'd caused."

My heart aches for them, for their pain and lonliness. Their dreams shattered, their hope taken, bound to a life of misery in the dark, watching as Tuonetar destroyed everything they built. "What happened next?"

His frown deepens. "There came a time when we were visited by Väinämöinen, here to look for secrets and spells. He found where the child had been hidden away. He vowed to tell me where she was if I agreed to help him set her free."

"And did you?"

He nods. "It was the least I could do. She was never meant to live in this realm. She was too pure for us . . . too good. She deserved a life with the living, surrounded by mortals and their dreams. I knew it, and so did her mother."

His story tallies with Loviatar's, and something in my chest loosens. "I've heard the songs of great Väinämöinen and Antero Vipunen. They say he turned himself into a serpent and swam away through your river's iron nets. They say he stole secrets."

"He stole more than secrets. I helped him steal her away. We created a distraction while Loviatar got her out from under the hill. It's how I got this," he adds, gesturing to his eye.

"He hurt you?"

He frowns. "I pretended to be trying to capture him. It was a ruse, and Tuonetar saw through it. We had to improvise. Loviatar came to my aid while Väinämöinen and the girl barely managed to escape. As punishment, Tuonetar bound me to the alder tree and trapped Loviatar here in death."

I sigh, my heart hurting for them both. I relax my hold on the knife in my sleeve. "I'm so sorry, Tuoni. What pain you've endured, what sacrifice you've made."

Tuoni nods.

"And the prophecy? You knew there would be a child."

He stills.

I step forward. "Please, Tuoni. I must know. There can be no secrets between us."

He turns his face to the fire, lost in memories. "Before she left, my sweet girl granted me a parting gift. She showed me a vision of my future."

"And . . . what was this vision?"

His mismatched eyes find mine. "She showed me a wife who shone like the sun . . . and in her arms, a child."

"Am I the woman in the vision? Am I the one who will give you that child?"

"She had no face," he admits. "The light shone from behind her like a rising sun."

This thought gives me hope. "So, I could still go free."

His frown deepens. "Go free?"

I take his hand in mine. "My lord, I would beg that you let me go. The woman in your vision has no face, you said it yourself. It doesn't have to be me. Please, if you care for me at all, you'll let me go before the witches finish what they started and kill me. Tuonetar will never let me live, I know that now.

And I want to live. If my time in death has taught me anything, it's how tenderly I care for life. *Please*, Tuoni—"

He shakes his head, turning away.

"Why do you turn your back to me?" I cry. "Why do you refuse to even consider letting me go? Perhaps I am not the one—"

"You *are* the one," he shouts, turning back to me.

"No—"

"You *are* the one, Aina. You *chose* to be the one. This is your doing as much as mine."

I shake my head. "No."

"You fulfilled the prophecy, not me."

"How?" I cry.

"You came willingly to Tuonela," he shouts. "You said it yourself: you offered death your hand. You chose your fate to save your friend. Just as you came to me in the woods and married me to save her again, to save all the mortal girls from suffering the same fate."

"I had to, my lord. It was my *only* choice."

"Yes, you bound yourself to me, blood and soul. You let me place the driftwood crown on your head as you claimed your throne. You gave me your body freely. You are my lover, my wife, and my queen. You are my light. From you will come my son—"

"I am a mortal, and every witch in this realm now has reason to see me dead," I shout. "If I am already pregnant with your son, and he shall claim dominion over death, then we are both at risk. No death god seeks to share power. They will hunt me all my days until this child is born. Then they will hunt *him*. We aren't safe here, Tuoni. You can't protect us—"

"Do not doubt my power!" he bellows, making every flame in the room roar to twice its height. Heat overwhelms me, burning my cheeks and singeing my dress.

I stand my ground, recalling the words I spoke to Loviatar in the sauna. "And do not doubt mine. You know nothing of a mother's fierce love. If I carry your child, I defy even the All-Mother herself to stop me from keeping him safe. Stand in my way, and you will become my foe, too, husband."

He leans away, looking down on me as if I were a stranger. "And what will you do if I keep you here?"

I hold his gaze, chin held high. Slipping the knife from my sleeve, I hold it to my throat, arching my neck back. "I would do anything to keep from bringing a child into this chaos. Anything at all."

He sighs. I can almost feel his heart breaking through our bond. He raises a hand and snaps his fingers. I cry out as the weight of the knife in my hand disappears in a wisp of smoke. It was that easy for him to disarm me.

"If you dare to make threats on your life, then you must be watched at every moment, wife. I cannot risk losing you or my child. I've sacrificed too much already to find you both. I will keep you safe . . . even from yourself." He turns for the door, and I feel my hope draining away.

"You were honorable once, my lord," I call after him. "You saw the light and goodness in Loviatar's girl, and you let her go."

He turns back to me, his hand still on the latch. "And I have regretted it every day since. Ask Loviatar, and she will tell you the same." He turns away to face the door. "My daughters will this night be bound in iron and cast into the bog. Tuonetar is locked in her tower. I ask that you make no attempt to leave this room. I will not come to you again until you ask for me."

The door shuts, and I'm left alone. I sink to the floor, unable to hold back my sobs.

I am nothing to the gods. A mere mortal they use in their

tricks and games. Expendable. Replaceable. Forgettable. The power I thought I'd taken is an illusion. I am on my own. I am alone.

When all my tears are shed, I fall back into my habit born from weeks of captivity. Like a caged animal, I pace from wall to door. I need a plan. I will be the mother of a death god, and many of the gods are aligned against me—against us. Any son of Tuoni will need a fierce mother if he is to survive. Aina and Ainatar must become one. These witches will come to know just how fearsome I can be. I dare them to come for us. I will be the one tearing out hearts with my teeth.

By the time my fire burns down to embers, I am resolved. I must leave Tuonela, marriage oaths be damned. Before the witches can break more of my bones. Before Tuoni breaks my heart and soul. I'm going back to the land of the living.

And my son is coming with me.

Part Four

Suns may rise and set in Finland,
Rise and set for generations,
When the North will learn my teachings,
Will recall my wisdom-sayings,
Hungry for the true religion.

—Rune 50. *The Kalevala*

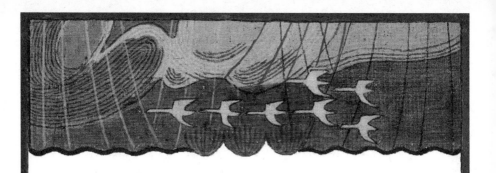

Siiri

44

I COME TO CONSCIOUSNESS in utter darkness. Heart racing, I lift a tattooed hand, brushing my fingers through the black. It hangs in the air like an unnatural, shadowy curtain, stretching as high as my mortal eyes can see. This is the veil, the barrier between life and death.

I drop my hand and smile, taking a few confident steps forward until I pass through it.

I am in Tuonela.

The smell greets me first: brine and moldy decay. It must be the river. I take a few more steps away from the edge of the veil, and my vision clears. A ribbon of glossy black water stretches before me.

Patting my chest and arms, I take stock of my itse. Weapons hang comfortably on my body—at my hips, down my boots, even between my shoulder blades. The dead man's smelly coat stayed with my body in life, acting as a guide only. Now I'm wearing an elk-skin coat with a fox-fur-trimmed hood. I reach inside my coat pocket and feel for my map. The small wooden box is in a leather satchel at my hip.

There's a whisper of a sound behind me. I turn and jump back as two figures emerge from the veil. My hand goes to my hip, ready to draw my short-handled axe. An elderly man with a shuffling gait walks right past me, followed by a young trapper in head-to-toe furs. I blink in surprise: the trapper has an axe sticking out of his back. They're newly dead. They walk away from me, uninterested in my presence.

With a calming breath, I follow them. We all walk to the water's edge, heading for a dock brightly lit by torches. Väinämöinen prepared me for this too. All the dead must wait and gain passage from the ferrywoman. More dead congregate here. No one hurries. No one pushes. They amble forward like sheep, completely uncaring that they're dead.

Splish. Splish. Splish.

From out of the darkness, the high prow of the ferry comes into view. I try to keep my head down and stay to the back of the group, putting a few bodies between myself and the edge of the dock. Tuonen tytti is older than death. Short and stocky, she wears a fur-trimmed cap over her white hair. Her milky white eyes are utterly sightless . . . another secret Väinämöinen told me. She cannot see a thing. It makes it easier for a shaman like me to slip onto the island.

Getting into Tuonela was never the problem. The trouble will come when we try to leave.

The ferry taps the edge of the dock, and Tuonen tytti opens a narrow door in the side of the boat. I let a few bodies fill the space between us before I climb on. The boat rocks beneath my feet as all the dead shuffle in. When the boat is full, Tuonen tytti shuts the door. More dead wait patiently on the dock, their shoulders slightly swaying.

I suppress a shudder. Is this all I can expect in death? No

wonder gods seek to live forever. I grip the boat wall with a tense hand, bracing as it lurches. Tuonen tytti works her pole against the bottom of the river, slowly turning the boat. We launch out into the deeper water.

This is one of the broadest points in the river. I won't come back here with Aina. Even from the middle of the river, I can hardly make out the opposite shore. A faint yellow glow slowly brightens. I watch and wait as more features begin to take shape. The lights in the foreground must be the dock. There are more lights high up on the hill—the palace. A dense stretch of deep darkness separates the two. My gaze darts left and right, taking in as much as I can.

The boat enters the ring of light cast by the torches on the dock. This is it. After everything I've survived, I've finally arrived in the land of death.

The boat lurches to a stop. In moments, Tuonen tytti opens the door and all the dead begin to amble out. I follow, watchful for armed guards. The dark, snow-covered forest looms just ahead. I hadn't even thought to ask Väinämöinen about weather in the underworld. Snow is less than ideal. I'll leave tracks.

Tracks are a risk I'll have to take.

The dead in front of me turn left, following the curve of the river. Already I can see the bodies of more dead dotting the wintry landscape ahead. But if I follow this group, they'll lead me away from the palace, not towards it.

It's now or never.

Glancing around again, I settle on a group of figures walking down the path from the direction of the palace. There are five in total. They carry simple staffs rather than swords or shields. They appear more like shepherds than guards—fittingly, since the dead move like sheep.

I pull an arrow from the quiver on my back and nock it.

Then I do my best to slink away from the group unnoticed, moving towards the birch trees. A hundred knotted eyes watch as I approach. Swallowing my nerves, I keep my fingers pinched tight around my nocked arrow.

The shepherds are getting closer. Can they see me?

Throwing caution to the wind, I break into a sprint, letting my strong legs carry me the remaining distance over the snow into the trees. I run as silently as a shadow, eyes and ears open for any sign of movement. I'm always in my element on a hunt. Nothing makes me feel more like myself, more alive.

And this will be the hunt of my life.

The fox is in your forest, mighty Tuoni. And I've come to reclaim what's mine.

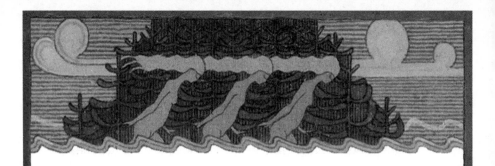

Aina

I WAKE ALONE IN my wide bed, sheets twisted around my legs. I slept fitfully, my nightmares full of chasing and running. I dreamt of Surma and Kalma in the woods. I dreamt of Tuoni too. He called my name, looking for me as I cried out. But he couldn't hear me, couldn't see me. One of the witches held me down, her hand to my mouth.

I shake off the nightmares and sit up, jerking aside the curtain. Kukka is in the room, dutifully adding logs to my fire. The comforting scent of porridge fills my senses. Without being asked, Kukka brings me a cup of tea.

"Thank you," I murmur, accepting the cup. I take a sip, enjoying the notes of spicy nettle and berry leaf sweetened with honey. With each sip, my mind clears. I take one last swallow, letting the warmth of the cup seep into my hands before setting it aside.

The time for wallowing is over. If I'm to plan my escape, I can't stay trapped in this room with only Kukka for company.

I'll have to find a way to sneak to the river and cross it. Only Loviatar knows of the tunnel that leads out under the weaving room. If I can get to it unseen, perhaps I can get to the river. I'll take my chances and swim. Siiri has always been the better swimmer, but I think I'll manage, knowing my life depends on it.

And I have fate on my side. In Tuoni's vision, a woman is standing in the sun, her child in her arms. I have to believe that Tuoni is right; that I'm the mother in the vision and I'm meant to return to the land of the living, the land of sun.

First, I have to get out of this room. The only way I'll be free is if Tuoni lets me out. He has to trust me enough to let me go walking around the palace on my own. He has to let his guard down. I have to give him a reason to trust me again.

I have to trick him.

The thought sickens me. Aina wouldn't even think of it. She's far too principled. But Ainatar now has more to live for . . . more to die for. Perhaps the death gods must be forgiven for playing their games with mortals. More than our fleeting lives are at stake when prophecies are invoked.

I close my eyes, brushing an invisible finger along the threads of our bond. It's almost impossible to comprehend the degree to which Tuoni has already woven himself into me. First as the raven, now as the man. Even when he's not physically in my presence, I feel him, as he surely must feel me.

I glance around my tower room, now as much a prison as my first room was. The box holding my crown rests on the mantel over the crackling fire. The other box containing the jewels from Loviatar waits on my dressing table. Kukka has laid out a new dress for me. This one is far more sensible than the coronation dress, a simple thing of soft wool dyed moss green. She helps me dress and braids my hair.

My clothing feels like armor, and I'll need it for what comes next. I must protect my heart at all costs. I'm already too vulnerable where Tuoni is concerned. He has the power to break me, to make me stay. He said he'd not come for me until I asked. Closing my eyes, I call to him.

"Tuoni," I whisper to the room. "I need you."

I feel a tight ball of tension loosen in my chest, and I know he's heard me. This connection between us could be my undoing. How do I control it? Will he notice if I try to hide my feelings from him?

In moments, a knock at the door has me turning on my stool. Kukka opens the door to reveal the death god. He's dressed as the hunter again. His long black hair is loose around his shoulders. He takes me in. "You didn't sleep."

"I slept a little," I reply.

"Your dreams haunt you."

"My nightmare is not yet over," I reply. "So long as I'm not safe, I won't sleep soundly again."

"My love, you *are* safe," he says, striding across the room. "I dealt with the twins. Kivutar and Kiputyttö cannot harm you. Tuonetar is locked in her tower. What more must be done to assure you that you will come to no harm? Tuonela is not just a realm of nightmares," he goes on, his tone pleading. "It is a realm of dreams. There is beauty here, possibility too . . . if you will but open your eyes and see it."

I take the opening he's offering. "Show me," I whisper.

"Show you?"

I nod, holding out my hand. "Show me something beautiful, husband. Show me one of your dreams."

He smiles. "Get your cloak."

Snow lies thick on the ground, but I don't feel cold. Tuoni and I are bundled up in wool and fur, our hoods pulled up against the chill. Our feet crunch through the snow as he leads me away from the palace walls. Behind us, the lights of the palace cast a golden haze over the snow.

"Where do you take me?" I say, my voice soft.

"Not much farther," he replies, leading us towards a thick stand of fir trees. He pushes his way through, uncaring that he'll cover himself in snow.

"My lord, what—" I cry out as he pulls me after him. I use his larger frame to block the slapping branches, snow dusting my face. One branch pulls my hood back. "Tuoni—"

"Come, love," he says on a laugh. "Nearly there."

I stumble through the last of the firs and gasp, spinning around. We're no longer in a dense forest on a cold winter night. We're in a forest clearing, and it seems to be spring. At the far end of the glade, a small waterfall flows into a babbling brook. A path along the water's edge is lit with lanterns. The mossy clearing is dotted with ferns and wildflowers in every color—lily of the valley, bluebells, pink anemone, violets.

"Where are we?" I whisper. "Why is it so much warmer here?"

"This is the Grove of Eternal Spring," he replies, smiling down at me. "It was made for my daughters long ago. On cold winter nights like this one, they'd come here and bathe in the pool, picking flowers hour by hour."

My heart flutters. "You made it? This is your magic?"

"This is the magic of Tuonela," he corrects. "Even death can be beautiful. It can be a blessing, a relief. It is the twin of life. All that is good and all that is bad; they are reflected in each other. They balance each other." He takes a step closer, placing a hand on my shoulder. "Thus far, you have seen only the bad. Tuonetar and my daughters made sure of that."

"Why do they fear this child so much?" I whisper, my hand going unconsciously to my stomach. I look up at him, tears in my eyes. "What harm can he do?"

The death god brushes his knuckles against my cheek. "They fear what they don't know, my love. You heard Mielikki's words. Our son will wield power over death. Can you imagine such a thing?"

"But you already control death . . ."

He shakes his head. "No, we control the dead, and we can influence the act of dying. Tuonetar weaves the threads of chaos, Kiputyttö turns her stones of pain, Kivutar stirs her boiling pot, Loviatar casts forth plagues . . . and Kalma collects the tortured dead and brings them below."

I suppress a shiver. "And you, husband? What do you do?"

He sighs, closing his eyes. Then he tips his head back, his body going still. A pained expression crosses his face. He's trying to hold something back from me. It's like a curtain waving in the wind blown through an open window; it makes the fire hiss and dance.

It's pain. The deep, throbbing pain of dying, bone-deep and exhausting.

"Oh gods . . ." Reaching out, I squeeze his hand. "You hold it back . . . don't you? You delay death. You carry it on your shoulders, breathing it in, giving the living more time."

He trembles with weariness, his eyes blinking open. His face takes on a mournful look. "I am the Great Fading, Lord of Blessed Death. But don't you see? I can delay it only. I can't stop it. I certainly cannot reverse its course. None of us can."

I drop his hand and step back. My hand flutters over my abdomen. "You think this child . . . you think he'll be able to stop death?"

His eyes flash with excitement. "Think of it, my love. A child born to a mortal mother and the god of death. Living and dying, in one body. Mortal and immortal. He shall be the embodiment of the great balance. Such a child would have magic truly fearsome to behold."

Death shall be powerless in his hands.

Could this child be the unmaking of Tuonela?

She will free us.

Loviatar's words shouted at the Witch Queen echo in my mind. The goddess is so sure of my fate that she risks her own life to protect mine. She needs me alive. She needs this child alive. What will happen to us? Can there be a world without death? Will that not upset the balance even more?

"You are fierce, wife," Tuoni says, his tone gentle. "You want to keep fighting me." His lips brush my cool brow. "I feel it in the bond. I felt it all night. You can keep nothing from me."

I go still, heart in my throat.

He knows.

His hands squeeze my shoulders. "Yes . . . you think on it even now. You think of crossing that river. You think of escaping and taking my son with you." Leaning away, he cups my jaw, tilting my face up.

I search his mismatched eyes, looking for his rage, his indignation. I see only sadness. My heart breaks for this lonely raven, this lovesick man. His end of the bond is a riot of conflicting emotions. Those calculating eyes stare through me, rooting me to the soft, mossy soil of this enchanting eternal spring.

"Very well," he says at last. "Your body may be supple as a reed, but your will is a bar of iron. You wish to leave me." His expression is one of anguish. "I cannot bear to see you suffer, my love."

"What are you saying, my lord?"

He holds my gaze. "I will grant your wish. I will return you to the land of the living."

My heart drops. "Oh, Tuoni—"

He raises a hand to silence me. His dark eye smolders like a burning coal, and his white eye seems almost to glow. "I will release you to the realm of the living," he intones, "only after the child is born."

I close my eyes, knowing what he'll say next. "Tuoni, no—"

He slams the door of our bond shut, knocking the wind from me. He's forcing me from his soul and his heart. He doesn't want me to witness them breaking.

"Tuoni—"

"You will stay, or you will go," he continues.

"Please don't do this." I press at the door of our bond, pounding with my fists, begging to be let back in. "Tuoni, *please.*" I drop to my knees, hands digging into the mossy soil. "Don't make me choose."

He ignores my tears, his emotions now locked deep in an iron box in his heart. "Stay or go, Ainatar, Queen of Tuonela . . . but my son stays with me. He shall never leave the realm of death."

Siiri

I'M RUNNING OUT OF time. I've circled the main palace structure twice, looking for entry points. A door Väinämöinen drew on my map is no longer there, and a crumbling tower on the western wall has been refortified. It's lit like a beacon with guards on the wall. There will be no getting in that way.

Unseen, I pass another set of guards. They move along, unhurried and inattentive. How long has it been since a shaman to rival Väinämöinen's power has dared to enter this realm?

I can't keep circling this fortress. I need an easy way in! If only the hand of hope would place Aina *outside* the walls. I could—

"Oh, gods . . ."

I duck back behind the closest tree.

Two figures emerge from the woodland edge. As soon as the light of the palace shines on the smaller figure, my heart stops. I would know the shape of her—the *feel* of her—anywhere.

Aina.

My Aina walks arm in arm with the god of death. I step around the tree, needing to see her more clearly. I feel dizzy, exhilarated. Aina is alive. I could call out to her, and she would turn. She would hear me.

Pulling my gaze from her, I take in the death god. He looks just as Väinämöinen described him—tall and broad and dark of hair. Neither of them wears a hood around their faces. If I get close enough, will I see that jagged scar on his face? He received it from Väinämöinen's hand during the battle they staged to distract the Witch Queen while Loviatar spirited her daughter away from her underhill prison. The gods may have staged the battle, but it had to look real. Väinämöinen landed a swing of his mighty sword, costing the death god the use of his eye. Tuoni gave as good as he got, nearly severing the shaman's head from his neck. Väinämöinen showed me his scar, hidden under his long white beard.

I growl low in my throat, watching as Tuoni places an arm around Aina, leading her towards that door in the eastern wall. He's touching my Aina, and I could kill him for it. I hope that damned eye pains him every day.

The pair pause as Aina pulls on the death god's hand. Her face is hidden from me by his larger form. Soon enough, the death god walks away, leaving her in the snow. A quarrel? A lover's quarrel?

I smile.

Aina stands alone, her features cast in shadows. With both hands, she pulls up her hood, hiding her face. But then she turns, her gaze sweeping the edge of the woods where I stand. I can't see her face inside her hood, but I swear by all the gods she's looking right at me. A recognition of being seen by her burrows deep in my chest.

My Aina is alive and looking at me.

In a blink she turns away, following the death god. He leads her along the base of the wall. Reaching behind himself, he takes Aina by the hand, pulling her in close to his side.

I drop my own hand to the quiver at my hip, my fingers itching to draw an arrow. I brush them along the fletching instead. I could make the shot at this distance easily. An arrow right through his head. I've made longer shots in worse conditions. I'd have another arrow nocked by the time his body hit the ground. Then Aina and I could run.

I mentally count the arrows in my quiver, imagining all the places I might bury them in his flesh before he falls. I will burn him. I will tear this island down around his head—

No, comes a soft voice, Väinämöinen's voice. I recall our parting words: *get your girl and get back here.*

No heroics. No mistakes. This is for Aina. Everything I've done, everything I've survived, has been to reach this moment. Long nights alone in the dark. Battles with witches and men. All the blood spilled, the pain endured.

I cannot fail her now.

And what has Aina suffered in the waiting? What has she been forced to do? What has she sacrificed to stay alive?

Tuoni leads Aina up to the thick wooden door. It swings open, and he stands back, making room for her to pass through first. Her eyes are averted as she steps past. He takes her gently by the wrist, pulling her to a stop. She turns, looking up at him. Gods, if only I could hear what he's saying to her! There must be some magic for that, some secret spell. What I wouldn't give to have the ears of an owl at this moment. But no, I have only the soul of a woodpecker.

The pair exchange a few more soft words. Then, to my horror, Tuoni raises Aina's hand. Turning it over, he kisses her wrist and lets her go. She turns and disappears through the open door. The death god doesn't follow. Instead, he continues to walk along the wall in the direction of the road that leads down to the ferrywoman's dock.

I stand there, using the tree as my new legs, trying to remember how to breathe. Aina and the death god have shared intimacies. He kissed her with the casualness of a lover. Which means I'm too late. He's worked his claws into her.

Forgive her everything, comes Väinämöinen's whispered warning.

I close my eyes, taking a few deep breaths. This is what he meant. Aina's alive, and that's enough for me. She wants to be saved. She wants to come home with me.

And my home is with her.

Opening my eyes, I take in the scene, my body tensing like a fox on the hunt. Tuoni is about to turn the corner. I can follow Aina into the courtyard garden. I tuck the arrow into the quiver at my hip and sling my bow across my chest. I'm about to leap from the trees when a sound has me stumbling back.

Crunch, crunch, clank, crunch.

Marching feet shuffle through the snow. Metal creaks against leather and swords clank against shields as four dead guards round the corner beyond where Tuoni just disappeared. In moments, they'll pass right in front of the door I need.

No more waiting. The woodpecker doesn't think. It's time to do.

I unsling my bow, after all, and pluck another arrow from my quiver. Waiting a few more seconds, I let the guards pass the door. Now I have the element of surprise. Taking off at a sprint, I close the distance to the wall. Nothing but a fierce blow to the head will take down the dead. Sliding to a stop, bow raised, I loose my first arrow. As I feel the twang of the bow vibrate down my fingers, I'm already reaching for the next arrow.

Thunk.

The first arrow lands in the back of a guard's head. With a grunt, he drops to his knees in the snow, then falls forward on his face. He doesn't hit the ground before I release the second arrow.

Twang.

The other guard turns to see at his companion in the snow, a vacant look on his face, as the second arrow slams through his temple, piercing his opposite cheek. He drops like a heavy bag of grain. The two guards in front turn to look at the pair of fallen bodies. They draw their swords, peering through the darkness with unblinking eyes.

The closest guard grunts in surprise as I launch myself at him, axe in hand. Ducking right, I slam my axe into the forehead of the guard. My momentum tumbles us both to the ground. I roll on my shoulder, pulling my knife free as I clamber to my feet.

The last guard takes up a fighting stance, sword held in a rotted hand. He's tall and broad-shouldered, like Onni. He'll have strength on his side. I need to use speed. The Onni-like guard steps forward, ready to swing his sword overhand at me. I dart to the side, passing my knife into my other hand. Dancing around him, I stab it into the guard's barrel chest. He howls, dropping to one knee. His gangly arm reaches around with unnatural flexibility as he grabs me by the throat.

I gasp, kicking, as he lifts me into the air, squeezing tight. I wrap both hands around his wrist, trying to break the iron grip of his fingers. The guard's vacant eyes lock onto mine and his head tips back. His mouth opens wide, and I know he's about to sound the alarm. Reaching for his face with both hands, I grab him by the lower jaw and jerk it downward with all my might, tearing half his face away as he screams. His unnatural howl is cut short.

He drops me onto the ground, and I scrabble in the snow, leaping to my feet with a discarded sword in hand. With a mighty swing, I lop his head from his neck, and he falls forward. I barely get myself out of the way as his heavy weight thumps down.

I stand amidst the carnage, dead bodies strewn about me, and take a few deep breaths, swallowing around the sharp pain in my throat. That was too close. I was distracted and clumsy. I can't let it come that close again. Remembering myself, I turn around to face the wall, my eyes narrowing on the heavy wooden door that Aina just passed through.

I smile.

The door is ajar.

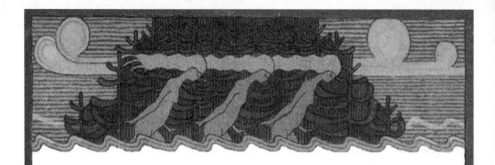

Aina

47

I STAND UNDER THE snowy branches of the willow tree, heart racing. Tuoni is prepared to cast me out, which means I got my wish. I can return to the land of the living. I can see the sun rise again. I can see Siiri again.

But at what cost? What mother could accept her own freedom at the expense of her child's? How could I ever agree to wait here, nurturing Tuoni's son, growing him in my belly, only to give birth and place him in the tender arms of Kalma?

"I will die first," I say to the willow's barren branches.

I have his oath, at least. Tuoni will return me to the land of the living. That gives me nine months to stay alive, seek alliances, grow my power, and convince Tuoni to let me leave with our son. I've already survived almost two. With Tuoni's son inside me, he and his allies will be overprotective. Nothing can reach me inside these walls. He has assured me of it. He goes now to review all his fortifications. I'm safe—

I frown at the hollowness of the words in my own mind.

The chill that overtook me out in the field rushes over me again. I can't pass through those woods without thinking of the first night . . . the night Inari died.

The night you killed her.

No, I can never be safe here, not even from my own memories. It happened again just now, standing out there in the snow. I looked to the trees, and I saw *her* standing there. The birch trees always watch me with those unblinking eyes, but this time a woman stood in their shadow. I know it was Inari, forever lurking in the hunting wood. Dreaming or waking, I can never be rid of her ghost.

A sharp rustling makes me turn. "Gods—Kukka, you scared me," I say with a little laugh.

The dead maid holds a foraging basket out to me.

I search her face, noting her hollow expression. "How strange is life that a dead maid is now my one true and loyal companion?"

She makes no response.

I take the basket from her hand, and we both walk towards the herb garden. "My mother always says that in troubling times, there's only one thing to do," I say. "Make a good cup of tea. Would you like to help me?"

Kukka sways slightly, which I've come to interpret as her sign for "yes."

I drop to my knees at the edge of the first flowering bed and begin to collect herbs. Lowering my face, I breathe in the comforting smell of marjoram. It reminds me of my mother's kitchen. That little memory has a soothing effect on my soul—

Twang.

I go still, all my senses suddenly tingling. I know that sound.

Beside me, Kukka drops to her knees. An arrow is buried in the back of her head, the sharp tip protruding from her eye. A look of surprise is frozen on her face as she falls forward into the snow.

"Kukka!" She's heavier than she looks as I fight to turn her over. I already know what I'll see if I look in her face. She's gone. Dead again. I'm alone and exposed in this courtyard. It would only take one arrow to finish me too.

A firm hand clasps over my mouth, and I squeal, my whole body going rigid. "Tuo—"

The hand stifles my scream as a strong arm encircles my waist. My assailant hauls me up out of the snow, dragging me away from Kukka's body. I fight, jabbing with my elbows and kicking with my feet as I'm dragged back under the dark curtain of the willow tree.

"Shut—*up*—Aina."

That voice. My heart stops as my body goes limp.

"It's me. It's Siiri."

No. This isn't happening. This is some trick.

"I'm going to take my hand away now, but you can't scream," says the voice. "You'll call the whole castle down on our heads. No more screaming. Do you understand?"

Oh gods, I've dreamed of Siiri's voice so often. Now, the soothing music of it washes over me. I give a curt nod. Strong hands let me go, and I scramble to my feet, turning around. I stifle a cry of relief, my own hand covering my mouth. Even in the shade of this willow, I'd know that silhouette any-where—the strong shoulders, the curve of her ears that point slightly out. The shadow steps forward into the narrow strips of light filtering in through the snowy boughs of the willow.

Siiri.

She's somehow older than I remembered, even though it's only been a couple months. She looks harder too. She wears a man's hunting outfit—a bow across her chest, axe and quiver at her hip. Her hair is odd. Where is her braid? There's something about her that feels strange. She's like something out of a dream.

"You're alive. Oh, thank the gods." Tears choke Siiri's voice. "You have no idea what this means. To see you . . . I *feel* you, Aina. Even standing apart like this, I . . ." She's clearly struggling to find the right words. My Siiri never had a problem expressing herself before. "I couldn't breathe," she manages to get out. "With you gone, I couldn't breathe."

This can't really be happening. In the depths of my loneliness, when I feel wholly lost and trapped, Siiri comes? It's too convenient. Too cruel. It reeks of magic. I don't trust it. Siiri watches me, waiting for me to give some response. "I couldn't breathe, either," I reply, watching her shoulders relax.

She reaches for me. "Come. I'm taking you home."

I go utterly still, my gaze locked on Siiri's hands. They're marked with runes. I can think of only one witch who would dare use this kind of magic on me. She's done it to me once before. But this time, the impersonation is too good. She has Siiri down to the last detail—her spray of freckles, the slant of her cheekbones, the music in her voice.

But those hands. The witch slipped up. This is not my Siiri. The only way Vammatar would be able to impersonate her so well is if she found her. Vammatar has captured my Siiri. I can only imagine what she did to her.

Rage boils inside me. "What have you done?"

Siiri's face falls. "What?"

"Where is she, you heartless witch? What have you done with her?" I peer through the tree's boughs. "Is she here? Did you take her?"

"Who?" Siiri steps forward. "Aina, tell me what's wrong. Who are you looking for?"

I lunge, throwing myself at the witch. I scratch and slap, ready to tear her throat out.

"Aina—*ouch*—"

"What did you do to her?" I cry. "Where is Siiri?"

We fall to the ground in a ball of thrown elbows and scratching fingernails. I wrestle myself atop her, letting my rage burn within me like a holy fire.

"Aina—*stop*—"

"Where's my Siiri? I'll kill you for this, Vammatar. *Tell* me!"

With a grunt, the witch rolls us over, pressing me into the snow. She gets her hips around mine, locking me in place. In moments, she has me pinned, her strength utterly overpowering me. "Just *stop*."

My rage burns out, and all I'm left with is the taste of ash in my mouth. I sag with defeat, stifling a broken sob. "Please, don't hurt her. Don't hurt Siiri. I'll do anything. Kill me, feed me to your mother, cast me into the bog. Just don't hurt my Siiri."

The witch loosens her grip on me. My eyes dart to her tattoos again. She follows my gaze, and her force on me relaxes. "Oh, Aina." She releases one of my wrists to cup my cheek. "I *am* Siiri. Don't look at my hands. Look in my eyes."

I shake my head, eyes shutting tight. I can't let her in. She'll break me, body and soul. Such a perfectly cruel torture. I could withstand anything but to have Siiri used against me in this way.

"These are not Vammatar's runes," she says, gently. "I thought the same thing at first, but no death goddess gave them to me, I swear it. Aina, *please*." Her warm hand is still on my cheek. "You know it's me. You *know* me. You know what you felt when you saw me at the edge of the woods just now."

I gasp, peering up at her freckled cheeks. "That was you?"

She lets go of my other wrist and climbs off me. "I thought

you knew. I felt it too. I was so sure. Aina, I felt you seeing me." Her voice trembles. "Am I really so changed? Aina, you are the only one who would always know me . . . please say you can still see me."

I take a hesitant step forward. "I knew it was you," I whisper. "In the woods . . . I knew. But I couldn't dare hope—" My words catch in my throat, and I close the space between us, burying my face in her shoulder.

"Oh, thank the gods," she says on a breath, her arms wrapping around me. "Thank you, All-Mother."

I let go of all grief and fear and cling to her. I breathe her in. She smells strange, like cardamom and wood smoke, nothing like my Siiri. And yet I feel her beneath my hands and know who she is. I don't know how she did it, but she's here.

Siiri pulls away first, her lips brushing over my brow. "Come, we have to go. They'll soon have this entire realm out looking for me."

"Why?"

"I've felled five dead and counting. And the death gods don't take kindly to intruders. They really don't take kindly to thieves."

"You're here to steal something?"

"Yes," she replies with a soft laugh. "*You.* Now, come on."

Siiri is here, and she's come to steal me away back to the land of the living. Fresh tears fill my eyes as I look down at her outstretched hand. Things are so complicated now. How will I ever explain what happened? Would Siiri still extend that hand to me if she knew the truth? If she knew the risk she was taking?

"Aina, come," she says again. "We haven't time to delay."

"I have to tell you something."

"You can tell me later." Dropping her hand, she unslings her bow from her shoulder. "Come on. This way. Quietly now."

"Siiri," I hiss at her retreating form.

She turns.

"I'm married," I whisper, letting my truth free.

"What?"

"The death god . . . I married him. I married Tuoni. There were reasons for it, I swear it. And I'd do it again," I admit, raising my chin. "But things are complicated now."

"So, we uncomplicate them," she says, crossing back over to my side. "He doesn't get to keep you like some prize. Return home with me now, and all can be as it was—"

"Nothing can ever be as it was."

She steps back, eyes narrowing as she searches my face. A tense moment stretches between us. "There's more. Say it all."

"I'm pregnant."

My words pierce through her thick armor. Siiri is always so easy to read—her grief, her frustration. "Are you telling me you mean to stay here?"

"I'm telling you that he will not let me go easily." I reach for her. "I can explain—"

"Don't touch me." She swats my hand away. "You have no idea what I've done. What I'm *still* doing—the sacrifices I've made, the scars I've earned, the people I've *killed*—all to find my way to you. To rescue you—"

"And what do you think I've suffered?" I say, my own resentment rising. "I killed someone too, Siiri. I have scars now too. I outfoxed the Witch Queen of Tuonela. I stole her crown. I fought a kalman väki with my bare hands. I've done everything I can to survive. I married Tuoni to protect *you*, to protect our families, to protect countless other women from falling prey to the death gods' schemes. And he's not all bad," I admit. "He's nothing like the stories, Siiri. He's kind and good, and he loves me."

"And you mean to stay," she whispers, her heart breaking

in the tone of her voice. "You mean to stay here and be Queen of the Dead. No more sunrises for Aina Taavintyttär. You mean to stay and raise a death god's babe in a cradle of bones?"

"I mean to protect you from *me*," I press. "Siiri, you must go. Now. If you are caught trying to help me escape, I doubt I'll be able to save you. And I will not watch you die. I will suffer any other pain or torture they can devise, but not that. Never that—"

"I'm not leaving without you."

"I'll find my own way," I assure her. Reaching out, I take her hand. "Tuoni has already promised to release me after the child is born. I just need time to help him see reason. I need him to see that our son must come with me when I go."

Her eyes go wide. "Your son? How can you already know what the child will be?"

"A prophecy foretold his coming. And Tuoni saw us in a vision. It was gifted to him by Loviatar's daughter."

"The hope goddess? She saw you with Tuoni? She saw you bear his child?"

Her words sink deep in my heart. "Oh gods . . . Yes, she is hope, isn't she?" I smile, relief flooding my heart. "Her daughter is hope." I drop Siiri's hand and turn away, puzzling it out in my mind. "Tuoni's most prized possession, taken from him too soon. He had to set her free so she could find me and set me on my path." I close my eyes, My hand rises to brush over my abdomen. "You're not a bad omen, my little love. You are the embodiment of hope."

Siiri steps closer behind me, her hand on my shoulder. "Aina, as much as you may love the death god now, you know you cannot trust him—and he can't keep you safe here."

I turn around. "Whether I love him or not doesn't matter anymore. *This* is the only thing that matters now," I say, gesturing to my abdomen. "The prophecy must hold. This child must live. The other death gods don't understand him. They want us both dead. I have to get us out."

"Then let me help you. Aina, put your trust in me again. I know I let you down before. In the woods with Kalma, I wasn't strong enough. I didn't protect you—"

"That wasn't your fault."

"I couldn't protect you," she says over me. "But I can now. Aina, I swear it. Come with me, and I'll bring you under the protection of Väinämöinen himself."

"You know Väinämöinen?"

She smirks. "Who do you think taught me how to sneak in here? He's been teaching me the ways of the shaman. He gave me these," she adds, gesturing to her tattoos.

I smile, my heart lightening. "I met Mielikki. And Kuutar and I danced with Nyyrikki."

Siiri gasps. "You did not."

"I did . . . at my coronation feast."

"Well, naturally," she teases. "You're a queen now. Pardon me for not bowing."

I roll my eyes.

"I met Nyyrikki's sister in the woods, and a nasty forest witch named Lumi. What was Nyyrikki like?"

"He's an absolute cad," I reply with another smile.

She grins. "The most interesting men always are."

I laugh. "If ever you were to marry a god, I think it would be him. Either marriage or mortal enemies, I see no other alternative."

We're both silent for a moment, gazing into each other's eyes.

I give her hand a squeeze, whispering the words that sit heaviest in my heart. "Do you hate me, Siiri?"

"No."

"Don't say it if you don't mean it. Don't give me hope where there is none."

Siiri slips her bow onto her shoulder and takes both my hands. "I don't know how to explain myself here . . ." She takes a deep breath, her blue eyes softening. "All souls exist in three pieces, Aina. Only three. *Always* three. You have them too. I'm here now in a piece of my soul. It's the piece that loves you so fiercely, it will do anything to be by your side again." She steps closer, dropping my hand to cup my cheek. "Being with you now, I finally understand the truth of my life. I don't know what magic it is, but I know without doubt that my soul exists in *four* pieces."

Her face softens as she smiles, her thumb brushing the corner of my mouth. "You're the fourth piece, Aina. You exist outside of me. You are your own person, and you will go your own way, but I can't be without you. So, I beg it of you now . . . let me follow."

"Siiri . . ."

"I'll ask for nothing else," she says quickly. "Never, Aina. I wouldn't do that. Just let me follow you even into death."

My Siiri is here. My dearest friend, my truest north. She followed me to the very depths of death. Of course she did. How could I have ever doubted she would? If there was one person sure to find a way to get to me, even in this dark place, it would be my Siiri. Now she's holding out her hand, asking me trust her, asking me to follow her back to life. She wants to take me home. She wants to *be* my home.

Heart in my throat, I grab the front of her coat and pull her to me. She sucks in a surprised breath as I press my lips to hers in a soft kiss of thankfulness. I hold her there, breathing her in. Her lips have always been the only softness in her. Otherwise, she's all sharp elbows and harsh opinions. But her lips . . .

I've noticed them before—the way they frame her mouth when she laughs, the way she purses them when she's frustrated. I kiss them now, tasting them. She tastes like salt and honey and, yes . . .

Juniper.

Wisewomen call juniper berries the "shaman's fruit." Different parts of the tree foster connection, healing, and purification. Siiri, my fearless shaman, come to rescue her lost queen from the endless night. I smile against her lips, kissing her again.

Her hesitation only lasts a second before she cups the back of my head and finally kisses me in return, her lips parting against mine. It's soft and sweet . . . and over too quickly.

I break away first, my hands stiff on her shoulders. We stare at each other, lips parted, chests heaving. "Get us out of here," I say. "Siiri, take me home."

She nods, and I drop my hands from her shoulders. Taking her bow in hand, she turns. "Follow me. Quick and quiet as you can."

Before I can reply, a familiar sound has both our heads turning. It's the softest of sounds: gentle footfalls crunching the snow.

"Aina," a low voice calls. "Who are you talking to?"

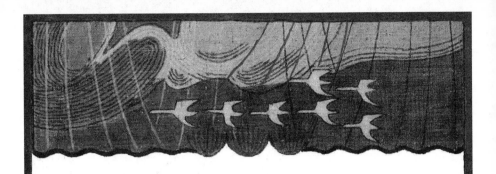

Siiri

MY SENSES ARE A riot of emotions. Aina just kissed me.
I can still taste her on my lips—sweet as a raspberry, soft as
cooling mint. But Aina is married to the death god. And she's
pregnant. She's scared and alone. She's fought so hard and suffered so much.

I knew this place might change her. It took me so long to
journey north and find Väinämöinen—too long. All the while,
she remained trapped down here, fighting to survive. My brave
Aina. She said she killed someone. She lured the death god to
her aid. She claimed the Witch Queen's crown. Is Tuonetar
dead? I don't intend to stay long enough to find out.

It will take all my cunning to get us out, and she's willing
to come home. That's all I need to know. I will get her to the
edge of the veil or die trying. "Follow me," I say. "Quick and
quiet as you can."

Before I can turn, all my senses fire in alarm. Someone is
here. I can feel them. I hear the soft crunch of snow.

"Aina," a low, female voice calls from the other side of the willow tree. "Who are you talking to?"

My hand falls to the quiver at my hip, but one sharp look from Aina tells me violence isn't an option.

"I'm here, Loviatar," she calls out.

My jaw clenches tight. The blind goddess of illness sweeps the willow branches aside, stepping under the shadows to join us. She's tall and austere looking, with thin lips, a narrow face, and long black hair trailing down her back. I expected the goddess of pestilence and plagues to look sicklier, but one might even call her beautiful.

But Loviatar took my mother. She takes so many—mothers from daughters, husbands from wives. So much death. So much pain and suffering. I want to blame her. I want to *hate* her. But I'm learning more about the balance. All gods must be respected. All gods serve a purpose.

And it was Loviatar who saved Väinämöinen.

The goddess stares unblinking at the space between us. "I assume you use my name to signal my identity to your companion," she says in greeting. "They clearly know you, but they do not know me by sight alone. Which means they are not from this realm, nor are they an immortal."

Aina take a step closer to her. "Loviatar, please—"

The witch raises a hand to silence her. She shifts her raised hand ever so slightly to the left. Then she curls her fingers down and points directly at me. "Who are you, little fox?"

I glance to Aina, readying for a fight.

Aina shakes her head again. "Just tell her," she whispers.

I face the goddess. "My name is Siiri."

The corner of the witch's mouth twitches in what I assume is meant to be a smile. "Ah . . . the one and only Siiri." Her white eyes narrow on Aina. "Your Siiri is a shaman? You kept that quiet, little mouse."

"I didn't know," Aina replies honestly.

I take a step closer. I won't be able to breathe until I put Aina safely behind me. "Goddess, I was trained by Väinämöinen himself. He waits with my body in life even now. He sends his regards—"

"Do not speak of him," she hisses.

"You helped him once." I inch my shoulder in front of Aina. "You helped each other. Please, goddess—"

She scoffs. "Is that the word he uses? I shouldn't be surprised that he claims to have helped me. That shaman took everything from me."

"I know exactly what he took from you," I counter. "What he took *for* you—"

"We will not speak of it!"

Aina places a hand on my arm. "Siiri, this is not the way."

I shrug away from her, with eyes only for the goddess. "The ancient forest giant Antero Vipunen told him where to find your daughter. She was held hostage by the Witch Queen beneath the Kipumäki. You tried to free her, but spells kept the door sealed even from you. He taught you the spells needed to break her out."

A single tear slips down the witch's pale face. "Stop. No more."

"Hope no longer dwells in this dark place," I intone. "She is free. *You* freed her. We ask you to give this new hope a chance. Let me take Aina with me. Together, we'll work with Väinämöinen to restore all that was lost. We will restore the balance. We will bring peace to the Finns. Surely, that will please the death gods too."

Aina places a gentle hand on my shoulder as she steps around me. She looks tenderly at the witch. "I'm so sorry, Loviatar," she whispers. "I know the grief you've lived with these long years. It takes the bravest of mothers to give a child away."

Loviatar glares at her.

"But you don't regret setting her free of this place. Any good mother would have done the same." She steps closer. "I only ask for the same chance you had," she pleads. "Let me protect my son. Let me leave with him before the other death witches tear us apart."

Loviatar's face is impossible to read. She cups Aina's cheek with all the tenderness of a mother. "You cannot get something for free, little mouse. Not in this realm."

Aina stiffens. "Name your price."

"Set me free," the witch commands. "My daughter and I have waited a lifetime to be together again. Now it is you who thwarts me. You've proved to be no more merciful than my wretched mother."

I glance between them, confused.

Aina's gaze is resolute as she mirrors the death witch's stance. "My mercy is boundless," she counters. "As are my love and fidelity. But I must be met halfway, Loviatar. I will not negotiate with you on that score. That price has already been set."

Loviatar hisses in frustration. "You still doubt my love?"

"Just tell me her name," Aina whispers. "Trust me as I am trusting you. We can all escape here together. We can be free. Please, Loviatar, meet me halfway."

I try to puzzle out their argument, glancing between them. "Your daughter? Is that what this is about?"

The witch stands across from us, her eyes unblinking.

"You want to see your daughter again?" I press. "We can make that happen. I'll talk to Väinämöinen. Between the two of us, we can find a way. We can bring her to you—"

"No," the witch snarls. With a sweep of her arm, she grabs Aina, pulling her in against her chest, her clawed hand at Aina's throat.

Aina cries out in surprise, her hands clasping the witch's wrist.

I drop my hand to the top of my axe.

"Don't even think about it." The witch tightens her hold at Aina's neck, her fingernails pinching Aina's fair skin tightly enough to draw blood. "You will not bring my daughter back to this place. Swear it, shaman."

I search her face, sensing her fear. "You're scared. You know she's not safe here."

"None of us are," Aina says through the hand at her throat.

"*Swear* it," the witch presses.

"I swear," I reply, taking this bold chance. This witch is spilling my Aina's blood. There's nothing I won't do to make it stop. "I shall never bring your daughter to Tuonela . . . on the condition that you let me leave now with Aina."

The witch hisses in rage, black magic creeping down the veins of her arms. Her eyes shift from pools of fog to orbs of darkest night. Her voice takes on a breathy rasp. "You challenge a death goddess, mortal?"

"I offer a bargain. Give me Aina now, and I swear on the All-Mother, I will do everything in my power to keep your daughter from this place." I take a step closer, all my hunting instincts humming inside me. "But keep my Aina from me, and I will personally shove your precious child through the veil and drop her squealing at the Witch Queen's feet."

The witch snarls, her teeth sharpened to deadly points. "There is no threat to my daughter's safety if you're dead, shaman. And my father will suffer no rivals to live. Say goodbye to your precious Siiri," she taunts at Aina, giving her cheek a kiss.

"No—" Aina struggles, tugging at the witch. "Siiri, go—now—"

I use the distraction of Aina's movement to tug loose my axe. With a single lunging step, I swing high, bludgeoning the goddess in the side of the head. Aina cries out as the witch's hand at her throat goes slack. The goddess looks briefly surprised, almost impressed, before she drops to the snow in a tangle of white robes and black hair.

Aina

LOVIATAR LIES IN A crumpled heap at my feet. "What did you do?" I shriek, turning on Siiri.

She tucks her axe in at her belt. "She'll be fine."

Blood is on the shaft, but the blade is clean. Dropping to my knees, I breathe a sigh of relief as I feel the goddess's slow pulse at her neck.

Siiri ducks out from under the willow and comes back in moments, dragging the limp form of Kukka through the snow. "You heard her. She refused to help us. We can't trust her, Aina. We can't just walk away from her and risk her sounding the alarm." With a grunt, she drops Kukka's limp form next to Loviatar.

Frustration surges through my veins. "You didn't have to hurt Kukka."

"Kukka?"

"My maid," I say, pointing at the dead girl's body.

Siiri jerks the arrow free from Kukka's skull, and I wince, looking away. She wipes the tip on her breeches before returning it to her quiver. "She can't feel anything, Aina. She's dead."

"You don't know what they feel. You didn't know her, Siiri. She was my friend."

Siiri stands over me, hands on hips. "We'll have to argue about it later. I don't know how much time I just bought us, but that witch probably has a thick skull. We must go."

I get to my feet and unclasp my hood from my shoulders, tossing it to Siiri. "Put that on and pull up the hood." I step out from under the willow.

Siiri catches up quickly. "We need to go to the river—"

"I know." I keep walking.

"We'll go the way I came in. Väinämöinen says the river is narrowest at the Kipumäki—"

"I know," I say, louder this time.

"Well—but you're going the wrong way—"

I stop and turn, glaring at her. "Siiri, for once in your life, shut up. Stop mothering me, stop protecting me, and stop trying to control everything. *Trust* me. I've lived here for months. You want out, and so do I. Just this once, trust that I know more than you."

Siiri opens her mouth to speak but shuts it again quickly. Her mouth sets in a firm line, her eyes blazing with the words she's leaving unsaid.

I gesture to my cloak around her shoulders. "Hood up, head down, and walk in my shadow. Try to shuffle a bit. Act like you're dead. And *do not speak*. Understood?"

With a scowl, Siiri flips up the cowl. The rest of the cloak hangs in folds around her shoulders, hiding her bulky weapons.

Giving her a nod, I turn. "Let's go then, handmaid."

We sweep across the garden and through the entry courtyard. The wooden doors, wide enough to admit Tuoni's great iron horse, stand firmly bolted shut. We pass through to the busy kitchen courtyard.

I stop in the doorway. Smoke rises from the ovens, filling the air with the scent of savory bread. Somewhere within the stables, horses whinny and cattle low. The dead shuffle back and forth, carrying bundles and trays, readying the hall for supper.

Behind me, Siiri grabs my arm. "They'll see us," she hisses.

"They'll see me," I correct.

Aina would never have been brave enough to do what we are about to do, but I am Ainatar now. I have power and presence. Holding my head high, I set my shoulders, and stride into the hall. I do my best to mirror Vammatar, who enters every room as if she owns it. This thought makes me smile. She doesn't own this palace. I do. I am Queen of Tuonela . . . for a little while longer at least.

All around us, the dead move out of my way, bowing their heads in deference. Siiri stays right on my heels. I have to hope she's keeping her head down. We walk right across the middle of the courtyard to the weaving room door. As I approach, a thin woman with wispy brown braids shuffles forward to open it.

"Thank you, dear one," I say, patting the servant's shoulder.

As soon as Siiri passes the threshold, she shuts the door. Then she's rounding on me. "You've moved us deeper into the palace! We need to go the other direction. We need to—Aina, you're not listening."

I know I'm not listening. I've already crossed the room, down the row of looms, my gaze locked on the floor as I find the right spot.

"Aina, what are you doing?"

"Stop bleating like a sheep and come help me."

Siiri watches me shove at the loom with my shoulder. "Aina, what—"

"Help me move this. There's a trap door."

She untangles her bow from the folds of my cloak and sets it aside. "You pull, I'll push."

We shove the heavy frame. It scrapes across the floor. The weights swing and clack.

Siiri gives it another shove, and the door is revealed. "And what's waiting underneath?"

I pant, hands on hips, as I look down at the faint seams in the floor. "This is the tunnel Loviatar used to secret Väinämöinen to the Kipumäki to rescue her daughter. It's the same tunnel I used to free Tuoni. The river waits just beyond."

Siiri gives me a sharp look.

I smile at her. "Trust me yet?"

Ignoring me, she pulls something from inside her coat. It's a piece of tanned skin that she unfolds. "Look here. Väinämöinen knew there was a tunnel, but the sneaky witch blindfolded him. He didn't know where it started, only where it led." She points to a rounded mark on what I'm sure must be a map of the land of the dead. "This is the Kipumäki. The river is narrowest just beyond it. There's an island in the middle. We swim to it, then swim again. Then there's nothing left but to pass through the veil." Siiri tucks the map away. Then she drops to her knees and wrenches open the trap door, exposing the narrow set of steps.

"Get a candle," I say. "I'll find myself another cloak."

Siiri scrambles to her feet to take a candle from the wall.

Before I can take three steps towards the storage room, the door to the weaving room bursts open. "Don't turn around," I manage to hiss.

Siiri tenses, raising a hand to give the hood of her cape a tug forward. Her other hand disappears inside the folds of the cloak, no doubt drawing a weapon.

I step between the row of looms, trying to pull attention from her standing in the shadows . . . and more importantly from the open trap door. "Vammatar," I call out, my heart sinking, as the witch sweeps in. A pair of dead guards flank her. She flicks her long, silky hair off her shoulder, gazing imperiously around. "What are you doing in here?"

Her eyes narrow on me. "I should ask you the same thing. Where is my sister?"

I try to control the racing of my heart. "Loviatar?"

The witch scoffs. "What other sister would I look for in this wretched room?" She takes a step closer, her voice dripping with venom. "Besides, we both know where my *other* sisters are, seeing as you successfully dispatched them into the bog."

"That was Tuoni's justice, not mine."

"It's no matter," she replies. "He frees them as we speak."

I blink, heart pounding in my chest. "They have paid for their treachery so cheaply?"

"We have need of them," the witch replies.

"What need?"

She smirks. "A true queen of Tuonela would know the threats to her realm. I tire of wasting time with you. Tell me where my sister is. You're always hidden away together."

"She just left," I reply, shifting another step further from the trap door. "If you leave now, you can catch up with her."

Vammatar's eyes narrow as she glances around again. "Why are you in here?"

"To weave," I reply coolly. "You gave me this assignment, remember?"

"Now is no time to weave, you silly fool. My father may delight at keeping you in the dark, but danger is danger. I'll not let it be my skin he shreds if he finds out I let you sneak around unattended."

I go still, not daring to look at Siiri. "In danger from what?"

Vammatar raises a finger to her lips. From far beyond the

walls, I hear it. *Horns.* They blast from east and west. "Do you hear that?" the witch teases. "Someone has entered our realm uninvited. Some treacherous snake is slithering through our garden. Father has us all on alert. Frankly, I don't care if a snake swallows you whole. You've been nothing but a nuisance. And I don't give an apple for prophecies. My sister witch can keep them. I only care about the here and now."

"Surely, I'm safe in this room," I say. "I'll bar the door when you leave. I'll hide in the storage room."

"Don't be ridiculous," she scoffs, striding forward. "You're coming with me. I'll take you directly to my father."

I duck to the right, hoping to keep her from looking towards Siiri and the trap door. "If there are dangers beyond this room, you should just—*ahh*—"

Two things happen at once. Vammatar grabs my arm and jerks me forward, and Tuoni throws open the door of our bond. I cry out as I feel every fiber of him demanding to know where I am. Vammatar lets me go. "What's wrong with you *now*, bonebag? Are you afflicted?"

I groan, pressing a hand over my chest as I soothe down the bond at Tuoni. *I'm well. I'm unharmed. I'm with Vammatar, and she brings me to your side.* I don't dare let myself think or feel anything else.

Down the bond, one feeling overwhelms me. It's strong enough I practically hear him shouting it in my ear. *Stay put.*

"Have you gone deaf?" the witch hisses, reaching for me again.

"It's him," I pant, rubbing at my chest. "He knows I'm here. He wants me to stay."

She glares down at me, looking for the lie. Could this be enough? Could she believe me and walk away? She closes her hand around my forearm. "Come on, bonebag. Let's lock you up tight in your tower." She pulls me along at such an angle that she cannot possibly miss seeing the open trap door.

"No," I pant, trying to steer us away. "Unhand me, Vammatar. I can walk myself—"

The witch stops, her body going still as stone, and I know she knows. I know she *sees*. The loom stands off-center. Slowly, she turns, her claws pressing into my flesh. She glares down at me.

"You're hurting me," I say, wrapping my hand around her wrist.

"I will ask you only once more, little bonebag . . . what are you doing in here?"

I don't dare let my eyes dart to Siiri. "You hate me, Vammatar," I begin, my voice soft. "Rightfully so, for I've upended all your lives. You hate the turmoil I've brought to your family—sister turning against sister. You want things back the way they were. Before prophecies, before all these lies and intrigues."

"And?"

I hold her dark gaze. "What if I said I could give it to you?"

The witch doesn't move. Her face is suddenly impossible to read.

"Let me go, and everything will be as it was before," I whisper. "I am the thorn in your side, so let me remove myself."

A quiet moment stretches between us as the witch calculates. Slowly, her blank expression turns to a sneer. "Where is she?"

"Where is who?"

"My wretched sister. Only she would put these thoughts in your head. Does she go to prepare the way for you? Is this tunnel how she did it before? Will she help you swim to the veil?"

"Loviatar had nothing to do with this," I say quickly. "I found this door on my own. I asked for her help, it's true. But she denied me. I attacked her. If you go now, you'll find her knocked insensible under the willow tree in the garden. Kukka is only helping because she's bound to me," I add, gesturing dismissively to Siiri. "She doesn't know any better. She had no choice."

Vammatar's expression changes. "You really are that treacherous, aren't you?"

"Don't help me," I plead, casting around for my last hope with this witch. "Help yourself. Let me go, and you'll have everything you want. Let me go, and you'll all be free again. You'll be a family again."

For one blessed moment, I think the goddess is actually considering my words, but then she smiles. My blood runs cold. "Did you really think that little act would work? Preying on my vanity? Appealing to my wretched selfishness?" She laughs. "You're a blundering fool. Nothing will ever be the same. You made sure of that. You are married to my father, and now you carry his child. I can wish you a fiery death, but the truth is that I'm curious enough to want to see what happens next."

"Oh gods." I search her wretched face. "You *want* everything to fall apart. You want to watch Tuonela burn and dance in the ashes."

She shrugs. "I'm the goddess of evil."

"If you want to watch it all burn, then stand aside," I reply. "You're blocking my way."

Her smile falls. "Take one step towards that hole, and I'll cut off both your feet."

As soon as the words leave the witch's mouth, Siiri steps between the looms and throws her axe. It slices into the witch's shoulder and clatters to the floor. Vammatar lets out a scream. She presses a hand to the long cut, already staining her robe with deep red blood.

"You," she hisses, her hand dropping to her side as Siiri strides forward, lowering her hood. "You're the shaman?"

"And you're a dead witch," Siiri taunts. "That's the last time you threaten Aina and live."

Vammatar's eyes light with excitement. Sharp knives slip from her sleeves. She twirls them with confident hands, squaring off against Siiri. "Oh, I shall dearly love skinning you alive. There is nothing more delicious than the taste of roasted shaman flesh."

Siiri is unfazed, tugging her knife from her belt. "Kill me if you can, witch. All-Mother knows I'll be aiming for your cold, bloodless heart."

The witch looks delighted, almost eager for this fight. The women lunge for each other and I shriek, my shoulder hitting the frame of a loom. Siiri's hood flutters back, exposing her messy blonde hair. She grips her axe with a tattooed hand, swinging wide. The goddess ducks, swiping with her sharp blade.

Siiri is too slow. The blade cuts into her upper arm, making her wince.

"Restrain this meddling shaman," Vammatar orders. "Tuoni will have questions for it."

The guards march forward. Siiri can't possibly fight them in this confined space. I look around, desperate for a way to help. I pick up the only thing I can find: a long, thin pair of knitting needles.

Slipping behind the closest loom, I let a guard pass. Behind me, Siiri and the witch trade blows, slamming into the looms. I duck into the aisle and leap onto the guard's back. He roars, reaching for me with a large hand. With one arm around his neck, I bring my other hand around, jabbing my knitting needle into his cloudy eye. He screams and drops to his knees.

I clamber off him before he sinks to the floor, sending a stool rattling away. Siiri is too focused to see it as she parries the witch's vicious attack. The stool hits her ankle, and she trips.

"Siiri, no!" Her knife clatters out of her hand. She grunts, rolling to her side as the witch lunges. Before Siiri can dart away, Vammatar grabs the hem of Siiri's cloak. Siiri gasps, jerking away with her neck to break the silver clasp—but it holds fast. With a victorious grin, Vammatar wraps her hand tighter into the cloak, reeling Siiri closer. The other guard advances to her front, his sword drawn.

"Siiri," I cry again.

They have her boxed in. I'm certain they'll kill her. Rage erupts from me as I grab another stool. Throwing it with all my might, it hits the guard in the side of the head. It's all the distraction Siiri needs to bend backward and free her neck from the cloak. She rolls, snatching up one of the witch's discarded knives. Armed once again with knife and axe, she strikes at the advancing witch.

"I can't wait to see how my father will torture you," Vammatar taunts me. "There is nothing he likes more than breaking traitors' bones."

The guard lurches back to his feet, sword raised in Siiri's direction. She's too busy blocking the witch's relentless attacks to notice. She ducks and weaves, using the looms as shields. This guard is clever. He passes left, ready to meet her around the other side as she dances with the witch.

I cry out, launching myself into the melee. With no other thought but to spare her the blow, I throw myself between Siiri and the guard.

"Do not touch the queen," Vammatar commands.

"Aina, no!" Siiri shrieks.

Too late. The guard's arm is already swinging before Vammatar can give her command. His fist collides with the side of my head, and the blow sends me tumbling to the floor. I didn't even realize how close I was to the trap door. With a shriek, I drop right through. I tumble down the stairs and land in a heap on the tunnel floor.

"Aina," Siiri screams from above.

I whimper, sucking in sharp breaths, my shaking hand going to my belly as I roll to my side. "You're safe," I whisper to myself and the baby. "We're all right."

"Aina!" Siiri calls again.

I peer dizzily up the stairs and press lightly on the spot just above my temple, wincing at the sharp pain. I look at my hand.

Blood.

"Don't pass out," I whisper to myself, stumbling to my feet.

I've barely taken a second step when Siiri's legs appear through the trap door. She drops through the hole and catches herself, sliding down a few steps on her bottom until her head clears the door. I cry out at the mighty swing of the guard's sword passing right over the opening where her head had been.

"Aina," Siiri says again, hurrying down the stairs to my side.

"M'fine," I murmur, one hand still pressing the wound on my head.

"Stay back," Siiri commands. "Stick to the shadows."

Vammatar charges down the stairs, a ball of fire floating at her shoulder. The light is disorienting. We both wince, blinking in pain. The witch is monstrous in her rage, knives ready.

Chest heaving, arms and shoulders marked with nicks

from the witch's blades, Siiri faces off against Vammatar again, ready to do battle in my name. Vammatar meets her in the middle of the earthen tunnel with a slash of sharp metal.

The guard stumbles down the stairs last, his sword clattering on each step, dangling uselessly from his half-severed arm.

Siiri is tiring. She can't fight them both. She needs me.

I drop my hand from my bleeding head and step forward, facing the guard. "As Queen of Tuonela, I order you to stop."

Without hesitation, the guard halts on the bottom step, swaying as he stands.

I sigh with relief, shoulders sagging. Gods, I was a fool not to think of it before.

"No," Vammatar shrieks. "Kill the shaman. Kill her—"

"Protect the shaman," I call over her. "Kill Vammatar."

Siiri slams her knife hilt-deep in the goddess's chest.

Vammatar growls with the ferocity of a wolf. White light pulses from her chest, knocking Siiri clear off her feet. But the guard doesn't stop advancing, so Vammatar is forced to deal with him. "No, you fool. Kill—the—shaman," she shrieks, hacking at the dead guard.

Siiri recovers, rising shakily to her feet. I gasp at all the places from which Siiri is bleeding. Vammatar sees it too. She flashes Siiri a victorious smile. "Surrender to me now, shaman, or your precious Aina will watch how well you scream as you die."

Siiri raises her weapons. "I can't die. But *you* can, you miserable witch."

Vammatar snarls with rage and both women lunge. As they collide, the light at Vammatar's shoulder goes out. I blink, panicking as white spots fill my vision. The witch cackles.

Siiri needs my help. I fumble in the dark, the clang of their weapons a warning in my ears as I push the dead guard off the blade trapped under his body. The stairs creak, and I turn.

Siiri and Vammatar are too distracted to notice the shadow now creeping down.

"Siiri, look out," I call, wrenching the sword free.

The shrouded figure sweeps forward and grabs Vammatar by the shoulders, wrenching her bodily away from Siiri. The witch shrieks in surprise.

My eyes adjust enough for me to make out white robes and long black hair. Loviatar lets her sister go, and the witches face each other.

"All this time, you were Father's pet," Vammatar hisses. "Now you defy him?"

"We all must choose our own path," Loviatar replies. Blood stains her temple and the collar of her robes, but she looks confident, steady. She frames her mouth with her tattooed hands and blows a gust of air from her lips. Her breath shines glittering green in the darkness. Like a noxious cloud, it swirls around Vammatar's face, imbuing her pale skin with an eerie green glow.

Vammatar's eyes are wide with panic as she chokes on the green smoke. All color fades away from her cheeks. "You—*witch*," she chokes out. "I'll—" Before she can finish her threat, her body sways, and she collapses.

Siiri

I PANT, ARMS AND legs shaking with fatigue, as I look down at the prone form of the goddess of evil on the tunnel floor.

"What did you do?" Aina whispers at the witch.

"I'm the goddess of illness, am I not?" Loviatar replies. "It seems my sister came down with a sudden and debilitating case of the fainting sickness."

"She'll kill you for this," Aina warns.

"She can try," Loviatar replies. "Goddess knows she's tried many times before."

I smile. Is it possible I'm starting to like this witch? But then Loviatar turns on me. She takes a step forward, hands raised. "Look," I say, "it wasn't personal—"

The goddess hisses.

"Please, don't hurt her," Aina cries. I'm not sure who she's talking to at this point.

Loviatar points a tattooed finger at me. The air around us stills. "If you ever raise a hand to me again, little fox, I will plague you with boils inside and out. They will pop and fester all over your lily-white skin. Your death will be slow and agonizing. Do we understand each other?"

I lower my axe, but not my defenses. "Why are you now helping us?"

Loviatar turns to Aina. "Tuonetar is gone. We believe her shackles are intact, but she's not in her tower."

"Oh gods," Aina whispers.

"I think Vammatar is to blame," the witch adds. "She reveals her hand at last. She is on the side of chaos."

"She said she wanted to watch it all burn," Aina replies.

"Kalma patrols the river's edge, the twins search for the shaman, and my father now searches for you. You'll never get out of here alive without help."

"And you're going to help us?" I can hear the tears in Aina's voice.

The witch inclines her head.

"Why?" I press. "I can't imagine it was the bump on the head I gave you."

The witch turns with a snarl to face me. "Actually, it was."

I blink in surprise.

"Why?" Aina asks again for both of us.

"I thought Tuonela was the safest place for Aina and her child because I didn't know Väinämöinen survived his curse. I've been trapped down here, cut off from the world above. And there's been little enough spoken about him. I didn't know he was training new pupils. And I never expected one so fierce . . . or so loyal to my queen. If you vow with the shaman to keep Aina and the child safe, I will help you escape."

Before I can reply, Aina steps forward. "Prove you mean what you say. Prove you trust me, so I may trust you, Loviatar."

The witch closes her eyes. In this darkness it's hard to make out her expression. I can only imagine it's one of torment.

This is a power struggle between Aina and the witch. Aina asks for something the witch clearly doesn't want to give.

"Toivotar," she says on a soft breath. "Her name is Toivotar."

"Toivotar," Aina repeats. "The tenth child of Loviatar is the goddess of hope." She smiles, brushing a hand along the witch's shoulder. "It's a beautiful name."

"She's a beautiful woman," I add.

They both turn my way. "You've met her?" asks Aina.

I nod. "She appeared to me moments after you were taken by Kalma. She helped me to my feet and set me on the path north to find you."

"And does she look like Loviatar? Black of hair, pale skin?"

"Yes," I reply. "But she smiles more . . . and she laughs."

Next to Aina, the witch is motionless.

"She came to me again when I had great need of her," I go on. "She offered me more provisions and told me how to find Väinämöinen. She is fierce, Loviatar."

"I knew she would keep fighting," the witch murmurs, tears slipping down her cheeks. "She wants to make a better world for us all in life and in death. You fight for it too . . . both of you."

Reaching into the satchel at my hip, I pull out the box Väinämöinen gave me. "Reach out your hands," I say to the witch.

She hesitates but then does as I ask. I set the box on her palms, and she stiffens as she feels the dimensions of the box. "What is this?"

"You know what it is," I reply.

"How did you get it?" she whispers.

I smile. "I told you, Väinämöinen sends his regards. Now we may trust each other too."

Loviatar stills, clutching her daughter's keepsake box.

"He's never turned from you," I go on. "He never will. He

lives out the days of his long dying, tortured by the Witch Queen for daring to bring hope to the mortal world. He cannot die, even though he suffers from an affliction that should have killed him ten times over. Just as you are trapped here in the dark, tortured forever by your own loneliness."

"Just as Tuoni is tortured," Aina whispers.

I turn to her. "What?"

"Tuoni helped Väinämöinen and Toivotar escape," she explains. "The Witch Queen fashioned her curse to punish Tuoni too."

"How?"

"You spoke of the long dying. Tuoni's power is to prolong life. He is the Great Fading, Lord of Blessed Death. By cursing Väinämöinen not to die, Tuonetar knew that Tuoni would bear the pain of his dying, prolonging his life. Don't you see? Tuonetar yoked them together and cursed them both—the shaman not to die, and Tuoni to bear the pain of it."

"Only Väinämöinen's death will fully free him," Loviatar adds. "Just as only you can free me from this realm. The Witch Queen has worked swiftly and surely, trapping us all in her web."

"Then we shall all break free at last," Aina replies. "For yourself and for your daughter, for my son, for the shaman, for the death god. Let us work together now. Come with us, Loviatar. As Queen of Tuonela, I free you from all ties to this place. You may leave Tuonela as you will."

Loviatar sighs with relief, clutching to her daughter's keepsake box. "Come. I will show you the way."

Before we move three steps down the tunnel before I cry out, a searing pain burning the back of my hand. "*Ouch—*"

"Siiri?" Aina whispers in alarm. "What is it? What's wrong?"

"I don't know. My tattoos feel strange. They feel . . . hot."

"Fire," the witch whispers. "Wherever you are in life, there's a fire near your body. It burns hot enough for you to feel it through your tether." She turns to me, her sightless eyes unblinking. "You are in grave danger, little fox."

"I have to get back. I've already been gone too long, and Väinämöinen needs me. It has to be Lumi." I groan. "Gods, I'll never forgive myself if I get him killed."

"Lumi?" the witch repeats, a curious tilt to her head. "Ajatar's irksome flea of a daughter?"

"Yes, she followed me north, intent on killing him."

"And . . . is he whole?"

"Yes, and Lumi knows. She's coming for him. We have to get to the veil."

As one, we take off down the dark tunnel. I don't know how long we run before Loviatar says, "Stop!"

Aina and I wait, panting, standing side by side, as the witch climbs up the narrow steps and throws back a trap door. The witch exits first, not waiting for us. We follow. With my axe in my right hand, I hand Aina my knife with my left. I have no bow. I left it in the weaving room. That makes the quiver at my hip useless.

Next to me, Aina shivers in the cold. We neither of us have a cloak.

"This way," Loviatar whispers.

We're in a densely forested wood, the trees dusted with snow. Through the gloom, I can make out the shape of a hill. It must be the Kipumäki, the famed hill where the twins weave their magic of pain and suffering. At the mere thought of them, the scars and wounds on my body cry out in pain.

"Nearly there," Loviatar says.

The rich smell of conifers and clean scent of the snow become overwhelmed with a new smell. It's briny, like water weeds left out to dry.

The river of death.

Aina holds tight to my hand as we push through the last

of the trees. Before us, the black water courses silently past, lapping at the pebbles of the shore. My gaze settles on something looming in the middle of the river. The water ripples around it. This must be the island. And the veil waits for us just beyond. We're so close.

"Hurry," the witch whispers, standing at the water's edge. "From here, we must swim."

I tuck my axe into my belt and wade in. Aina takes the witch's hand and they walk into the water together. I'm knee-deep, ready to brave the freezing water, when a shrill cackle rends the air.

"I thought I might find you all here," a voice behind us purrs.

Dread sinks down to my bones. There, on the banks of the river of death, a haggard-looking woman stands in sweeping robes of glittering gold. Her corded grey hair is piled high on her head. She has a haunting, skull-like face, with dark eyes framed in shadows. I know she is Tuonetar, goddess of violent death.

The Witch Queen sneers, her lips curling over blackened teeth as she beckons to us with her willow wand. "Why don't you step this way, and we can all have a nice little chat? It's time to talk about actions . . . and consequences."

Aina

TUONETAR SMIRKS, BECKONING TO us with her broken hand. Her wrist is marred with bruises and scorch marks. The cuffs of her golden robes are crusted with dried black blood. She's free of her manacle, but it cost her dearly. Even now, her broken hand can barely clutch the wand. She keeps the other hand hidden in her robes; I have to believe it still wears its chains.

A witch at half power is still formidable.

"Mother," Loviatar calls from the shore. "You don't have to do this—"

"Silence!" Tuonetar shrieks, swiping the air with her wand. Loviatar reels as if slapped.

"And who is this?" Tuonetar points at Siiri with her wand.

"My name is Siiri," she calls over my shoulder.

Tuonetar takes in the tattoos on her hands and scowls. "You're the shaman they're all looking for?"

"Väinämöinen sends his regards," she taunts.

The Witch Queen hisses at her before turning to me. "And where do you think you're going, little maggoty mouse queen?"

I step in front of Siiri. "You have no power over me, witch. I wear the driftwood crown now. The dead answer to me."

Her eyes narrow. "If I have no power over you . . . then why does your voice shake?"

Swallowing my nerves, I brush at the threads of my bond to Tuoni. He left the door ajar. He's angry and he's hurt, but he's on the hunt. He fights for my safety. It's all he wants. Will he ensure my safety even if it means losing me? He must see now that there is no way to secure his realm against the powers that threaten me.

Reaching out with an invisible hand, I pluck on the threads of our bond. He will come. I have to keep her talking until he does. This witch loves to hear herself speak.

Triumph glints in her eyes as she takes my silence for fear. She laughs, a high, rattling sound. "Oh, I have you cornered at last. I prepared all my traps, but you walked right into one of your own making." She pulls a face of mock concern. "What will our poor, brokenhearted king say when he learns you mean to leave and take his unborn whelp with you?"

"Why should you care if I am gone?" I challenge.

"Because the whelp cannot be allowed to live! Have you learned nothing from your time here, you rotten wretch? I will not have my power eclipsed by a devious, grasping little mortal and her worthless mewling babe."

"You interpret the prophecy looking only for your loss," I counter. "What if this child is a *gift* for Tuonela? Any new power given to a death god is power you will all share in. He could transform this realm. He could make everyone here better off—"

"I don't want them better off!" she shrieks. "They must pay for what they've done. Actions must have consequences."

I hold my ground, buying us more time. "You had no right to Toivotar's power, and you certainly had no right to keep her caged. You want to speak of actions and consequences? Where were yours, Tuonetar?"

She scoffs, turning to Loviatar with a sneer. "Are we saying her name again? I have missed those days."

"You stole a child from her mother," I go on, taking a step out of the water. "You locked that child away for fear that others might benefit from her awesome power. You are selfish, Tuonetar. You are weak-minded and cruel."

"I will skin you and squeeze your eyeballs for my jam," she taunts.

I pluck at the threads of my blood bond again, taking another step out of the water.

You are strong, Tuoni sends down the bond.

"It wasn't enough to steal a child from your own daughter," I call across the clearing. "You punished Loviatar for wanting her back. You're a bully, Tuonetar."

"Now you're just flattering me," she sneers.

I pull again on the bond.

You are powerful. You are a queen. A goddess. Fight.

I am powerful.

Siiri's life is in danger. My child's life is in danger. It's my turn to fight. Squaring my shoulders at the witch, I step out of the water. She watches me approach with hungry eyes.

"Aina, don't," Siiri rasps.

Raising a hand to her in warning, I take another step out of the water. For too long now, Tuonela has been ruled by Tuonetar's corrupting influence. She brings only chaos and death. Tuoni may be her opposite, seeking peace, order, and control, but they both fail to see that there can be a third way. A way between chaos and control. A way between the unexpected death and the long dying.

I am Ainatar, the mortal death goddess, Queen of Tuonela. I am the third way.

I seek out the very center of myself, the calm and strength. I hold it in my belly like a burning flame.

Power is made.

I hold the witch's gaze as my fire burns, heating me to my very fingertips. Rooting my feet in the pebbles at the water's edge, I raise my hands towards the Witch Queen. "Your time here is done, Tuonetar. Siiri and Loviatar are under my protection now, and I am not afraid to die for them. I am Ainatar, Queen of Tuonela, and I embrace death as my equal."

"You will never be my equal!" With a snarl, Tuonetar slashes her willow wand through the air, sending out a jet of white sparks towards me.

Pulling on every source of ancient power I can feel in this place, I brace both hands in front of me. Tuonetar's magic slams up against a shield that shimmers in the night-sky colors of Revontulet the firefox. Its light shoots upward, arching over Loviatar and Siiri, protecting them, protecting us all.

Tuonetar gasps, eyes wide. "What magic is this?"

I hold my ground with a smile. "*My* magic."

In her fury, she slashes the air with her wand again and again, stalking closer to us. Her wand's sparks reflect off the dome-like shield that glows with an aurora's hues—purple, green, and blue.

Across from me, the Witch Queen's bony chest heaves. Fresh blood flows down her mangled wrist. Black drops sizzle on the snow. "I will *kill* you, Aina Taavintyttär," she calls, her voice simmering with inhuman rage.

"That's not my name anymore," I call back.

Hold on . . . hold on.

I close my eyes, breathing deep. I am a goddess. Tuonela is a land of magic and monsters. There is enough power to spare for this mortal queen. Opening my eyes, I stare down Tuonetar, the witch who has brought so much suffering to so many. She is envy. She is rage. She is the chaos of the unexpected, the wholly unwanted.

And she must learn her place.

"I am Ainatar, Queen of Tuonela," I proclaim into the darkness. "I am the goddess of righteous death, and I call on you now. All of you dead who have suffered at the Witch Queen's wretched hands, rise! Wake from your sleep, and come to the aid of your goddess." I feel the fires of my own righteous indignation burning in my throat as I call up all the magic I can from this sacred earth, spinning it into power. "Rise, and protect your queen! Rise, and take your just revenge!"

With a snarl, Tuonetar's gaze darts to the dark wood.

Siiri takes her chance and steps out of the water to my side. "Aina, what are you doing?"

"Claiming my power," I reply.

Loviatar stands at my other side, her eyes glowing white as she tips her head back with a smile. "They come."

Tuonetar laughs, her wand dangling in her mangled hand. "It would seem you are still powerless! It was a fine speech, but you cannot claim what you have not been gifted by the All-Mother—"

"They come," Loviatar says again, louder this time.

Through the trees come the sounds of marching feet, clanging steel, and pounding drums.

"I took nothing that Tuonela did not freely offer me," I call to the Witch Queen. "You have upset the balance for long enough. Now, face your consequences."

As we watch, a horde of the dead bursts from the woods at a run. Some hold weapons—swords and axes—but many are women. The women of the wood. All those girls she tortured and killed to prove to Tuoni that he would never have his way.

They are mine now. I will give them a goddess worthy of their worship. There are reasons to fight and reasons to die. There is power in making that choice, in life and even after death. "Protect your goddess," I call to the dead. "Capture the Witch Queen. Rip that wretched wand from her hand!"

Tuonetar slashes with her wand, sending out more jets of light. But just as before, her magic bounces off my dead, reflected by my shield. "How are you doing this?" she screams. "You are mortal!"

I stand at the river's edge, solemn as the grave, as the dead surround her. She still tries to fight them, even though the magic from her wand cannot touch them. She bellows as they force her down into the snow, ripping the wand from her hand.

"Aina, you must go now," Loviatar says at my side, her hand on my shoulder.

But I can't go. Not yet. I wipe the tears from my eyes as Lilja, Salla, and Inari approach. Lilja has the Witch Queen's wand in her hand. She holds it out to me. I take it with shaking hands, and the dead girls back away.

"Thank you," I whisper to them.

They bow their heads in deference.

Looking down at the wand, I think of all the horrible things it's done—the lies it sustained, the lives it destroyed. Gripping it with both hands, I snap it in two. A few faint sparks hiss from the tip, but the heat in the wood fades. I drop the pieces onto the pebbles at my feet, letting the lapping water pull them into the river's black depths.

"Aina, it's time," Loviatar urges again. "The way out is now clear. You must go."

"I can't stay here," Siiri adds. "Väinämöinen needs me."

I turn away from where my horde of righteous dead bind the shrieking Witch Queen in chains. "Come," I say, taking

Siiri's hand. I hold out my other hand to Loivatar, but she doesn't take it. My heart sinks. "Loviatar, come with us."

"Do not stop," she replies, her tone solemn. "Do not look back."

Tears well in my eyes. "Please," I whisper. "Don't do this. Come."

She stands calm and resolute. "Tuoni needs me here more than my daughter needs me there. Go, Aina. Now."

"No." I shake my head, even as I let Siiri pull me deeper into the river.

"Go, Aina," Loviatar calls again.

"Come on," Siiri urges, tugging at my hand.

"Come find us," I call, gasping as the icy water hits my hips. "You are free, Loviatar! As Queen of Tuonela, I grant you safe passage."

She nods, raising a hand in farewell.

Teeth chattering, I swim after Siiri, taking long strokes with my arms. My thick woolen dress weighs me down as I kick my legs, swimming for the island. When my knee hits a rock, I wince and stumble to my feet. Next to me, Siiri wades out too, reaching for my hand. Her fingers are as cold as mine as we step onto the island. I glance over my shoulder to see the dead crowding up to Loviatar, presenting her with the Witch Queen bound in chains.

Next to me, Siiri tenses. "Oh gods, no."

I turn to her. "What is it?"

She points through the dark, down the beach, away from the dead.

I follow the direction of her point, my eyes narrowing on the figure of a massive black animal with flaming red eyes. "Surma," I whisper.

Siiri puts a firm hand on my drenched shoulder. "Aina, he guards the river."

Foreboding fills me. "We must cross," I pant. "Come, Siiri. We must cross. *Now.*"

Before Siiri can respond, Surma lets out a deep, mournful howl. We both go still, listening as it echoes across the surface of the river. The dark water ripples from shore to shore. The sound hits us, and my whole body erupts in shivers that have nothing to do with the cold. This isn't just any howl.

It's a summons.

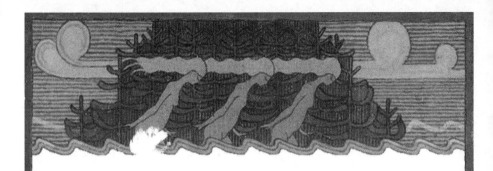

Aina

"WE'RE SO CLOSE," I pant, straining towards the river's far edge. An echo of magic still surges through me, making me shiver along with the cold. "Siiri, we can still make it." I hold tight to her hand, pulling her to the other side of the narrow rock island. "Come on, we can make it—"

"Aina, wait. Listen."

From deep in the shadows of Tuonela, an ominous sound begins to grow. All the fine hairs on my neck rise. It's a rattling, humming, roaring sound. "Siiri . . ." I reach for her hand. "What's happening?"

"Surma has summoned our doom," she says, her voice flat.

"Our doom?"

The roaring grows louder by the second—screeching metal, groaning wood, the pounding of hammer to anvil, the awesome roar of a crashing waterfall. All around us, the black water laps higher, threatening to swallow our little rock island and us with it.

"You remember the songs of Lemminkäinen?" Siiri calls over the cacophony of the roar.

"Yes, but—the wave hits the water, surely," I reply. "We are on land."

"No, Aina *look*." She points down with a tattooed hand.

The stone island on which we stand is jagged and grooved, as if the rock has been cut away in long, narrow slices, hacked by a great many blades.

"Oh gods." I look up, meeting Siiri's gaze. We both know what's coming. It's Tuonela's last and greatest defense. The river swallows up all the swords and axes of the mighty who have fallen in battle, all the hunters' iron-tipped arrows, even the sharp tips of sewing needles. The river takes them all and makes them into a wave of inescapable death. "It cut Lemminkäinen into a thousand pieces," I shout over the din. "His mother had to sew his body back together."

Siiri presses her forehead to mine. "I'm sorry—Aina, I'm so sorry. I tried. Gods know I tried, and I failed you again. I did everything—"

"It's all right."

"I failed you," Siiri says again.

I try to block out the crashing wave. "Siiri, look at me," I say, cupping her face. "Look at me!"

Slowly, Siiri lifts her chin.

"Look in my eyes." My gaze is steady and clear, for I have no more tears to shed for Tuonela. The goddess of righteous death wants to keep fighting. She wants to burn the metal in that wave to ash. Whatever magic remains in me, I will use it. I will keep fighting.

The wave bears down on our little island, surging taller than the tallest tree. "Don't look at the wave, look at me," I command, cupping Siiri's face with both hands, pulling her closer. "Look only at me now. It's only us two here. It's always been us. It's always been *you*."

She wraps her tattooed hands around my wrists, holding me fast.

"Together in the end," I shout. "There is no Aina without Siiri. Go, and I will follow."

She nods, pressing her forehead to mine once more. "Go, and I will follow."

My last words bloom in my chest, bringing me no small amount of peace. I speak them into this moment of our shared death. "I love you, Siiri."

She melts against me. "Oh, Aina. Gods hear me, I love you."

Just as the wave peaks, a blinding flash of light sends both of us reeling. I scream, throat burning, as we're blasted apart by the heat. Rolling to my side, I push up shakily to my knees. The jagged rock cuts into me, but I don't care. I stare up in awe. A massive wall of flame has just appeared in the dark sky. It snakes around our island, cutting us off from the wave's promise of crushing death.

Siiri scrambles to her feet, her freckled cheeks blooming pink with the heat of the fiery wall as she turns to me, wide-eyed. "Is this more of your magic?" she calls out, her voice nearly swallowed by the roar of the flames.

If it is, I don't know how I'm doing it.

"Oh gods," Siiri cries. "Aina!"

I follow the point of her outstretched hand again, tracing the fire to its source. There, at the black water's edge, stands the god of death.

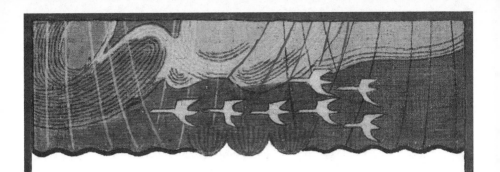

Siiri

I LIMP OVER TO Aina's side, my body aching all over. With one hand on her shoulder, I try to take in what I'm seeing. Tuoni stands at the water's edge, both hands raised, holding the wall of flame steady as the wave crashes against it. The sound rattles my bones with the fury of an earthquake.

This fire is hot enough to melt the metal of swords and axes. The white-hot flames hiss and steam. Aina and I are showered with a mist like rain that stinks of molten metal. Above the wall of fire, the sky fills with acrid, billowing smoke.

Across the river, the death god's face is a tortured grimace, lit by the fire shooting from his hands. He fights to hold the wall in place, keeping the wave from tearing us apart. Flames creep up his arms, burning away the black cloth of his sleeves, melting his skin.

"Tuoni," Aina sobs. Her face is twisted in horror as she watches him burn.

I throw my arm around her.

"It—hurts—" she sobs. "He—can't hold it. Can't stop

it—" Her eyes open, now two black orbs, as her head tips back on a silent scream. Then her voice changes. It's lower and deeper, singed with ash and smoke. "Swim."

I lean away, watching as she channels her deathly husband.

"No," she cries in her own voice. "I cannot leave you like this—*ahh*—" The shadows overtake her eyes again. Tuoni's voice calls out through her mouth, "Take her. Go. Now."

The wall of fire sweeps outward, reaching for the far side of the river. He's making a path for us. He's letting us cross over to the veil.

"Aina, come on." I pull her to her feet.

She fights me. She has eyes only for her death god, who seems to be weakening. He cannot control the magic of his own realm. "Tuoni," she screams. "You are Tuonela! Fight for us, my love! Fight for our son!"

At her words, the death god goes rigid. Before my eyes, his body begins to change. The power he needs to control this wall of flame is so all-consuming that he cannot maintain his veil of mortal beauty. The man disappears, leaving only the god. Tuoni's body elongates, his limbs twisting and stretching, his shoulders narrowing. All at once, he's taller, strong as iron, but skeletal in form.

I can't tear my eyes away from this new, haunting creature. This is the true form of the god of death, unbound from all attempts to mimic mortality. His black hair flutters around his shoulders in wild tangles. With a roar, he seems to pull on the fire. I gasp, watching as flames engulf his arms. In moments, the fire dances behind him like a cloak caught in the wind.

All around us, the wall grows taller, its flames stronger, as he channels the very essence of Tuonela.

"Aina," I say, pulling at her shoulders. "Aina, come on!" I keep a tight hold on her hand as we wade into the water on the far side of the island. Once we're in deep enough, I let go of Aina and dive forward, kicking for the opposite shore. Aina takes long strokes at my side, her wet braid fishtailing behind her as she swims.

We stumble up onto the far bank. She's weak and exhausted, overwhelmed with grief. As soon as we're past the water, there is a roar loud enough to fell a mountain . . . and then the fire disappears. I wince in the darkness. Without the fire to hold it back, the wave crashes past us, the metal within rattling and clanking its way down the river. As our eyes adjust, Aina steps back to the water's edge.

The death god is still in his haunting, unbridled form. He kneels at the river's edge, gazing across the black water at us. Loviatar stands just behind him. Kalma and Surma too.

"Oh, thank the gods." Aina places a hand to her heart. "I feel you, my love," she whispers. "I will always feel you. You will always be with me." She closes her eyes, her head tipped back.

I place a hand on her shoulder. "Aina?"

She stiffens, her black eyes opening wide. "Don't touch her," she hisses in that strange voice. Across the river, Tuoni's true voice rings out, echoing his command.

I drop my hand away.

Aina whimpers, her shoulders sagging as she nods. Slowly, she gets to her feet.

"Aina . . ."

"We will do him that one courtesy," she says, her eyes clear. "Do not touch me while he can see us."

I peer back across the water, and I know he's looking at me, taking me in. "He knows who I am?"

She nods. "He knows everything about you, Siiri . . . about us."

Reaching for the top of my axe, I hold his piercing gaze. "Aina, get behind me."

"No." She steps forward, placing herself between me and the death god. "You must stand behind me now."

"Aina—"

"I bound him to me by sacred oath. He cannot harm you." I can hear her heart breaking in her voice. For as much as she loves me and wants to return home, she will grieve him until she dies. That's who Aina is. She is constancy itself. Loyalty. Faith. As she gazes across the water at her deathly husband, he waves his hand.

She gasps. There, on her soaking wet head, is perched a crown. With trembling hands, she reaches up, her fingers brushing its sides. The crown is a simple thing of wood, soldered with thin lines of gold. "I came to Tuonela as Aina, a mortal girl from Lake Päijänne," she murmurs. "I leave as its queen."

"He's letting us go?"

She nods. "Back away slowly. Take me to the veil, only do not touch me. He can't bear it." As she moves back, she places a hand over her stomach, her soft gaze locked on the death god.

I walk backwards too, working my way up the short slope of the river's edge. The veil awaits, mere steps away. It hums with magic. It wants me to touch it. My tattoos sting and burn, calling me back. I'm running out of time. Väinämöinen needs me.

"When I say, reach back with your hand," I whisper. "I'll pull you into the veil."

She gives a curt nod, not turning to look at me.

"Waking can be disorienting," I warn her. "But I already know my body is in grave danger. You may have to be ready to run, ready to hide, ready to fight. Do you still want to come home with me?"

"You are my home," she replies, her tone steadfast. "I go where you go."

I feel the hum of the veil. It all but reaches out for me with eager fingers. I focus all my energy on the runes of my left hand—the bear-riding girl, the lake, the trees. I focus on the shaman holding a drum. Väinämöinen. Home.

"Aina, give me your hand."

The last sound I hear in Tuonela is the death god's haunting wail of grief as Aina reaches for me. I take her hand and step back, pulling us both into the eternal darkness of the veil.

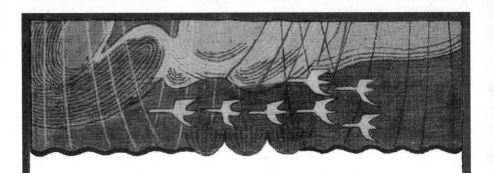

Siiri

54

"COME ON, GIRL. WAKE up," Väinämöinen shouts. "Gods, why did I ever let you talk me into this?"

I rouse, groaning as I feel the familiar weight of the drum on my chest. My nostrils fill with the smell of pungent smoke, making me cough. My eyes shoot open, and I bolt upright.

"Finally," the shaman shouts with relief. "What took you so long? I was about to have to drag your body out of here, girl or no girl. We've only got moments to spare."

"What's happening? Where's Aina?"

The shaman is already kneeling at her side, his rune-marked hands cupping her face. Her gives her cheeks a light tap. "Come on there, girl. Cross over. Wake up now." He's gentle, but insistent.

In moments, Aina stirs.

Väinämöinen chuckles. "So, you're what all the fuss has been about, eh? Well, you're pretty enough, I suppose. Right now, you look like a drowned rabbit. Up you go, lovely."

She groans, barely able to roll to her side.

He glances over his shoulder, flashing me a knowing look. "You did it."

It doesn't feel like a victory. It won't until I know she can be safer in life than she was in death. "What's happening?" I say again.

"Lumi is here," he replies. "She's trying to burn the damn roof down over our heads. It's taken all my magic to hold her back. We have to get out."

I push up to my feet. "I've had enough of meddling witches today. Step aside, old man, and I will tear her rotten black heart out."

"Siiri?" Behind me, Aina sits up, her eyes panicked as she coughs. "Siiri!"

I hurry to her side. She's weak and disoriented. I awoke in my body, which has been kept safe and warm here in Väinämöinen's hut. Aina wears what she wore in death— layers of soaking wet clothes and no cloak.

Väinämöinen is busy rushing around the hut. His eyes glow blue-white as he hums low in his throat, speaking words of strength and resilience to the roof. The heat from the walls is so intense, I'm sure one touch would burn my hand to cinders.

Aina looks wildly around, her eyes locking on the shaman. "Is that—"

"Väinämöinen, yes," I reply.

She coughs in the smoke. "Are we—"

"On fire?" Väinämöinen supplies for her. "Yes. So, it would be a rather good idea for you to get up now." He tosses me my axe. Then he picks up his massive broadsword. Reaching for the hooks by the door, he grabs his jacket and shoves it at me. "You need to get her ready to move."

"Where are you going?" I say, tossing the massive coat over to Aina.

"Get the girl, get the drums, and get outside," he shouts over the roaring fire.

"Väinämöinen," I call after him. "What are you going to do?"

He crosses the room to me, gripping me by the vest. "You remember what I told you? You remember my curse? *Do you?*" He shakes me hard, nearly lifting me off the ground.

"Gods—yes," I grunt, coughing. "You can't die, you can only be killed. Lumi means to be the one to kill you, so we've got to kill her first. This ends tonight."

"We'll end it together," he says. "You're ready. Now, come on. Grab the drums." Without another word, he pulls Aina up with one hand, slinging her over his shoulder. With his sword in the other hand, he kicks open his front door. The flames blast out over the snow as we run from the hut.

I fill my lungs with the fresh winter air, but my relief is soon eclipsed by the sight that greets me. The clearing echoes with the howls of wolves. There must be three dozen, maybe more. Behind us, the flames from the cabin's roof burn high into the night sky. On the far side of the clearing, Lumi waits next to her sled, a ball of white flame glowing at the top of her magical staff. When she catches sight of Väinämöinen, her eyes grow large with excitement.

"Get her out of here," he grunts, depositing Aina into the snow at my feet.

"I'm not leaving you—"

"Of course not! I need your help, fool girl. But we didn't go through all of that for you to lose Aina. Make sure she's good and safe." Without another word, he charges towards the wolves.

With a muttered curse, I help Aina away from the burning hut. Lumi torched the barn too. The whole roof is ablaze. The doors are shut, trapping the dogs inside. They yip and cry, desperate to be set free.

I leave Aina halfway between the hut and the woodland edge. Racing across the clearing, I wrench open the door of the barn. A massive plume of smoke billows out, choking me. I drop to my knees, covering my face with my arms as I cough. All around me, the dogs leap out the open door, panting and rolling in the snow.

"Help him," I cry. "Help Väinämöinen."

The sled dogs all take off, barking in a frenzy at their first sight of the wolves.

"Aina, I need you to get up." I pull her up with me. "Remember what I said? The fight isn't over. It's barely begun. Move, Aina. Run to the trees."

It's all she can do to stand on her shaky legs, blinking in the bright lights of the fire.

"Take this," I say, thrusting a knife into her hand. "And these." I shove the straps of the shaman drums at her. "Do *not* lose them."

"Where are you going?" she cries through chattering teeth. Väinämöinen's coat hangs on her. It's comically large on her slender frame.

"I have to help Väinämöinen. I need you to fend for yourself. Can you do that?"

She nods, trying to control her trembling.

I cup her head and pull her close, planting a quick kiss on her frozen lips. "Die, and I'll kill you."

She nods again, stepping back. "Go, be a hero."

Turning away, I run back across the snow, axe in hand. I come around the side of the burning hut. Väinämöinen stands in the middle of the clearing, swinging his sword in graceful arcs, swiping at any wolf that dares to get too close. All around him, his sled dogs grapple with the other wolves.

They're no match for the larger beasts, but they're a good distraction. Several wolves already lie dead in the snow.

Lumi has yet to join the fray. She stands back, lobbing balls of fire, keeping Väinämöinen's movements contained as he ducks and bobs, fending off flame and fang. Tucking my axe in at my belt, I race over to the shaman's pack, unrolling a stockpile of all his other weapons from the hut. I take the full quiver and belt it at my waist. Then I grab the bow and stand. I nock an arrow and pull back on the string.

Twang.

The arrow whizzes through the air, landing with a squelch in the eye of a large white wolf. It yips in pain and crumples at Väinämöinen's feet. The shaman follows the direction of the arrow to where I stand, framed by his burning hut. Smiling, he swings wide with his sword, spinning just in time to knock a leaping wolf from the air.

"Come on, you witch," he shouts across the snow at Lumi. "You came here for me, so kill me if you can! Stop sending these mongrels to do your work for you."

I loose another arrow. This time it sails over the shaman's head, landing with a thud next to Lumi's hand on the rail of her sled. The witch jerks her hand away, scowling at me. I loose another arrow.

Lumi snarls, batting it from the air with a swipe of her magical staff. With eyes only for Väinämöinen, the witch jams the end of her staff deep into the snow. Flipping the edges of her white cape off her shoulders, she strides forward, unsheathing a pair of short swords. Her intention is clear: she doesn't need magic to best the shaman in a sword fight. "It's over, Väinämöinen," she calls. "Great hero of Kalevala. Surrender yourself to me, and maybe I'll let the meddlesome girl live."

Before the shaman can respond, a trio of wolves descend

on him. I loose an arrow, felling one, but two more close in. I take off at a run and loose another arrow, but it flies wide, barely grazing the beast's hip. It's just enough to make him angry. He turns on me with a guttural snarl, fangs bared.

Racing to the shaman's side, I scare the two wolves back. Dropping my bow at my feet, I pull my axe, and swing wide. A russet wolf dodges and circles back in front of me. I back several paces, facing the burning hut, until I'm back-to-back with Väinämöinen. The wolves continue to circle us as Lumi crosses the snow, her swords raised.

"Take care of the wolves," he grunts at me, pulling a shorter sword out of the scabbard hidden at his back and handing it to me. I barely get my fingers around the hilt before he's slamming a dark wolf in the ribs with a blast of blue light. He strides across the open snow, daring the witch to face him.

I'm distracted for a moment by a growling wolf. He's young and overeager, hardly more than a pup. I make quick work of him.

"It doesn't have to be this way," Väinämöinen calls out to the witch. As he walks, he blocks the lunges of two desperate wolves with more blasts of his light magic. "Ajatar is a poison in your mind. Stop letting her control you. There is still time for you to go in peace."

The witch snarls, flicking her long hair off her shoulders. It flutters in the wintry wind like a banner. "You think my mother guides my steps? I want this for *myself*, shaman. Your magic is all I've ever wanted!"

"Possessing my magic won't bring you what you seek," he says calmly.

For the briefest of moments, Lumi pauses. Her face shifts from agony to sadness . . . then to rage. "You don't know what I seek." Her eyes flash with white-hot need. There will be no walking away from this. She's set on her course. Väinämöinen knows it too. His shoulders dip in resignation. When Lumi starts running, he does too. As he runs, he grazes a hand up the blade of his sword from hilt to tip. Flames erupt down the metal.

The shaman and the witch meet in a clash of iron. Sparks fly off his flaming sword as she parries and lunges, cleaving the air with her two sharp blades. He ducks and spins in the ankle-deep snow to match her.

They're both masters. Each time I think he has her, she dances away unscathed. Twice, Lumi's blade connects to his skin at leg and elbow. Blood seeps from his wounds. He can't get close enough to strike her, his long sword requiring wider strokes.

I do my best to reach him. I fight back a grey wolf, matching him snarl for snarl. Too late, I see another wolf leap from the darkness to take Väinämöinen from behind. But the wolf yelps in pain, crumpling to the ground with an arrow in its side.

I spin around to see Aina standing before the flaming hut in Tuoni's crown and Väinämöinen's too-large jacket, bow in hand. She lets another arrow loose. It goes wide, but close enough to scare a wolf away. It opens the space I need to break through and join Väinämöinen. He swings low again, forcing Lumi to dance back. Then he swings high with his powerful backhand. Lumi jumps to the left, escaping the blow.

It's just the distraction I need.

Raising my axe, I plant my feet, square my shoulders, and throw. The axe spins haft over blade. Lumi screams in pain as it thuds into the meat of her shoulder. She drops her right-hand sword with a whimper and staggers back. I cover the distance, picking up her discarded sword. Now I have two, and she only has one.

With a panting breath, Lumi jerks the axe free from her shoulder. Blood runs freely from the wound, staining her pristine white clothes. Her right arm hangs uselessly at her side. "I'll kill you for that, you irksome little insect."

"You can try," I taunt, daring to give her sword a twirl with my wrist.

Lumi raises her other sword and points imperiously at me. All around the clearing, the remaining wolves howl. They have a new order. *Kill the girl.*

Väinämöinen faces the injured snow witch while I fight the wolves. The clang of swords rings out across the snow. I block countless attacks. As I drop and spin, I slip on a patch of ice. It gives a bold russet wolf the opening he needs. He lunges for me, teeth bared. Väinämöinen lunges to the side, placing himself between me and the charging wolf.

"No!" I scream.

He can't swing his weapon without hitting me, so he lets the wolf knock him to the snow. Väinämöinen's sword falls from his hand as the wolf sinks its teeth into his shoulder, shaking its head to tear his flesh. Väinämöinen cries out, blue light glowing from his open mouth. He punches the wolf in the muzzle again and again.

I regain my footing, and swing at the wolf. "Get off him!"

Behind me, Lumi shrieks too. "No! The shaman is mine. Let him go!"

The massive russet wolf releases Väinämöinen, and the shaman pulls himself across the snow, trying to escape Lumi. He pushes up to his knees, his hand covering the gushing wound at his neck. He has no weapon. He needs time to recover. As much time as I can give him.

Rushing forward, I throw myself between Väinämöinen and the witch. She takes in the pair of swords I wield and smiles. The dance is on. We circle each other, parrying and jabbing. Lumi is so fast, even using only her left hand. I'm no match for her. But I don't need to beat her. I just need to give Väinämöinen time to get to his feet and get his sword. He can use his magic. Together, we can finish the witch.

Lumi's blade flashes through the air. I overcorrect, and she jeers, cutting deep into my arm. I cry out, the sword loosening in my grip. I let it drop to the snow. Lumi steps forward, eyes flashing with victory. I stagger back, lifting my remaining sword to block her next blow.

The witch suddenly stumbles away with a shriek. An arrow sticks out from her injured right arm.

"Nice shot," I call over my shoulder.

"I was aiming for her head," comes Aina's reply.

Lumi raises a shaky hand to the arrow, wincing in pain as she pulls on it. She looks from me to Aina, her eyes narrowing with rage.

Väinämöinen has found his feet. He bleeds freely from the neck. Placing a firm hand on my shoulder, he plants himself behind me. I square off to face Lumi with only one sword, ready to defend him to the death.

"Siiri." His voice is quiet. "I'm ready."

My eyes flash with rage as the witch approaches. "I won't let her take you from me."

He leans against me, his massive frame nearly three times my size. His breath is warm on my neck. "Siiri . . . I choose you."

I look over my shoulder into his clear blue eyes. The color is draining from his face. In this moment, he looks truly ancient. His eyes are full of tears. They aren't tears of sadness or anger. They're tears of joy. Tears of peace.

"You saved me the day we met in that pit," he says. "You brought light back to my life and made me whole. My fierce, wild Siiri." He brushes my cheek with a bloody hand. "Take what I offer. Finish this witch, and keep your Aina safe. Keep the people safe."

"Don't you dare," I cry, tears thick in my throat. "Don't do this, old man—"

"I was never going south again," he says. "I've been dying for years. So, finish the job. Become the new Väinämöinen. Set me free."

Across the snow, Lumi jerks the arrow loose from her shoulder. "You're mine, Väinämöinen! For so long, I've waited for the moment when you would be whole again. You and your little shamaness cannot thwart me now. *I* found your itse. I trapped it in that bear and drove it north. I've earned the right to claim your magic!"

"You'll never take him from me!" Raising the witch's sword, I flip the grip of my left hand on the hilt.

Lumi charges me, snarling like one of her rabid wolves. I hold my blade with both hands and swing high. Lumi has no choice but to lift her own and parry. But I shift direction midswing. Anchoring my foot in the snow, I plunge the blade backwards.

Väinämöinen is ready. He steps into it, bracing against me with both hands. I let out a sob as the blade meets resistance. The sword pierces him straight through. His hands tighten on my shoulders as he takes a gasping, pained breath.

"Nooooo!" Lumi releases a primal, haunting scream before she lunges for me.

Aina's next arrow whizzes past my shoulder, piercing the witch in the chest. She stumbles, still screaming, and tries to jerk the arrow free.

"Siiri . . ." The shaman grunts against my ear. "Let me call you 'daughter.' Just once—let me—"

Closing my eyes, tears falling, I twist the blade in his gut. "I love you, Father."

His hands weaken on my shoulders. I can feel the life leaving him. I jerk the blade free, and he sinks down to his knees. Blood pours from his neck and his gut, staining the snow red. He looks up at me, the light of his magic flickering in his eyes. "Daughter," he says again, trying to raise his trembling, bloody hand. I take it in mine, pressing my cheek to his palm. "Needed—will we be—again—"

I nod. "I will go south," I whisper. "I will return your wisdom to the people. I will fight for them, Father. I will fight to free the Finns."

He nods, closing his eyes, relief washing across his face. Slowly, he falls back into the snow.

"No," I cry, dropping to my knees. I close my eyes against the pain of watching him die, but a blinding white light has me opening them again. Väinämöinen's whole body is glowing. I glance from the shaman to Lumi. The witch sways like a reed, blood pouring from her wounds. She blinks to keep her eyes focused. As we both watch, the ghostly form of Väinämöinen rises up from his body. He looks down at me and smiles, his mustache twitching.

"Your henki," I say in awe. By the power of Tuonetar's curse, it now belongs to me. The Witch Queen's curse came with a cost she failed to calculate: she will never claim his soul. Väinämöinen's henki places his hands on my shoulders and pulls himself forward, stepping inside me.

Lumi wails, hand falling away from the arrow still lodged in her chest.

All around us, the few remaining wolves howl with her in her grief.

The power of Väinämöinen's magic courses through me, burning like a fire, even as it roots itself like a tree. It weaves into every part of me—my muscles, my bones. I feel it rising up my throat and shooting down to the tips of my fingers.

The strength of twenty men courses through me. Lightning crackles at my fingertips. I am not the Väinämöinen who could barely lift a sword, ready to succumb to the long dying. His body lies next to me in the snow. I am young. I am strong. I am the Väinämöinen of the stories and songs. I am the shaman of the ages.

Bending down, I pick up my fallen sword. It feels like an extension of my arm. I face Lumi, taking in the witch's many injuries. Her bloody fingers slacken on the hilt of her sword. I can see bone through the torn flesh of her shoulder. Her right arm hangs limp and useless. If she doesn't use what power she still has to save herself, she'll likely bleed out and die.

I lower my sword. "I'm done with killing for today," I say, my voice rich and powerful. "Väinämöinen's magic is safe. Take your wolves and go. Never return."

"There is no honor in retreat!"

"There's no death in it either, you rotten witch! I've seen enough of death for ten lifetimes. You don't want to go to Tuonela. There's no victory for you there."

I can see the anguish etched on the beautiful lines of her face. "This was my path," she says hopelessly. "You've taken everything from me. I can't walk away. I can't change course now. It's not in my nature."

I sigh, shaking my head. "You witches and your twisted natures. Why do you bring this pain on yourself? What dark power possesses you? Look around. Nature changes all the time. Dare to think your life could be more. It could be different."

She glares at me, still swaying on her feet.

"I'm giving you one chance to walk away," I call to her. "Take it, or perish, Lumi."

For a moment, the witch considers. With tears in her eyes, she looks at the carnage in the clearing. So much blood. So much death. Her injured shoulder sags, and she drops her sword. "There is nothing left. I have nothing."

"You were as much a slave to Väinämöinen's curse as he was," I say, realizing the truth of my words. "But you are more than this failed quest. You are powerful and beautiful, Lumi. Go live on your own terms."

She swallows, her eyes shutting tight as she winces in pain. "And watch from afar as you wield my magic?"

I stiffen, my hand gripping my sword more tightly. "It was never yours. Väinämöinen chose his fate. He chose *me*. You cannot have this power. So, I repeat, leave now . . . or die."

Lumi snarls at me, her face a mask of sorrow and rage. I can feel her wolves pacing in the darkness, waiting for the word from their mistress to strike again. The witch holds my gaze. "Give me a clean death, shamaness."

My mind courses with all the memories I now share with Väinämöinen. I remember Lumi in all our past battles. I can feel Ajatar's hand at my throat as she sealed Tuonetar's curse on me. I fight a moan, biting my lip, as memories of the pain of the long dying make me want to weep. Gods, he was in so much pain for so long. I truly was his deliverance. I ended his suffering.

Just as Väinämöinen chose his death, I must now extend the same courtesy to Lumi. "So be it." Stepping forward, I raise my sword. The snow witch stands her ground, determined to die on her feet. Väinämöinen's light crackles over my shoulders and down my arms to my massive blade. "Lumi, daughter of Ajatar, I return you to the warm embrace of the All-Mother."

I swing once, high and fast. Lumi's knees buckle, and she drops. Her expression doesn't change as blood from her neck pours down her chest, staining her white robes. It doesn't change when her severed head topples from her neck. The witch now feels only relief. Tired, blessed relief. Her body falls forward into the snow next to her sword.

Aina

THE HEAD OF THE beautiful snow witch falls from her shoulders. Siiri stands over her, Väinämöinen's sword in hand, looking down at her body. The few remaining wolves howl as they tuck their tails and run back to the safety of the forest. As the witch's body falls forward, Siiri lowers her sword.

With a desperate sigh of relief, I drop my bow and run. "Siiri! Are you all right?"

Slowly, Siiri turns. Her eyes still glow with the light of Väinämöinen's spirit.

I take a hesitant step back. "Siiri, your eyes . . ."

She blinks, taking a few deep breaths. The light fades until her blue eyes meet my green ones.

"What happened?" I whisper, glancing to the shaman in the snow. "Is he gone?"

Siiri shakes her head. "No, it's not . . . Ahh—" She grips my arm for support, her head tipping back as her body tenses. "Oh gods—he's here with me," she pants. "He's inside. It feels so strange. I suddenly feel as if I've lived two lives. Everything that was me—my life, my stories—and everything that was him. They're both mine now. I feel his memories like I made them."

"Oh gods . . . the battle with Iku-Turso? Ilmarinen and the forging of the Sampo? Antero Vipunen?"

Siiri's face is a riot of expressions as she feels it all, lost in a sea of memories. "Everything," she whispers after a moment. "Everything."

"Oh, Siiri." I run my hand down her arm, avoiding the deep cut that still bleeds.

Siiri drops to her knees at the shaman's side, letting her heavy sword fall away. She lifts his tattooed hands and folds them over his chest. Her fingers brush over one of the runes on his hand, and she sobs.

I place a hand on her shoulder. "What is it?"

She touches the mark again. "It's me. I'm the girl who rides the bear north in search of a lost shaman."

"We should close his eyes."

Leaning over his body, Siiri closes the shaman's lifeless blue eyes. "I killed him," she whispers. "I killed Väinämöinen."

"Why did you do it?"

"To take his magic. To keep it safe from Lumi from anyone who sought to break Tuonetar's curse. He wanted me to have it. He was planning it all along. Crazy old man," she mutters. "Tuonela was a test. If I returned with you, he was going to give it to me."

"But why would he want so badly to die? He was immortal."

Siiri glances over her shoulder at me, giving me a soft smile. "The goddess of righteous death should understand his reasoning better than anyone. Tuonetar took away his choice to die. He wanted to choose who would kill him and claim his magic. He chose me. I am Väinämöinen now."

I hug myself tight inside his large coat. "What are we going to do?"

Siiri looks around the clearing, dotted with the corpses of Lumi's wolves and Väinämöinen's dogs. The hut and the barn are little more than embers at this point. The snow runs red with spilled blood. "First, I'll build a pyre for Väinämöinen," she replies. "We'll return him to his mother in the sky."

"And then?"

Slowly, she gets to her feet, wincing with pain and fatigue. Reaching out, she cups my cheek and smiles. "And then we return south, my queen." I roll my eyes at her, and she grins. "You are a queen, are you not?"

I raise a hand to touch the crown still balanced on my head. "Can I call myself the queen of a realm I no longer inhabit?"

She grows thoughtful, her eyes flickering with the light of the shaman's magic. "Perhaps *this* realm could use a queen."

"What do you mean?"

"Well, I certainly can't do it," she says with a shrug. "I'll be far too busy returning the wisdom of the ages to our people. But it will be no easy task, uniting the Finns and pushing back the Swedish invaders. A queen might be useful for the people to rally behind."

"I've had enough of crowns at the moment."

"We don't have to decide anything right now. Tonight, we return the shaman to his mother. Tomorrow, we'll make our plans."

I nod.

"All that matters in the end is that we're together, yes? Come kings and queens, shamans and gods, witches and wolves, Siiri and Aina will always find their way back to each other."

I smile, nodding again. "Yes. Always."

We work together to prepare a pyre for Väinämöinen. I'm tired and cold, heartsick and hungry, but still, I don't stop. With her axe, Siiri fells a tree and cuts off the branches. We put Lumi's body beneath the pyre, along with her magical staff. Siiri slips a pair of silver bracelets off the witch's wrists and puts them on her own wrists.

"What are you doing?"

"These were my mummi's," she replies, showing them to me. I recognize the woven-braid pattern. "Lumi stole them. I intend to see them safely returned."

The last thing Siiri does is place the shaman's drum atop his chest and put his mallet in his cold hand. She'd explained that the drum would never work properly for another shaman. It deserved to return with him to the All-Mother.

Siiri lights the pyre and steps back, returning to my side. Taking my hand, she begins to hum. The song is low and deep in her chest. It has no words, but she pours all she's feeling into each sound—her pain, her loss, her love for the man she burns, her tender hope for a brighter future. I wait at her side as Siiri sings out her grief, a last song for Väinämöinen, greatest hero of the ages.

We stand in the clearing until his body is gone and all that remains of the pyre are embers. Siiri drops my hand and turns away, but motion in the darkness has me grabbing her arm. "Siiri look."

Siiri turns around, following the direction I point. One hand is already at the scabbard on her hip, ready to draw her sword. She places an arm before me, her eyes glowing as she mutters under her breath.

A figure emerges from the darkness, walking towards us across the snow. She wears robes the color of an aurora. Her skin is milky white, her long black hair flowing unbound down her back. The wind whips at it, pulling tendrils across her face.

With a chuckle, Siiri drops her hand away from her sword.

Stepping around the remains of the pyre, the woman stops before us. She has slender, long-fingered hands that bear no tattoos. Her eyes are bright and clear, almost white. She looks unmistakably like a young Loviatar.

"Oh," I say on a breath.

"Now you arrive," Siiri chastises, even as she smiles. "The fighting is over and now you bother to show a little interest?"

The goddess ignores her cheek. "Hello, dear ones." Her voice dances across the clearing with the grace of a bell.

"Toivotar," I whisper, taking a step forward.

The goddess of hope inclines her head in greeting.

I feel overcome with relief. My hand comes to my abdomen as tears slip down my cheeks. "Your mother saved us, Toivotar. She freed us from Tuonela."

"Yes, I see that," she replies.

"She was so brave. And she loves you so much. She did everything—" I choke back my words, too overcome to speak.

Toivotar simply smiles, glancing between Siiri and me. "I see I am indeed a little late . . . but you clearly didn't need too much of my help." She turns to Siiri. "Hope is a fickle thing, isn't it? We find it in the oddest of places. You found it in a lost and lonely bear. You got more than you bargained for, didn't you, Siiri Väinämöinentyttär?"

Siiri glares at the goddess. "I loved him," she says defensively. "I was as much a daughter to him as you ever were. I set him free. I've earned the magic and the name."

"You did well," the goddess replies gently. "It was always meant to be yours. 'Suns will rise and set in Finland, rise and set for generations,'" she intones, speaking the words of

Väinämöinen's last song. "'Until the north learns my teachings . . . hungry for the true religion.' You fulfilled his last prophecy, Siiri. You are now the light that was promised. You must return to Kalevala."

"I know," says Siiri.

"The work ahead will be tireless," the goddess warns. "And I fear rather thankless."

"I know that too," Siiri replies solemnly.

"But the fate of Finland hangs in the balance," Toivotar goes on. "Our blessed Finland is under attack. Religious zealots seek to claim this land and her people. The tide will be unyielding. The snow will run red with our blood. There will be days when you feel certain that the true religion is lost, sunk to the depths of the blackest sea. Do not give up, Siiri Väinämöinentyttär. You are the light. You are the hope."

Siiri swallows, giving the goddess a curt nod.

Then Toivotar turns her smiling face to me. She glances up at my crown. "And you, Ainatar, Queen of Tuonela? What hope did you cling to in the dark months of your capture?"

Closing my eyes, I reach out for the invisible threads binding me to Tuoni. They're weaker now, but still there. He keeps the door wide open. I can't feel his thoughts and emotions as clearly as I could in Tuonela, but I catch glimmers of him, like the reflection of moonlight as water ripples in a dark pool. I open my eyes, looking to the goddess. "That I was strong enough to survive," I whisper. "That Tuoni would love me enough to let me go."

Toivotar smiles. "He loves you, aunt. Never doubt it. He always knew his happiness would come at a price. He knew he couldn't keep you. His happiness would be fleeting, like a glimpse of the sun on a cloudy day, gone too soon. Your child belongs in the land of the living . . . as does his mother."

I nod, sharing a look with Siiri.

Toivotar slips her hand inside her robes and steps forward. "On the night I left, he gave me something. He said that when the time came, I should give it to his son."

The goddess places something on my palms. I look down, tears welling, at a small wooden carving of a raven.

"A sielulintu," the goddess says. "So your son always knows the way back to his father."

I close my fingers around it.

"I know what we must do," Siiri says. "And I know what it will take to do it, but we need your help once more. Please, Toivotar. We are tired and wounded. We have nothing—no food, no supplies. And this winter will only deepen before it eases. Grant us your favor once more, goddess."

"I hear your plea, and I grant you favor." She waves a hand over the snow.

I look around, surprised to see a homestead appear. All remnants of the battle with Lumi and her wolves are washed clean. No blood mars the white winter landscape. A fresh powder of snow blankets the clearing. Smoke rises from the chimney of the cabin, with a barn looming behind.

"A gift for you both," she says. "The shaman and the queen. May this restore your hope and bring you both some much needed rest. You must do all you can to prepare for the fight to come." Before either of us have a chance to thank her, the goddess disappears, floating away with the winter wind, her last words drifting through the air.

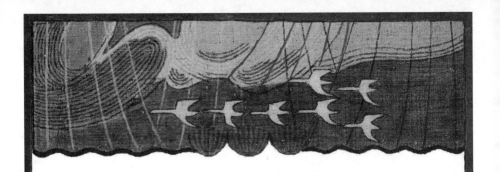

Siiri

I OPEN MY EYES, orienting myself as quickly as possible to my new surroundings. Well, they're not *new* surroundings. In fact, I know them as well as I know the tattoos on the backs of my hands. I'm home again, lying on the shores of Lake Päijänne. My body is safe in the north, guarded under Aina's watchful eye.

After many long discussions over our evening fire, I finally convinced her to let me send my itse out again. It's time to speak to our families and tell them of Aina's safe return. It's time to tell them of our plans.

It was never a question of Aina wanting her family to know we're alive and safe; she's simply new to soul magic. When I tell her that souls can become untethered, she panics, terrified she'll lose me to the long dying. "You are the strongest tether I'll ever need," I assured her. "I will always find my way back to you."

In the end, this was enough to mollify her. She watched over me as I drummed into the darkness.

And now I'm back where it all began.

It's a mild spring morning, and the snow lies thin on the ground. All around me, the *drip drip* of melting ice. I walk down the well-worn path, weaving between the birch trees along the south side of my family's homestead. It's late enough in the morning that the men should be away. That was one of Aina's other stipulations. I'm not to repeat the chaos that was my own brother trying to burn me at the stake.

I smile to see my little sister in the yard feeding the chickens. She looks taller after all these months apart. "Hello, Liisa," I call out softly.

She drops the basket of chicken feed with a gasp. "Siiri? You look different . . . your hair."

I laugh, raising a hand to smooth it down. I got Aina to fix it so now it hangs evenly above my shoulders. Liisa's never seen me with anything but a long braid. "You look different too. You look strong. Is Mummi finally making you do chores?"

Liisa surveys me with sharp eyes. "Are you really here, or is this like before?"

"I'm here in the only way I'm able," I reply. "I've come to see Mummi."

"She's in the house." She hurries away towards the open door. "Mummi," she calls. "Siiri is here."

I follow Liisa inside the house. Mummi sits at our large family table sorting the laundry. Her hands hold up a pair of breeches. "Siiri? Oh, thank the All-Mother." She hurries around the table, wrapping me in her arms. The scent of home envelops me—fresh-baked bread and cardamom. "Oh, my brave girl. My sweet Siiri. You're here."

"She's doing that disappearing trick again," Liisa says from her stool. Her cat hops up on her lap.

"I've come to see Milja," I say against Mummi's shoulder. "And you," I add, giving her another squeeze.

She lets me go. "Yes, of course. We'll go there now." She wipes hurriedly at her eyes. "The men are all out. Your father will be sorry to have missed you. The last time was . . ."

"I'm sorry for that too," I say. "Did you suffer after I left?"

Mummi pats my cheek. "It does no good to dwell on the past."

I stiffen. "What did the priests do, Mummi?"

"It doesn't matter—"

"They ransacked the house and barn looking for you," Liisa says.

"Liisa, that's enough," Mummi orders.

"Then they accused Mummi of being a witch," she goes on. "Father had to pay a fine to the Church, so they wouldn't send her south for a trial. We lost half our cattle. When the priests learned Milja and Taavi were giving us extra food, they fined them too."

My gut twists. "Mummi, I'm so sorry."

"I said it doesn't matter," she replies, glaring at Liisa. "All that matters is that you're safe. You *are* safe . . . right?"

I nod. "I'm safe, Mummi."

Liisa still watches me. "Why have you not come back to us? Is it Aina? Is she dead?"

Mummi rounds on her. "Liisa, did you finish feeding the chickens?"

"Now that you're here, you should meet Aksel's new bride," she says over Mummi.

I glance between them. "Aksel is married?"

Mummi slips her blue cap on and grabs her favorite wool shawl off the peg by the door. "Not yet. It's all been a bit sudden, but love always rings true in the end."

"Who is he marrying?"

Mummi smiles, holding out her hand. "Liisa's right. You should meet her."

We take the long path through the trees to get to Milja's house, to avoid being spotted by the other villagers. "What does Milja know?" I say to Mummi.

"Oh, goodness. Everything. More than even you, I suspect."

I pause my steps. "How—"

"Hurry up," she calls out. "All will be revealed soon."

We step into the yard to find Milja on the back step peeling vegetables with a young woman with long, blonde braids. Both women look up as we approach.

"Good morning," Mummi calls.

Milja's eyes fill with tears. "Siiri? Oh, blessed mother, be praised." She hurries over to wrap me in a tight embrace.

The young woman behind Milja looks at me with joy in her eyes. "This is Siiri?"

Milja inspects me, her fingers brushing over the scar on my neck. "Is Aina alive?"

I smile, taking hold of her hand. "Let's go inside."

We all settle at Milja's table. She fusses over my thinness and my cut hair as the young woman pours us all cups of tea.

"My Aina?" Milja says again.

"I have her," I say with a smile. "She's free of Tuonela. She's with me in the north."

Next to me, Mummi squeezes my shoulder, while Milja and the young woman fall to pieces, crying and hugging each other. My own smile dims as I watch the stranger cry. "Who are you? Why do you act as though you know Aina?"

The girl laughs, wiping away her tears. "Oh—forgive me. I never said. My name is Helmi."

I go still, heart racing. I know this name well. She was all Aina talked of during the first days of our reunion. I've committed all the girls' names to memory: Lilja and Salla, Riina and Helmi, Inari and Satu. Most nights, Aina has nightmares. She wakes up screaming, her body drenched in sweat. I hold her and ask the same question: "Who was it this time?"

Someone is always dying in Aina's dreams. Someone is always fleeing. Someone is tortured with a little round stone. Aina has dreamt of Helmi's death many times.

"You've heard of me," she says gently. "Aina told you?"

I give a curt nod. "How did you get here?"

"Aina freed us. She made a deal with the death god and—"

"I know what happened down there," I say over her. "I'm asking how you got *here*."

She holds my gaze. "We made her a promise, Riina, Satu, and I. We promised we would find her family and tell them what happened. She wanted you to know how much she loved you, Siiri . . . and that she didn't blame you for what happened."

"I blame myself enough for the both of us," I reply.

Milja places a hand on my arm. "It was the will of the gods, Siiri. No one is to blame. The girls arrived at the break of winter," she goes on. "They were such a gift to us, a balm after those dark times."

"And Riina?" I press, desperate to give Aina any good news. "Satu?"

"She returned home," Helmi replies. "As did Satu. But my parents are dead. I was living with an aunt who never cared much for me. She thought I was a burden. I came here and met Aina's people and felt so at home. You've all been so kind to me," she adds, glancing around.

"You're a good girl," says Mummi. "You've found your place here."

Helmi smiles, blushing as she takes a sip of her tea.

I lean back in my chair. "Ahh, you're my brother's intended?"

She nods.

"When do you marry?"

"In a fortnight," Mummi says for her. "And we'll all be made very happy by it. Helmi has been living here with Milja. But when they marry, she'll come live with us."

I reach for my cup of tea, and all the women look at my tattoos. "You don't need to be afraid of these," I say with a smile. "They're not the marks of Kalma or a witch. They're the marks of a shaman. To rescue Aina from Tuonela, I went north to find Väinämöinen. He taught me how to cross over the realms. He gave me the marks."

"How did you break her free?" Helmi whispers.

"In the end, Tuoni let her go," I reply. "He realized she was safer in life than in death."

"Gods be praised," Milja says, eyes closed.

"There's something you should all know," I add.

They all look to me, expressions wary.

Aina gave me her blessing to do this. It has to be done. They have to understand. "Aina is pregnant with Tuoni's child."

Gasps go up around the table.

"That is why we haven't returned to you sooner," I explain. "We've decided to wait until after the child is born. Aina needs comfort and rest and safety. We have that where we are now."

"And where is that?" Milja presses.

I give her a weak smile. "North . . . that's all I'll say for now. But we *will* return," I add before she can protest. Reaching out, I take her hand. "Aina and I are returning south. The gods have given us a sacred mission."

"A sacred mission?" Liisa echoes from her spot at the end of the table, her fair brows arched high.

I nod. "We're going to free our people from the Swedes

and their god. We're going to unite the Finns. We're going to fight . . . and we're going to win."

Silence meets my pronouncement. Four sets of eyes gaze at me in fear and confusion.

Mummi breaks the silence first. "Siiri . . ."

"I'm not Siiri anymore," I say, letting the last hammer fall. "Well, not *only* Siiri."

"Who are you?" Milja whispers.

Pulling on the ancient wells of magic pooled deep inside me, I raise my hands and begin to hum, singing a song of spring—fresh rains and budding flowers and new blades of grass. I let my music pour out of me, filling the air. The women cry out as they see the light of my magic in my eyes. I wave my hand around the room, quickening my spring song. Garlands of flowers snake around the rafters and up the walls—great blooms of fireweed and purple harebells, daisies and yellow irises. Water lilies bloom from our teacups.

I let the song fade and stand, placing my hands flat on the table. The women look all around in shock. The inside of Milja's house now looks like an enchanted garden. Bees and butterflies flutter amongst the blooms. I smile, reciting the last few lines of my farewell song. "Watch for me at dawn of morning, that I may bring back the Sampo, bring anew the harp of joyance, bring again the golden moonlight, bring again the silver sunshine, peace and plenty to the Northland."

Mummi nods with tears of pride in her eyes.

"I am the new Väinämöinen," I say. "His magic is mine now. And I am here to tell you faithful few: I am coming. Look for me journeying down from the north. A queen will walk at my side. Tell everyone: Väinämöinen returns."

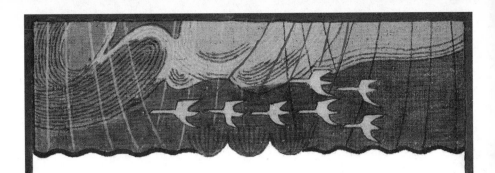

Siiri

A MILD SPRING GIVES way to a charmed summer. Together, Aina and I do the work of collecting nature's bountiful harvest. We forage and fish and hunt. Each day, I train Aina in the use of the sword and the bow. By the time her months of waiting pass, the beauty of summer is beginning to fade into a golden autumn.

Her labor is long and painful. Once her waters break, we pray the baby comes quickly . . . but he doesn't. She strains for hours, sweating through her clothes. I make teas of willow bark and chamomile, trying to ease her pain. I hold compresses to her forehead and neck, cooling the fires that burn in her.

"He's never coming out," she cries, nearly delirious.

"He will," I soothe, kneeling between her legs. "He wants to come out; he just doesn't know the way. Just like a man—he'll try every door but the right one."

Aina tries to laugh, but it comes out as a groan. She grips the furs, the knuckles of her hands white as another spasm takes hold.

"Oh, Aina," I breathe, bracing her legs. "The head is coming now. You're doing well. Keep pushing."

Aina gives one last push and the baby lands in my waiting arms. I pull the child to me, cradling him close. Aina sinks back against the furs, panting for breath. She lifts a weak hand towards the quiet baby. "Is he hurt?"

I wrap him in the cloths we prepared, rubbing his little body as his first cries break from a weak mewl to a squall. I laugh, handing the baby over. "He's fine, Aina. Angry and healthy."

"And he's a boy?" She peeks inside the cloths, looking him over for herself. He's already calmer in her arms, his eyes closed.

I come around and sit on the side of the bed, brushing the sweat from her forehead with a damp cloth. "He's perfect." Leaning down, I kiss her brow.

"Oh, my beautiful boy," she murmurs, her lips pressed against his wet hair. "My perfect, sweet boy. You are mine. My treasure. My victory."

The first few days of the baby's life are quiet and joyous. I thought it might be difficult to love him. My resentment of how he was created runs deep, no matter how often Aina chooses to tell me about the death god's "good qualities." But one look at their child washes all that away. He is beautiful and blameless.

And he's *mine*.

This child will have two mothers. All-Mother, hear me, I'll love him and protect him like he's my own flesh and blood.

Aina can hardly bear to put him down. The only way I can get her to rest is if I take him. But then she lies awake, watching us together. I tickle his toes and talk to him, singing softly the songs of sleep and good health. Most of all, I sing him songs of strength. I hold him by the hour, stroking his petal-soft cheek, pouring all the love, hope, and strength I can into his little soul.

Unbound from his swaddling, he kicks his legs, enjoying the temporary freedom.

"He needs a name," Aina says with a laugh, watching him squirm.

I'm busy at the table, fletching new arrows. I work methodically with a stack of white feathers and my sharpest knife. "What name is fitting?"

"Hmm, we could name him Taavi after my father . . . or Tuoni after yours." She tickles the baby's chin. "Jaako and Kaarl are the names of my brothers . . . or Aksel and Onni after your other uncles."

My smile falls. "Quiet."

Aina quickly wraps the baby in his swaddling, holding him close. "What's wrong?"

"Listen."

Aina listens, her eyes locked on me. Aside from our crackling hearth, there is no noise. "No birdsong," she whispers.

It's midday in summer. There's always birdsong. I rise slowly, moving away from the table to the wall where my bow and quiver hang ready. "Someone—or some*thing*—is outside."

Outside the cabin, a raven caws.

"Oh Siiri, it's Tuoni," Aina whispers in excitement. "He's here."

"You said he had no tattoos," I chastise. "You said he couldn't come here."

"He doesn't—he *can't*," she counters. "But he can take the shape of a raven. It's his luonto, right? You said all luonto are birds. He did that all the time. It's how we first met."

I search frantically through Väinämöinen's memories. Tuoni and the Witch Queen are both tethered to Tuonela with ancient magic. They cannot leave, I'm sure of it. In a way, Tuoni is death, as much as he is its lord and master. I set aside my bow and quiver, picking up my sword instead. As I cross towards the door, the raven caws again.

"Don't hurt him," Aina pleads. "You heard Toivotar. He loves me. He just wants to see the child."

I wrench open the door, sword at the ready. Väinämöinen's magic hums under my skin. The words for a repelling spell are already on my tongue. I taste them, bitter like a sour apple. I peer out into the front yard, and my stomach squeezes tight. "*You.*"

"Who is it?" Aina calls from behind me.

I storm out of the house into the yard.

Kalma stands in the clearing, a massive raven perched on her arm. The death witch looks as beastly as ever, eyes like pits of darkness. She wears fresh blood smeared down her neck with artless fingers. I can smell her from here.

Pointing my sword at the witch, I let my magic fill me, spilling from my mouth as I make my oath. "You should know, witch . . . I am no longer the child you once frightened on the beach. My name is Siiri Väinämöinentyttär. His magic is mine. Be a witness to these words: Aina and the baby live under *my* protection now."

I gesture with my sword to the raven on her shoulder. "Tuoni, if you ever send Kalma to me again, I'll cut off her hands with my father's blade. I'll keep her rotten itse locked in a room, as you kept Aina locked away, and I'll take little pieces from her. Your daughters are good at weaving, so I'm told. Let it be their project to sew the thousand little pieces of her soul back together."

Kalma scowls, saying nothing, but I watch with satisfaction as she shifts her stance, her free hand disappearing inside the folds of her robes.

"Siiri," comes Aina's soft voice behind me. She stands in the doorway in a simple wool dress dyed oak brown. Her long hair is plaited, draped over her shoulder. The raven caws at the sight of her, ruffling his feathers. She smiles at him. "Let him come." She holds out her arm. "He wants to see his son."

The raven swoops in a wide arc past me, fluttering onto Aina's arm. She strokes his feathered back as he clicks his beak. She gives Kalma a long look, still petting the raven. "Come on, then," she calls out to the witch.

Kalma dares to take a step forward, but I point at her with my sword. "Stay right there. You're not coming in this house."

Aina places her hand on my arm. "I invited her, Siiri. Lower your sword—and your hackles. I owe this witch a life debt twice over. She won't harm us. She's curious," she adds, glancing over at the witch. "She wants to see the baby, too, don't you?"

I scoff. "Aina, have you forgotten what this witch did?"

"Of course I haven't. It happened to me, remember? If I can forgive her, so can you. And if her stench makes you uncomfortable, you can wait out here with the chickens." She steps back into the house, taking the god of death with her.

Slowly, I step aside. "After you, witch . . . apparently," I add under my breath.

The death goddess walks on bare feet over the grass, her torn and soiled robes dragging over the ground. She steps past me, ducking to fit her headdress under the doorframe.

I'm the last inside, shutting the door behind me.

Aina is already on the bed in the corner. She picks up the baby, whispering softly to the raven. "I'm not sorry it turned out this way," she tells him. "And please don't blame Loviatar. She did what she thought was right to protect me and our child . . . our son, Tuoni." She holds up the baby, wrapped carefully in a blanket. "He's a happy little thing," she says with a laugh. "He was born into Siiri's arms. He was so angry at first. But as soon as we wrapped him up warm, he stopped crying, and he's been content ever since."

Aina strokes his cheek. "Toivotar says he'll be beautiful. Black of hair, like you. And tall. She gave me the sielulintu you had made for him," she adds, reaching over to where it sits by the baby's cradle. She holds it in her palm, showing it to the raven. "When he's strong enough, Siiri will bring him to you. He will know his father. I will never keep him from you, Tuoni."

The raven caws softly. Like the death god, he has one black eye, one cloudy white. Even in his luonto form, he bears the scars Väinämöinen gave him. I smile in satisfaction. I no longer wear his scars on this body.

From the corner, Kalma watches us.

"You can come closer," Aina says. "I want him to know his sisters."

Kalma casts a look in my direction before she steps away from the hearth, her dark eyes now locked on the child. I watch each step she takes with my hand on the hilt of my knife.

"I hope you'll be a good sister to him," Aina tells the witch. "I want him to know and love you all, as a brother should. Does he look like his father?"

In answer, Kalma reaches into the folds of her robe and pulls out a piece of parchment. Moving slowly, she extends her hand out towards Aina.

Aina sets the baby down on the bed by the raven and takes the note. With wide eyes, she unfolds it. "I can't read this," she admits, glancing from the raven to Kalma. "Is it from Tuoni? Can you read it for me?"

Kalma scowls and moves back over to the hearth. Task fulfilled, she's disinterested in helping any further.

Aina looks down sadly at the letter, stroking the raven's

silky black feathers. "I'm sorry, my lord, but you know I cannot read."

"I'll read it," I say.

Aina, Kalma, and the raven all look to me.

"What?" says Aina. "But—Siiri, you can't read either."

I smirk, running a hand through my shoulder-length hair. "Väinämöinen can read, so I can read." It shocks and delights me. My smile falls as I look at the hopefulness on Aina's face. "I'll read it for you," I say to the raven. Let this be my peace offering. He let us leave Tuonela. I'll let him say a proper goodbye.

The raven clicks his beak as I take the letter from Aina. The words are scrawled in a confident hand, the ink heavy on the page.

"Well?" Aina asks. "Can you read it?" She already has tears in her eyes, the baby nestled protectively in her arms.

Sighing, I begin. "It says, 'I, Tuoni, Lord of Death, entrust the care of my son and heir to his mother, Aina Taavintyttär, hereafter known as Ainatar, Queen of Tuonela. The child will be raised in the realm of the living. So I have spoken, so I am bound.'"

"Thank you," Aina whispers at the raven. "I will never forget this kindness, my lord."

"There's more," I say.

Aina glances up, her free hand stroking the raven's feathers. "More?"

"He says, 'My only condition is this: Each year, on the longest day of summer and the longest night of winter, Ainatar must bring the child to me. My son will know his father.'"

"Yes," Aina rushes to say. "Tuoni, of course. I want him to know you."

The raven clicks his beak, leaning his head into her touch.

"There's more," I say.

She looks back at me. "More? Well, keep reading, Siiri."

I grimace, reading through the words once first. I glance over the parchment at her. "Aina, I really don't think I should be the one to read this—"

"There's none other here," Aina cries. "Please, Siiri. You must read it for me. *Please.*"

I sigh again and nod, regretting my generosity immensely. "Right . . . well, next he says, 'Aina . . . my wife, my Aina. Your name is a blessing. Please leave me with hope. I cannot dwell in this darkness without your light. Lie to me if you must, only say there is a place in your heart for me. Let me hear the words from your own lips just once. Tell me you love me.'"

The words hang heavy in the air as we all wait for Aina's response.

Aina blinks back her tears, looking to the raven. "Tuoni, there is no lie in my heart. You know the truth already. You feel it in the blood bond that sings now between us. I will love you until I die." She strokes their baby's soft black hair. "My heart is yours . . . as yours is mine."

I sink against the wall, feeling my own heart breaking. I don't know why I expected anything less. The intimacy between us has grown over the months since our return from Tuonela. We kiss and touch. She sleeps nowhere but by my side. She loves me as her friend, and that will have to be enough.

Aina surprises me when she continues. "If we were only hearts and minds, my heart beating for you would have been enough. I would have stayed and braved your world." She glances over to me. "But a clever shaman has taught me that we are more than hearts and minds. We are souls too." She looks to the raven. "You have my heart, Tuoni . . . but Siiri has my soul."

My breath catches in my throat.

"Our hearts are broken now, my love," she murmurs to the

raven. "The pain will remain. It will be a constant reminder of what was . . . what could have been. But you *will* live, Tuoni. I swear it. People live with broken hearts. They cannot live with shattered souls."

I can't look away, too afraid to believe the words I'm hearing unless I see Aina's mouth move to make them.

Aina strokes the raven with a gentle hand. "Without you in my life, I'll be a cup that is eternally half-empty. This bond in me will ache for you." She glances up again, her green eyes soft and warm as she makes her declaration to us both. "But without Siiri, I'll die."

A tear slips down my cheek, and it takes everything not to go to her.

Aina wipes her own tear away. "So, you see, I had to leave. It wasn't about you, Tuoni. It was never about you or my love for you. I simply want to live. And my soul cannot thrive in Tuonela. I belong *here*. I will always belong here. I belong with Siiri."

We're all quiet for a moment. Even the baby is still, content to be held by his mother.

"There's more," I say, breaking the silence.

Aina lets out a heavy breath. I can tell on her face that she can't take much more heartbreak today.

"It's just a question," I say. "Rather a good one."

Aina raises a curious brow.

I smile, folding up the parchment. "He asks for his son's name."

"He doesn't have a name yet," Aina replies.

I cross the room to her, handing her the parchment. She takes it, our fingers brushing as she looks up at me. Suddenly, her gaze softens, and she smiles wide.

"I think there's a reason none of the names I pick seem to fit him," she says.

"Oh, yes?" I reply.

"Yes, I don't think I'm supposed to be the one to name him." She looks to the raven. "It will be Siiri who teaches him how to return to you. She'll help our son grow in his powers. She will protect him and love him as a second mother, equal to me in the raising of him. Siiri will name our child."

I stiffen as I feel all the eyes in the room look my way. I haven't bothered to tell Aina that I already named the boy in my heart. I first met Väinämöinen in the form of the bear. He was all quiet strength and serenity. I first loved him in that form. I will love him forever. Thanks to his curse, which may yet be my blessing, we will never be parted. I wear him inked into my very skin.

Vaka vanha Väinämöinen.

I close my eyes and smile, letting all the stories and songs of the ages wash over me, filling me with hope and promise. The road before us will be long and treacherous. But I have my family to ground me and guide me. Aina, who is as much a wife to me as a wife ever could be. And now we have our son, who will restore the balance of life and death. He'll help me bring Finland back to its former glory.

The shaman's magic flows through me as I open my eyes, gazing down at my dark-haired, beautiful son. "His name is Kalev," I say. "We'll call him 'Kal' for short."

"Kalev," Aina whispers, testing the name. "Is that your name, my little Kal?" The green-eyed baby coos at the raven perched on her mother's knee. "It suits him," she says with a smile.

Kalev, son of Aina, a mortal queen. Kalev, son of Siiri, the new Väinämöinen, shaman of the ages. Kalev, only son of Tuoni, god of death. Kalev, Prince of Tuonela.

The End

The story Aina and Siiri began continues in book two

South is the Sea

Join Siiri, Aina, and Kal in their next adventure as they fight to expel the Swedish invaders and finally bring the true religion back to the people of Finland.

Acknowledgments

This story was born out of my lifelong love of mythology, my fierce pride in my Finnish heritage, and a global pandemic. All those stars had to align for Siiri and Aina to find their way into my heart and onto the page.

I want to thank all the people who read various drafts of this project over the years: Emily Beach, Molly Ardin, Devon DeSimone, Amy Morse, Joss Diaz, Lauren Searson-Patrick, Margaret Rose, and Alex Dawning. Special thanks to Jessa Wilder: you saved Tuoni. Seriously, he owes you a fruit basket. Susan Wilkerson and Kirsten Davis, you helped me find Siiri's voice, and made the pandemic feel less lonely.

To my agent, Susan Velazquez Colmant, thank you for giving me a chance. Thank you as well to my amazing editors, Sarah Guan and Anne Perry. You trusted me to rework this story and offered so much insight and guidance. To my teams at Erewhon and Kensington, I'm so grateful to you all for helping me bring this book to life with amazing covers, formatting, editing, and interior art. To all my other partners at JABberwocky—Stevie, Valentina, Christina—thanks for all your hard work and dedication behind the scenes.

To Ben, I love you. I hope someday you read this and you're proud of me.

To Bernice, my mummi. You gave me my first Finnish phrase book and your copy of the *Kalevala*. You always believed in my storytelling gift. Minä rakastan sinua.

To the rest of my extended family, I love you all. You listened to me talk about publishing for hours on end, you kept my gin and tonics refreshed, and you always asked for updates and cheered me on.

To Meg, my stalwart friend. Your kindness is a deep well of strength. You embody so much of my sweet Aina.

To Katie, my ideas woman. You dark and twisty weirdo, you know what you did. Your ideas took the plot to the next level.

To Ashley, my number one fan (who has definitely read worse). I can't even put into words what your support has meant to me. This book would not exist without you. I wish everyone had an Ashley in their life. The world would certainly be a more tolerant and beautiful place.

To Jordan, you put up with so much from me, and you ask for so little in return. I'm sorry for all the times I didn't just take the trash out when it was full. And I'm sorry I stole your office. And I'm really sorry I'm too afraid to try night diving. I wish I could be different for you. But you've always known who I am, and for some reason you love me anyway.

Lastly, to you, my dear readers. As I've stumbled my way through this career, changing tenses and exploring new genres, you've been right there by my side. An author is nothing without their readers, and I am the luckiest person on earth to have such a fantastic readership. Whether you're new to the Emilyverse, or you've been with me from the beginning, I'm so profoundly glad you're here.

XO,